PIERCE HER

PIERCE HER

COME FOR ME, BOOK ONE

KELLY FINLEY

Edited by Judy Roth and Nora Esthimer
Proofreading by Kat Wyeth, Kat's Literary Services
Cover by Caroline Johnson

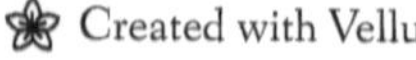 Created with Vellum

ALSO BY KELLY FINLEY

Come for Me

Protect Her, Prequel Novelette

Pierce Her, Book One

Hunt Her, Book Two

Chase Her, Book Three

All for You

After Him, Book One

With Him, Book Two

And more...

GET MORE

WANT A FREE COPY OF *PROTECT HER*,
THE *COME FOR ME* PREQUEL NOVELETTE?

Join my monthly news tease for this special gift, bonus scenes, sneak peeks, and a BTS glimpse into my author adventures. I share it all.

Join at KellyFinley.com, and this gift is coming your way.

To my Marine with a French manicure, a survivor, a like-sister and a sweet badass who told me to write something sexy she'd like

In humble gratitude and with great respect, ten percent of all proceeds gratefully earned from this book will be donated to the non-profit organization AMVETS-Sheroes on the Move.

PIERCE HER PLAYLIST

"Pretty Waste" by BONES UK
"Haste" by RY X
"Saving All My Love" by Empara Mi
"Watermelon Sugar" by Harry Styles
"Say It" (feat. Tove Lo) SG Lewis Remix by Flume
"Mallorca" by RY X
"Beneath Your Beautiful" (feat. Emeli Sandé) by Labrinth
"Talking Body" (Gryffin Remix) by Tove Lo
"How to Let You Go" by Benson Taylor, Carolanne Busuttil
& Yoed Nir
"Falling" by Harry Styles
"Army of Me" by Björk
"Better" by SYML
"Death of Me" by PVRIS

Listen to the PIERCE HER playlist on Spotify

CHAPTER ONE

CHARLIE RAVENEL

Pretty Face by BONES UK

How do you mark the anniversary of the day you were shot? Three times. Six years ago.

You don't.

I got up and did the same damn thing I'd done the day before. For hours. Now that was a celebration.

I aimed the bow of my kayak dead center through the paparazzi blasts of lights off the water, my paddle lashing fast slices across the surface. Exertion. Sweat. And yes, the pain. Pure Zen in my veins. Alone again on the brackish Calibogue sound. Nirvana.

The moon lingered in the clear day sky above. A constant haunting companion warning me that one day mine would collide again in another bloody show.

Until then, I closed my eyes. Coasting forward, pulling

a deep breath in, swimming in the silence, my mind sought peace.

"Hey, blondie. We'll give you a hard tow!"

Eyelids firing open, I clocked them. Three drunk young men leaving the island marina. My destination and home. Their boat slowed in a bobbing prowl nearing me.

"No, thank you," I said. "Y'all ain't got anything I need." My smile? Kind. My tone? Syrup. My glare?

Fuck off.

They didn't retreat, sloshing even closer to me. I wanted to punch their dicks for ruining my day on the water. My daily church.

The youngest guy, red plastic cup in hand, swayed port side, wearing sunburned cheeks as flaming as the blood shot through his eyes. Staring pupils. Shoulders wobbling. "Damn bitch, what happened to your face?"

The insult was praise to my ears.

I lifted my gaze higher. Quick calculations—how I'd take down each one of them.

"Why don't you and the little shrimp in your pants jump in with me, and I'll show you what a bitch I am?"

My smile crinkled the long scar across my right cheek, wearing it like a proud badge of, "Go to hell."

The biggest guy threw his chin up. Amused. "Leave her alone, dude." Smart.

Red cup dude with the logo T-shirt that might as well read, "NOT SURE OF MY COCK OR MY MASCULINITY" stumbled back on his feet when a wake rolled under us.

The third guy. A brunette at the center console steering the boat leered at me, brown eyes trickling a shiver down my spine. *Yes. He's one of them.* Guilt in his eyes with a desire to do it again. To violate. To hurt. Women.

My molars bit down in recognition. My stare locked on him, memories shooting through my mind.

Blood in your mouth, trailing behind you. A girl grabbing your hand. A baby's soul-shredding scream.

Their boat swayed silent with his glare aimed at me. I didn't move a muscle. No retreat or waste of another word. I had all the patience in the world to stay in this moment.

"Fuck you, bitch." The youngest wordsmith tossed his drink over the side. The evil captain punched the throttle down, churning a hefty wake behind the boat.

I smiled, "Stand in line, assholes," tossing the invitation over my shoulder with a leisurely stroke home.

Throwing my orange kayak onto the storage rack at the marina's dock, ignoring the partying day-trippers, I loved my five-mile run home. It soothed my nerves, the rhythmic pounding of my shoes down sandy roads under a canopy of oaks draped with Spanish moss.

Bounding through my back door, silence and a cold glass of water from the fridge greeted me. I checked my phone on the kitchen island. A missed call thrilled me. Nestling earbuds in, I called her back, sounding off the second she answered.

"It's a Saturday night in London for you, bitch. Shouldn't your hot ass be on a date or getting laid?"

I lived vicariously through my best friend, joking, but missing her so much. Juliette was shooting a movie in London, going to glamorous weekend parties and dinners, calling me with the salacious Sunday morning details.

Meanwhile I was alone, up to my eyeballs renovating my home in South Carolina and perfectly content in my solitude.

Our weekend ritual kept me sane and smiling. Most of the time.

"Charlie Fucking Ravenel, I could say the same for you, my sweet." Juliette's warm voice filled my soul. "Let me guess. You're alone in your rash guard, been on the water all day, and you have a book and shots of Tito's for company tonight."

"Yep. Hot pages and a cold drink. The perfect date."

"A six-year long lonely date for you. And a lonely month for me. It's about time for both of us to get properly laid."

No, it wasn't. Alone I was safe, gazing out of the windows of my home at the dunes and the steel blue ocean outside.

"For now, my love." Juliette read my silence. "Let's just get you in a bikini."

"You still coming to see me when you wrap?"

I needed our Miami trip like a dose of heroin—euphoria to replace my memories.

"Yep. I have two bikinis, and now I'm on the hunt for a scandalous one piece. I want a red, plunging something. But everything so far makes my bum look like a pancake."

"Bitch, please, you have the cutest ass on the planet, and ten million people have posted about it."

"You're one to talk with that kickass booty of yours. Did you do it?" Juliette asked. "Did you go shopping yet?"

"I bought a bikini, like I promised."

It actually looked kinda pretty when I'd tried it on at the store last week.

Until I saw my scars in the dressing room's wrap-around mirrors under the cruel fluorescent lights. Pressing my suddenly sweaty forehead to the cool mirrors—*you can't do this*—I felt sick.

Exposing myself scared the shit out of me. I was fearless

about everything... except my body. The sight of it always provoked stares and rude questions.

But I'd promised Juliette. I'd do anything for her—for any woman or girl. Even take another bullet for one. But I didn't give a shit for the attention of men. I didn't want it anymore.

"You'll be proud." I opened the French doors, stepping out into the warm winter day. "It's a crocheted string bikini." I almost didn't do it. But I kept my word, going as sexy as I could find. "And the top lining comes out if I wanna get arrested."

"Yes, bitch. Or laid," Juliette blurted in my ears. "I love you! We're doing this. If not getting you properly fucked by a hot bloke, at least you'll lure one over for me."

"I have no followers, and you have forty million. I think it's your gorgeous face luring them over."

"Charlie." Juliette got serious. I knew why. "I know you don't want to talk about it, but I know it's today. And I know what's tomorrow. Six years ago. I'm just sending you my love."

"Thank you."

It was all I could say, tears threatening to fall over my lashes.

It wasn't the kind of anniversary you celebrate. It was the kind that dropped you to your knees.

A *ping* pierced my ears.

I walked back to my phone on the counter and tapped the screen. JEREMY glowed back. Shit.

"Hey chica, sorry. I gotta get this. Love you."

"Love you. Cheers."

I pressed ACCEPT on my phone. "Your hair better be on fucking fire calling me on a Saturday," I half joked.

In the year since I'd last worked for him, Jeremy stayed

in touch, calling to talk about fishing, football. Really, he was keeping tabs on me. But he never called on the weekend.

"She says to the man with a bald head." Jeremy sounded amused, clicking his pen. "Did you get my package? It just arrived. Should be on your front steps. It takes bloody special delivery getting something to you since you hide from all civilization over there."

"Ah, babycakes, you shouldn't have. My birthday isn't until November."

I kept goading him but caught the urgency. Opening my front door, securing the bud in my ear, I bounded down the steps to the driveway. "Happy fucking birthday to me." I snagged a box from the bottom step, running back inside.

"You're welcome," he said. "Lorraine Morris sent this to me last July. She was in Madrid, showrunner for the first season of *The Druid*. One of her cast members found it in her trailer the day they wrapped shooting."

I ripped the box open. Shaking out a manilla folder, I flipped it open, finding photos. Two taken of an A-4 sized note penned on a piece of vellum paper. The handwriting read clear, but it looked like a printed font. The ink, blood red.

You. Will. Be. Mine.

"Huh. Somebody likes drama, even if they aren't original," I said, examining the image for any other information. "Unusual choice of paper. Architects or DIYers usually only use it. They put a little effort into it too. Who found it?"

"Kierra Williams. She was fifteen and it shook her up. Madrid police opened a case last summer but still have nothing. There's been a cock-up. I spoke to her mother who's been throwing fits about her daughter's safety. Her mother said Kierra won't say what, won't give specifics, but the girl is adamant this is about more than a note. Now they're beginning to shoot season two, and the studio has agreed to scale up cast security."

Oh, hell no. I waited for the big ask.

"The studio manager swears his lot was secure," Jeremy said, "but someone bloody got in and out without being seen. Or maybe they were on the inside all along. Which is worse? Some nutter sneaking onto set or a creepy sick fuck with easy access?"

"What do you think?" I asked. "Is it a prank or legit?"

"That's why I'm ringing you, Charlie. Nobody has better instincts for this than you."

He was right.

I could suss out someone in seconds. Rarely, if ever, was I wrong.

I'd been right about the grip in Belfast who stalked Juliette. He was in my sights in a week, caught in two. And the young woman on the catering truck who took pictures on set and sold them? I caught her red-handed.

Jeremy had recruited me to work on the mega-hit show *Fated* four years earlier. I protected Juliette until the show wrapped a year ago. And I earned a reputation. Toward the cast, I was funny. Toward a threat to them, I was ruthless. My military experience working with women and girls in bad situations and gathering intel didn't hurt either.

I looked at the pictures again, knew what I thought. What I sensed mattered more. Pictures weren't enough but I trusted my instinct.

"*You.*" An othering of the stalking subject. He craved hunting an object. "*Will.*" Not a wish. A command. Sure of his power. *"Be."* Cruel. Arrogant. Women existed for him. *"Mine."* He needed to possess, entitled to have everything.

YOU. WILL. BE. MINE.

The effort was amateur. It twisted my gut. The threat to this girl wasn't.

"It's not a fucking prank," I said.

Beside the photos, the file held a sheet of paper. I studied the client profile with a headshot of Kierra Williams. She was the perfect ingénue to cast—a stunning Irish girl with full berry lips, long copper hair, porcelain skin and lush brown lashes rimming emerald eyes. She had an old-world beauty with a seductive look of emerging womanhood, sure to attract viewers and the attention of many... particularly perverted assholes. But no matter how old she looked, Kierra was sixteen now, still a child in many ways.

I swallowed hard. Jeremy knew my past, knew my weakness. I could taste the manipulation.

"Rob's your best bet for the job," I said.

Now now. I wouldn't go back. Six years of crawling my way out of pain; my body was strong again. And my mind... I had control now. Almost. It was a peace I paid for and it was priceless.

Especially today.

"Don't be stubborn, Ravenel. You were my ace in the hole protecting Juliette. And I need you again," he said. "I can't send Rob by himself."

I winced, hating he was right. Yes, this girl would be unnerved with only men on her security detail. And yes, *this* girl was hiding something.

I studied Kierra's picture again, inhaling a deep instinct

to protect her—or any girl—from a dangerous man. But taking this assignment would challenge every breath of peace I now drew.

Something compelled me to ask, "What's the timeline?" Then I kicked myself for giving Jeremy hope.

He hissed a not-so-silent, "Yes," then said, "Pre-production is underway. Kierra, her mum, and team arrive in Madrid in one week. Shooting wraps in July. It'll be five months, tops. Rob just arrived to sort his lodging. He can help you find something."

I said nothing.

"I know it's short notice," Jeremy added. "But Lorraine says they can't rely on the locals, and Kierra's parents say she's not going back without real security." He paused.

Again, I waited him out.

"Oh, and," he said, "I almost forgot to mention. Anders Nylund is cast for seasons two and three."

Forgot, hell. Jeremy knew I was tight with Anders and his family. We'd all grown close working on *Fated*. That's where I'd met Rob too. Having both Rob and Anders on *The Druid* gave Jeremy a strong hand to play.

Truth was, friends were my only family. And Madrid? Returning to Spain after all this time... I thought of my mom.

"Let me sleep on it." I finally spoke.

"All right." Jeremy sighed. "We have a couple of days. Take your time."

His patience rang false with anxiety.

I showered. With my hair still damp, I went to bed alone and tried to read. No go. Thoughts of Kierra kept taunting me.

Yet another girl tormented by a man.

Finally, I slept, but awoke to my scream and soaking wet in sweat.

My fucking nightmares? As certain as the sunrise.

Tossing and turning, I awoke next to the sound of a Tibetan chime from my phone's alarm. The sun wasn't up but would appear on the horizon soon.

I opened the doors to the balcony. A raw breeze frosted my naked skin. I never covered my body for meditation. Learning to sit. To wait. Any discomfort, it was part of my discipline. My bare legs crossed, pressing against unforgiving wooden boards, finding their familiar pose.

A rhythmic breath released my haunted mind. Minutes I lost until time returned along with my thoughts, compassion for Kierra filling my soul... and a sick concern.

Torment was all I knew for the uncertain fate of the last girls I'd helped. I'd do it all again, flipping my middle finger to my own life to protect them, but I paid a damning price. Every morning, I prayed they were safe, but I'd never know.

But you can protect this girl. This time can be different.

My eyes flew open.

Heading back inside, flipping over my phone on the nightstand, I laughed. Two missed calls from Jeremy. One from Anders. One from Rob. Jeremy had enlisted them. They were doing a full court press.

I didn't need to hear exactly what they'd say—each with their own reasons why I should join the show.

I group-texted all three:

Relax fuckers. I'm coming

CHAPTER TWO

DANIEL PIERCE

Trapped. Uninspired. Overwhelmed. I needed to shoot something.

"Mate, you forgot this." Lance tapped me on the shoulder. I'd forgotten my phone in the car.

As we walked across the parking lot, I glanced down. The screen lit up with a constant barrage of texts and notifications—all wanting me.

"Cheers." I dropped it in the pocket of my shotgun bag.

Lance introduced me to skeet shooting. With every shot fired, it helped me explode my stress, every bloody weekend.

We came to this shooting club while filming the first season of *The Druid* here in Spain. We're reunited, here again for season two.

I couldn't trust many people, but Lance was discreet, loyal. He was the lead horsemaster for the show and one of a few who asked nothing of me. Most others sharked around, hungry for a bite... or more.

A black 4x4 pulled into the parking lot, the driver leaning on his horn, parking next to my 4x4. The sudden blare made my driver sitting inside, jump.

"Who's the wanker?" I asked.

"It's Anders." Lance threw his arm up, waving. "I told him about this yesterday. He asked if he could come."

I watched, amused by Anders's dramatic leap out of the car, roaring a loud "Argh!"

Wanker? No. Anders was a riot. I'd already enjoyed several doses of my new co-star's antics this past week in table reads.

The passenger's side door of Anders's 4x4 opened. Someone wearing a straw cowboy hat hopped down from behind the door, black cowboy boots hitting the pavement.

Too small to belong to a man.

"Lance! Daniel! My men!" With a mischievous smile, Anders boomed our way, a rifle case resting on his brawny shoulder.

"About fucking time," Lance called back. "We've got a rugby match to watch today too, mate."

"Don't I fuckin' know it." Anders laughed. "My money's on any team playing against your English Roses." His grip pulled Lance into a smack on the back.

Then Anders turned to me, green eyes dancing with a devil deal. "Wanna make it a little interesting, Pierce? Put a tenner down on your boys?"

"A fool and his money are soon parted." I laughed, closing the deal with a vigorous handshake.

Stroking his long, strawberry blond beard, Anders turned to introduce his friend. "Charlie Ravenel, come meet these two tossers. One is a supergod, and the other one is a super horse's arse."

A petite figure stepped out from behind Anders.

Bloody hell, Pierce. The sight of her slapped my mind. *Not like any Charlie you've ever met.*

Long, blonde waves fell from under the old cowboy hat. Her chin lifted, revealing arresting sea-glass speckled eyes, fringed by thick lashes under dark eyebrows. A dusting of freckles across her tan face made her look young. Wrinkles bracketing smiling eyes suggested experience, I hoped.

Her full pink lips cocked in a defiant grin. When she turned her face to Lance first, extending her hand, it shocked me—the jagged, blush scar scraping across the side of her cheek.

Crikey Moses, Pierce and catch your breath. She's so fucking beautiful.

"Hey y'all." She greeted us, shaking Lance's hand first. "Nice to meet you."

"I'm Lance Moore. Horsemaster on set and supergod in the flesh." Lance nodded toward me. "That's Daniel Pierce. He's the tosser."

When her eyes landed on me, lips challenging, "Oh, I can tell," a smirk crimped her cheek... and that scar.

So much for polite, so much for professional. The twitch in my trousers, instant.

The joke was on me. I didn't need reminding that my bloody face was one of the most recognizable in the world.

Her hand reached out for mine. Her grip, firm and strong. And the heat from her palm? It grabbed my skin... and much more.

Hundreds, thousands of hands I'd shaken. None ever grabbing me like hers. All I could mutter was "Nice to meet you."

That was a lie. *Nice* didn't describe the urge owning me that moment.

"Y'all ready to shoot? Or are we gonna sit here and listen to Anders's verbal diarrhea all day?"

Her lady-like Southern accent delivered that smart-arse joke and my breath hitched.

Anders laughed. "Yes, ma'am." He tried a horrible Southern accent. "Let's get to shootin'."

We walked toward the first station. I couldn't help it. "Tell me, Charlie. What's a woman risking out here with two strange men and a big, crazy Viking?"

I wanted to hear more of her voice. I wanted to die, sounding like a creep instead.

"Charlie worked on *Fated* with me," Anders answered for her. "She and her team saved our fuckin' arses in Belfast. Maja, the kids, and I couldn't leave the house until they came to help. I told Lorraine I wouldn't step foot on set if Charlie wasn't on the show."

"That's bullshit," Charlie said. "But I'd do anything for Maja and the kids."

"Ah, you're with HGR Security," Lance said. "I heard you guys were being brought on this season."

"Yeah, just got here yesterday. I'm here with my partner Rob Vasquez. We get up and runnin' Monday."

What? New cast security for the season? The news threatened my sudden pleasure in her company. A twitch hit my shoulder.

She'd be focused on her work, no doubt. Work no one told me about. That our showrunner, Lorraine, had upped the security level on set.

"I suppose you'll be working with my team too," I said, masking my probe with pleasantries.

I employed a strong team guarding my privacy and life. But the buzz on *The Druid* was getting intense. More security meant more scrutiny. More surveillance of the comings and goings of everyone on set. More limitations over already restricted freedom.

That's the price I paid for the job.

I was first on the call sheet, bringing a huge following to *The Druid*. The streaming show had one of the largest audiences ever. My fellow cast member, Mason Hunt, had his own fan base from his child-actor days and teen films while our young and beautiful Kierra Williams was the breakout star.

With Anders Nylund joining the principal cast too, the hype would skyrocket for everyone.

"Yep," she said. "We're doing audits the next couple of weeks. Rob is working with the studio manager, and I'm meeting with all the cast's personal detail."

"You'll like my team." Drawing nearer, her hair smelled like vanilla. "Glad to have you on board."

I swept my arm forward with a bow, intending for her to walk ahead. To be polite. To admire her ass.

She grinned. "Supergods before mortals." Mimicking my gesture, she refused my control with her cheeky rebuke.

I relented, stepping to catch up with Lance. We reached the long line of tables under the metal awning, setting our rifle bags down.

I leaned over, "What do you know about HGR Security?" trying to sound casual with Lance. Then I felt like a prat; it was a legitimate question.

Waiting for his answer, I glanced left at Charlie with Anders at the other table, loading their shotguns.

Fuck, she's fucking stunning.

Shit, I darted my eyes back down before she caught me.

"I know they're one of the top firms." Lance slid on his protective lenses. "A lot are former military. A few get into some pretty dodgy shit with nutter fans. I heard they were brought onto *Fated* after their first season. That Juliette Jones had some sick psychos targeting her. That someone from the HGR team took down a lot of threats to her and the cast."

"Wonder why Lorraine brought them onto the show."

"Guess she wanted the best."

Every production has security on set. As part of their work, they disappear into the landscape. At least, that's how it always seemed to me.

But not this season. Not now.

Charlie Ravenel joining our production gamed my every nerve.

Who she was intrigued as much as to why she was here. And the story behind that scar on her stunning face? Intrigued was a beige understatement for what suddenly roused my senses.

CHARLIE

I HAD TO TURN AWAY. Away from Daniel Pierce to find my breath.

What the holy fuck was that, Charlie Girl?

My body howled awake at his handshake, at his touch. The first time in six years it responded to any man.

The sets I've worked? I'm used to being surrounded by beautiful people, men and women. Hell, I had to fight off how beauty was as much a burden as a blessing for many of them.

I treated actors like nobodies. Or anybodies. It's one of the reasons they trusted me.

But bless my heart. Daniel Pierce, famously the sexiest

man alive, possessed so much exquisite physical DNA it required a full audit.

Sure, I'd seen him plastered across covers and screens. I blushed. Okay, fine. I'd given myself solo pleasure at the sight of his photo. Three times. But that was a screen, a fleeting fantasy. This was him, palpable and in person.

And oh, where his staggering bounty of beauty stopped, his sexy charisma raced, lapping my body for the win.

Charlie Girl. I adjusted the scope on the rifle. *Slow your roll. You've got a job to do. A girl at risk.*

And I'd fucking asked for this. Asked Anders where the cast hung out. Wanting to meet each one of them. Off set. In a setting where their guard was down. In a setting where a stalker might betray himself.

I wasn't wheels down in Madrid for twenty-four hours, kissing my relaxing trip to Miami with Juliette goodbye, before I found myself jumping into the deep end of this job.

Right into the ocean of Daniel Pierce.

And it was raging wet.

Over six feet of hulking muscles wrapped down a body that famously took discipline to achieve. Black hair fell in soft waves, framing aqua eyes as deep as a cenote, enticing anyone to jump in. Stubble blanketed a square jaw and deep cleft chin. Pillow lips formed a perfect soft bow, almost feminine, until they flashed a white-hot, hungry smile.

He was cast as Zeus, the god of gods who had no equal, many enemies and could bed any woman in a comic book series turned movie franchise. Two films had dominated the box office in the blockbuster series. A third was rumored. And everywhere Daniel Pierce went, he was "Zeus" to his fans.

I read how many followers and press also branded him
—"Sex God."

He sure as hell looked like it.

Inhales like I used in mediation subdued the shock of
him. And his question? About what I was *risking* out here?
Well, that pissed me off.

I wasn't risking shit. Not for any man. My mission clear;
I racked my rifle. *Protect the girl.*

Putting my nose down, peering covert up through my
eyebrows, I studied his heart-stopping profile while he
stuffed shells into his shooting pouch.

A hunch hit me.

He'd gone from *Zeus* to *The Druid.* I'd watched both
that week as part of my research.

On *The Druid*, he disguised some of his beauty behind
the auburn wig, emerald contacts, prosthetic facial scars,
and scowl for his character, Carric Morrigan. It gave him a
temporary escape from being Daniel Pierce.

My synapses fired up without prompting. It never took
long.

He's hiding something. More than his beauty. What?

The question scratched my brain, making me dismiss
the tingling between my thighs the proximity of him invol-
untarily caused.

I'd get used to Daniel Pierce. Eventually.

I'd gotten used to all the eye candy on the set of *Fated.*
To me? The male actors were boys playing with swords,
having no real concept of war. They did stunts. I did real
missions. They were sheltered. I'd been targeted. I was
never intimidated... and rarely impressed.

My thoughts, my gaze wandered over his peach ass in
jeans.

And never be fooled. Beautiful humans can commit ugly acts.

Shots brought me back to the moment, to how Daniel shot first. He hit two single clays but missed the double. Same for Lance. Anders took out both singles and one of the doubles.

I waited to shoot last. Counting my inhale, exhaling into the percussion pushing the air, skeet held safe memories for me. With my dad. I begged him to teach me how to shoot my grandfather's rifle. Every weekend found us at the range.

The sound of exploding clays didn't trigger me, though an unexpected gunshot could. Anticipating the sound helped.

But something else. Something had me breathing on a razor's edge.

"Char, no more hiding. Time to play." Anders signaled it was my turn. Like a brother, I loved him. He'd done more than see me shoot before.

I didn't shoot like most men. All three of them fired with their rifle ready at the shoulder. Not me. I shot out-of-shoulder with two clays launched from opposite directions. The first clay had to appear before I could shoulder my weapon.

It was how my dad taught me.

My jaw clenched, seizing my heart. It's what saved my life.

A life that in that moment stepped back into the line of fire. To protect another girl? Yeah, I couldn't be stopped.

Closing my eyes, I inhaled. With my exhale, opening them, I called, "Pull!"

Fire, pump, hit. Fire, pump, hit. Getting the pair. Not a flinch of recoil. Out-of-shoulder again. The second pair flew. *Shoulder the weapon.* Again. Fire, pump, hit. Fire, pump, hit.

Clay exploded into dust everywhere.

"Bloody hell!" Lance yelled.

I turned, seeing his grin. Daniel Pierce's face recorded shock and awe.

Anders looked satisfied, proclaiming, "If you think her aim is fierce, you should see what she can do with her fists." That embarrassed me some but by the time we finished the sixth station, my right hand shook. I squeezed it tight, gaze locked up on Anders. We shot together working on *Fated*. He recognized the signal.

I had to stop.

The guys finished the two final stations but couldn't beat my score.

"Who's buying my first Guinness?" I pulled off my hat, then earmuffs. "Seems I'm owed three and will need to suffer through rugby on a flatscreen to enjoy them." I shook my hair out too.

"Oi!" Daniel exclaimed. "You dare to insult the greatest sport in the world?"

Oh shit. His panty-wetting grin told me otherwise. Eyes sparkling curious, roaming with an intensity over me, stirring panic with pleasure. Not trying to hide it, Daniel Pierce was anything but insulted by me.

Careful. With a look like that, you'll have a lot more to protect than a girl.

CHAPTER THREE

DANIEL

She loomed a few meters behind me.

A man knows it. When he meets a woman who doesn't fuck around. In any way.

I avoided them. Their toe-to-toe stance with me gave them too strong of a peek into my world, challenging everything I hide. Usually, I was attracted to those who posed no threat, to pliable women who acquiesced. To my whim. To my life.

Yet today, I was ambushed. My relaxing weekend was turned upside down by the arrival of my new colleague. One whose assignment and allure intimidated me.

I sat on the sofa in Lance's flat. Eyes on the match.

Mind on her.

She hung back with Anders, sitting on a barstool at the breakfast bar in the kitchen. They weren't interested in the match, laughing like old friends. Their affection for each other didn't seem sexual. Still, it surprised me, how it snapped me with jealousy.

I jumped off the couch, strolling over as if I needed a snack too.

"Good job, mate." Anders, snacking on ham, offered his approval to Lance. "Jamón Ibérico. Best in the world."

Charlie tossed olives in her mouth like popcorn. "God, I've missed the food here," she said. "I haven't been back since I was a kid. I swear, I'm gonna eat my way across the Iberian Peninsula."

She folded a slice of jamón across her tongue. And moaned.

Fuck me, that sound from her throat twinged my cock.

Anders laughed. "How long is that list of restaurants you and Maja have now? I don't think Madrid can handle you two women and your appetites."

Charlie flicked her eyebrows up. "It's a damn long list. My family moved here for two years when I was eight. I'm gonna see how many places are still open all these years later."

The first half of the match ended. Lance paused the game.

"Hey mate." Anders nodded to him. "Come check out my new Krieghoff. It's as handsome as it is powerful."

Anders cradled his rifle cocked open over his arm, heading out to the balcony for an after-action review. Lance followed. He could geek on guns for hours.

Charlie remained perched on her barstool, picking over what food remained.

Grinning, I had her all to myself.

Pouring another Guinness, summoning every cocky role and real-life arrogant ounce in my body, I dared myself. *Take her on, Pierce.*

"You know much about rugby?" I asked.

"You throw the ball backwards, and people get the shit beat out of them. That's all I know."

She ate another olive and spat the pit in a bowl she designated for her aim.

Her lack of lady-like manners besotted me. "So, you're into American football then?"

She washed the olive down with beer before answering, "Yeah. American football makes more sense. I like it. As well as women's soccer. But if I had to pick, water sports are my jam."

"Surfing, right? You look like a California girl."

It was true. She wore that don't-give-a-shit, American surfer look like a pair of perfectly worn flip-flops. Random streaks bleached white in her golden mane. A four-season tan. Relax fashioned over her small frame.

The look of her; it disarmed me.

"Carolina, not California," she replied. "I've surfed, but we don't really get a lot of good waves where I'm from."

"Where is that?" Hoping that sounded nonchalant, my feet shuffled. Fuck, like I was twelve years old again, nervously chatting up a girl at school.

"A little island off the coast of South Carolina that you've never heard of. Most folks know the one next to it—Hilton Head—because of the golf."

"I know Hilton Head. Never been, but yeah, I've seen the golf on TV. Looks like a beautiful place." Struggling for the perfect next line, I went for the taunt. "*I* grew up on an island too. Walney Island off the west coast. Now I bet *you* haven't heard of *it*."

"Nope." She played along. "Have you heard of Daufuskie Island?

Fuck's sakes, my cock just noticed how she tongues her back teeth in a lips-parted challenge. Eyes firing right back at me. Not intimidated. Not impressed. Luring me to reveal more, I tried even harder for her.

"Nope. Never heard of it." I stuffed the last piece of jamón into my mouth. Chewing. Wondering. Worrying. Was she into me? Or on to me? "So, we're just two kids from no-name islands." I nodded toward the flatscreen. "We played rugby, of course. And my brothers, sister and I got into a bit of wind-surfing."

"Wind-surfin' sounds fun." She smacked her lips after her next gulp. "I never really got into it. It was more sailin', fishin', giggin'—that sorta thing for us."

After she drank three beers, I counted them, her face relaxed. So did the guard of her accent... in full bloom for me now.

"Gegging?" I asked, smiling, my body drawn toward her voice.

She grinned at my sad attempt. "Giggin'." She tossed the word back. "Like flounder gigging. You've never heard of it?"

"Gegging," I tried again, laughing at my Southern accent, floundering with *my* failed attempt.

But she leaned in, coaxing me to try again for her. "Like 'fig' say 'gig.'"

I studied her mouth, her lush pink lips, wanting to plunge in. "Gig." I leaned closer, beckoned by the blues and greens in her eyes.

"Now 'in' like you want to go 'in' something."

My breath quickened under her command to enter. "Gig. In."

"That's it! Giggin'." She rewarded me with a smile. "We grew up giggin'. Or flounder giggin' to be exact. It's like spear fishing at night. We spent hours doing it. Then we had fried flounder and French fries the next day with mountains of ketchup as our prize."

"Giggin." I nailed it that time, wanting to please her. "We have flounder on Walney, but I just shore fished. But anything with a spear sounds fun." I was staring. I couldn't get enough of the view. "Who's 'we?' Brothers and sisters?"

My cheeks started to ache from smiling back at her. Not with the practiced grin I wore for the camera or the one I deployed with a wave, masking the nervous twitch of my shoulder whenever I stood in front of crowds.

Usually, I was guarded around new people. Giving measured responses to every question. Never really knowing what would remain personal and what would become embarrassing-to-career-ending press.

But this afternoon, the tables turned. Interviewing her excited me. Probing her with questions and wanting more. How every time she answered me, her eyes fucking lit up. It surged my body from hot to incendiary, burning my guarded act to ash.

"No brothers or sisters," she said. "Can you grab me another beer, please?"

I'd grab anything she asked for.

My sweaty palm pulled the fridge door open, a cool beer bottle offered it relief. When I turned back, steps drawing me closer to her, the pulse in my chest tripled. She sat within my grasp.

"For you." I offered her the beverage.. and so much more.

Her fingers wrapped, unhurried, one by one, around the bottle's base. "Thanks." She smiled. Oblivious to my invitation? Or ignoring it?

Pouring a ruby black stream from high, she answered,

"I'm an only child. I've been on my own since my parents died."

That shuffled me back, "Bloody hell, I'm sorry," shocking me with a pain from my childhood. One I don't talk about. One that left me exposed. But this nakedness? I craved it with her. "How old were you when they passed?"

"I was eighteen, just started college." Her gaze dropped to the foam in her glass. "And now... it's just me." She deployed a singsong "let's move on" tone.

But I studied her posture at the painful reveal.

How she blanketed her long hair over her right shoulder. How she kept her head cocked to the same side. How both the hair and gesture hid the scar on her cheek. Was it practiced or unconscious?

The secret behind the scar was far worse than her parents' early death, I suspected. It gouged a horrific contradiction across her otherwise perfect face.

A contradiction I lived too. But I didn't have a scar across my cheek betraying the secrets hiding underneath. They were too deep and damning for anyone to know.

I didn't care. What was happening to me? I was a moth to her pain. To her secret. It drew me closer, unable to resist her.

"What's Charlie short for?"

But I took the hint, pouring another Guinness, needing more of the elixir to quell whatever the fuck was coursing through my veins.

"Charlotte," she confessed with an eye roll. "Named after my grandmother." She flexed me a, "Don't even think about it," look. "And *no one* ever calls me that, *Daniel Pierce.*"

Fuck's sakes, the sound of my name, dripping from her

lips wet with the sheen of beer in that honey accent almost made me moan aloud.

I drowned the sound with a long swig of beer before licking foam off my lips, my logic amusing.

"Charlotte Ravenel" sounded like a Southern lady who had manners in the parlor and no fear in bed. "Charlie Ravenel" was a French football player who didn't count his drinks and got into scraps at a pub.

I wanted both.

"Where'd you learn to shoot like that?" I asked. "It's bloody impressive."

"My dad. He competed in college. Wanted me to go Olympic. I liked it because it was our time together. Our last few times together actually. But it got too competitive and ruined it."

Her jaw clenched. Her trigger finger wiped condensation off the glass, grief flashing across her eyes, pain sliding down her face.

My heart. My questions. Every part of me but one softened to her. It was a surrender to a woman I'd never felt before. "So, why did you shoot today?"

"A Marine always improvises and adapts."

Surprise hit me again. "You were a Marine?"

"Semper fi and all that."

There was a burden in her tone.

Anders and Lance walked back inside. That game paused and the rugby resumed, demanding half of my attention the rest of the match.

CHAPTER FOUR

CHARLIE

My eyes aimed at the screen while my periphery scoped more.

That exchange in the kitchen?

His delving questions. His smile firing heat across my skin. The attraction arcing from his presence, jolting me—Daniel Pierce crept closer to me in minutes than any man had in years.

How? The attraction, it's obvious between us. Why? We have a lot in common, and a lot we're not saying. What's next?

Pain. Grief. That's all I've known.

It stilled me stoic in the chair, drawing up my defenses. I was here for a reason. One I'd never forget. *A girl is at risk.* It always owned my mind despite what immediate thought rented the rest.

Push him away. If there's one thing you know it's when a man is aiming for you.

England won and bets were paid. Anders stood up, the

first to say it, stumbling back a bit. "I got no business driving my arse home."

"Simon can take us all back." Daniel rose from the sofa, offering his driver and large SUV.

"No mate, I'm in the opposite direction," Anders said. "I'll call for my driver. Take Charlie home. I'll be fine."

"Your drunk ass is gonna bail on me?" I joked with Anders but had to get home somehow, preferring Daniel's trained driver to a random one in a cab.

I glanced up at Daniel, cringing to need anything from him. "Mind if I get a ride?"

"Please do." The delight in his eyes rattled my core. His phone pinged. "That's Simon. He's outside."

I thanked Lance for the afternoon and great food before Anders wrapped me in a bear hug.

"Night, love," he said. "Thanks for kicking our arses today."

"Night." I squeezed him back. "Give my love to Maja and the kids. I'll drop by later this week."

Daniel held the back door to the massive SUV open for me, like he enjoyed being chivalrous. Like I needed it. "Thanks." I tried dismissing the gesture.

But oh hell, passing so close, inches from his gravitational pull, it did it again. Purring my body awake. Pissing me off at the rush.

He crawled in behind me.

I buckled in, giving Simon my address, noting the fuzzy on my brain. The Guinness hit me. I'd lost track at three before the second half.

"Why did you join the military?" Daniel asked, already buckled in and focused on me again. Hard. "Can't be easy for a woman."

Fuck. He remembered exactly where our game paused

and he was seeking more. Of me. And this man always got what he wanted.

Not this time.

"I don't do anything easy." I faced him. "That's why I picked the Marines." His pursuit pushed into the chain-link of my defense.

"What about you?" So I pushed back. "Being a celebrity isn't easy either. It's heaven until it's fucking hell. That's what I've seen of it."

"Yes, but I can't complain. I wanted it."

"That makes two of us."

Remembering my research on the flight to Spain, I reviewed his profile along with all the cast's. I knew... he did want his celebrity life.

The public story about him? He grew up a skinny kid with a handsome face. In his teens, he bulked up playing rugby. A local photographer at a game told him he should model. Next thing, he was eighteen and all over London billboards in a men's underwear campaign that literally stopped traffic. For two years, he graced magazine covers. It wasn't long before he was offered roles. At first, he was cast as eye candy. But he took it seriously, thriving with acting lessons. Now people regarded him as a talented actor, still always wanting his shirt off or a sex scene.

But no matter how naked he appeared on screen; he was covering up something.

That I knew.

The silence between us only made the attraction in the air heavy, painful. And he was staring at me.

I flinched. "Why did you want it? All the fame and success?"

"Acting was an escape. It was the only thing that made me happy."

"Does it still?"

He shrugged his massive shoulders, looking away, reluctant to admit more.

There. That settled it.

But nope. My beers kicked in and I saw it.

How pain flashed in his eyes when I mentioned my parents' death. Yes, he lost something too. What? Who?

And we shared another pain—being objectified. Daniel Pierce was the rare man more objectified than most women.

Curiosity flew out of my mouth.

"Does it ever bother you?" I asked. "How they talk about you? Every article I read or interview I saw for this job talks about how you look. Calling you 'Sex God.' They talk about you like you're just a pretty face and not a person with a soul."

His shocked focus turned toward my lips, to the candor pouring from my mouth.

I needed him to admit it. How he relished it.

With too many years on the sidelines of this industry, I'd witnessed what beauty like his could do. Women screaming for him. Millions online posting graphic descriptions of what they wanted to do with him. Press giddy, hanging on his every word. Everyone rushed to serve him. Men like him expected to get whatever they desired. And all gave it to him with orgasmic delight. It fed egos and wallets.

I needed Daniel Pierce to be an arrogant asshole. It would make pushing him away easy. Because while my mind warned me to stay away, my body ached to be nearer to his.

He had to fail this test.

But he only drew closer toward my harsh sincerity, leaning on the armrest, closing the distance between us.

"No one's ever asked me like that before."

Swimming in the pause of his words, his eyes roaming over me, sweet shivers rose over my flesh.

"What about you, Charlie?" He never answered. Instead, the rich butter of his voice turned back on me. "You're a breathtaking, sexy woman. I can imagine how many times *you've* been told that."

Fuck, he terrified me. Confessing his admiration. Eyes so alluring. Face so handsome. Lips so close. Shocking my pulse up.

I turned away. I wouldn't take it. "I hate it," I said, confessing to the window, "my face has always been a liability for me."

What the fuck just spewed from my mouth?

The truth. One I had bottled up for so long. Yet the mere pressure of Daniel Pierce twisting at the right spot in my resistance burst me open.

"People talk about how I look," I said to the night. "Staring like they're entitled to a piece of me. You're 'such a pretty girl' growing up. Girls are bullies about it. Guys at school make comments, try to grab your ass. The only time they leave you alone is when a rifle is in your hands.

"Then you're a 'female Marine,' not just a 'Marine.' And then a 'wounded vet' with a 'what happened to you' cruel question." I cracked my knuckles against the cool glass. "You're a fucking object to people."

I turned back to him. To my pain. I couldn't hide it. "No one ever sees through to your truth."

Shut the hell up now, Charlie Girl. Keep him away.

But sympathy painted over his gorgeous face, silence holding his pillow lips. The ache in his eyes lured me out even more.

Was it honest or an act?

"I'm not alone." I had to know, unmasking us with my brutal honesty. "I've watched your interviews. How you raise your jaw and lower your voice to every question. When they talk about how you look or ask you something personal, you tap your foot and pull your shoulder away from the inquiry. You smolder a side grin in defense and deflect. Like letting anyone in and telling the truth is too painful for you."

His right eyebrow shot up at my observation.

"Same goes for me, Daniel. Telling the truth hurts too fucking much, doesn't it?"

The navy sweater he wore heaved, inches up, with a trapped breath. I found it. His scar. His vulnerability. It was beautiful, dizzying my logic, unleashing more of my mouth.

"But not today." I couldn't help myself. "Why were you honest with *me*? I made you nervous, shifting but always smiling. But you weren't afraid. You dropped your shoulders, chin, and the act. And you actually talked to me. Why?"

"You saw all that?"

"I see lots of things. The truth is in the small details."

"What else do you see about me?"

His gaze trapped me there. Enthralled. Asking to be seen. No, desperately needing it.

Was I any different? Did I really want to be known? All my pain and truth?

No.

I wanted to stay safe, alone. And this man threatened me with more than interest in his eyes. He kept advancing, kept coming for me.

I gave one final verbal shove, pushing him away. "I can see that your ego craves the attention, but your soul is burdened by the adoration." That bobbed his neck back, widening his eyes. "Am I wrong, Daniel?"

Please say, "Yes." Please don't be human. Don't be so damn gorgeously strong and vulnerable. Any woman's kryptonite.

"No. You're not wrong."

His face. His muscular frame. His facade. It all collapsed in the seat. Like I hit my target, killed his ego, and he was finally relieved of its burden.

And his defeated gaze wouldn't let me go, clinging to mine. "You see me, Charlie. Now let me see you. What burdens you?"

Were we really doing this? Being so fucking honest the day we met? Like we were in a damn confessional and all truths would be revealed with a wafer, cross, and a prayer?

What the hell? Usually this works. Usually, they run. No one gets this part of you.

But he kept grasping for me like a life jacket on his sinking ship.

I shoved him back with judgment. Shaming him so far away he'd never come back again.

"We don't share the same burdens, Daniel. We live in parallel worlds. Ironically flipped given our genders. You're the pretty face of a god, and I'm the ugly scar on a face. Your body is beautiful, to perfect and perform. Mine is wounded, to defend and protect. And in the end, you got all the profit, and I got the pain."

It worked. Hurt blasted across his yielding face.

Shit. Why'd you do that? You don't like hurting people.

No, I had to. Had to be so damn honest he couldn't take it. So he would leave me alone and let me do my job.

But his eyes wouldn't relent. Pushing right back for

more. Like he crawled on top of me, mounting me for the win.

"That's what you think, Charlie." Fuck, I'd never met a man like this, one I couldn't intimidate. "But that's not what you feel between us right now. Admit it. It's too strong."

"You don't know what I feel."

"I don't need to know it." Tilting his chin, he twisted into me. "Suddenly, I feel it. I feel everything. I believe we both do."

He hit my target too, the impact of him exploding through my body. It was instinct. I fired back.

"No. I believe in two things, Daniel. Science and karma. One gives you beauty." A strangling in my throat. "The other makes you pay for it."

"We're here, sir," Simon called out.

The car stopped in front of the small, white Spanish villa with a terra cotta roof I rented. It looked like every other on the street. I glanced down, unbuckling the seat belt then picking up my bag.

When I looked back at him, I saw too much and said, "One thing I will admit. How we are alike." I felt too much. "I believe you've suffered the price too. Question is, are you strong enough to admit it?"

Yanking the door handle, I bolted out of the car, slinging my bag over my shoulder, escaping as fast as I could. The hum of his SUV sounded behind me, waiting for me to open my front door.

I wouldn't look back. Closing the wooden arched door behind me, I collapsed against it with more emotion in one day, in one brutal conversation, than I'd felt in years.

Scanning the scene around me—terra cotta floors, white walls, Miró paintings and plants—the rest of me... questioning...

What the hell just happened with him?

DANIEL

WATCHING HER UNLOCK HER DOOR, raw emotion surged through me. I told Simon to wait. To make sure she got in safely. To study her. To recover from her. Her words cracking through my mind.

I thought I questioned her today. She read me the whole time.

Whatever she just did to me—it bloody hurt with emotions I'd been acting for years but living numb to.

My fucking head was spinning. No, my whole world was.

No one challenged me. No one spoke so raw, so honestly with me.

Bloody hell, she intimidated me... and I loved it.

It was a new sensation. Charlie Ravenel's words took razor blades to my skin, and yes, I could finally feel again.

She was right. I was real with her today. Why?

She made me nervous, so fucking alive around her.

And yes, I fed on adoration; needed it for my ego and bank account.

How did she know?

For years the millions my supposed beauty rewarded me with, it forced down a pain that plagued me with a lonely void. My vanity. All for profit. Not for purpose. The superficiality of my life. One of excruciating isolation in a hotel between one screaming fan interview to another. Millions worshipping me like a god, and yet, I'd never felt so alone, so empty. My only companion—the bloody secret I hid from the world.

I did my job. Acting happy. Looking handsome. Being strong. All with an ugly, hollow ache in my chest I could never fill.

Until now. She dropped a match on me, and I blazed full of pain.

She saw it and saw me, past my bullshit celebrity, straight through. How my body tried telling me what my mind didn't want to admit.

This life? It had me gagging on my soul.

In one day of meeting this woman, she'd pierced the veil of my facade with divine accuracy. It fucking terrified me. And I only wanted more.

More of her.

CHAPTER FIVE

CHARLIE

"Wow, a Walmart is more secure than this place," I whispered low enough for only Rob to hear.

The only thing that felt right? Working with Rob again.

We're a strong team. We went through Quantico. We served tours in Afghanistan around the same time. We'd protected Juliette. Each of us had dark ghosts. And we each had wicked tongues for jokes, making long days and dangerous threats bearable.

The rest? This Monday? I started down a familiar perilous path.

It was our first day on set, before dawn, before any cast and crew were scheduled to arrive.

The transportation captain, Hugo, met us at the gates of the studio. Everyone went through them to get in. Credentials had to be worn. Names had to be on the list for the day to be permitted in. It ensured safety.

Not by my estimation.

We walked the entire studio lot with the on-site security team. There were multiple points around the wall anyone could jump over.

I imagined it—shimmying up the palms beside the wall and leaping inside. Not hard to do.

And don't get me started on how the guard at the gate was more interested in his phone than checking if our credentials were legit. Anyone with a printer and some audacity could hack that faulty system.

The studio lot was huge, with four other productions being filmed. Each had their own basecamps of trailers and trucks for operations and services. All scattered over sprawling acres with mammoth stage buildings in between.

At any given time, hundreds to a thousand or more people worked within the studio gates, all crammed into their own villages of unlocked trailers and trucks, creating easy access with alleyways where anyone could skulk in between without notice.

I imagined that too. Sneaking into a trailer. A big, hairy hand smothering a small mouth that tried to scream. No one would know until the violence was done.

It thinned my breath with sick unease.

The Druid had dozens of trailers at basecamp. We had to take all of them into consideration as we made a plan.

Surveillance cameras weren't allowed on any basecamp or stage building. They're too much of a hackable security risk, violating the privacy of the cast and crew, risking the costly secrets behind any production.

And while social media and smartphones were vital in promoting any film or show nowadays, they were also a significant security risk. They had to be silenced if brought on set. Everyone had to sign a strict non-disclosure agreement prohibiting photos and posts to social media.

Still, some broke the rules anyway.

In this world, you had to trust people.

The exact problem.

Hugo, the transpo captain, arrived every morning before anyone else, unlocking the trailers. Before the cast arrived, the costumer hung their first scene's wardrobe in the closet of their trailer. Catering fired up their truck for breakfast and lunch. Hair and makeup prepared potions and palettes for the day. All while a basecamp production assistant stood by the cast trailers, knocking on their doors when it was time to shoot, keeping an eye on who went where, and when.

Our tour ended in front of Kierra's white trailer. A sign reading "2 – BRIGID MORRIGAN" hung on the door—Kierra's trailer and cast number along with her character's name. Hers looked like most others at basecamp. It was next to Daniel's.

"1 – CARRIC MORRIGAN" hung from his sleek black door. The outside of his swanky custom trailer signaled his high status.

Mason Hunt had his own on the other side of Kierra's. And now Anders's posh trailer took up space on the other side of Mason's.

I scanned all four principal cast trailers lined up like targets in a row. That sight? I wouldn't take my eyes off all season.

Kierra's was a two-banger trailer—a bang for the sound each door on the side of the trailer makes. Her trailer was divided in two parts. One half was her classroom with her teacher. The other half was for her private use.

As a minor, an adult had to be on set with Kierra. Last season it had been her teacher. Now—with this stalking threat—her mom would be coming to set too.

HGR Security insisted on an office for us near the principal cast members this season. We had a third of a three-banger beside the hair and makeup trailers, going down the path to the catering truck.

Hugo pulled the door open to Kierra's trailer before leaving us to our work. I took the two metal steps up into the space, pulling my breath and instinct in.

Rob followed me. He unpacked his counter surveillance gear and started using it to comb Kierra's trailer for electronic devices.

I looked around, using a gut feeling to spot threats.

It was the usual. Small sofa. Banquette table with seating. Kitchenette. Wardrobe closet and mirror. Small door into a microscopic bathroom.

But something threatened.

Hovering over my right shoulder, I sensed it watching me.

I whipped around.

Lights flashed on the device in Rob's hand when he climbed up to the blinds over the window by the banquette table. I saw it too. We stayed silent while Rob pinched the small camera and tiny wire out from the top casing of the blinds.

It was recording our every movement and word.

He moved to disconnect the wire, but I stopped him with a grin, whispering into the micro lens, "Fuck you," before Rob severed the connection.

The trailers for season two had been open on basecamp for days now for pre-production.

Rob raised his eyebrow at me. Our assessment?

This was an inside job.

We called Jeremy from their secure trailer office. "Fuck!" Jeremy spat out. "There goes the bloody budget." He started going down the list. We knew what to do. "I'm sending Joaquin. We need someone local for the team." The clicking of his laptop keys filled the speakers on my laptop. "I'll contact the studio and Lorraine. We have to lock this down."

When our video chat ended, agitation had me reaching down, yanking the laces on my boots tighter.

"Let Jeremy worry about the budget," I said. "You know what I'm gonna do."

Rob kicked his boots up onto the drop table-turned-office desk. "Yep, saw it before with Juliette. Many times. God help the poor fucker."

"I'm gonna catch his ass. Fucking red-handed. I'll call Kierra's mom tonight with the update. Otherwise, it's a need to know only."

Rob stretched back in his office chair. "At least we know Lorraine, the studio and the producers won't talk. Gotta keep a facade of a secure workplace."

"They got their motives"—with a final yank of my laces, I darted my glance up at Rob—"I got mine."

I only cared about the girl I hadn't even met yet.

The girl some perverted fuck wanted to watch undress with his hidden camera. The thought of all he could steal from the girl scorched rage through me.

STARING at the dark ceiling that night, I lay in bed, willing my mind to be as still as my body.

It didn't work.

Today on set, confronting the camera, confronting the threat to a girl, it left my heart pounding with the truth.

This job? I wasn't only protecting Kierra.

I was protecting myself. Whether I was hiding in my secluded island home or in the shadows of a set, focused on the threat to an innocent girl instead of the one tweezing my vertebrae; it didn't matter.

The instinct still haunted me.

For six years.

Ever since the horrific day that marked me forever.

Sitting up, I turned on the bedside light, taking the envelope out of the drawer. It held Kierra's picture and the photocopy of the note she'd found.

I had to focus, I had to deal with the present, the future.

What did I see? Kierra's stalker was on set, fixated on having her.

What did I know? Two of us were being stalked now.

CHAPTER SIX

CHARLIE

I warned, "Y'all ain't gonna like this news," sitting beside Rob in front of my laptop on our video call to Jeremy after a long day. Hell, a long week. And it was only Thursday afternoon.

We had divided our tasks.

Rob met with the studio manager, with Lance at the stables, with transportation and the location managers. I reviewed police and personnel files before filling my calendar with meetings with the protection detail of the principal cast: Kierra, Anders, Daniel, and Mason.

Until we completed our assessment, Kierra wasn't to come to set. No scenes were scheduled for her. It's a legitimate protocol. One that secretly allowed me to delay what would surely rip my skin off with recall.

I needed more time. Before I met Kierra.

And my past.

"Bring it." Jeremy clicked his pen on the call. Bad news always fired his thumb up.

"When I called Kierra's mom to schedule our meeting, she shared something with me," I said. "Something she doesn't want Kierra to know."

I had mixed feelings about keeping my mark—the person I'm tasked to protect—in the dark about threats. But since Kierra was a teenager, there was a delicate balance between information and innocence.

"The owner of the house Kierra's family rented during season one called her mom," I reported. "The owner discovered that the window screen outside Kierra's first floor bedroom had been sliced open, clean, like with a razorblade. But the windows are so old, so much paint on them. Her mom said there was no opening them."

"So, he stood right outside her window?" Jeremy's head shook. "Wanting her but not able to get in."

"Yep," I confirmed.

The closeness of the threat to Kierra troubled me too.

"Glad they're renting in a gated community now," Rob said. "We got a vulnerable location though. Lance showed me around the stables. The cast rehearse there with their horses, some locations are scheduled there next month too and that place is Swiss cheese. Too many holes to count."

"Joaquin is en route," Jeremy said. "We got more backup here in London if you need them."

"Good," Rob said. "And Charlie gets to put on her cowgirl hat and go horseback riding tomorrow."

"What?" Sounded like horse shit to me.

"Someone needs to ride the stable's perimeter"—Rob couldn't stop grinning—"to see where fans are trying to sneak in."

"Fuck you and your allergies to everything with fur." I slouched in the chair. "How early?"

Rob leaned back, delighted in his. "Lance is there at seven a.m., mi prima."

"Fine." I changed the alarm on my phone. "Lucky for you I'm a country girl, you city fuck."

I didn't mention I hadn't been on a horse in over fifteen years.

"All right. That's sorted," Jeremy said. "Anything else?"

"Nope," we replied in unison.

Nudging my SEAT León sedan up to the gate of the stables, I checked the dashboard clock. 6:50 a.m. glowed back. I always rented the most common local car in white for the job. Blend in. Never stand out as a target.

Swiping my access card, the gate opened. In my rearview mirror, I saw Lance pulling up behind me. He parked by the front of the stables while I parked under the shade of some trees.

Lance called out, "Good morning!"

With cowboy boots crunching across the gravel lot, I shouted back, "Mornin'!"

My hair still hung damp from a rushed shower that morning. It took me forever to find my black riding tights before grabbing my HGR tactical jacket and rushing out the door.

I gave Lance a handshake, pronouncing, "I'm ready to ride."

He pointed to my feet. "I like the boots. But I don't think we'll be roping cows today."

I cocked my chin up to his joke. "Well, I gotta lasso somethin'."

Not giving a shit, I was no equestrian. These were my mom's boots.

"I'm game."

A baritone voice rumbled behind me, whipping my head around.

Daniel Pierce leaned against the stable door in a black fleece jacket, jeans and a red baseball cap, lips smacking with a smile and the last bite of an egg bocadillo.

I assumed it would be just me and Lance. Daniel here knocked me off guard, curling my lips up in pleasure before I could stop myself.

I already clocked him a few times on set from afar that week, noting how he spent most of his time alone in his swanky trailer.

It was my job to observe people. Getting paid to watch Daniel Pierce? A true bonus. One a few southern parts of me enjoyed.

"Okay," I answered, "ride one click ahead and we'll see if I can rope ya."

We dared each other with half-cocked grins.

I thought he'd hate me after I psychologically pillaged him, hurting him on purpose to push him away.

But no, he stood there, grinning back like he wants more pain. "Yee-haw," he teased me more, tipping his hat.

Fuck. And fine. I can dish out salty all day long.

I strode past him into the stables. "I just wear the damn boots, y'all. Not every Southern woman is a cowgirl." I threw the words over my shoulder. "I don't do ropes and cattle. I do lines and a jib."

I was aware Daniel was following me, aware how my jacket sat high on my waist, so aware of how my ass felt served up like a buffet to him in these tights.

Eat it up, Pierce. It's as close as you get.

"Well, I'm glad someone can ride to report back on this," Lance said while they walked through the stables out to the paddock. "We need more security out here."

The stable master was saddling three horses up. "Who's riding with us?" I asked Lance, fearing the answer I already knew.

"I am," Daniel said. "You don't mind, do you?" He patted the gray neck of the imposing Andalusian, giving the elegant horse his caress while staring me down. "This beauty is new this season. I have two weeks to master her ride."

Mind? Hell yes, I did. Especially at the sexy double entendre he just dared. It blushed my cheeks.

Was this man going to be gum on my boot? Stepped on and following me around, horny for more?

Together, the three of us rode for an hour around the perimeter paths.

As we slowed to round the top of a hill, Lance caught up to me, warning, "Up here is the biggest problem. It's where paparazzi and fans hang out for pictures of Daniel. Mason and Kierra too. They yell out and spook the horses. Almost knocked Kierra off last season."

Sure enough, as we rode side-by-side over the hill, there they waited. Two cars parked in the grass behind two women and one man shouting, "¡Hola Daniel! ¡Ven aquí! ¡Ven aquí por favor!"

Lance's horse spooked. Daniel leaned in, calming his. My horse tensed under my thighs too.

"All right. Let's deal with this." I rode toward the fence, gesturing for them to follow.

The man at the fence cried out, "¡Daniel! ¿Por favor puede tomarnos una foto juntos?"

Daniel looked at me, his eyebrow raised, questioning what's next.

"Stay here a sec," I said.

Calmly, I jumped down from the horse while the guys stayed on theirs. Approaching the three fans, I stopped twenty-five feet away. Close enough to shout, far enough to react if one made a run toward Daniel.

Noting their faces. Memorizing the model of the cars, their front plates. Scanning their hands. Just phones. They weren't a threat. Just a nuisance.

"Hola. ¿Cómo están?" My tone was polite tone, asking the obvious. "¿Son aficionados del programa? ¿The Druid? ¿Vinieron a ver a Daniel?"

"¡Sí, sí!" they exclaimed.

I hooked my index finger, twice, signaling for Daniel to join me.

He jumped down from his horse. As he walked over, all three squealed, jumping up and down. How adult fans lose their damn minds around the objects of their worship; I was embarrassed for them.

I whispered to Daniel, "Do you speak any Spanish? You can thank them for being fans but tell them they need to stop coming to the fence because it's scaring the horses. It's dangerous. You or someone else could get hurt."

He looked surprised at my simple tactic. "I don't speak Spanish well enough for that."

"Say it in English. They may understand. I'll translate."

He spoke with warmth and a dazzling smile. I recited in Spanish, adding, "Nada más una foto."

"Sí, sí. Claro. Perdónanos, Daniel." They repeatedly apologized, looking ashamed for upsetting Daniel, for putting him in harm's way.

Yep, I knew the power of guilt all too well.

Daniel waved for their photo. The fans went crazy. Then they caught my fierce eye and stopped at one photo like I instructed.

"Está bien," I declared.

Daniel turned back toward his horse while I explained to the fans that next time security would be at the fence. Thanking them for being fans of the show, I warned, if they came back, they'd get fines or jail. I'd be sure of it.

When I climbed back up on my horse, Daniel laughed, saying, "I don't know what you said to them, or if you sounded more like a mum or a Marine. But either way, you sounded like a woman not to fuck with."

I tugged the reins, turning my horse toward the paddock, replying, "Most of the time."

Riding beside Lance, we talked about my report to HGR and the studio about security out here.

Those fans were harmless. I didn't trust others would be.

DANIEL

PRETENDING to check messages on my phone, I waited for Charlie to finish with Lance.

All that past week, I thought about her. How she gutted me open in the car and left me gasping for more.

That woman dominated my brain and body. Every spare thought I had landed on her. Then I'd glance up, look out my trailer window... and a long, blonde ponytail under a black baseball hat would swish by.

It was like my thoughts were fated to find her every time.

Lust for her threatened to obsess. The only force stemming its power? The word "lust" failed to name it.

What was taking residence in my being for her? So fucking fast the terror of it thrilled me?

Once she walked toward the parking lot, I tried to casually follow, admiring the view. Her spectacular ass, a magnet for my gaze.

She got to her car then turned around suddenly. "You aren't following me, are you?"

Fuck, busted. "Just waiting for Simon to pick me up."

She shrugged and resumed ignoring me.

The sun beamed high in the sky, raising the temperature. Peeling off her jacket and tossing it into the back of her car, she wore a white crew-neck shirt underneath. It hung loose, showing little skin, but it gave me hints of ripped arms, taut abs, and as she moved, ripe breasts, her nipples firming as her body cooled.

My eyes roamed again over those fucking tights, appreciating her firm bum and hamstrings. It looked like she was a strong rider of something. Galloping my pulse, I wished it was me...

And her, riding you so tight, so wet and hard right now. With muscles like that? She could fuck you all night, Pierce. The view of her naked on top of you, those pert tits, her firm ass in your hands. Fuck, how you'd hang on to her, coming for your dear life.

I dropped my stare, yanking my cap off and pulling my fingers through my sweaty hair. Anything to distract thoughts quickly going south on my body.

"Sorry to disappoint you," she said.

Fuck, busted again. "Disappoint about what?" Simon pulled into the parking lot.

"No rope." Her tone? Hard. Her smile? Soft. "No lassoing."

"Ha!" I whooped, relieved. *Not busted.* "Remember, I'm an island kid like you. I'd rather run lines and a jib too."

My car stopped in front of me. My randy mind teased me with a, "Maybe you can rope me later" request, but thankfully my thirty-seven years stopped my mouth before my dick spoke nowadays.

Climbing in the car, I conjured visions. After seeing her with those pants and nipples, my imagination was very generous. As soon as Simon pulled into the studio lot, I escaped straight to my trailer, desperate for a shower and to indulge in my new-found fixation.

Charlie Ravenel, bound for me.

CHAPTER SEVEN

CHARLIE

No more putting it off. Early Monday morning I drove through the security gates into Kierra's neighborhood. After the cut to her window screen update, I thanked the family's wisdom for renting in this community. I approved, also noting the cameras monitoring the house when I parked outside.

Rob pulled up behind me and got out of his car. He'd audit existing surveillance, suggesting upgrades if needed. I'd handle the human side.

"Sup, fucker," he said with our usual greeting.

"Sup, fucker."

Rob always made me feel better. We could read each other's moods like a menu—like, *oh, I see we're having pissed off with a side of impatient today.*

I rang the camera doorbell. It took less than a minute.

"Hello there." Kierra's mom, Anne, and her Irish lilt sounded through the speaker. "HGR?"

"Yes, ma'am." We held our credentials up to the camera.

"I'm Charlie Ravenel. We spoke on the phone. This is my colleague, Roberto Vasquez."

The door opened. The concern Anne tried disguising on her face flooded me.

Her daughter was being stalked. It was hell for her too.

"Good morning, Ms. Williams." I shook Anne's hand. "Nice to meet you in person."

She led us inside where we met Kierra's team. "My husband and son are home in Galway. This is our Madrid family." She introduced Kierra's assistant, manager, and driver.

"I heard you were Juliette Jones's protection on *Fated*." Grace, Kierra's assistant, asked me, "That was you in London with her, wasn't it? Outside that club?"

Yeah, that was my famous shot. It went viral.

The time I throat punched a pervert, dropping him to his knees for grabbing Juliette's breast outside a club in London.

Paparazzi got the picture, but never got my face. They only got my back squatting before him while I twisted his balls and whispered in his ear, "Back off my girl, dick. Or next time, I'll rip it off."

I smiled. "Mr. Vasquez and I worked on *Fated* for several years, yes."

That's all I was willing to disclose.

It took fifteen minutes for Kierra to walk into the family room to greet us. Her delay wasn't rude. It took bravery to confront this now.

But nothing prepared me for the Kierra's beauty, even after studying her photograph. Transparent skin, large liquid green eyes, masses of copper waves. Knees buckling as I stood, I shook her hand.

"Hi, Kierra." My voice choked. "I'm Charlie."

Kierra looked into my eyes. Fear hid behind her unnatural composure. It split me open with a lightning strike of painful memories.

Dear God, Charlie Girl, you must do this. Keep your shit together and protect her.

"Howya." Kierra's Irish greeting and touch was so light, I barely felt it. She turned, greeting Rob with the same subtle resentment.

I was glad to see some anger in the girl's eyes.

She'd need it.

Rob started the meeting with a conversation about the option of putting a camera inside Kierra's trailer, one with a range set to monitor her trailer door only. We already told Kierra, her mom and team about the hidden camera we found aimed toward her dressing area. Even though cameras weren't allowed outside at basecamp, Kierra could do what she wanted in her own space.

"Kierra, it's an option, but I must share my reservations about it." I warned, "Nothing is one hundred percent secure. It can be hacked. We can protect you without it, but it's your call. No one else's."

"Kierra dear, don't you think it's a good idea?" her mother urged. "It's for your safety."

Kierra's face twisted at the intrusion. I didn't care that Kierra was technically a minor. It was her privacy and body. And her decision.

Kierra shook her head emphatically. "I don't want any cameras in my trailer."

That's my girl. Way to be stubborn.

Rob frowned. He'd prefer to use the technology, I knew, but he kept his protest silent. He focused next on logistical issues with transportation and security protocols.

All while I studied her.

How Kierra picked at her cuticles, leg bouncing, scared, and annoyed by the conversation. How her mother noticed it too. After an hour, she gently suggested we break for more tea.

"Would you mind if I talked to Kierra privately?" I asked Anne in the kitchen, sipping the tea she offered. "We can go for a walk." Anne furrowed her brow, seeming reluctant to let her daughter out of her sight. I set my cup down. "Ms. Williams, I promise. I'm here to protect her."

Anne dropped her shoulders. "If Kierra is comfortable with it, then yes."

I found Kierra sitting in the living room, scrolling through Instagram. I peered over her shoulder. "Any good dish?"

"No, just doing my daily stalk of Harry Styles."

"Yes, girrrllll," I sang out. "I can't wait for his next album."

Kierra's lips lifted at our shared fandom.

I nodded toward the front door. "Can we go for a walk and chat?"

Kierra's shoulders winced up, her knee still bouncing.

"Don't worry." With every cell in my body, I promised, "I won't let anything happen to you, Kierra."

We walked down the manicured street of the wealthy Madrid neighborhood.

I asked about her favorite foods in Spain, favorite shows and music. I shared stories of living here as a little girl. How I drove my parents crazy with my obsession with Flamenco dancing, stomping around in my mom's high heel shoes.

That made Kierra laugh.

When Kierra's fists weren't balled up anymore and swung relaxed, I asked, "So, how are you feeling about all this?"

"I don't know. Scared, I guess." Kierra gazed into the distance. Tears started rolling down her cheeks. "I can't sleep. I'm scared to be alone. I don't understand why someone would do this to me.

"I got in a big row with my parents about coming back to the show. They wanted me to quit. But I was lucky to get the role. My parents have sacrificed so much for my career. My Nana too. She passed last year. She was so excited about this."

Kierra's steps halted, her face flush with tears. "I'm not giving in." She turned, eyes and words pleading to me. "It's embarrassing though. I don't want people to know. I don't want to be the girl who needs special treatment."

"I understand." I liked this girl's strength. "I served in the military. Giving women 'special treatment' meant to some we weren't equal."

I reached out, touching Kierra's arm.

"*I* take you seriously, Kierra. As far as other's know, we're extra cast security because of the success of the show and because you're a minor. Secretly between us, I'm your protection officer. Rob and Joaquin are my back up. Only a few will know. They'll keep it quiet too."

Kierra's face softened in relief.

It was a fine line I had to walk, honoring Kierra's feelings and needing her trust me. I had other motives too. I needed to give the stalker a chance to fuck up and try again.

I'd be ready for him.

"Tell me about the cast and crew," I said. We started walking again. "How does everybody treat you?"

"Lorraine, the producers and directors, they're all great to me."

"What about the crew? Anyone ever make you feel uncomfortable?"

"No, not really."

"Anyone in the cast or the day-players?"

Kierra may not have noticed last season, but I needed her watching now. All the people on set? It was hundreds. Too many to watch all the time.

But many times, you didn't just watch, you felt. You regarded everyone with Zen-like suspicion.

"Umm." Kierra's lips pressed together; her steps hesitated.

"Kierra, it's between us. I promise. I just want to know your feelings. Your instinct. You need to learn to listen to it."

The entire list of all the cast, crew and extras from season one—it was long. I needed someone to aim for.

Kierra glanced my way; forehead wrinkled. "I guess Daniel makes me nervous. During our scenes or sitting together in the green room on set."

"Daniel?"

"I don't know," Kierra said. "He's always nice. Professional. Doting even. But I don't know." She shook her head. "He makes me nervous. Maybe it's the whole Zeus thing. I fancied him when I was a girl."

"Kierra, do you notice how you say, 'I don't know,' followed by exactly what you *do* know? Take away the 'I don't know' and you hear your instinct, your truth."

"Huh." Kierra's chin bobbed back. "Well, I know Daniel's a stunner. But now that I work with him, it's weird. Not romantic. Just weird. He's"—she lowered her voice to a kind whisper—"he's too old for me."

A grin slid across my face.

Daniel's "too old" for Kierra? If I were picking men, he's finally ripe for the pluck.

Maybe it *was* the Zeus thing. His staggering looks intimidated many. I hoped that explained Kierra's discomfort.

Still, I didn't dismiss it.

A kid's instinct can be more reliable than an adult's. Particularly for a girl. Like a survival instinct she has before it gets numbed by the pursuit in this world of men.

"What about Mason?" I hadn't met him yet.

Mason Hunt was the staggeringly handsome younger man cast to look like Daniel's little brother. Twenty-one years old. Only five years older than Kierra. Maybe the good-looking guy effect plagued Kierra.

Hell, since I left my safe world and landed in Madrid... I knew the feeling.

"Ha!" Kierra tossed her head back. "Mason can be an eejit. Always on his phone. Always going on about his nights out. He and his mate, Lorenzo, our basecamp P.A. Mason pals around with him, acting better than everyone, trying to impress Daniel and the stunt team."

Typical, pretty-boy actor full of himself. I'd seen the kind on the set of *Fated*. Anders ate them for lunch. I'd enjoy watching him put Mason in his place this season.

I'd met Lorenzo already, the morning we found the camera in Kierra's trailer. He stood post, doing his job outside the cast trailers. He was a handsome, local guy. Eager to please. Rob had joked around with him while I noticed how many times Lorenzo asked about HGR and our jobs on set. Questions we laughed off.

When we started walking back toward her house, "Kierra," I touched her hand, stopping our steps. "I know what you're going through. How it feels to be targeted, so I need you to trust me. Tell me everything. I won't think you're crazy. I've seen you assert yourself with your mom. I get it. But I need for you to follow my instructions. Okay?"

Focusing on Kierra's emerald eyes, I flashed back to

another girl's eyes full of terror. It squeezed my throat but I gritted out the words, "I won't let anyone hurt you, Kierra."

Kierra stared at the scar on my cheek. "I believe you."

Just as the touch of my hand left Kierra's, "Charlie, I need to tell you something," she pulled it back. "I kept a secret from my parents because they never would've let me come back to set. But it's why I insisted on more security this season."

I steeled myself, having suspected this all along. "Okay. I'm listening."

"It wasn't just the note I found the day we wrapped. There were several left in my trailer. I thought they were sweet. One told me I looked beautiful. Another said I was doing a good job. It's embarrassing but they flattered me at first. But then they got creepy. The second to last note talked about my body, about tying me up with rope."

"Do you still have the notes?"

They could be evidence. I could have them sampled for prints or DNA. Because, what I learned this week? The police found nothing on the last note. *Not so amateur after all.*

"No. I threw them in the bin." Regret bent Kierra's face. "My mam was there when I found the last one. That's how this whole thing started."

She's hiding more. "What else happened, Kierra?"

Kierra paused, looking surprised, then relieved. "That same last week we were shooting, things went missing from my trailer."

I nodded, asking, "What was taken?" I listened to the pattern of grooming Kierra described, masking the alarm on my face, the surge in my pulse, noting it all started the last week of filming.

I had to find out what else happened that week on set.

Kierra's brow pinched. "The blue scarf I knitted on set last season. The necklace my boyfriend gave me."

A boyfriend back in Galway. I already checked him out. Not a threat. "What did the necklace look like?"

"It was my initial 'K' with my birthstone for May. A little emerald."

Kierra glanced down. The pause, warning me, *there's more.* "Kierra. I'm not mad. Is that all you need to tell me?"

Tears returned to her eyes. "My knickers were taken the last week on set. I got back to my trailer, and they weren't with my other clothes in my wardrobe closet."

I bit down every warning flooding me, calmly asking, "Kierra, what did they look like?"

Not able to mask the fear set across her face, she answered, "A white cotton thong. Nothing fancy."

After a long exhale, balancing all the shoulds with strategy firing my logic, I said, "Kierra. This is between us. For now. But I want you to find the courage to tell your mom. Soon. She loves you and is doing all she can to protect you too. I'm not a fan of secrets. They're a real danger. Especially when we're trying to keep you safe."

Kierra nodded; lips pursed.

I cut my eyes at her. "Tell her. Okay?"

"I will," Kierra said. She wouldn't let go of my hand. "Charlie, is it going to be okay?"

"It is now."

That was a half-true.

LATER THAT AFTERNOON, I woke from a siesta to the breathless screams of a little girl.

My heart pounding, I was drenched in sweat.

In my dream, a little girl's pudgy hands reached for me. She was fascinated by my blonde hair under my black head scarf and helmet. I snorted like a little piglet at her touching my strands.

It made her giggle.

Those giggles morphed into howls of torment in my nightmare. Screams of pain no one could stop. Someone had to stop them.

I had to stop them.

I jolted up, drawing deep breaths. Counting to four. Over and over.

Why this nightmare again, why now?

Kierra, of course.

I'd endure anything to protect *this* girl now.

CHAPTER EIGHT

CHARLIE

It was later that same Monday night. The producers of the show hosted a cast dinner in a private room at a swanky Madrid restaurant.

I attended as incognito as possible while Kierra and her mom took their seats, following my instructions. "Just act like I'm not here."

The presence of these bodies gathered heated the sinews in my neck.

The principal cast were encouraged to bring a plus one. Most did.

Though I cursed myself noting how Daniel arrived alone, how it flushed relief across my heart.

Anders brought Maja. Mason brought Lorenzo, the two of them boasting about how they were going out for "real fun" after the meal.

It made my stomach flip, how Daniel, sitting across from Kierra, stole glances at me before he forced his gaze to other guests. He was the ultimate professional, disappearing from the table for a while, returning with the restaurant's sommelier and a round of Don Perignon for everyone.

Mason, sitting to Daniel's left seemed distracted, sidetalking with Lorenzo, but when he did engage with others, his charisma was potent, practiced.

And Anders, to Daniel's right, was the life of the crowd with jokes and Maja laughing along with him.

I surveyed the room.

I noted who spoke to Kierra, the contours of the conversations. Most were jovial, though a couple of the male producers leaned in as Kierra spoke, raising my eyebrow. Either they actually respected Kierra as a talented actor—I hoped—or the girl's beauty enraptured them.

Daniel's comments toward Kierra were warm. Anders's? Familial. And Mason's? Chin up, provoking. Lorenzo tried chatting with Kierra, but he twisted awkward, intimidated by her.

Poised, Kierra politely smiled, replying to them all, though I clocked her black sandaled foot bouncing under her chair.

She was nervous.

Everyone treated Kierra like an adult woman. No one treated her like a girl.

The fact itched my trigger finger. The range of regard for Kierra, my responsibility to protect, it fired my senses.

I could smell the guile, taste the deception served.

Fuck, Charlie Girl. He's right here in the room with you.

When Kierra and her mom stood up to go to the restroom, I followed. Once we were alone in the narrow corridor, I checked the women's restroom. Three stalls. All clear. Kierra and her mom entered. I covered the hallway.

While I texted Kierra's driver with a departure update,

the corner of my eye caught it—a hulking silhouette suddenly filling the narrow space.

"I wanted to thank you, Ms. Ravenel." Daniel neared. The aroma of him—cedar, apple and something pulse raising—filling my air. He stopped outside the men's restroom.

The inches between our bodies, not enough.

"Just doing my job, Mr. Pierce."

Don't look at him. You know what you'll see. Aqua eyes that fucking drop a bomb on your resolve to keep him away.

"I don't mean about the fans at the stables. I mean for what you said to me in the car." His voice coaxed my reluctant gaze to rise. "About the night we met."

And my eyes met his. The way he looked down at me. Not amused. Not angry. It was admiration searing to attraction. He licked his bottom lip... before biting it.

Holy shit, fucking tingles fired up my legs. Was that sweat in my palms? Was that shame gnawing at my heart for being such a brutal bitch to him? And he was thanking me for it?

I swallowed it down, gunning my gaze right back at him. "Yeah. Sorry 'bout that. My mouth can be as lethal as my aim."

"No one has ever come that hard at me." Staring down, no lines troubled his stunning face, only a ravishing smile that took my entire being. "I liked it very much. It gave me a lot to think about."

"Don't think too much on my words, Mr. Pierce."

"I wasn't merely thinking about your words." He neared another inch. "I've been thinking... about you." Fuck, leaning even closer. "A lot."

Heat flushed my cheeks and everything between my thighs. I watched it flame up his neck too.

"Do you do that often, Ms. Ravenel?" he asked. "Drop a man to his knees?"

"Can you handle it, Mr. Pierce?"

My question pulled his chin dangerously close to mine. "I'm man enough to want much more of it." He stole my breath. "To be on my knees in front of you, Charlie. It would be a massive honor."

My clit screamed. I could imagine his beautiful face buried there. His lips, his tongue, tasting my...

A shuffle approached. Lorenzo entered the narrow corridor. Daniel glanced over his shoulder at him before taking one more look at me and then he disappeared behind the swinging door to the men's room.

Putting my nose back to my screen, hearing the sinks flowing in the women's room, the floor wobbled beneath me. Kierra and her mom were almost done. Good... because I needed air. Fast.

The crowd finished the night with final toasts for a great season two. A lively spirit was in Kierra, laughing all the way out to the parking lot. We were some of the last to leave.

Malcom, Kierra's driver and another HGR Security employee, had grabbed dinner around the corner. He was walking across the parking lot to meet us at the car.

"You'd be a right dinger all made up, Charlie." Kierra taunted me with the red lipstick from her bag. "You're so stunning. And that scar is dead sexy. Do you have a boyfriend? Or a girlfriend?"

That made me laugh. "No. And if anyone gets me Kierra, they'll take me as I am."

Our steps halted, shocked by the sight on the passenger door.

Kierra's necklace. A "K" with an emerald twinkling in the parking lot light.

It hung from the passenger door handle. It hung by a white zip tie handcuff.

My hand flew up, blocking Kierra. Scanning our surround. No one. Just a gaggle of producers across the parking lot plopping into their cars. Malcom stood on at the driver's side door, witnessing our sudden halt, Kierra's terror, and my tactics.

"Malcom, call Jeremy. Tell him we need a detective out here. Now," I instructed.

Fuck, we couldn't call the police with lights flashing. It would only draw attention to Kierra's stalking threat, the last thing we needed.

Jeremy knew the Madrid detectives who had opened the stalking case. One of them could meet us, check the door for prints, take the necklace for the same treatment.

I secured Kierra and her mom in the car before siting in the driver's seat. Malcom stood guard outside. Kierra had to do it now, explaining to her mom what was stolen from her trailer last season.

Watching in the rearview mirror, I listened as they descended into a heated discussion while the detective quickly arrived. He took pictures before starting to swish a brush across the door and handle.

I got out, looking over the detective's shoulder—nothing as the bristles and black powder brushed over the car paint. No prints.

"What are we to do?" Anne's arms folded across her chest, seeming ready to yank her daughter onto the next flight out of Madrid as our car headed back home. Kierra sat beside her, hands shaking, scared but eyes desperate to stay.

"We stay smart and watch and wait," I answered,

turning around from the passenger seat now. "No more secrets. Right?"

Kierra nodded, looking at her mom with pleading eyes. "No more secrets, Mam. I promise." She looked down before glancing up, asking me, "Those cuffs? He's saying he's going to use them on me?"

Terror flared Kierra's nostrils. It broke my heart. And pissed me off. "Not on my watch, Kierra. He'll be the one in cuffs one day. I promise."

On the way back to Kierra's house, I started a list. Seventeen names of who it could be. Yes, maybe one of the crew knew about the cast dinner and location, had spotted Kierra's car in the parking lot. It was the same one she had arrived in and left from set earlier that day.

I sucked my teeth, dismissing that theory.

He was leaving no prints, no DNA. Taking items he knew were personal to Kierra, to her body and heart. And leaving them now with zip tie cuffs? Restraints that were easy to hide. Used to bind hands, feet, arms, legs—making any victim easy to control.

The certainty infuriated me. He was no amateur. That fucker had sat at the dinner tonight. Across from Kierra. Across from me. Smiling the whole time.

Smiling... because he had planned this.

CHAPTER NINE

DANIEL

A text woke me. It was Anders.

Dinner tonight at 7.
Match at 8

I smiled, replying...

What can I bring?

Your arse and Guinness. I'm not
bringing that Irish swill into my
own home

Normally I declined Tuesday night invitations, especially after last night's cast dinner. After work and the gym, I go home, crashing before the sun set.

But one thought enticed me to accept.

Charlie Ravenel will be there.

I arrived with Lance on time. Simon dropped us in front of the sprawling villa Anders rented for his family. I didn't blame him for the splurge. If I had a family, I'd do the same.

Platters filled a rustic dining table, a true smorgasbord with pork roast, rye breads, cheeses, and more. The table sat beside an open kitchen, next to the large family room with vaulted ceilings, a huge flatscreen, sofas and sweeping views of the gardens and pool outside. Anders had the doors open to the almost spring evening.

I searched the small crowd gathered. No Charlie. Mason was also missing. This was too tame to be his scene. And Kierra and her mom were absent.

But I noticed another beefy bloke chatting with Anders's driver. Curious, I made my way toward the massive man who reached his hand out.

"Hey man. Nice to meet you." His words and face sincere. "Rob Vasquez. I'm with HGR."

All the man's bright white teeth sparkled in his handsome, teddy bear grin, though his Popeye forearms and death grip warned, he could fuck me up in a second if he wanted to.

"Cheers, mate. Good to meet you." I held my grip and ground firm, taking inventory. Dark, short hair, fashionably styled. Olive skin with ebony eyes and a disarming smile.

What was that shitcake of emotions I last ate decades ago? This was the Rob I'd heard about from Lance? The tech geek? The one who'd suffocate over a kitten or horse? And the partner Charlie worked so closely with every day?

Remember that taste, Pierce? It's delicious jealousy iced with insecurity. Eat it.

I sank into the sofa by the open patio door with a Guinness in hand. Between this Rob bloke and Charlie being MIA, my night turned to shit.

Was she even coming? I dared not ask.

A loud squeal whistled outside by the pool a half hour later. "Auntie Char!"

My neck snapped right.

Erikson, Anders's five-year-old son ran toward Charlie, who knelt, arms out to embrace him. Linnea, Anders's almost two-year-old daughter, echoed her brother's squeal.

Charlie hadn't come through the front door. She went through the backyard to the pool where she'd find the kids, like she'd been here many times.

Erikson jumped into her arms, soaking wet. Throwing his arms around her neck, he flopped like a little wet fish in her embrace.

"Hey, Minnow," she cooed in such an American way it had to be from her childhood. Burying her face in Erikson's neck, she snorted, making him squirm with laughter.

Little Linnea reached up with her wet, chubby hands from the top of the pool stair she played upon. "Me, me," the toddler said.

I faked watching the football game on the screen.

Really, out of the corner of my eye, I watched how Charlie kneeled, scooping the girl up in her other arm. Linnea giggled when Charlie wriggled her nose over hers. Then, with a mountain of kids on her, she wandered over to Maja's mother by the pool, offering her a kiss on the cheek and a warm greeting too.

Who is this woman, Pierce?

I didn't recognize her.

She wore a long red, flamenco-style skirt with a white midriff cut-off T-shirt reading, "Carolina" in faded lettering. Her hair fell free, tousled from the kids. Gold dangling earrings, rings and bracelets caught the light. The black tactical boots she wore on set were replaced with tan flip-flops, revealing tiny feet.

The sight? My heart hammered.

She was so blazingly beautiful, doting on kids, laughing freely. This was not that tomboy, fuck-you look that had amused me so far. Instead, it looked like she'd wandered off a summer beach in California (or Carolina to be sure) into a place where she felt at ease.

I closed my eyes, my head buzzing, dizzy with warmth, though I'd only had one Guinness, the hot truth branding my chest.

I hardly knew Charlie, but I wanted to make her smile like that.

I wanted to make her laugh that way.

This stunning woman had walked into my numb scab of a life, picked it raw and I sat gushing for her. Every fucking feeling bled from me to be that place of ease for her.

Maja appeared, rescuing Charlie from the kids. "You two, she's not a gymnasium." With a mum tone, she took Linnea from Charlie's arm while Erikson proudly remained perched on her hip.

"I'm soaking wet." Charlie glanced down at her shirt, laughing. "All right, Minnow." She put the boy down. "Go swim and let me eat. I'll read you a story later."

"Go, go." Maja gently pushed Erikson toward the pool with his grandmother.

Charlie said, "I need a sweater or something."

"In there." Maja pointed to the front library room over my left shoulder by the front door.

I couldn't help it. I watched as Charlie tried darting behind the sofas without anyone noticing the wet T-shirt contest she'd win. With no bra on her in the cool evening?

Her nipples became little Eiffel towers under a thin cotton shirt.

That sight? A sure wonder of my world, spinning my mind and firming my cock.

She emerged with Maja's long, black sweater wrapped around her.

"Maja, where are my favorite meatballs?" Her path headed straight for the dining table. "And where's my Tito's? I've been saving my appetite all day, and this bitch needs a drink."

She nudged Maja's shoulder for a quick peck on the cheek before the two of them descended into whispers I couldn't hear.

Anders hit pause on the game. Raising his beer stein to the small crowd gathered, he boomed, "Thank your arses for joining us in our new casa. Here's to a great season. And here's to my beautiful Maja for feeding us." He leaned down, giving her a grateful kiss before proclaiming, "Let's eat!"

Rising to my feet, I took a deep breath, hoping for a chance to talk to Charlie. But Rob beat me there, giving her a fist pump. "Sup, fucker."

"Sup, fucker."

I wished she talked so easily with me.

When Rob asked her with an amused grin, "You cold," my jaw clenched. Guess Rob was a fan of her wet T-shirt contest too.

"Fuck off." She laughed, pushing him away with a step and a twirl, turning around... and colliding with my chest. "Oh." Her nose, then her body, crashed into mine.

God, how I wanted to grab her and take more. "Sorry." I cupped her arm instead, steadying her, my palm tingling at the silken warmth of her bare skin.

I dressed for her tonight, going for the casual poison of a white T-shirt, jeans, brown leather belt and boots. A curated look I was confident in after dozens of magazine covers.

But confidence left me at the inhale of her perfume: honey, subtle patchouli and something that smelled like dessert.

It fucking stoned me.

She stumbled back from my touch. "Too many big ass dudes in this small ass kitchen," she said.

"Welcome to my world." Maja returned to the kitchen with an empty platter. "Anders is the worst one. He's like a big damn tree." She set a platter down, picking up another full one from the counter, gesturing for me to follow. "Daniel, better hurry before those men eat all my gravlax."

"Yeah, mate!" Anders shouted from the edge of the table. "Come get it before I eat it all." He grabbed a piece off the full platter Maja set down for the guests.

She grinned, swatting his hand. "Stop it."

I missed my chance. Charlie started helping Maja wash the dishes. And I needed to recover from the torpedo of her touch.

Chewing down two plates full of salmon and meatballs, I chatted with Lance about plans for the gym tomorrow.

Rob stood within earshot. "Hey, I need a good gym. Where do you guys go around here?"

Lance said, "Alta Gym. It's less than a kilometer from the studio. Join us sometime."

The evil green monster on my shoulder wanted to protest the company of Rob. But the gentleman angel on my other told me to *shut the fuck up.*

"Auntie Char!" Erikson's little voice yelling from the

kitchen turned me around to see the boy standing in front of Charlie with his fists on his hips.

I found myself smiling, nearing the scene, wanting to see what Charlie would do.

"Auntie Char promised me her stories." Erikson stomped his foot in his dinosaur pajamas. Charlie scooped him up to her hip, burying her nose in his curls wet from his bath.

"All right. One story and then it's bedtime," Maja said.

"And I want Zeus to come too." Erikson pointed to me standing there.

Charlie and Maja stifled grins.

Yes, I was used to this from kids, enjoying it most of the time. All the action figures, toys and marketing bonanza over the *Zeus* movies made lots of kids shout that name at my face.

"All right." I used my American accent for the character. "But only if you promise to stay in bed and go to sleep."

Charlie's smiled at me. I felt like I got a gold star sticker from the hot teacher.

"All right," Maja said. "Char and Zeus can put you to bed. But no pool tomorrow if you get back up." She mouthed to me, "Thank you."

I followed Charlie through the family room to the grand staircase by the front door. Erikson proudly pointed. "This way," he said, looking back over Charlie's shoulder, making sure Zeus followed too.

Walking behind Charlie up the stairs, I was captivated. A little boy rested comfortably on her hip, his foot dangling down her firm, swishing backside. Her skirt was long. It charmed me—the very lady-like way she gathered it up with her free hand in front. Like Scarlett O'Hara ascending Tara in my mum's favorite movie, *Gone with the Wind*. A light jangle drew my eyes to her ankle bracelets. She walked barefooted now.

Suddenly, I felt stodgy in my leather boots and silk socks.

How could I reconcile the two sides of Charlie?

By day, a smart-ass tomboy in tactical gear. One who could snipe me from a thousand meters. By night, a carefree young, bohemian woman who was generous with her affection.

I didn't know which I fancied more. But tonight, my body was absolutely intoxicated by this one.

Erikson took to eagerly pointing out his new toys, doing anything to stay awake.

"All right, minnow," Charlie said, "jump up in that bed if you want a story."

Too excited to listen, Erickson commanded, "Zeus, you sit here." He patted the upholstered rocking chair with his hand. "And you can hold my *Triceratops*." He shoved his stuffed animal into my hands.

"And Auntie Char, you sit on my bed." He patted the bed at the exact spot he expected her to sit before climbing in.

Charlie cut her eyes at me, amused. We recognized the performance. Erikson was a miniature Anders.

The little boy sat straight up in his bed, yanking his blanket up to his waist, insisting, "I want the one about the mouse."

Bloody hell, Pierce, he belongs in a director's chair.

Charlie leaned toward Erikson, bargaining, "You better lie down faster than a hot knife through butter if you want a story."

Her Southern phrase surged a smile up my cheeks. Or was that my heart?

Erikson flopped back into the bed with a "hmph," pulling the covers up to his chin.

Charlie scooted closer to him.

CHARLIE

"ONE DAY there was a *biggg* lion who got soooooo sleepy that he laid down to take a nap by the foot of a *huge* ol' tree," I said before making loud snoring sounds.

Erikson giggled.

From the corner of my eye, Daniel's head tilted, his lips turning up.

I knew all of Aesop's fables, delighting Erikson with my drama, voices and accent. My dad had told them to me, just this way. And I'd entertained Erikson many times before.

"That big, ol' lion slept awwlllllllll day!" I exclaimed with a deep Southern drawl. "So lonnng that the mice livin' by the foot of the tree didn't know *what* to do. His big 'ol *butt* blocked their home."

Erikson rolled, laughing. "'Butt' is so much funnier than 'bum'! Do the mouse voices! Do the mouse voices!" He tried sitting up.

"Shhh." I patted his head back down to his pillow, loving to twirl his soft curls.

Chirping in a high-pitched, Southern granny mouse voice, I said, "Well, now that silly, ol' lion done gone and fallen asleep in front of our house!"

A movement caught my eye. I glanced at Daniel. He had the *Triceratops's* foot stuffed in his mouth, eyes twinkling while his towering body racked, suppressing his laughter.

In a deep, old Southern grandpa mouse voice, I blustered, "That dumb ol' fat lion gonna sleep hah all night. Ain't no way we can get in! What we gonna do, Mabel?"

A snort hit the air. It turned my head again.

Daniel was wiping tears from the corner of his eyes, before giving another cute snort.

Holy shit. A million pictures of him. And none ever looked more beautiful than he does now.

Like years of watching the same sunrise over the ocean, but this time, the dawn finally warmed me.

He glanced up at the pause in the entertainment and found me admiring him. I didn't stop. And he didn't look away.

His laughter ebbed. Lowering the toy from his face, he just held my gaze, softly smiling back at me.

This moment. With him. It breached my high walls. Climbed up my ribs. Crawled into my solitude. Unlocking my ache, it tried to liberate something guarded deep within.

What is it about this man?

"Finish, Auntie Char," Erikson pleaded in the molten silence of the room.

For a moment, I shook my gaze and heart free.

Taking a deep breath, I avoided the word "butt" and taking the accent down a notch or two. When I got to the end of the fable and the lesson, "When someone has helped you, you should help them too," Erikson finally looked heavy-eyed.

Stroking his hair the whole time, I leaned in to kiss his forehead. "Night, Minnow."

"Don't leave," he murmured.

Daniel stood, joining us by the edge of the bed. He laid the *Triceratops* in the crook of Erikson's arm. "I enjoyed being your guest, little man. I gave *Triceratops* special powers to help you sleep." He reached out. Little blond curls wrapped around his thick index finger like a silk ribbon. "Keep your promise. Stay in bed or no pool tomorrow."

"Okay." Erikson pulled the stuffed animal close to his little body. He cuddled it while I glanced back one last time, blowing him a kiss before leaving.

Daniel pulled the door closed behind us, chuckling. "You put on quite a show, Ms. Ravenel."

I leaned against the wall, chuckling too. "Couldn't have done it without Zeus's help."

The look in his aqua eyes changed, humor fading, replaced by a heated question on his lush lips, nearing mine. My pulse tripled; desire rushing between my thighs.

His laughter, his tears, his forgiveness for my lashing out, his gentle way with the little boy, and now the unmistakable heat of his question freed me.

I lifted my chin to his, softening my lips in silent answer. *Yes.* I closed my eyes. *I want him too.*

"Charlie." My name sighed soft from his lips, steaming even closer.

Flash!

A grenade. A memory exploded, ripping my lips from his before we could touch. I shoved his brick body back, a strangle taking my throat. I tore free from the gravity between us, staggering down the hallway.

Not here. Not here. Not here.

Grabbing the wooden banister with both hands, my bare feet moved heavier than with combat boots. World shaking. Ears ringing. Vision blurring, tunneling. I aimed for the library doors at the bottom of the stairs.

Escape.

CHAPTER TEN

DANIEL

*W*hat the fuck, Pierce?

I thought she wanted to kiss.

Following her to the top of the open stair-well, I watched her disappear into the library across the front foyer. It collapsed my chest.

She was crying, shaking.

Fuck, I crossed a line. And I bloody knew better. After all these years and painful mistakes. Dreadful behavior I ceased years ago after a late-night drink and candid conversation with my little sister, Tess.

"You know big brother," Tess had said. "You better be careful. I know they throw themselves at you, and you get caught in all sorts of cocked up messes. Pun intended." She'd raised her scotch to me, telling me more candidly than anyone dared because I was "so fucking handsome and all that bollocks," she had said. "You don't know what it's like to hear 'no,' so you think that's a 'yes.' And it's not."

Tess schooled me. How silence wasn't consent. How it was often a terrified response to power. And power? I had it. I could exploit almost any situation.

"What do I do?" I had asked Tess. "Get every single woman here forward to sign a consent form?"

The notion didn't sound ridiculous. I knew the lengths other celebrities went to, keeping their privacy, dalliances and even crimes protected with non-disclosures and money.

Bloody hell, I'd done it too.

"Maybe," Tess had said. "Just don't be that kind of man. Celebrity or not. That's not the brother I love. Just bloody ask a woman. Make sure it's what she really wants. It's that fucking simple."

It troubled me, what my sister had said.

I assumed I'd always been a good man. Apart from one horrific mistake... I was beyond good. I was a hopeless romantic. Yes, I could get a bit too passionate, truth be told. Wooing women was harmless, amorous sport, and I loved making every play—flowers, notes, dinner. It was always what they wanted. Or at least, that's what I believed.

Until now.

And lately? Since that talk with my sister, I was careful with the target of my affection. I kept it to one girlfriend, making sure to get her consent. Fuck's sakes, she asked me up to her hotel room on our second date. And I asked all night long while she moaned, "Yes" over and over as we both got what we wanted.

We'd been dating for a couple of years now, off and on. But my career was my priority and I wasn't changing. Not for anyone. That's why we hadn't spoken in two months. Honestly, I didn't care for her anymore.

But staring now at the door Charlie hid behind, shaking

and crying because of me, I did care. I found a new target for my affection.

All I had to do was ask if I could kiss her. Then again, I was an arrogant prick, assuming she wanted me.

A cringe twisted my gut.

You're acting like the entitled "Sex God" people call you, Pierce.

Charlie finally let her guard down to me, and I exploded her trust into a thousand pieces.

Fuck, you're a selfish, arrogant, randy arse.

Making my feet move, I bounded down the stairs, texting Simon to bring the car around, declaring to the crowd, "All right mates, I'm knackered. I've got to get home."

The game clicked down to the last minutes. All eyes were glued to the screen, not hearing me.

Only Maja seemed to notice. "Where's Charlie?"

I pointed to the library, giving the "cold" signal with my arms, hoping she'd buy it. Hell, I didn't know. I thought on my feet.

The crowd gave a stifled cheer for Real Madrid's win. My phone pinged back. That got Lance's attention. He popped off the sofa, gave Anders a quick big hug and Maja a thank-you kiss.

I just stood, twisting awkward by the front door. Staring at the closed library door across the hall, my stomach soured with shame at my latest fuck-up.

Lance ambled out the door while I waved, shouting loud enough so Charlie could hear me too. "Thanks again! Cheers!" And closing the door behind me.

She could come out. The monster was gone.

CHARLIE

A SOFT TAP sounded against the library door. "Charlie. You in here?" Maja opened it and took in the sad sight—me, shaking with wet cheeks on the sofa.

"Oh, sweetie. Sweetie." Maja rushed to my side. "What is it?"

I sat up, raking fingers through my damp strands. "I fucked up, Maja."

"What do you mean, you 'fucked up'?" Maja sat next to me, reaching out to stroke my hair. "What the hell happened?"

"He tried to kiss me, and I ran away like a freak, crying."

Maja questioned with a smile. "Daniel tried to kiss you?"

"God, what was I thinking? We were having such a fun time with Erikson. Laughing so much. Then we were in the hallway. Next thing I knew, he got quiet with this look in his eyes and I knew he was going to kiss me and I shocked myself. I wanted him to... and then..."

And then. What?

How could I describe it? How the sensation knocks me down with a sudden, big wave that crashes over my back, slamming me into my past and pain.

Maja knew my story. After my episode skeet shooting with Anders in Belfast a few years ago, there were no more secrets between us. It bonded us even more.

"Oh, come here." Maja wrapped her arm over my shoulder. "It makes sense, my love," she whispered. "You know why it happened."

Parts of my brain knew as much between sobs. But when the sensation hits, it floods me. Sometimes I blacked out. Sometimes I hallucinated. Other times, it gripped my heart so tight, drowning my breath and voice.

"Maja, I heard Kai's voice."

I gazed up at the plastered ceiling. Kai would want me to move on. Guilt wouldn't let me. I came home to the VA hospital, wounded, and my husband came home in a flag-draped coffin.

After all these years, I wasn't ready to love again. But for now, surely just a damn kiss? And please God, eventually, really fucking good sex.

"You heard Kai because Daniel is the first one, isn't he?" Maja asked.

"Yes, he would be."

Wiping tears away, I tried getting my shit together.

I'd joked with Maja in the past about the men flirting with me, asking me out. I pushed them away.

This was different.

"What the hell am I thinking, Maja? You and Anders know why I'm really here. Because Kierra's got a stalker on set."

"You don't think it's Daniel, do you?"

"I'd be a fucking idiot to rule anyone out so soon." The truth knotted my stomach. "There's something about him. Something he's hiding. I can't place it, but I fucking know it."

"Not him. I can't see it."

"Stalkers don't come with signs around their neck. It's the opposite. They're delusional but smart. Obsessive and narcissistic. Jealous but charming. Falling in love instantly."

The sick stalking shit I'd seen so far protecting Juliette; it would make Maja's blood run cold.

"I'm sorry," Maja said. "Daniel's not like that. That's

not what I see in him." Her glance bounced from the library door back to me. "But I can see how he fancies you. In the kitchen. Tonight. He's gobsmacked." An amused grin pulled her lips. "I think you are too."

"Oh hell, Maja. Come on. Even if it's not him. Even if he is the perfect man millions think he is, I would be a piece of ass to him. It'd be the biggest fucking mistake. I'm here for Kierra. To protect her. If I get caught with him, I'd get reassigned. And I'm not a woman who shits where she eats."

I used the crass phrase often issued during my military service, and I agreed. No sex was worth fucking up your career. The man got high-fives. The woman got called a "slut." Being married to Kai, a fellow Marine, protected me from that sexist bullshit.

I shook my head at my own stupidity. "And he's Daniel-fucking-Pierce, for God's sake. He's fucked hundreds of women. Why the hell would I get involved with that mess?"

"Yes, he's Daniel-fucking-Pierce and makes us all swoon." Maja grinned. "But you're Charlotte-fucking-Ravenel. And you my sweet, are no man's piece of ass."

"Well, now I have to work with the man, and it's gonna be so damn awkward." I flopped back on the sofa already exhausted by the problem. "I'm not used to this shit drama. How am I gonna fix it?"

I knew how to control my mind—most of the time. I'd already dragged myself through worse, literally, to stay alive, nurturing myself back from hell.

No one could take that from me.

But this Daniel thing? It felt new. New to my heart scarred with loss. New to my body silent for years. New to my mind I was apparently losing.

Oh, Charlie Girl. The irony. Starving all these years.

And now the chance of a cornucopia of sex with Daniel Pierce—a bounty of masculine beauty. Your forbidden colleague, at best. A perverted stalker, at worst.

You're fucking kidding me, right?

"Well, you can do two things." Maja used that no bull-shit tone I loved. "You can act like nothing happened. Joke around with him. Or you could just tell him. Not every-thing. Just something so he might understand."

She grabbed my hand. "Besides, you did it for those girls. There's no shame in it. And you've suffered and waited long enough." With a long pause, she squeezed my hand and said, "And he wanted to kiss you, bitch. You deserve at least a night or two with Daniel-fucking-Pierce. Better yet, fucking Daniel Pierce. No one has to know."

The absurdity made me grin. "Thank you." I squeezed back. "I'll figure it out. Until then, I've got work to do. I've got meetings with Lorraine and the executive producers tomorrow."

Maja walked me to the kitchen, pulling open the back door. "Call me." She pressed the button to open the garage door.

"I will," I said, descending the stairs, walking out into the driveway to my little white car waiting there. "Love you." I waved as I climbed in.

"Love you too." Maja waved back, pressing the button to close the door behind her.

DANIEL

I WANTED TO FUCKING DIE.

Lance and Simon rehashed the game on the ride home.

But Simon kept glancing back at me in the rearview mirror. Was my acting failing? Was guilt written all over my face?

We dropped Lance off at his flat. Alone now, I gazed out the car window, glad for the music Simon played until U2's "With or Without You" came on. Bloody hell, it made me sick again.

I mumbled, "Cheers, mate," to Simon when he parked the car in front of the estate I rented in Madrid.

"Night," Simon replied. But before I could close the door, Simon asked, "Hey, mate. You all right?"

His kindness forced my smile. "Yeah, thanks. Just knackered."

Swinging my front door open, I stood in the foyer, feeling like I'd broken something so beautiful before I could even cherish it.

Lumbering upstairs, I undressed, mindlessly walking into the shower. Water poured over my thoughts of Charlie again. Not with the lurid fantasies I'd enjoyed so far.

It looped in my mind, in my heart...

You made her cry, Pierce. Goddamnit, you're not this kind of man anymore. You swore. Never again.

My fists met the hard tile, not in a foolish, young punch. They pressed against a surface that wouldn't yield to my force, pushing back with the hard truth.

It's too late. The harm is done. You and your randy impulses. You cocked up. Again.

Habit checked my phone alarm set for four a.m. when I stood by the nightstand. My heart schemed the only thing I could do, scrolling, looking for her name in my contacts.

The sight of it hurt. "Charlie Ravenel."

My assistant, Colleen, always updated my phone with the crew and cast for every production.

I texted:

It's Daniel. I'm very sorry

CHAPTER ELEVEN

CHARLIE

Haste by RY X

The morning alarm on my phone demanded my tap. I picked it up, checking for texts. Juliette often sent something overnight.

I groaned. Daniel's apology glowed above me in bed. A storm of feelings blew in.

Which do you want? His cocky, practiced grin? Or his genuine, disarming laughter?

Either would be the biggest and best mistake of your life.

I dug a little deeper for patience.

Remember what Mom used to say? If it's a good idea today, it'll be a good idea tomorrow.

I needed a plan. How to get my body and head together. And how to get my heart straight. And how to tell the horny little devil between my thighs to shut up.

If thoughts of Daniel crossed my mind, I'd push them

away. I was trained for this, a damn ninja at compartmentalizing. *Focus on the job.*

Swiping through my calendar, the screen filled with meetings that week. Today was Wednesday and our meeting with the executive producers. Tomorrow with Daniel. Friday with Mason.

Nerves twisted my gut. Not a lot of time to plot a next move.

Sure enough, during my lunch meeting that day, a text lit up my phone, winding down the clock on my resolve.

It's Daniel again.
Can we please talk?
Just a few minutes.
Promise

One hour later. Meeting done. Driving back to set. I was still deciding. Could I do it? Could I play with fire like it wouldn't play back?

But we had our meeting with his team tomorrow. And I'd rather blister my feet in stiletto heels for a year than suffer through that awkward shitshow.

I parked my car, grabbed my bag, and headed toward basecamp. Another *ping* sounded while I debated. A look down at the phone in my hand confirmed...

It was Daniel again:

Please Charlie

Fuck, could he see me from his trailer?

I glanced up at his behemoth black home on wheels, wondering if he was staring right at me. If he could see how his beg shot heat through my body. How the thought of him watching me; it turned me on.

Why resist it? Like Maja said, I could do this. Just one bite. Just one night.

Nose down, typing a reply, I walked right past his trailer. Kierra's was empty. She hadn't come to set today.

6pm. Security trailer

His immediate reply:

Copy

Promptly at six p.m., his knock on the banger door sounded a polite *tap-tap*. I opened it rather than call out for him to enter.

"Hey, Mr. Pierce, whatcha got?" A casual pitch coated my voice in case anyone on set stood within earshot, seeing him enter.

Laughter. I glanced up to catch Lorenzo standing three trailers up. Exchanging words with Mason. Exchanging a look over Mason's shoulder. Watching us.

I scanned down at the folders in Daniel's hands before he climbed up the steps into the trailer. It looked like architectural renderings on vellum paper were folded inside of them.

The door banged shut behind him.

It was just us.

Together now.

And alone...

A navy hoodie and matching sweatpants draped over him like a cozy blanket. A black licorice tendril of hair hung wet over his eye. The smell of the shower he'd just taken, his soap and cologne, it filled the tiny, nondescript space with the scent of cedar and sexy. Even the tortured look on his face softened the harsh fluorescent lights zapping us from above.

Shit. He's too much. You can't do it.

My pulse agreed. I turned my back to him. The orange I always brought to work begged for my nervous peel.

Tell him. End this little flirt now. Before it gets worse. My logic insisted. My vocal cords disagreed.

"Charlie."

His butter-rich, deep voice could beckon me to play in traffic with him.

Forget the orange. I put it down, turning to face him, hiding my eyes under the brim of my baseball hat.

The fire in my throat; I couldn't speak.

The folders in his grasp were getting crimped, strangled by his grip.

"I want to apologize for my conduct at Anders's party," he said. "I should've just enjoyed the moment with you. Just enjoyed your story with Erikson and the giggles and let it be that. I'm sorry for being inappropriate and I'm"—I glanced up to aqua eyes begging down at mine and his face fell, making his voice crack—"I'm ashamed of my behavior and deeply regret upsetting you."

I stood at attention, at my only position of strength trying to resist his disarming words.

Sincerity etched deep across his brow. He said, "I promise it won't happen again. I will be nothing but respectful and professional with you. Please accept my apology."

God, look at him. As real as his laughter. He means it.

I closed my eyes, wincing and swallowing hard, forcing

my voice to work. "I'm not mad at you, Daniel." I opened my eyes—the sight of him before me, bewitching.

But again, the strangulation. The next words I needed to say wouldn't come.

Fucking say it, Charlie!

Pushing through the choking blaze in my neck, I said, "I wanted you to kiss me. But I have PTSD. And something triggered me last night. But it wasn't you. And I'm embarrassed by it."

I stood naked in a storm of vulnerability I hated. Hating the tears that threatened next.

He stood in a gentle pause at my confession before shaking his head. "I'm so sorry, Charlie. I should have known better. I'm the one who should be embarrassed." He leaned toward me, halting, looking too afraid to move any closer. "I've been coming on too strong. You've been trying to tell me. And I'm the bloody prat for not respecting that. It's my fault."

Wiping the tears from my damn cheeks, I reached to take off my hat. The trick of tipping my chin up to make them stop didn't work. The harsh lights on the ceiling blurred my watery eyes.

"It's not your fault, Daniel." *Look him in the eye.* "I have PTSD from my tours and from six years ago when I got shot."

"Is that the scar on your face?" he asked without hesitation. "Sorry. I shouldn't ask."

I didn't mind. "Yes." Skimming my fingers across my right cheek, I traced its familiar raised edge. "I think it makes me kinda sexy."

Surprising myself, of course I fucking joked about it. Then again, smart-ass comments were my defense.

The scar on my cheek? I didn't hate it anymore. When I

looked in the mirror, I was proud of how I earned it. Problem was it distracted people when they first met me. I tested them. How long will it take before they look me in the eye?

Daniel passed the test the day we met. I realized it then. His gaze lingered on my eyes... or my lips. I'd been so busy pushing him away, I'd failed to notice.

"I would agree," he said. "I'm thinking of getting one of my own to be as fit as you."

His smile back was the one that got him named sexiest man alive. And it worked. My body rose to the bait.

"Keep up your shenanigans, Pierce, and I'll give you one."

The grip on the folders relaxed in his grasp.

"Charlie, I love joking with you like this, but I mean it. It gutted me to upset you. I want you to know that I respect you and will admire you silently from afar. No more shenanigans, I promise."

Dear God, his vulnerability was a siren call luring me to the edge.

Jump off the cliff. You can't fall halfway. Go!

"You didn't hear what I said, did you, Pierce?"

It took him a second. Then he grinned. "You said you *wanted* me to kiss you."

Did he just blush? Yep, he just went from thirty-something to fourteen at the realization. *Too sweet. Too hot.*

And the mere words "kiss you" across his lush lips.

My God, my pussy wet while the possibility terrified my heart. Lust and fear colliding, I didn't know which to fight and which to let pull me under.

A nod of my head—yes—answered for me.

Tears came again. I couldn't stop them. This time, they rose from some place deeper. A place no one had touched for years. "I just need time." It left me unguarded. "I need to go slow."

"I like slow." His voice smoothed with a tender smile. "We can do slow." He took a small step toward me.

"Charlie, I can't stop thinking about the other week in the car. What you said, how it hurt, but it was true. And so fucking real. I've never felt that before. Millions of people look at me but you're the first woman to actually see me. Even if it's not pretty; at least you fucking saw me. And I'd go a lifetime without a kiss from you if I could just be so bloody lucky to have more time with you. Just to talk with you."

The rip current of his exposure started drowning me, pulling me down with him, soaking me everywhere. "Do you want me to make you wait a lifetime for a kiss?"

"I'd prefer not." Even his chuckle lured me to salacious thoughts. "But for you, I'd be willing to try."

"What would you prefer to have with me?"

"That would be highly inappropriate for me to discuss with you in the workplace, Ms. Ravenel."

"Well, you can confess willingly to me, or I can put a couple painful moves on you, Mr. Pierce, and torture it out of you."

"Promise?" His grin reached between my thighs. "To respectfully answer your question, I desire much more than to kiss you. But I'll humbly submit to wait for whatever you want, Ms. Ravenel."

His words? Perfect. And to have him want me, to be willing to wait for me? Shocking. Delicious. Also... frightening.

I shook my skull, making my brain work instead of my tingling pussy.

"Daniel, seriously though." I scanned the bare bones

office. "How are we going to do this? We can't get caught together. It doesn't matter even if we just talk. I'm not allowed to be with you. I'll lose my job over it. And I'll never risk that."

"Can I make you a picnic on my patio?"

"A picnic?"

"A friendly picnic on my patio. No shenanigans, I promise. No one else will know. There are no cameras."

"You don't have security cameras on your patio?"

Why weren't cameras aimed at every entrance to his home?

"As you will discover in our meeting tomorrow, Ms. Ravenel, no cameras are on my patio. I have my boundaries too. I spend my life in front of them and know how to use them. The fence around the property has them. But between us, and in the shared spirit of disclosure, I like enjoying my patio in the sunshine au naturel, and no one is getting that on camera."

"Damn shame."

Yep, that vision I'd revisit alone in bed—Daniel Pierce, nude and lying bathed in golden light. His shredded, muscular body and got-to-be gorgeous cock, soft and asleep in the sun.

He continued with his plan. "You can drive over in that white Tic Tac car of yours and hide it in the garage. I only have my bike and Volvo in there. It'll fit."

"Volvo?" I profiled him again. "I pictured you in something more expensive and sporty."

"The bike, my Ducati motorcycle, is sporty and posh. I needed to rent something here for all my bags and me. I'm a big guy."

"I bet you are."

"Good one." He gazed at me, shaking his head. "You

know, if we're going slow, Ms. Ravenel, you must show me mercy. I can control myself but not my stiffy."

"Sorry. You control your stiffy and I'll control my mouth."

"There you go again." He laughed at my dirty pun. "You've got a deft tongue, Ms. Ravenel."

I licked it across my back teeth with a grin before answering, "Indeed I do, Mr. Pierce. But I'll behave at this picnic of yours, I promise."

"All right then. I don't know how long it will take to orchestrate but leave it to me."

"That's okay. I like waiting." I pulled my hat back on, concealing my eyes again. "Speaking of. You better get going. Joaquin is coming in soon."

"Ah. Right." His steps pivoted, aiming toward the door.

Once he pushed it open, I called out, "Night, Mr. Pierce."

"Cheers, Charlotte." The words crooned over his granite shoulders.

One minute later, a text from him:

And thank you for the honour
of our first date Ms. Ravenel

One hour later, I replied:

Hear that cracking sound
Mr. Pierce?

He pinged right back:

What is it?

> The sound of the ice you're skating
> on if you call me Charlotte again

Indeed. I'll need lots of cold
showers with you, Charlotte

I informed him:

> And lots of white Tic Tacs

He fired back.

LMFAO

CHAPTER TWELVE

DANIEL

I woke up a new man.

Roused from erotic dreams of blue water and Charlie, I stayed in bed until moans of her name came with powerful release.

Later, I smiled through a workout, slamming battle ropes, whipping them against the floor in excitement to see her in a few hours. A meeting or a picnic? I'd relish any time with her.

Back home, showered, shaven, and dressed, it was only polite for me to put some effort into the meeting.

While coffee brewed, I ventured into my courtyard, cutting long stems of the little, bright yellow flowers blooming on the low bushes. They'd dress up the breakfast bar along with trays of light snacks. While I arranged them, their honey bouquet filled the air from the vase I found under the sink.

The doorbell chimed three quick times. That was Colleen.

"Hiya," she called out.

"In here," I called back from the kitchen.

She appeared in the doorway. "Well, don't you look smart today. I'm used to finding you in sweaty gym clothes."

Her look approved of my crisp, white button-up tucked into light tan dress trousers. No tie and a few buttons left undone, as usual. My hair was styled back, though a piece kept falling while I fussed with the electric kettle. Colleen always teased me how I could go from handsomely elegant, to devilishly handsome, depending upon the state of my "tendril" as she called it.

"Thought I'd dress me and the house up for the meeting." I finally plugged the kettle in, my nervous hands turning to fuss again with the vase of flowers.

"Far be it from me to stop you." She set her bags on the countertop. Eyes down to her tablet, she swiped through the morning's emails, not failing to comment, "The flowers sure are a special touch for just a security meeting."

Fuck's sakes, she was on to me. I held my tongue.

Colleen was my second mum. For over ten years, she'd been my personal assistant. We met a year before I was cast as Zeus and together ever since. Sadly, she was retiring soon. Our trip to Comic-Con this July would be her last.

Letting people go; there were painful reasons why I never reacted well to it.

I adored my team. After years together, we were close. Simon and Matt provided my personal protection detail, running an odd errand for me too. Elaine handled my stylist, wardrobe, hairdresser and some of my appearances. She was being groomed to take over when Colleen retired.

Another triple ring of the bell and Elaine appeared. "Hiya." She even sounded like Colleen. It wasn't lost on me how she had Colleen's haircut and Savile Row style too.

Minutes later the rest of the team stood assembled. "Elaine," Colleen said. "I believe you're point person for the meeting."

Elaine nodded, taking charge.

"Got the kettle on? Good." Elaine observed. "Let's meet in the living area. Simon, pull some chairs from the breakfast table please." She gave me a looking over. "Those turned out nicely."

She pointed to my trousers. Since I took up running, half of my wardrobe had to be altered this season because this woman did not tolerate ill-fitting jackets or trousers.

I patted my bum. "Thanks." Elaine was mum number three.

She gave me a "pish" and started rearranging the food.

"Uh! Why are you messing with it?" I know I sounded like a child, laughing, so she gave me an elbow to go away.

"How many should we expect?" Colleen asked, peering over her glasses at the large living room by the open kitchen.

"I was told two," Elaine said, lining the cheese slices into an appetizing row. "HGR is sending two men: Charlie Ravenel and Roberto Vasquez."

I smiled from my toes to my "tendril" at the assumption Charlie was a man.

"Charlie is a woman," Simon replied, pouring water for his tea.

"Oh?" Elaine said. "All right then." She paused. "Have you already met with studio security, Simon?"

"No. Ms. Ravenel was part of my transport two weeks ago, Saturday."

"Your transport? Why is studio security traveling with you, Daniel?" Elaine's tone stressed. "Is there an active threat?"

"Nothing like that," I said. "We gave Charlie a ride to

her villa from Lance's flat after skeet shooting and watching the match. Her ride had too many beers. We all did. And Simon took care of us," I assured Elaine with a side squeeze. "Normal weekend shenanigans. Nothing to be concerned over."

"Ah. Good, then." She folded linen napkins for the guests.

Right on cue, the doorbell chimed once.

"I've got it!" Colleen called out, already halfway there.

I heard her ask to see credentials before opening the door with a greeting. "Hello. I'm Colleen Douglas. Mr. Pierce's executive assistant. Please come in."

Rob and Charlie entered the kitchen with smiles and handshakes for all. After greetings and belongings were set down, Colleen offered, "Please take a coffee or tea before we sit."

I tried desperately not to notice the firm curve of Charlie's bum in her impeccably tailored black pants suit. Or her perfume that smelled like sex and pralines when she stood beside me, accepting the hot coffee I poured for her.

Tried... but failed.

When we reached for a napkin, our hands brushed. The skate of her flesh across mine shot straight below my belt. She acted oblivious to it.

"I thank you all for your time," Charlie said to the room. Taking our seats in the living room, she continued, "We'll work as quickly as we can today. And of course, we'll remain available to you all in regard to any questions or concerns you may have."

Pierce, pray she remains available for your desires too. Every single seductive inch of her.

Leaning back on the sofa, I reveled in the show.

How her Southern accent sounded subdued. How she

didn't say, "y'all," like I enjoyed. No tomboy before me. Instead, she displayed an elegance to how she gently set her coffee cup down on the glass coffee table, crossing her legs and slightly adjusting her suit jacket.

Was this yet another version of Charlie for me to meet? Military posture. Feminine manners perfect but clipped and businesslike. The high heel of her black dress boots snuck out from under the hem of her pants, catching my eye.

Yes. This is Charlotte Ravenel, prim and proper in your parlour.

I'd had an audible taste of her naughty mouth yesterday. Now my body screamed rabid to meet the one fearless in bed.

Yes, taking her hard from behind, that hair tight in your grasp while you pound into her pussy.

No, Pierce!

Not with her.

You'll take your time, see how wet you can get her, hear her cry your name in that sticky, sweet voice while you watch her come for you, over and over. You'll make her yours. All fucking night long...

A lifetime without her kiss? Bollocks. I wouldn't make it a week. Oh, but the promises I made to try.

Her eyes caught my indecent musings. "Mr. Vasquez and I appreciate the information your team provided in advance, Mr. Pierce." Her words kept the meeting on target.

Thankfully I had a strong team in place. I was a pro, making no mistakes. My boring routine of gym, studio, home and an occasional gathering with vetted cast and crew was already locked down, making HGR's work easy.

Rob suggested I install more cameras on the patio. I

compromised aloud with ones monitoring the exterior courtyard walls.

Once that was sorted, I glanced at Charlie typing on her laptop, remembering the intel I'd confessed about my nude sunbathing. The "I told you so" smile across her face was cheeky... and sexy.

The meeting wrapped. Charlie and Rob left. Simon and Matt headed out while Colleen and Elaine stayed behind discussing my schedule for the show's hiatus next month.

Most cast and crew took the week off to relax. Not me. I had to jet the globe for more meetings—home to London, then to New York for dinner with a director, next to Miami for a potential brand sponsorship meeting, then back to work in Madrid. No rest, always work.

I opened the fridge, hungry for Charlie. Something else would have to satisfy until then.

"So, you were skeet shooting with Ms. Ravenel?" Elaine asked.

I smiled with my face in the refrigerator, knowing where the conversation was headed. She couldn't disguise the approving tone in her voice.

"Yep," I said. "Anders Nylund brought her along. They worked on *Fated* together and became friends."

"I wonder if she liked the yellow flowers you set out for her." Colleen went in for the real jab.

I grabbed a glass bowl and turned around, snapping off the lid to the leftovers. My glance across the kitchen island caught Colleen's amused eyes scrutinizing me over the top of her glasses, both she and Elaine prodding for more.

It made me grin, waiting for the follow-up, casually sinking a spoon into the black lentils with shredded chicken, tomatoes, and feta.

"I bet she's a good shot," Elaine said. "Former military?"

"Helluva shot," I answered with a mouth full of lentils and chicken. "Former Marine." I knew it would get their goat.

Colleen snapped a rag at me. "Don't talk with your mouth full, young man."

I laughed. Bad manners always made them cross. Though I'd just turned thirty-seven, they still treated me like a kid sometimes. I fucking loved it.

"Well, I admire a strong woman like that," Elaine added. "Not the sort you can fool with. She makes us all proud." She dropped her tablet in her shoulder bag. "Maybe you should go skeet shooting more often. Could be the smartest thing your pretty little head could do." She offered her cheek to me for a peck before heading toward the front door. "See you tomorrow. Cheers."

I shoveled three more bites in before throwing the bowl in the sink, proclaiming, "I'm off to the gym, again." I gave Colleen a quick peck on the cheek too before running upstairs to change.

She shouted, "Have you reviewed these fabric samples and renderings from your architect in these folders yet?"

They'd been sitting on my kitchen island since I moved into the rental last season. "Nope, not yet," I answered, bounding up the stairs.

She called out, "The folders and drawings are all crin-kled now."

Knowing exactly why, I didn't answer.

CHAPTER THIRTEEN

CHARLIE

The third time I had to ring the doorbell, I wanted to punch it.

Rob stood next to me, grinning with a side-eye glance. It was obvious. I was already pissed off.

The door finally swung open in a flurry to a young woman winded from a rush to answer it.

"Hi. Sorry. I was in the office and thought Mason would get the door." Tucking her long brown hair back behind her ear, she asked, "HGR?" glancing down at the badges we offered before she reached out her hand. "Krystle Davis. Mason's assistant. Please, come in."

We exchanged introductions while I peered over her shoulder.

Mason Hunt sat like a techie mastermind in his dining room-turned-gaming suite. Swiveling in a gaming chair, headphones on, barking at someone in the head-set, his gaze was immersed in the images on the high-end tri-monitor.

The set-up was a video gamer's dream. A glass-front, gaming tower desktop, special lighting, pulsing speakers, a paper printer, a 3D printer, and other tech clutter and gadgets strewn across the massive table.

"He'll just be a few more minutes." Krystle led us into the large living area with even more flat-screens and a huge sectional sofa.

Noting the time on my watch, I started the countdown.

Krystle asked, "Can I get you anything?"

"Yes, please. Water would be great," I replied. "Thank you very much."

I was raised to accept a host's offer with a small request for something. Simple manners. Manners Mason Hunt clearly cared nothing about.

A man came in and introduced himself as Kevin, Mason's personal guard. He was a friend of Mason's family in Texas, he said.

When Krystle returned with the waters, Rob asked about her background. She said she had started with Mason a few years earlier after he shot his most successful movie—a beach flick in which he never wore a shirt, of course.

I checked my watch. Five minutes. Time was up.

"Well, it was a pleasure meeting you both." I stood up. "I thank you for your time, but I gather our meeting was not a priority for Mr. Hunt, so we have other important work to do."

I had zero tolerance for rudeness. No man could disrespect me or Rob. He followed my lead to the front door.

Mason looked over his shoulder, ripping his headphones off. "Hey, dude. I'm coming"—he looked back, distracted by the screen—"let me just..."

Fuck this. I reached for the door knob.

"All right." Mason dropped the headphones on the table, swiveling in the chair to face us.

"Mr. Hunt, don't get up." Softly, I smiled. "If your security isn't a priority for you, we're happy to leave and tend to more important matters."

"No." His frame hunched up, gesturing for us to return to the living room, never offering a handshake or greeting. "We'll meet now."

We went through the usual protocol.

The security cameras Mason had around his house, we liked. The lifestyle Mason enjoyed, we didn't. It was a liability to the security of the show. Night clubs. Pubs. Private bars. Exclusive parties.

You name it, Mason devoured it.

And I feared one drunk escapade with a right word said to the wrong person and Mason wouldn't be the only one getting screwed that night.

Secret locations could get disclosed. Transportation times and routes could be divulged. Phones with famous contacts or credentials to be copied could get stolen. I didn't underestimate how the smallest act could put Kierra and the entire cast at risk.

I cooed the sugar-coated compliment. "Mr. Hunt, we know that you appreciate the popularity of *The Druid* now. Thanks in great part to *you*."

Of course, that got his attention. Eyes up now, roaming over me, he listened for more. They landed on my scar and wouldn't leave.

I said, "So, now the studio is issuing stricter protocols for everyone's safety, especially for our biggest talent like *yourself*." Biting my bottom lip, I widened my eyes.

Sex oozed from Mason's pores. His allure? It bordered

on lewd. And his gaze mounted over me like he fucking knew it, relishing it to its fullest power.

I noted his resemblance to Daniel, why he was cast as his younger brother. The green contacts and auburn wigs their characters wore made them appear related. Mason's brawn made him older while Daniel's extreme fitness made him look ten years younger. The two men appeared a few years apart to the naked eye.

They had matching cleft chins under full lips that knew how to turn up and turn on anyone in their path. But Mason's nose was smaller, cuter even, giving him that alluring feminine aspect necessary for his character.

Side-by-side, Daniel and Mason were an imposing dose of orgasmic eye candy—making anyone desperate to watch and coming back for more.

The only thing greater than Mason's looks was his ego.

I plucked it like a harp string and Mason's tongue lapped up my compliment while his scrutiny continued.

Ah, it's that look. *You know it well. He's measuring how fuckable you are in his book.* Play him like a fiddle. All strings. Too fucking easy.

"I appreciate the *attention* you must *enjoy* on your evenings out, *Mr. Hunt*." I drizzled honey over his inflated ego. "And we know that you appreciate the increased level of discretion in public that will be required now for *your* show."

I raised a coy eyebrow to him.

The tip of his tongue licked the middle of his bottom lip. "Yeah, I hear ya. I gotta protect my show. Daniel and I are both feelin' the heat. I have like thirty million followers now. It's fucking fire." Reclining back on the sofa, he cocked a side grin. "What'd you say your name is again? Jamie? Sammie?"

His Texas drawl hissed Ss.

"Charlie Ravenel." I gestured to my backup. "And this is my partner, Roberto Vasquez. We are here for *you*, Mr. Hunt."

I looked at his team, Krystle and Kevin, standing behind him. I didn't envy their jobs. Mason must be a fucking peach to work for.

"*You* have a good crew in place who may appreciate some help given your surging popularity," I said. "HGR Security would like to recommend one of our best protection officers for you. He'd be great backup detail for your team, though I know no one better mess with Texas."

"Damn right." Mason woofed. He pursed his lips, considering my offer, calculations coiling across his face. The thought of increased scrutiny growled down his cheeks before he grinned. "Nah. We're good. My team's locked down."

Shit, I wanted a HGR person on each of the four principal cast's team.

John, Anders's driver, was from HGR. Kierra's driver, Malcom, was our staff. I had Daniel covered. And I wanted one of our own on Mason's team too.

We could only suggest it, never force it.

Standing up along with Rob, I offered my hand with the biggest smile I could fake. "We remain at *your* disposal, Mr. Hunt." Mason slipped his palm into my grasp. "Please let us know if you *need anything*."

I was petting a pit bull. His touch—soft, warm, sinewed, able to bite, to maim. One shake and I pulled away.

At least I could rely on his ego to muzzle some of his behavior. He now believed as I'd suggested. The show ranked hot because of him and Daniel. It was their show. They were the *men* in charge of protecting it.

"Thanks for the kind offer, Charlie." Mason stayed seated, returning my smile, his sapphire eyes groping my tits again until I turned to leave.

Rob laughed out loud on the way back to his car. We'd ridden together with plans for the gym afterward.

"So, mi prima." He drove, summarizing our week's meetings. "Mason's the liability. You should see his Instagram. That bitch is out on the town every night. Can't fucking help himself."

I unzipped my heeled boots, dropping them on the passenger floorboard like a snotty tissue. Rubbing my pinky toe, I watched the now familiar villas and buildings whiz by.

"Drop me off at home," I said. "I forgot to put my sneakers in my bag. I'll meet you at the gym."

Rob continued summing it up, pointing his car toward my villa. "Kierra's the job. Anders is locked down. The producers know to keep quiet. And Daniel's easy."

No, Daniel wasn't easy. He was perfect. So fucking perfect. I didn't say it.

And I didn't want to trust it. Every kind word. Every heart-melting smile. Every vulnerable share. Every heap of respect he showed me.

Nothing was wrong with him. Only everything oh so beautifully fuckable and right.

Except, he's your forbidden colleague. You'll get reassigned from protecting Kierra if you get caught with him. And you're hunting an evil, elusive stalker. Don't blow sunshine up your ass. Daniel Pierce is hiding something. Best muzzle your lust too.

Rob stopped in front of my villa. I zipped my boots back on before reaching for the door.

"All I know is," Rob said, "you had Mason eating out of the fucking palm of your hand today. Too easy."

"Well"—I laughed, turning around with a smart-ass grin—"you don't get a bad dog to stay in his cage without a good bone."

CHAPTER FOURTEEN

DANIEL

The sky hung low and dark.

I wanted to ride my Ducati to the gym but checked the forecast. Heavy rain. Grabbing car keys instead and throwing my bag in the Volvo, I headed out.

The front parking space marked "Propietario" at the gym was open, per instructions of the owner, Armand. The guy took care of me. Gym members were also under Armand's strict rules forbidding photographs, videos or approaching any of us on *The Druid* cast.

Armand buzzed me in with a wave. It was a quiet Friday evening—only serious athletes here at the time.

Walking toward the treadmill, I glanced across the gym... and froze.

The sight? One I hadn't dared hope for.

Charlie.

Pushing a weighted sled down the turf-run. Quads straining under black, shiny leggings. Sweat dampening her white T-shirt while a sport headband held back her thick, braided ponytail.

God likes you, Pierce.

I aimed toward the vision. With her back to me, thrusting the heavy sled away, every nerve in my body admired her glute and leg strength. She turned to come back and paused at me standing there, watching her with a hungry smile.

I couldn't help it.

Brushing her hand like swatting at a fly, "You're in my way, sir," her tiny gesture moved my entire body.

"My lady." I bowed, stepping back as she pushed the sled up to my toes. "Well done. One of my favorites too."

A lucky towel wiped the sweat off her neck. A lucky bottle met her lips with a swig of water before she confirmed, "I love doing lower body."

"I can tell."

By an athlete's measure, her form was in top shape. By my measure, I craved its every carve and curve.

"Hey man, you gonna join us?" An American voice boomed behind me. I turned as Rob strode up with a dripping water bottle in hand.

"We're playing Call It." Rob set the bottle down. "And I owe Charlie ten of these." He dropped three more heavy plates on the sled before taking off down the run.

I was glad to see him go, not so glad to see how the man's muscles in his black shorts showed to good effect as he strained away from us.

"I knew Rob works out here," I said. "Do you come often with him?"

"We come when we can." Charlie stood beside me. "We play Call It—Ten, Twenty or Thirty. One of us calls the exercise, sets and reps, and you do it. No bitching." Lifting her chin, her fists met her waist like a superhero. "Join our game if you dare, Pierce."

Her epic body and beauty? A super league of their own.

And fuck's sakes, her challenge—sexy. Urging me to take her on? Yes, right now, every stitch of clothing I'd rip off her, taking her so hard up against the gym wall, her legs wrapped around me.

I'd try waiting for her, but dear God, my compulsion. How I craved her, imagining how good it would feel to have her all to myself, every part of me, thrusting deep inside her.

It wasn't fair. Rob spent all day, almost every day, with her. Why did I have to share her tonight?

Quit being a tosser, Pierce. They work together. Besides, if just you and Charlie publicly work out, a shitstorm of press will rain down on you both.

Rob barreled back up the turf, crushing the sled runs. I took her challenge. "You're on, Ravenel."

I set my bag and bottle on the gym floor while Rob turned around for another run and Charlie started slicing through jumping jacks.

"Is this part of the game?" I copied her. "Plyo while we wait our turn?"

It would be a hell of a workout, blasts of cardio then weights. Fuck yes, I liked the idea of Charlie giving me an ass beating.

"Oorah!" She sounded the Marine call, not even breaking a sweat doing them.

Rob finished up his turn. "You up, Pierce?" He toweled his face, sounding like an excited kid asking his best friend to come out and play.

"Ten, right?" I dropped two more plates on the sled and charged down the run.

"Burpees!" Charlie called to Rob.

Quick minutes later, I finished my reps. "Who's next?"

"Your turn, Pierce," Charlie said. "Whatcha got?"

"Watch out man!" Rob laughed, his eyes admiring Charlie. "Don't be fooled. She's fucking stubborn as a mule with ant-like strength—small body, big force and she'll kick your ass."

I grinned, searching the gym for my next move. "All right, Ravenel. Let's see what *you* got. Pull ups, thirty. Two sets."

Me, and probably Rob judging by his shoulders, could do pull ups for days. But they weren't easy for the average woman. It took serious upper body strength. I admired her now, thankful I wasn't lusting after average.

We headed toward the power rack. I grabbed a belt, handing it to Rob, assuming we'd do weighted pull ups, and she'd do hers without. Rob took the challenge, loading the belt up. I called "mountain climbers," enjoying anything that had me sweaty and breathless on the floor beside her.

When it was Charlie's turn, she started putting on a belt, tightening it around her small waist.

Rob's chin bobbed up like a protective boyfriend. "What are you doing?"

She snapped back, fastening the belt. "My reps."

Rob warned, "Charlie, you put weight on that and you're gonna fuck your shoulder up."

Her face shot him an irritated scowl. "I'm fine."

"Be stubborn now, Ravenel," Rob said, "and we're both gonna pay for it. Neither one of us can afford for you to get injured. We're a fucking team, remember?"

Charlie glared at Rob, sucking her teeth. "All right, fucker." Unbuckling the belt, she threw it down. "Have it your way."

They sounded like a bickering couple. I heard it clear, tasting sick envy again.

Rob knew her body. How well? He cared for her. How much? They were a team. How so?

Charlie jumped high to grab the bar. Once she did, she started banging out wide grip, L-sit pull-ups. Nothing but upper body power with serious ab and hip strength. No way me or Rob could do them like her in perfect form, not with our heavy legs.

It was an impressive "fuck you" to Rob who didn't seem mad. He seemed relieved.

The close bond between them? It was painfully obvious. But the grueling workout had all three of us prodding each other on. By the time we finished, I was high on desire, endorphins and a wicked cocktail of dark emotions.

We grabbed our bags and headed toward the glass front doors. The sky poured.

"Man, it's raining cats and dogs out there," Rob said.

"I'm parked out front." I clicked my car remote. It powered up lights inside and out as well as the engine. "Let me give you both a ride to your cars."

"I'm fine," Rob said. "I grabbed a spot up front too." He hit his remote, a car alarm beeped nearby. He offered his other hand out. "Good workout, man. Join us again if you can."

I shook it back. *Fuck, it's hard hating this guy.*

"Night, fucker." Rob offered a fist bump to Charlie.

"Night, fucker." She bumped it back before turning her eyes to me. "I'll take the ride."

I opened the gym door for her and she darted through the sheets of rain, jumping into my passenger seat. Despite the close proximity of the car, we got drenched.

Dropping into the driver's seat, I threw my dripping bag

and baseball hat in the back. She handed me an extra towel from her bag.

"Thanks." I took it.

But I couldn't look at her. Wiping off my face and arms, running fingers through my damp hair, fuming, there was no denying it...

Rob loved Charlie. Maybe they'd had something years ago. Maybe they never did but wanted to. Maybe they did now. It didn't matter. There was something strong between them. I couldn't fucking shake the maddening certainty. Couldn't shake the toxic jealousy.

God, how does she do this to you Pierce?

From the moment I'd met her, firing every emotion through me? So real. So raw. So intense. All the frigging time.

Charlie made me want to yell, cry, hold and fuck her— all in one desperate, frenzied clutch.

CHARLIE

I SAT NEXT TO HIM, reading him like a romantic thriller. Few people are easier to spot than a jealous man. They're red neon, blinking with warning signs.

"Where's your car?" he asked.

"Up there." I pointed. "Close to the street."

In dead silence he drove across the parking lot, stopping behind my car. "Thanks for the workout." He glared straight ahead.

"Daniel?" I turned in my seat to confront him. Wipers whishing back and forth. Rain pelting the roof of the car.

"Yes?" he replied, reluctantly turning to face me. No smile. Only hurt.

"Are you jealous of Rob?"

His hands strangled the steering wheel. "A bit, yes." A bit, hell? Looked like a megaton. "He's a nice chap, and I know you two are colleagues." Tone lowered, he tried explaining, "But he obviously cares deeply for you, Charlie."

I reached out for the wet tendril falling over his furrowed brow. Wanting to crawl on top of him, to fucking take him and his vulnerability.

"Daniel," I said instead, twirling his tendril around my index finger.

The playful gesture made him smile despite himself. "Yes?" He tilted his head up, inviting more of my caress.

"Rob is gay."

"What?" He pulled back away from my touch. "I... I didn't know."

"Of course, you didn't know." I started drying my hair with a towel. "What do you expect him to do? 'Hi, nice to meet you, I'm Rob and I'm gay?' You don't introduce your-self as, 'Hi, I'm Daniel Pierce. I'm straight and have fucked hundreds of women while a million more await.'"

He rolled his eyes. "I haven't fucked hundreds of women, Charlie."

"But millions more are waiting"—I volleyed back with a smart-ass smile—"men and women."

I caught Rob eyeing Daniel discreetly a couple of times in the gym. We both ogled Daniel's body all night.

"I don't want millions. Men or women." He leaned so close. "I'm waiting on one rare beauty—you, Charlotte Ravenel."

Breathe. You know the plan.

I had to rest my buzzing head back on the seat. "I'm flattered Rob made you jealous."

"Yes, he made me jealous and now I feel like a nob." His grip over the steering wheel let go. "I'd never assume Rob is gay. And I know that's a stupid thing to say. Like I could supposedly tell. That it even matters. Or that it's my bloody business."

He took the towel back, wiping it across his wet neck. "My older brother Michael is gay. He came out to me his first year at university. He said, 'I'm gay and hope you don't get all cheesed off about it.'"

"Were you?"

"No. I didn't get mad. I love him. Wanted him to be happy. And my family adores Brian, his husband. They're waiting to have my niece this summer via surrogate. So I should know better. Sorry."

"All of us are more than meets the eye." I started unraveling my wet braid. "Rob is out now. And you're right. We are super close. We both served at the same time. He in Kabul at the embassy. Me in Helmand out of Camp Leatherneck. We met in L.A. when HGR flew us in to recruit us for *Fated*."

I shook out my wet strands. He grinned, chin cocked, quiet—seeming amused by my hair care routine.

"And we've spent a ton of time together. He treats me like any other Marine, and I love him for that. He's had my six, I mean, had my back, many times. So we call each other 'cousin' because he's full Dominican and I'm a quarter."

"Dominican?" His brows flew up. "I thought you were tan from the sun. But that's another stereotype, isn't it?" Resting his head on the car seat, it was like we were lying in bed, talking all night. "Your mum or your dad?"

"My mom. She's half Dominican, her mom, and half

Finnish, her dad. And my dad is as old Southern white American from French descent as you can get."

Twisting my hair into a loose bun, I turned to stare out the front windshield. "I still miss them. I really miss my mom at night. And I think of my dad whenever I'm driving. It's crazy when memories hit you."

"How'd they pass?"

"In a plane crash." I winced. "My dad was a pilot turned aviation consultant. He loved flying with her in his Cessna. They'd fly to Miami and the Keys a lot. Mom liked all the Dominican food and the vibe there. She didn't always fit in at home, in South Carolina. Neither did I."

The rain meandered in little rivers down the glass. Why with Daniel, I didn't know, but I revealed more.

"I had just started college when their plane went down. The NTSB said it was a fuel system defect. I'd just talked to my dad that morning. He was surprising Mom with another Miami trip."

A memory swiped with the wipers across my mind. The last time I saw my parents? The day they moved me into my dorm. Our last hugs. Our last words of love.

Tears wet my cheeks, surprising me. Crying in front of Daniel; I wasn't embarrassed. It only relieved my grief, talking about my parents, keeping them alive in my heart.

He reached his hand out for mine, open, palm up. It paused my tentative heart.

For so many years, I had no hand to hold. Needing this now, my fingers, then my palm surrendered to his. The intimate feeling of his touch? It wrapped around me, calming and in control.

"So they died together and happy," I said. His thumb rubbing across my hand, back and forth, caressing my sadness, it lured me out. "That's how I try to think of it."

"What are their names?"

"Beau and Sophia Ravenel." Names that made me smile. "Sophia Karnonen dey Reyes Ravenel," I pronounced in perfect Spanish. "And Beauregard Duke Ravenel. Very Southern."

"What's your middle name?"

"Sophia." I smiled even more. "My mother was a feminist for sure. I had to have her name too."

"Charlotte Sophia Ravenel," he purred in beautiful French.

I laughed back. "No one in South Carolina says it like that." Flexing my free hand over my chest. "More like 'Shaaaaalut Raaaavenelllll'. My name has ten syllables at home, Daaaanielll Pierrrccce." I mocked with the deepest Southern drawl I could muster.

"You keep talkin' in that accent darlin', and I'm comin' across this car to take you now." He tried sounding like Rhett Butler in *Gone with the Wind* but didn't really get there.

It made me laugh harder until his gaze silenced me, his massive shoulders flexing up, drawing my hand up to his chin. Air lifted in my lungs when the heat of his lips brushed across my fingers.

I imagined his breath across my clit. His tongue...

Honk!

We jumped.

Armand pulled up alongside with his window down. "Is everything okay?" His heavy Castilian accent could make any interruption pleasant.

Daniel pressed his window down. The rain had stopped. "Yeah, mate. We're all right." He gave Armand a salute. "Just chatting about work and workouts."

"Está bien. Have a good night," he called out, pulling away.

"We're so busted." I wasn't mad.

He grinned my way. "No, busted would be my lips buried in your neck."

"Oh, we could get busted doing lots of naughty things in this car, Daniel." I dared, "Better your lips buried in my neck than my head buried in your crotch. *That* would be busted."

"Fuck, Charlie." He sighed, closing his eyes. "You're torture with that mouth." They flashed open with impatience. "Come over for that picnic I promised. Next Friday. I'm slammed shooting until then."

"This picnic will involve my tongue *only* tasting your food, Daniel."

"I'm not the one who said something about my cock in your mouth."

"That's not exactly what I said." Lifting his hand up to my lips, I floated them across his warm knuckles. "But I enjoy the image in my mind." Drifting down the pulsing veins on his hand. "Do you, Daniel?" Hovering over the tickling hairs on his wrist, challenging his gaze.

"Fuck yes. But only if I get a go at you too." His lips parted while my mouth danced over his skin. "Until then, just food." His lush lips curled in that grin that cast a million orgasms across the globe. "For now."

"For now," I agreed.

I had to let go of his hand before I put it where I was dying for him.

When I bent down, reaching for my gym bag on the floorboard, he asked, "What will you do until then?"

Stepping out of his car, I suddenly felt shameless, confessing to his curious eyes, "You know good and damn well what I'll do, Daniel. And I promise I'll moan your name over and over while I do it."

My truth threw his head back in surrender on the seat with a tortured moan.

I closed his door before I said more.

Can't believe you just said that. Yep, and don't give a shit. The lust. It's fucking yummy.

One hour later, his text.

I just moaned your name too Charlie
Over and over
And will twice a day waiting
Only for you

CHAPTER FIFTEEN

CHARLIE

When I couldn't sleep, I worked.

Wednesday morning had a six a.m. call time for Kierra.

I arrived on set shortly after four.

Dawn had yet to rise for the small crew also on set. I had to ask Hugo, the transpo captain, to let me into Kierra's trailer early.

Lorenzo wasn't here yet. He'd beaten me so far since Kierra had started shooting, always appearing over my shoulder, stopping me for early morning chats.

There was an odd mix to him, an awkward curiosity coupled with a desire to please. Yet, he had a subtle disdain for the cast. Given his ambition so far, it seemed unusual he ran late.

The costumer pulled up in her cart, following on my heels into Kierra's trailer. She hung up Kierra's wardrobe in the closet for the first scene before rushing out, off to Mason's trailer next.

I started a pot of coffee in the kitchenette. The smell. The dripping. The quiet. It all comforted me.

Turning the overhead light back off inside the trailer, I reclined in a chair, closing my eyes for just a moment. For the fifteen minutes it took for the pot to brew.

My mind was a yo-yo, dropping me down into sleep then yanking me back up into thoughts.

Of Kierra...

Since filming had started, I noticed how Kierra's hands shook on set. Then she'd fist them up. Angry at herself. Angry with her fear. It was an anger I understood.

It made me hover as close to her as I could. Protecting her. Willing my strength into her. Wishing I could give her peace so that Kierra could breathe calmly.

That was a joke. How could I give the girl a peace I didn't even have?

Deep practiced breaths. Please. Dropping me down into rest then thoughts snapping back up again.

Of Daniel...

The maze of emotions I felt near him, knowing he was forbidden to me, knowing he had a dark secret, knowing a stalker hid somewhere on set; the threat called to me. He called to me.

My compass? It was marked with more than lust. With every smile. With every story. Hands held and stolen glances at each other. Waiting for Friday. I wandered farther and farther into his...

Thump.

My eyelids snapped open.

Thump.

A gentle rock shook the trailer.

Sliding out of the chair, I snuck low to the window. Index finger curling over the blade of the blind, I pulled it down to see. No lights in the makeshift alley behind the trailers. Only generators buzzing. Snakes of electric cords winding left and right.

Movement. Coming from the left. A figure passing under the window. In a dark hoodie. Was it navy or black? I couldn't tell. Only that it was sneaking my way, aiming between Kierra and Daniel's trailers.

Whipping my gaze to the brushed steel doorknob of the trailer door, I waited for him to turn it, assuming Kierra's dark trailer was empty.

The doorknob turned. And turned.

Yes. I stood up. Five feet from the door. Waiting. For him to open it. And I would end him. His grooming, stalking notes. His theft of Kierra's things and sanity. I crouched to leap on top of him, ready to catch the fucker now.

Outside, the soft *putt-putt* of an engine hit the air. A cart sounded down the path, the sound nearing from the catering truck.

The turning of the doorknob? It stopped. Footsteps crunched. Running away.

I bolted. In three swift steps I banged the door open and leapt over the steps, landing two booted feet firm on the pavement.

My neck snapped right. The cart, two sound techs, clunking their way up the path.

To my left? Daniel's trailer and the path leading to another stage building and the parking lot beyond. Empty.

I ran left between Kierra and Daniel's trailers.

The fucking cables snared my boot, slowing my pursuit. Stumbling, I paused to yank my foot free. Five more steps and I stood in the alleyway, looking left, then right.

Empty.

Damn. So fucking close.

CHAPTER SIXTEEN

CHARLIE

I needed this. To forget the hellish week. To forget for one night how Kierra left the set with her hands shaking every day. We both tried to ignore the eerie lack of another taunt from the stalker.

What was he waiting for?

All I could do? Wait too.

And have a picnic dinner with Daniel Pierce.

Skimming my closet for date-like apparel, I cursed the slim pickings. I grabbed my red flamenco skirt again, along with a thin, pink, cashmere ballet wrap-sweater, loving the combo of red and pink. It was a proud "fuck yes" celebration of the femininity I rarely got to reveal. Still, it kept my body hidden and safe.

Reaching for a bra from the lingerie drawer, I smiled. Nope. Nothing on underneath. I closed the drawer.

I flipped my hair over for a quick blow dry. A little mascara. Coconut lip balm. First date with Daniel Pierce or not, I didn't do makeup. My feet slid into flip flops. My hands grabbed my old jean jacket and tan leather handbag before picking up a picnic basket from the kitchen peninsula. It held my surprise for the night.

But when I stepped out the front door, clicking my car fob, it didn't do that cute *beep* back. I tried again. Nothing.

Hey, horny lady. You were too distracted with thoughts of Daniel and left your damn car lights on.

With a quick search in the trunk then the back seat for jumper cables, I found nothing. *Fucking rookie mistake.* No one else could know about tonight. I had to turn to my partner in crime. Texting him:

Dead car battery. No cables
Need a ride, please.
I'll throat punch you if you
make a comment

One minute later, his reply:

Are you a damsel in distress
my lady?

Not in distress. Safe in my
home. Fine to stay here
tonight

Sending Simon right over
We can trust him
He keeps all my secrets

Fifteen minutes later, Simon pulled up to my villa and stepped out to greet me. "Good afternoon, Ms. Ravenel."

I didn't miss his approving smile, sharing our secret. I

closed the front gate behind me. As I reached to open the back passenger door of the car, Simon rushed over.

"Please allow me, marm." He pulled the door handle with a slight bow.

It was ingrained. My Southern manners found me picking up my skirt and stepping into the car while I thanked him.

We rounded a pebbled circular drive in front of Daniel's estate minutes later. Simon jumped out again to open the door for me. I accepted his hand, looking down, making sure I made a graceful exit from the high step.

When I glanced up toward the front walkway, Daniel was speeding my way.

Loose waves on proud display. Flip-flops on perfectly groomed feet. Dark blue jeans straining over strapping thighs and a tissue-paper thin, white linen sweater with boatneck collar hanging low, showing off his sexy-as-fuck carved chest and dusting of dark chest hair.

Oh God, you're in trouble tonight.

"Oi!" Daniel called out. "You beat me to it, mate." He took my hand from Simon's.

"I'll gather your things, marm."

When Simon bent over to retrieve my basket and handbag from the car, Daniel insisted, "Please, let me," reaching his other hand out to take them from Simon.

"Well, y'all. Who's gonna fight to carry me to the door?"

They were acting ridiculously, like I was the fucking Princess of Something arriving at the castle. Then again, these two English gentlemen seemed to enjoy competing for a medal in The Chivalry Olympics.

"I win that one for sure," Daniel said, scooping me up in his arms, my basket and bag dangling from his hand.

It shocked a squeal out from me that made Simon laugh,

watching the spectacle of Daniel carrying me up the front walk. My heart was pounding while I looked back over Daniel's shoulder, thanking Simon again.

Simon slightly bowed."Good night, marm."

Like hell, good night. Was that what he was used to with Daniel's guests? With his secrets? They stayed over on the first date?

Stand by, Simon.

Not part of my plan.

Daniel carried me up the front stairs like a twenty-pound sandbag, no burden against his strength. "Something smells delicious." He stepped over the threshold. "What treats are in your basket tonight, Ms. Ravenel?"

I wrapped my arms around his neck. "You won't be enjoying any of my basket treats tonight, Mr. Pierce." He stopped in the foyer with the front door wide open. "But you can have my fried chicken."

He beamed. But didn't put me down. His foot tapped the front door closed. Simon had seen enough of the show.

Brushing his lips over my hair, his voice was so low it almost whispered over my ear, "You look beautiful tonight, Ms. Ravenel."

His forehead nuzzled mine, his nose, his lips an inch away. Plunging us into a deep moment, silent with eyes open. Breath growing shallow. Pulling us down together. Deeper. Our wet world disappearing above.

Oh God, where are you going? Come up for air before you drown with him in this beautiful ocean.

I forced myself to break his spell.

"You're gonna have a helluva time eatin' fried chicken like this."

"I'm not letting you go, Ms. Ravenel," he said with the same certainty as water is wet, the sun is hot.

"All right then." I kicked off my flip-flops. "My toes shall not touch the ground tonight." I fluttered my feet, encouraging him to move.

He laughed, carrying me through his living room, out through the glass patio doors.

A lush blanket with a mountain of throw pillows on the grassy square of his courtyard welcomed me. Candles glowed in the sunset. Two bottles rested concealed under white towels in silver ice buckets beside a large picnic basket.

It's so romantic, Charlie Girl. It's so much trouble.

He set my basket and bag down on a lounge chair before he carefully laid me down on the pillows. "Can I take your jacket?"

Looking like that mounted over you? He can take your bounty.

Thankfully, he stood up.

"If you promise I'll get it back." I peeled it off, offering it up, my pink wrap sweater covering my breasts like a wet paper towel. Useless.

Shaking his head at the vision, he walked back into the house, wondering aloud, "Am I waiting in heaven or hell?"

He returned with a small tray of glasses and an ice bucket. The Bluetooth speakers on the patio started to play a Latin Lounge station.

Lowering his powerful body gracefully down, he sat cross-legged beside me. "May I pour your poison tonight, Ms. Ravenel?" He turned to the two bottles, unwrapping one, revealing a bottle of chilled Tito's.

"Daniel Pierce, how the hell did you know my poison?"

"I'm not just a pretty face, my lady. I can get my own intel too." He could only take the subterfuge so far. "I overheard you ask Maja." With a pop of the cap of tonic water, it spewed all over his sweater. "I did that just for you." The cutest smile mocked his goof, making me laugh at his soaked sweater, waking his nipples too.

"Now we match," he said.

I enjoyed the spectacle while he poured my drink. "Yes, but I won the wet T-shirt contest last month."

"Oh yes, my lady. I saw it." He handed me the crystal tumbler. "You certainly did."

"Hey, can you blame a gal? After years under a flak jacket with crushing SAPI plates over constricting sports bras. I go braless whenever I can. It's bullshit how you guys get to go shirtless, and women don't."

"I agree wholeheartedly. Be my guest, Ms. Ravenel." He set his glass down, reaching for the hem of his sweater, taunting. "I'll go first."

"You fuckin' wish, Pierce."

Don't stop him! Please God, take your fucking shirt off, Daniel Pierce.

He dropped his hem with a grin, raising his drink to mine. "Thank you for the sincere pleasure of your company this evening, Ms. Ravenel."

I sat up to with a *clink*. "Mr. Pierce, the pleasure is all mine." He took his first sip while I lightning quipped, "And you had me at Tito's."

He sputtered his wine. "Thank you for a proper ruin of my first sip of a bloody good bottle of Ygay I've been waiting a year to open."

"You're welcome," I sassed. "I don't go as fancy as your Ygay. Tito's is as highbrow as I get. Guess I'm not one to put on airs."

That stopped me. What I just said. "God, that's something my dad would say. He'd say, 'Don't put on airs. Graciously accept whatever's offered to you.' God help me if I refused something served. My daddy would have my hide. One time I had a stand-off with him over lima beans."

I took a sip, continuing. "I hate them. And one night we were having dinner at his colleague's home in Savannah. He made me wear a white dress and black, patent leather shoes. I must have been about six and hated every minute of being a little lady."

His grin at my rambling; it made me stop. "I'm sorry. You give me Tito's and story time begins."

"Keep going." Lying on his side, propping his head in his hand, he said, "I've got a whole bottle of Tito's and all night for you and that accent. And you had me at hating lima beans."

"Well, I remember it because it was like a battle of the mules. Who was more stubborn, me or Daddy? My mom said, 'Two asses don't make a right,' and stayed out of it. So my daddy kept eyein' me like 'eat those damn lima beans.' And I whispered back, 'I'll take any whoopin' over these yucky lima beans.'"

Another sip of his wine met the grin on his lips. "I reckon I know who won."

"Yep. Daddy gobbled quick spoonfuls of lima beans before the host came to take my plate. I got homemade butter pecan ice cream for dessert that night and an ass whoopin' worth every bite." I raised my glass to the memory. "Love you, Daddy."

He joined my toast, saying, "Tell me another tale in the *Adventures of Stubborn Little Charlie*."

"You need to pay me with dinner first."

"Ah yes. Right." He got up to kneel, fetching our meal from the large basket beside him.

The aroma wafted, recognizable the second he set the

bowls down. Saffron, capers and sea food. He'd made paella. For me.

It's too much. It's perfect.

I touched my hand to his. "Thank you very much, Daniel. I really appreciate all of this." He gazed up and held it back.

"You're welcome." His thumb caressed mine. "But you may want to save the 'thank you' until after you've tasted it."

We sat up to eat, about to enjoy the first bite when he exclaimed, "Wait, what about your chicken?"

"That's the second course. Now tell me some tall tales of *The Beautiful Boy from Walney Island.*"

He had them. Escapades of him and his older brothers playing along the banks of the channel. Apparently, they often resulted in a lot of sand thrown at Daniel. "I'd get a bit tired of their torture so would seek out my little sister, Tess, and torture her instead."

We volleyed tales of childhood and teenage antics through tears of laughter. Somehow, we landed on school dances.

He confessed to awkward moments and stiffies. I shared sagas of fox-trot lessons my father forced me to take, preparing me for Cotillion, and how I won every effort to thwart them.

"The irony is when I was a girl, my daddy said with a face like mine, he had to raise me to fight like a boy. Lord did he ever. Then I became a teenager, and he lost his damn mind trying to make me a proper young lady. All those bullshit lessons and no one ever asked me to a dance," I said, laughing in relief that Cotillion never happened, sadly because my parents died, but glad still the same.

"You were never asked to a dance?" His voice rose three octaves along with his face.

"Nope. No corsage. No grinding slow dances. No drunken after parties. No hard-ons or virginity lost."

"Well, we shall remedy that tonight. Excuse me, my lady."

He jumped up barefooted, aiming for the courtyard wall. Yellow wildflower bushes bloomed under red roses climbing up the stones. One rose broke off with his snap before he pinched the little thorns off upon his return.

You'll never forget this sight. How he's bowing with one hand behind his back, offering the rose to you with the other.

A gesture he'd surely mastered for some character. Corny and cute. It acted on me too.

"May I have this dance, Ms. Ravenel?" he asked before helping me rise gracefully to my feet.

"Yes, you may."

You may have more than a dance if you keep playing your cards right. You're a damn poker shark at romance, Daniel Pierce.

For a fleeting second, I wondered, no, I feared. *Is this a dangerous ploy, or is it pure romance?*

"Just a moment, please." He held my hand with the rose, taking his phone from his back pocket with the other, scrolling. I grinned, knowing his game. "Ah." He made his selection. "Perfect."

Once the beat dropped and humming started, I laughed, nervous and seduced. "Lady in Red" by Chris de Burgh.

I almost couldn't do it, letting his gorgeous body press against mine aching from years of loneliness.

But he took control.

Tucking the rose behind my ear, offering his hand in perfect form, resting his other against the small of my back;

we knew the song from our childhood. It was on any eighties' love song playlist and way too sappy to be real.

Not tonight.

By the first chorus, he let go of my hand, hooking his index finger under my chin and lifting my lips to his. Not touching. The allure and ache in his eyes mirrored mine, shocking my heart, making it hammer against my ribs.

By the second chorus, he broke form and the tension we couldn't endure anymore. Cupping my head to rest my cheek on his chest, he filled my senses. Hard muscles swaying gently against me. Bare feet stepping lightly next to mine in the grass. Arms holding me in a strong embrace.

How I'd missed this. We danced until... all songs ended.

After a long pause in a yearning silence, he whispered into my strands, "Can I please have another dance, Charlie?"

I smiled with my head at ease on his chest. "Yes."

You'd agree to waterboarding torture right now.

"Lady's choice," he said.

I pulled back, intrigued. "Really? Any chance one of your roles was a Latin Lothario who could salsa?" I didn't know his entire IMDB but couldn't think of any.

"I'm afraid not. I'm trained to cut an Elizabethan rug. But I'm man enough to hold on and follow your lead."

"Deal."

He took his phone out of his back pocket, unlocking it for me, "Be my guest," and surrendering it to my outstretched palm.

His arms wrapped around my waist. It took me a minute. The press of his body against mine didn't seem to mind.

Found it. "This is a classic to any kid of the nineties." I had to tense my lips down, suppressing the joke. "Maybe it made its way across the pond. A song sure to inspire any foxtrot."

When I slid his phone back into his pocket, my fingers grazed over his ass, lust flushing my body.

At first, he looked puzzled. It started like a rap song. I watched the recognition in his eyes when the vocals dropped. It tossed his head back in laughter. "I Wanna Sex You Up" by Color Me Badd.

"Hang on, Pierce." I coaxed his hips in tempo against mine. He answered back with rhythm of his own, seizing my hips in his strong grasp. I leaned far back, trusting his strength, grinding against him in cadence to the beat.

Another song, corny as hell, but hot as fuck now. Our foreheads met in a game of lurid stares while the lyrics put shared thoughts in our heads.

I pressed firm against his thick hard-on. One that made my entire body pound all reason from my head. "Does this remind you of that middle school dance, Daniel?" The dance of my hips against him intensified.

"Yes." His lips parted. The sound of his staccato breaths, ones of lust, they made me dizzy. He licked his lips before adding, "But I've grown much bigger since then." Grinding harder against me, he proved it. "At thirteen, I would have messed your lovely skirt before the first chorus." The friction between us screamed with heat. "Now I can wait much, much longer."

I grabbed a handful of his flexing ass. "We'll see, Mr. Pierce." He groaned, latching his grasp over mine.

We coiled into each other with knowing smiles, inches from the other's lips until the song faded. I laid my head back on his chest. He cradled me there with his damp hand; his heart thumping under my cheek. His hard length demanding against me. I melted in his embrace, almost weak from the wet swimming between my thighs.

Did you just dance with the Devil? Yep. It was exquisite.

"Don't they drink after school dances?" I dropped the hint, desperately searching for my willpower.

He chuckled against me. Another disarming trait; when he laughed, his whole colossal body rocked with joy.

"Thank you for the dances, my lady." He lead us back to the blankets. Another round of drinks was poured before we dove into my basket of treats.

Licking his fingers with his eyes on me, he said, "Your breasts are sin worth every bite." He grinned while he polished off almost all the chicken.

I rubbed my arms, shivering now in my thin shirt.

"Let's go inside and get warm," he suggested.

I started to get up.

"No, no, Ravenel." He scooped down to pick me up again. "What did someone say about their toes not touching the ground tonight?"

This was delightfully fucking ridiculous. "What about our dancing?" I argued the point.

He replied, "I'll make an exception for a randy bump and grind," while he carried me back inside.

CHAPTER SEVENTEEN

DANIEL

Saving All My Love by Empara Mi

I set her down, her bare feet dangling from my kitchen countertop. Claiming the space between her thighs, I spread them open to her skirt draped over her knees.

Every smile. Every story. Every laugh. Holding her body so close. My fucking world was rearranged in one night, making it sensuous hell going slow with her and I dropped my lips down to hers for more.

Where was that aching space between our lips again? Ah yes, right here.

"Are you going to kiss me, Daniel?"

My gaze traced the outline of her light pink lips. "Not until you ask me to." The high of the drug she'd introduced into my veins flowed like opium through my body.

The waiting for her.

Drawing my lips even closer, we were poetry, my favorite Keats poem. "Ode on a Grecian Urn." It laments of a woman and man painted on a pottery urn, suspended forever about to kiss, frozen there, never knowing the touch of the other's lips.

She sighed. "I need to wait."

"I'll wait as long as you want."

She met my gaze with an ache of desire fighting fear dancing in her eyes. The contradiction? Enthralling.

"I have to confess something, " she said, "and you can't laugh."

I took the rose from her hair, setting it down before cupping my hand to her soft cheek, trailing my thumb down her raised scar. Her shoulders dropped. I saw it; the tears she fought back at my gesture. "I won't laugh at you, Charlie. I promise."

Her stare fell, along with her cheek still cradled in my hand. "It's been six years since I've kissed a man." A deep breath filled her lungs. She raised her marine eyes, her teeth scraping over her bottom lip, confessing, "And he was the only man I ever kissed."

"Hmmm. Only one man... and no women?" I didn't care, relishing any truth about her, only wanting to make her smile.

"Cute." It worked. "No, just one man. I love women." She tickled her fingertip lightly across my top lip. My cock jumped. "Just never met one I'm attracted to."

I murmured, "Six years."

It wasn't a question. It was an exaltation.

Six bloody years. She must be starved for it. And God, how I could feed her appetite. Every slow, hard inch. And to be the only other man? I'd lie upon any altar and sacrifice all to satisfy her.

"Do you think you've forgotten how to kiss? A man?" I grazed the tip of my nose across hers. "I seriously doubt that, Charlie. But I'd be happy to teach you anything you've forgotten."

Our sexy banter and the promise of unleashing her passion after six years made me so fucking hard. Crazed imagination luring me with all I could do to her. Pleasing her. Fucking her. Making her mine. Over and over. I pulled back to start now, to beg for just one kiss.

Lust. Pain. Fear. It was swimming in her eyes.

Fuck's sakes. Control it, Pierce. Slow down. Now!

I exhaled the greed threatening to take me, reaching for her hand instead. "Charlie. I'm sorry." Resting my forehead to hers, peering down into my new bliss, I said, "Six years is a long time. And you don't have tell me why. And I promise I'll never push you."

Don't cock this up. Not with her. She's different.

I just wanted her, in any way, in any time she was willing.

She moved, nuzzling her cheek against mine. "I don't want to talk about it. Not tonight." We were silent for a minute before she confronted my eyes. "I just wanted a first date like a normal person. Like the perfect night you've given me." She traced her fingertip over my lips again. God, I was losing it. "And I promised myself if I ever did this again, I deserved someone worth the wait."

Clocks stopped. So did my heart.

I stood in a void of time and breath in fucking awe of her.

Humbled.

It came down to one kiss, one painful secret she'd been protecting for six years. And now I stood between her thighs, a breath away from her lips, hearing *I* was worth the wait.

No, you're bloody not. Far from it if she ever knew.

I never worried if I was good enough for a woman. I never cared. Waiting was not something I did. Any night out. Any woman. A flirt, drinks bought, condoms in my pocket, a discrete signature on an NDA and I always got what I wanted.

God, I'd been a callous, selfish arse so many times in the past, leaving an ocean of pleasure and pain in my wake.

Not this time. I was no fool. Thirty-seven years old and only three weeks into meeting her had introduced a new reality into my life.

Charlie Ravenel was worlds beyond any woman I ever met. Would ever meet.

But the baggage I came with wasn't as pretty as my bloody face.

This would all end once she knew what I'd done. She'd walk away. Or worse, she'd want to kill me. And I would lose the one woman I had to have.

But you can change, Pierce. Try so bloody hard on your knees for her.

It attacked my heart, erasing my inflated ego. I had performed this before—this feeling at first sight. That was an act.

This wasn't.

"I'll wait for you, Charlie." I was captured, inches from her lips and helpless in my truth. "If you think I'm worth it."

CHARLIE

I CLOSED my eyes and didn't recognize my world anymore. But I knew it, without deliberation. "You are, Daniel."

So many men I'd pushed away.

But Daniel Pierce was too strong. He only came back for more. Yes, he was a powerful alpha to millions. But with all I'd survived, I sat with him between my legs, more than his equal.

I could handle him. And have him. Risking just one night like Maja said. Maybe one week. For once in my life, I could do something for myself. I didn't want forever from anyone. I didn't believe in it. I knew loss and solitude on a visceral level.

No one defined me now.

I could say yes to all he awoke in me, letting my body devour all of him too. We could take. We could receive. And it would end as everything had in my life. Then I'd go back and walk my beach, safe and alone with memories for a lifetime.

And whatever he was hiding? It couldn't compare. Not to what I hid too.

"Ask me on another date and prove to me you were worth the wait, Daniel Pierce," I commanded, curving my hips, urging against his. "If you want to."

He sighed into the hair falling over my ear. "Oh God, how I *want to*, Charlotte Ravenel."

I glanced down. His stiff cock pushed to the edge of the waistband of his jeans. Tempting his hard truth and my resolve, I challenged him, "Show me how you want to."

Yanking my hips into his crushing grasp, he thrust firm into my center, over and over while the heat of his lips trailed down my neck. "Like this."

Thank God for his thick jeans between us, or it would be my end.

"Fuck, Daniel." More than my body howled for him. Six years of carnal need roared for the hottest man I ever met.

Gripping his hair buried in my neck in one delicious grasp, the other captured his flexing ass, luring him inside. I could imagine him. Yes, just like this, thrusting deep inside of me.

The lust in his voice matched his hot breath in my ear and the sweet pain of his clutch driving into me. "God, Charlie, I want you so fucking bad."

God, please. Yes. Now.

No, Charlie! Wait, goddamnit! Not like this.

"Daniel." I pushed his body, his touch away. He groaned, staggering back. Dazed with desire, I couldn't catch my breath. "I need to go before we get into trouble."

He peered into my eyes, panting. "It's no trouble." Reaching down, he adjusted the erection straining against his jeans. "I promise to behave until you leave. And then I'll need a long, hot shower thinking of you so I can hold a coherent thought again."

"That makes two of us."

He sighed. "Fucking hell. The thought of you touching yourself is more than I can take right now." His hand trembled, reaching for his phone in his back pocket. "I'm getting Simon to bring the car round... or I'll have to start with you here to witness."

"Promise me I can watch you one day. While you watch me too."

He pulled me off the countertop, holding me while he texted Simon. "Charlie, you're breathtaking, fucking torture." His thin shirt fell over his muscles with chest hair sneaking through the threads, tickling my cheek.

I was the one in sweet torment.

"Let me get your things." He let me go and ambled outside for my bag and basket.

Darting for my jacket and shoes in the foyer, I had to escape. Not trusting my body. Not trusting anything.

Stay in control. Don't fucking lose it now. Just enjoy the night. It was perfect.

He surrendered my things with reluctant hands before trudging to the front door, pulling it open like it weighed a metric ton.

I paused in front of him. "Thank you for a beautiful first date, Daniel."

"You're welcome. And good night, Charlotte Ravenel." He didn't smile. "I want to hold you again, but if I do, you're never leaving me."

CHAPTER EIGHTEEN

CHARLIE

The euphoria from my first date with Daniel thirteen days before became a distant memory. Though he texted and we talked on the phone every day, it wasn't the same. All the cast and crew were exhausted.

We had ten grueling night shoots in Solosancho, adjacent to an archaeological site. It was eerie, perfect for the scene, but remote for the cast and crew. No cast trailers at this location. Only a small basecamp. With restrictions due to the historic site, all cast members were corralled outside under a pop-up tent for two weeks.

The intense schedule and high risk away from the protected studio had me on high alert. Shadowing Kierra all night found me collapsing every day and over the weekend for sleep that never seemed enough.

And now, another threat stole my sleep.

Three nights ago on set, Kierra had jumped up from her cast chair, glancing nervously back at me, telling me she needed the toilet. The frantic nature of her announcement warned that wasn't the case.

I had escorted her to the honey wagon—the only multibanger trailer at the location for such needs. While we walked over, Kierra whispered, "Charlie, I just got this message request in my DMs."

She handed me her phone. It showed a message in Kierra's Instagram account from a user with a profile picture of Kierra's face with a blindfold imposed over the image.

That and the message disturbed me.

@you.r.mine.brigid
Waiting to bind you up in that necklace and bracelet I left you.
Bet your first boyfriend doesn't give you such breathtaking gifts

"Kierra"—I tried not betraying my frustration—"you were supposed to turn off all messages to your account months ago."

"Sometimes my fans send the sweetest ones. I feel bad ignoring them."

"You need to focus on your safety, not your fans." I didn't like the jealous reference to Kierra's boyfriend. "It lets that sick man feel too close to you. Trying to control you. Understand?"

Kierra had nodded her head. Fingers tapping across her screen, she shut down all messages for good.

I reported it to the HGR London office the next day. They were on it, trying to track down the account. I didn't hold my breath, suspecting the stalker wouldn't be stupid enough to leave a digital trail.

I was right.

It left Kierra on edge, her mom growing anxious, the security team getting frustrated and me itching with rage.

Though the weather was calm for production that week, it wasn't how I felt. Or Kierra. The notes, the camera, the necklace, the sneak up to Kierra's trailer, and now the creepy message.

The stalker was circling around, waiting for his chance. With delusional sick references to jewelry and bondage, his jealousy over the girl and her boyfriend worried me.

But his pathologic patience impressed me.

I had to respect it because I did the same.

The long wait brought pleasure and pain, addictive in its own way. The duality always gave me an edge. I was so fucking stubborn I'd wait an eternity for him to make his next move. Knowing, he'd strike again soon.

Now it was Thursday night and hopefully the last one production shot out here.

The entire ensemble had a pivotal scene to do—an argument between Kierra's character, Brigid Morrigan, and Daniel's character, Carric.

Carric mocks his little sister, Brigid, angering her, refusing to see their coming doom. Their father, Arzur, played by Anders, sides with Carric. Yet Arzur cannot ignore the foreboding sense his daughter's hallowed warnings may indeed hold true. Finally, Herne, the younger brother and Mason's character, quells his family's anger at the end of the scene. Herne is the peacekeeper in the story arc, and by the end of this season, the ultimate literal sacrifice.

While Rob shadowed Kierra from the hair and makeup trailer to set, I stood there already, talking with Jennifer Adams, the director of this episode. I asked her and the assistant director if we could play music between set-ups.

I hoped it would calm Kierra. And secretly, me too. They loved the idea.

The terrain was too rough for the golf carts. Rob drove Kierra and Daniel on an ATV from basecamp to the pop-up tent. Joaquin brought Mason and Anders on another.

All four actors walked shoulder to shoulder toward the tents in their full hair, makeup, and costume. They looked at home in the landscape with its Iron Age features. The set created mimicked the ancient Celtic stone fort and sacrificial altar nearby.

I shivered. The sight was ominous.

Anders, in the character of the Arch Druid, loomed over the others in his gold robe with black fur lining. His long auburn hair and beard were streaked with gray, giving his character sage presence. Makeup and special effects aged him twenty years.

Daniel and Mason appeared threatening in their red robes. They were Sacrificers. Daniel's handsome face hid under a shorter beard. His long auburn hair twisted into warrior locks along both sides of his head. Sacrificial and battle scars marked his face, arms, and naked torso underneath his robe. Carric had a warrior's body, built to fight as his father Arzur had before he became the Arch Druid.

While Mason as Herne Morrigan looked strong, he did not share his older brother's size and stature. He dressed like Carric but was styled to look out of place. His auburn hair fell in disheveled waves. He wanted to be a Blue Bard, an artist. But his father Arzur would not allow it.

Kierra as Brigid Morrigan looked the most striking. She was a young priestess. Her white robe flowed over ivory skin while long copper hair cascaded down her back. Her face appeared young, but her eyes possessed a bastion of feminine power the men ignored to their own demise.

I loved what Lorraine, the showrunner, had shared

about her concept for the series during our meeting with the executive producers.

Lorraine had said, "The fate of the Druids resides in the girl. Will the Morrigans realize Brigid's destiny as the chosen one to wear the gold robe of the Arch Druid? Or will they bestow it upon Carric in patriarchal tradition as the first-born son, angering the gods and goddesses and sealing their doom?"

I was definitely a new fan of the show.

They found their cast chairs under the tent, all listening to Jennifer as she explained her vision for the scene. I could see Kierra trying to focus on Jennifer's direction, but her eyes darted, distracted.

The stress on her innocent face broke my heart, reminding me of another girl's face, one who had suffered a silent, daily strain.

I stood by Rob and Manuel, Kierra's makeup artist. "Do you still have your speaker on the cart?" I asked Manuel. The makeup and hair artists had their palettes and supplies loaded onto it, but I thought I heard one playing the other night.

"Sí," Manuel said. "Here." He pulled the large, black square out from underneath a tissue box.

"Do you mind if we play some tunes now and during last looks for Kierra?"

Manuel smiled. "Sí. She's having a rough week. She's not having fun with me like usual."

I took out my phone to find his speaker on it, then I scrolled to find Beyoncé. Kierra loved Beyoncé. I cataloged all the girl's likes and comforts. With one touch, "Single Ladies" began to play.

Finishing up her chat with the cast, Jennifer shouted out from the tent, "Turn it up!"

Manuel cranked up the speaker while I turned up my phone. The music waved through the night air, shifting the energy around us.

Anders exclaimed, "Hell yes! Dance party!" jumping up to do a few Beyoncé, put-a-ring-on-it moves, making us all crack up. Jennifer added a few good moves of her own. Manuel followed with his own impressive steps while the rest of the crew started to sway, staying on task, enjoying the beat.

All while I watched Kierra's eyebrows go from furrowed to amused.

When the song finished, Manuel cried out, "In Español, por favor."

Rob shouted back, "Dale!"

He took my phone and made the next selection. "Bailando, Spanish Version" by Enrique Iglesias danced across the air.

Rob cheered, "¡Viva, Dominicana!" and grabbed my hand.

I didn't refuse. I loved dancing with Rob and threw my baseball hat on the cart, inspiring Manuel to shout, "¡Olé!"

Anders clapped the flamenco beat while Manuel approached Kierra for a dance, escorting her outside the tent to join us on our impromptu dance floor. Manuel showed Kierra a simple, traditional salsa while Rob held my hips, leading us in a shameless version of the dance.

Then Rob turned me with the rising beat of the chorus, sending my hair flying before yanking me back, dancing in alluring circles with our twisting arm holds and turns. At each repeat of the word "contigo" in the chorus, he'd whip-turn me again and again before pulling my hips in for a sexy grind.

My peripheral vision captured our admiring audience under the actors' tent. All stood, swaying to the music.

Except Daniel.

He leaned back in his chair, grinning. I wanted to pull him out to dance, but no way we could hide our attraction in a hot, public display.

At the end of the second chorus, I broke from Rob to go to Manuel. Rob put his hand out to Kierra. Manuel slowed with me in a formal salsa while Rob showed Kierra a few of the complex turns.

I adored the carefree grin on Kierra's face. It inspired my own, making me sing aloud to the very end.

We took our bows to the claps of our small audience and Jennifer shouted, "All right, let's shoot this!" She high-fived me and Rob, heading back to video village.

The actors took their seats, laughing. Hair and makeup let them get settled in before they came in for last looks. Any touches they had to do? Worth it. Everyone seemed ready for a great night now.

I pulled my hair back through my baseball hat, adjusting the brim and catching Daniel's eyes.

Even disguised as Carric, I recognized his gaze. It tickled my stomach, an urge building in my sex. It was the same look he had the last time he hovered inches from my lips.

Yep, we all needed a dance party.

With a smile, I turned away.

CHAPTER NINETEEN

DANIEL

I woke late the next morning. The song still singing in my ears. Her still dancing in my mind.

I plucked up my from the nightstand, texting:

> Thank you for the show last
> night, Ms. Ravenel. May I have
> a private one tonight?

Stretching my arms overhead, I waited for her reply. For her rolling hips. For her grinding ass. For another dose of her drug.

My hand traveled under the waistband of my boxer briefs. I smiled at the typewriter sound, the unique ringtone I gave her contact name. My free hand checked my phone, smiling at her reply:

Instead of a show, Mr. Pierce,
I'll teach you so we can do it
together

I grinned, one hand replying, the other stroking my morning wood.

Can you school me now
Ms. Ravenel? I'm in bed &
feeling randy to learn

What do you want to
master, Mr. Pierce?

Whatever your wet, lovely
hand is touching right now

Mine pumped faster at her reply:

Are you sure you have the
discipline for a hard drill?

I have a firm grasp, ready
for you to guide me

My hips thrust into my fist, seeking this pleasure and her reply:

It's wetter than water. You'll
need control

That quickened my breath, wanting to drown in her, typing...

> Under your command,
> I bone up quickly

Get on your knees Daniel
if you want to immerse
yourself

Every part of me stirred up, desperate for her.

> Gladly. Will you please
> give me oral instruction,
> Ms. Ravenel?

I knelt, throwing my head back in a moan under her rule. Pausing when I heard it, only needing her next reply.

Master that tongue and
I'll bathe you in it Daniel.
Good day

She ended the lesson and us both.

CHARLIE

I SHOWERED, still glowing from my text tryst with Daniel. Damn, how horny we were for each other.

Dragging a towel across my torso, I almost felt guilt. How I never acted like this with my husband, Kai. He was my first everything. Not like I waited out of stupid notions of purity. Apparently, I had intimidated the good guys away.

Until Kai.

We dated in college when I didn't know my body, feeling unsure with his too. Typical Kai with his books, he found some on Tantric sex, and together we learned the pleasure of delay, the use of breath and senses to heighten our lovemaking. It taught us the power of sex, making me confident with desire.

But that was ripped away from when we were stationed apart. Traumatized by war. Never to share it again.

I rubbed cocoa butter over my belly, massaging my scars to soften them, basking in the feeling again with Daniel. This desire resonated stronger with him.

That was the guilt.

And the reality.

This lust was in a different body. One that had been through hell, bore the scars, and now hungered for the heaven of pleasure. My body was more than ready.

Careful, your heart isn't though. It may never be.

And you've got a fucking job to do. Don't you dare let loneliness and lust cloud your vision.

I got dressed to go to the studio. My phone sounded again with a distinct ring while I laced up my boot. Something was wrong. Kierra never called. She texted everything.

"Hey chica," I answered. "You okay?"

"Charlie, there are flowers in my bag," she almost whispered. "Little bright yellow flowers all in my bag."

"Your bag sat on your chair under the tent all last night, right?"

I was sure but needed to hear it from her. They didn't have to move the actors' tent for any setups last night. Her chair stayed in the same place for hours.

"Yes. I left it there with everyone else's."

The terror in her voice scorched through me.

I knew Kierra's bag—a floral print, LeSportsac deluxe tote. She often left it sitting unzipped on her chair or hanging over the back of it.

And I knew the little yellow flowers Kierra described. The recognition rushed bile up in my throat.

Oh God. You saw them at Daniel's house. In a vase on his island. Growing in his courtyard.

But could he be that deceptive, that alluring and evil at the same time?

No. Surely my instinct would tell me if he was. It never failed me.

Besides, he wasn't impulsive. Or stupid. Everything he revealed to me so far was the opposite. Quite the opposite.

And those flowers grew everywhere. Piorno. Some called it "Mountain Broom". It grew wild on low bushes with long stems all over the Iberian Peninsula.

It was in bloom now and everywhere around the Solosancho location too. You couldn't see the flowers at night, but you could smell their honey in the warm spring air.

It hadn't been a windy night and Kierra's bag lay under the tent. No way the flowers could have drifted on a breeze into her bag.

Someone snuck them in.

"Is anything else in there or missing?" I heard the clatter of Kierra dumping the contents of her bag out onto a solid surface.

"No. I just see my normal stuff and these flowers everywhere. I like flowers, but not like this." Her breath huffed in fear. "It's so creepy, Charlie. The message this week and now these flowers. He's so close."

"I know. It's okay, chica."

It wasn't.

Little gestures may seem harmless. They weren't. They spoke to a pathology fixated. Obsessed with controlling. Impulsive to possess. And the threatening proximity it revealed?

Bile burned up to my mouth next. I choked it down, focusing on my tone to smooth Kierra's nerves.

"Kierra, we got this. Clean your bag out. Get rid of anything you don't really need. And from now on, remember exactly what you put in there. Every day, before you leave the house, take an inventory. Keep it zipped on set, and then check it every day when you get home."

Logic clicked through my mind, listening to Kierra organize her items back into her bag.

Why little yellow flowers?

They were symbolic of new beginnings, like their springtime bloom. Whoever put them in Kierra's bag didn't want to only scare her. He wanted her to know he adored her in a perverted way. Like a new phase of his wicked worship had begun.

What was next? How far could he escalate this?

I already knew what could be at the bitter end of this ritual. The pain. The suffering. Of an innocent girl.

"It'll be all right," I lied. "I'll meet you on set in an hour. I'm not leaving your side. I promise." That was true.

Kierra had only a few pages to shoot today with Anders. They'd wrapped at Solosancho last night. They had to film one interior scene back at the studio.

I'd be there until they were done, and Kierra was delivered safely home. If that meant all day, Daniel would have to wait. I'd never leave my girl.

I ended our call, whipping the laces tight up my other boot, smiling.

You won this round, Charlie Girl.

He couldn't resist the temptation last night. Tired of waiting, he was growing impatient. And careless.

Yes, I'd nail him soon.

CHAPTER TWENTY

DANIEL

Watermelon Sugar by Harry Styles

Finally, she stood inches from my chest. I asked her, "What treats do you have in your basket tonight?"

Charlie smiled at me in the doorway of my garage with a temptation over her arm.

She'd run late this evening. But a few hours were nothing to the days I'd been aching to get her alone again. I couldn't control it, remembering our texts that morning. My body roused the instant she stepped out of her car.

"Strawberries and things," she said. "I saw some at the market and got an idea."

I didn't move. Neither did she. We hovered in a close standoff.

"An idea? Don't you mean a dessert?"

I adored peering down at her. How she fit into my chest —tall enough to reach my shoulder, small enough so I had to bow down to have her.

"Nope." She swished past me. "Not dessert."

She tortured me again with her outfit. Another long skirt in a Spanish, floral print. Another long sleeve, wrap shirt. This one black and knotted high across her ribs, no bra, and thin enough to see through if the light was kind.

"Dinner smells good," she said.

I closed the distance between us while she unpacked her basket. Strawberries, cut to serve, appeared in a white bowl. Then she set out three small ramekins with lids.

Something possessed me, my hands seizing her hips, positioning myself behind her while I inquired down her neck. "What do we have here?"

Tonight, no thick jeans between us. I made sure of it; only wearing my black cotton pajama pants with boxer briefs underneath, trusting she could feel my length heavy for her now.

Two more weeks without her had driven me mad. Impatient for us to start. After last night's dance and this morning's texts, my body was pleading against hers to the point of gratifying pain.

"Is this what you want, Daniel?" She arched, grinding back on me. Her hand met mine clutching her hip. Her other snaked through my hair, luring me in.

"Fuck yes." I traced over the bare skin of her taut belly while bending my knees so I could urge into her. The instinct was owning me. "God, I need you."

It scared me. How not a minute more of this I could take. How my restraint diluted with every second she was near. How I craved her, needing for this to begin, more than anything.

With a nudge, she pushed me away. "Close your eyes." Turning, she jumped to sit atop my countertop.

I obeyed, panting in blind pain. I heard lids snapping

open on the ramekins. A snare of legs captured me, yanking me back into her at almost a matching height. I didn't know what she was doing, but it was killing me, and I loved it.

"Open your mouth to me," she said.

Tipping my head back, I opened my lips to savor anything she offered. It met my tongue—sweet with cream, juicy with something tart, making the flavor dance across my palate.

The heat of her breath tickled my ear. "What do you taste, Daniel?"

This was some sort of sexy-as-fuck game. "Strawberries with cream and something tart," I said, wanting more of it. "Lemon?"

Something landed on my lips at that last word. Hers. Like a butterfly alights on a flower. Warm breath. Fruit and sugar. Tickling touch.

God, please, a kiss.

She pulled away. "Your turn."

No, my play. "Close your eyes."

I opened mine to see what she had hiding behind her. Strawberries with ramekins. One with whipped cream. One with a brown glaze that smelled like fig and balsamic and another with lemon juice. I dipped a strawberry in two of them.

Lifting her little chin up, I said, "Open your sweet lips to me, Charlie."

I dangled the strawberry over her mouth. Her tongue licked the cream off the tip instead. The wanton act coursed a fierce rush of lust through my body.

"Open," I ordered again, wanting to rule more than the lips on her mouth. She parted wider, giving the strawberry another disobedient lick before I could put it in.

She was teasing me while I tried controlling her—an addicting, maddening struggle.

I dragged my thumb over her lips while she relished the flavor. Licking mine wet, I grazed them over hers. My eyes were open, admiring her thick mink lashes, brushing my nose against hers and those fucking sexy cute freckles.

"What do you taste?"

"Something warm and creamy with a luscious acid ribbon at the end." She held her mouth barely from mine, opening her eyes and challenging me. "Like I want to taste from your hard cock one day."

A moan escaped my throat. Thrusting hard against her naughty suggestion, I pulled back from her lips, focusing on her eyes with the torment in mine. Every nerve in my body throbbed, desperate for some piece of her.

"Charlie, I can't take much more. I want you too much. I'm going to fucking come right here in front of you."

"I want to make you come, Daniel." She tilted her lips up to mine. "And I want you to do it while you kiss me."

Oh, fuck yes, her sweet command and consent. My hands embraced her face, bowing my mouth down to her. "Are you sure this time?"

"Yes." She smiled and didn't need to say more.

My heart raced, but my journey was deliberate, moving slow. She could stop me... but didn't. Lingering my lips against hers, her hot strawberry breath was so close and melting me.

One. Gentle. Kiss. Her lips, supple. With a small quiver.

Fuck, I forgot to shave. "Am I hurting you with my scruffy face?"

"I like how it hurts." She kissed me back, offering more of her lips.

Yes, please, and not stopping now, I cradled her face in my palms, lifting her chin up and taking more of her kiss, again, and again. More of my passion. More of her lips. More of my breath. When my hands slid into her silky hair laced between my fingers, her body rose to mine. Oh fuck, I was gone, parting her lips with my tongue.

She moaned through my wet probe. Her fingers grabbed my hair, gripping what length I had and pulling me in, hard. Dear God, she wanted even more.

I had kissed so many women. In front of cameras and each felt like choreographed, awkward hell. And many more forgettable ones behind closed doors.

But this new world? With her? Lights popped inside me, not from cameras. It was flashes of my truth, waking everything numb within. Unwrapping her heartache and my heart, we were immersed in a dance of skating tongues, brushes of lips, breaths drawn together.

Halting for an inhale, for balance, searching her eyes, my fingertips traced across her right cheek. "Can I kiss you here?"

Her lips trembled but she said, "Yes."

I held her hands in mine. Her lips, her body, her secret, her pain—everything about her, I wanted. My kiss traveled along her fragile scar, tracing to her ear and back again to her lips.

Saline tears trickled over mine. I pulled back. "Are you okay?"

"Please don't stop."

I held her face, my world, in my hands now. "Charlie, I don't want to rush you. Just tell me what you want."

"I want you, Daniel, and that terrifies me." Her smile didn't waiver under her tears. "But fear won't stop me."

She surprised me. Drawing me by my neck back to her

kiss, taking my bottom lip in a delicate grasp between hers. It shot pleasure straight to my cock, dragging a deep moan up from my throat at the new sensation. She pulled back, opening her neck, offering me more.

My lips traveled down her damp jaw to her ear, whispering, "Do you want me to kiss you here?" Trailing my index finger down her neck.

"Yes, but that's as far as we both go tonight. And I go first."

I leaned down, submitting myself to her. Her gentle bites, kisses and tongue devoured my neck. The desire in her breath across my sensitive ear became all I heard when she asked, "Do you like my mouth on you, Daniel?"

"Fuck yes." I moaned, going mad. My knees noodled. My cock starved. Taking my turn next and what she'd allow, I devoured her lips, her tongue, her neck, her fucking moans urging me on.

I whispered in her ear all I imagined that morning. How my cock fucked my fist desperate for her. How I came moaning her name.

"Tell me, Charlie." I pleaded with seeking thrusts, but the tension in her thighs closed her center to me. It was part of her torture, and I was a fanatic for it, luring me to the verge. I could do this with her words alone. "Tell me what you want me to do to you."

She coaxed my ear with teases of her tongue and salacious details. I closed my eyes, descending into the shameless, hard-core images she painted across my mind. Beautifully lewd ones I could imagine with her, imagine to the point it would be real one day. I was going just by the sound of her voice, with her, now. Taking her mouth so deep while it spilled from me, I came without a touch, with only her kiss. Shuddering again over her sweet lips, I moaned as pulse after pulse of my desire finally found release with her.

Gasping for breath, should I laugh or cry? I was a teenager again, resting my forehead to hers, not believing what she just did to me. "Damn, Charlie. My God, that was breathtaking." I sensed my creamy, damp end between us and got shy. "I'm sorry," I said, struggling to open my eyes.

"Don't you dare apologize. I think it's beautiful," she said before offering a deep, assuring kiss. Then she looked down, admiring the stain on my cotton pants. "And so fucking hot."

I was relieved, elated she was free about it. Though we were doing a sexy as hell game of teasing the fuck out of each other, it wasn't out of shame. She needed to go slow, and I reveled in the opiate of it.

"I want to give you pleasure too. I'm not that kind of man anymore."

"It's okay."

"No, it's not. I want to make you come too, but all I know involves lines we haven't crossed." I laced my hands through her hair. "Just tell me what you need, and I'll try."

"Daniel"—her hand took my stubbled cheek—"I promise I'll let you do more than try. But when we do, one orgasm and a couple of hours won't be enough. After all this time, I'm going to want you for days. And I don't want promises for forever after. Just give me a week and we'll both get all we want."

She was right. For me, a few hours or one night with her would only leave me crushed, wanting her more. After six years, I could imagine sailing through her wet storm, never wanting to find land again.

I'd give her more than a week. I'd give her everything.

"Charlie, gift me with a week with you and I promise whatever you desire. We can start now if you like."

We grinned through kisses, knowing we couldn't. My call time was in twelve hours. The thought made me resent it for the first time. How I wanted her, not the job.

She pulled back from my lips. "Whatever we do, we can't get caught together. And let's not get stuck in your house for a week either. There's too many people and cameras."

"Where can I take you, my lady?" I smiled down at her, loving the idea of spoiling her. The money and power I had could lavish her. I just didn't know how I could buy time and privacy. Then I remembered. "We can go on hiatus together, someplace no one will see us. Just tell me where, or it'll be a roach hotel in Moscow."

She scoffed with a grin. "Oh, I'd rock your world in a roach hotel in Moscow."

I murmured through kisses down her neck, "I know you would." I wanted to start again.

"Look here, Sex God." She grabbed my hair, playing, pulling me nose-to-nose to her.

I spoke like Zeus. "Yes, Sex Goddess." Grinning at our game.

"Take me to a warm island of our own with bright blue water where we can fuck naked a hundred times in the sun and show the fish what wet really means." She grabbed a fistful of my ass with her free hand. "And I command you call me Sex Goddess here forward."

She said that last part laughing, like it was a joke. But not the first part. That was a deal.

"Yes, Sex Goddess," I agreed, scooping my arm under her legs and carrying her across the kitchen. "Your wish is my command."

"I command that this is the last damn time you're carrying me in your arms." My steps didn't stop, heading toward the stairwell. "Just where do you think you're taking me, Sex God?"

"Where any Sex Goddess belongs." Carrying her up the stairs, I chuckled with how far we could take the joke. "To my bed." I kicked open the double doors of my bedroom.

CHAPTER TWENTY-ONE

CHARLIE

"Wait please while I shower up. I still owe you dinner," Daniel said, lowering me down on his bed. Pulling the covers over my bare feet, he kissed me before disappearing into his ensuite bathroom.

I sank into the spot, into his smell on the pillow and little dark hairs scattered on his white sheets. They were the expensive kind, making any bed feel like luxury. Tugging the covers up to cuddle me more, I closed my eyes to the sound of water splashing off his body, imagining what he looked like naked in the shower.

A soft kiss woke my lips. The aroma of him swirled around me before I opened my eyes to find him sitting beside me, dressed in fresh clothes. He looked like a dream with damp hair falling in waves, with a bedside smile that could heal the dead.

He brushed my hair back. "Charlie?"

"Did I fall asleep?"

"Yes. Just keep resting here." He pulled the coverlet over me. "I'll sleep in the guest bedroom tonight."

I stretched like a kitten, complaining, "But I'm hungry."

He laughed at my pretend brattiness. "Well then, let me get you some warm clothes. It's a cool night and this house has shit heating." Walking into his closet, he returned with sweatpants and a sweatshirt, setting them on the bed. "These are the smallest I have. Far be it from me to cover you up, but I can't have you shivering through dinner."

I stretched again with a, "Thank you."

"You're welcome, my Sex Goddess. Dinner will be ready in five." He turned, closing the doors of his bedroom behind him.

His comfort. His care. It all enticed me to never leave his bed.

Get the fuck up. This is way too dangerous. Way too tempting.

I did. Getting undressed, chills crawled across my skin. Stepping into his sweatpants, chuckling at how they would swim on me, I glanced down. Amusement left me at the sight of the circular scar above my right hip bone.

No, not yet.

I hid it below any waistband of my pants or skirt. Tightening the drawstring of the sweatpants in a knot, I was desperate to secure them.

Wincing at the familiar pain, I lifted my right shoulder above my head to put on his sweatshirt. Always hiding this scar too.

I had three. Two of them were brutal. And Daniel, like most people, only knew the scar I couldn't hide from the world. They defined me now. I feared the sight of them would imprison me forever.

Damn, you can't do it.

Fear flooded me. To let Daniel see them? To spend a week with his hands on them? Would his touch trigger their story, robbing me of any pleasure, delivering only familiar pain?

My heart raced. My mind galloped, willing my feet to follow.

Grab your bag. Tell him you can't go through with it. Run out the door and never look back.

Don't you fucking dare, my lust insisted. I dare you to fuck him, my mind taunted back. Fuck you both, my heart warned.

My gaze fell on his pillow. Lingering my fingertips over the white cotton, it shut them all up.

He makes you happy.

Even in this fucked up job, even when you don't know who the evil one is, you know this—it's called joy. Just because one part of your life is dark and haunting, it doesn't mean all of it has to be.

Not anymore.

I looked up, praying to my mom. Her fierce spirit would find a way to kick my ass if I didn't at least try again. I had a family of ghosts, and my mother's always championed me to be loving. Shameless. Fearless.

And Kai? He'd want me to have this. He never had a jealous bone in his body. And it was a body gone. And mine still stood here. So painfully lonely and aching that if I let the truth of it wash over me, the sobs would destroy me.

One week with Daniel Pierce. That's all. Then back to solitude. And safety. Promise.

I lighted down the stairs, hungry for dinner and much more. The sound of my bare feet padding into his kitchen made him turn to see me standing with his clothes hanging off me like potato sacks.

"You're so bloody cute, Ravenel." He charged toward me, putting his arms around my waist. "Can I kiss you again?"

I reached for the nape of his neck. "Daniel, you don't have to ask me anymore."

"Quite right. I'll never stop then." His lips kissed mine again like he wouldn't. But then he did. Stop. "Look here, hungry Sex Goddess." He took my hand, guiding me toward the breakfast nook. "Dinner awaits."

"I think you missed your calling, Sex God."

Salt-crusted Sea Bass with patatas bravas, it was beyond delicious. We fed on food and conversation. I shared how my family had lived in Spain and then Turkey for years when I was a girl. My dad's work in aeronautics had us traveling all over the globe in growth markets.

He asked, "So, what languages can you speak?"

"Mmm." I took a sip of sparkling water before I answered, "Spanish, Turkish, Farsi, Pashto and a bit of German. I went to the language academy in Monterey with the Marines, mainly for the Pashto."

A memory flashed. *Lethal brown eyes. The bazaar of Marjah. The back of Jax's flak vest. A shock in your shoulder. Blood in your mouth.*

I changed the subject.

"What about you?" I asked. "Where has the world taken you? You can speak French, I can tell."

He shared tales of travels to locations around the world. Filming was fun. Press junkets, exhausting. I couldn't imagine the bullshit of screaming fans, selfies with everyone, having to answer the same dumbass questions over and over and over again. He had far more patience than I.

When he got up to pour another round of drinks, he grinned, handing mine back. "Did your only boyfriend teach you that game that has forever changed my relationship with strawberries?"

"Let's go sit by the fire and I'll confess all my witchy ways." The chill by the windows had really frosted my bones.

He offered his hand, helping me climb out of the bench nook. Like I needed help. It amused me as we crossed into the living room.

"You first." Playfully, I pushed him back on the sofa before swooping down to straddle him. "Supergods before mortals, remember?" Play turned to passion in his eyes. "Now kiss me," I said. "Just lips. No tongue. Then stop to breathe with me in between. Like this."

Parting my mouth, I embraced his with a tender suck of his bottom lip, then slowly, his top. I stopped and he did the same to me. Then I held his hands and gaze for four deep breaths together before another kiss shared. Back and forth. Every time he caressed my top lip with his, it seared through me. Each time I took his bottom lip, a groan lulled from his throat. And our breath? It was as powerful as the intensity deepening in our eyes, an erotic cycle of minutes upon minutes, kiss over breath over kiss, the ritual magnifying until my body felt ablaze and he reached for me, moaning my name and wondering aloud what was happening to him.

Hovering over his lips, I asked, "Have you not ever practiced Tantric sex before?"

How could this man who fucked so many women over two decades not know what we were doing?

"So, that's the name of your drug?" He panted. "I've heard of it, but no, I've never felt this before."

"You explore the senses. Connect with breath. You go slow and let it build, enjoying the power of it."

He closed his eyes, inhaling, a furrow etched across his forehead. His silence troubled me.

"You think it's a crazy, dick tease, don't you?" I only shared this with one other man and myself. Shyness. Shame. Hating the feelings pelting me, I fought against his embrace.

It jolted his eyes open. "Come here, Charlie." Pulling me back, he spoke with an intensity I hadn't heard before, with a possession I never felt, grabbing me hard. "Don't ever push me away again."

I relented, back in his arms, looking down at him, stunned by how vulnerable he made me, not knowing if I should feel warned or wonder.

Cradling his hand to my cheek, he exposed me even more. "I don't think you're crazy. I think you're the most remarkable woman I've ever met. I think your mouth and strawberries shake my fucking core. I think your dick tease is the most erotic thing I've experienced. You have me melting into the sofa with an orgasm I didn't even have. So, if Tantric sex is your drug, I'm a fucking addict now." He kissed me again and again, the way I taught him, melting away my fear.

He stopped with a devilish look on his face. "Can you recommend some Tantric reading though? I'm a competitive man. If we do nothing else for a week but see who can outpleasure the other, it would indeed be nirvana."

He laid us down on the sofa, holding me in his arms. "You never did tell me who taught you about the strawberries."

"No, I didn't." I played with the soft dark hairs on his forearms. I couldn't tell him. Fearing my truth—of being wounded *and* a widow—it would steal all the joy from the little time I had with him.

He squeezed me tighter, letting quiet fall over us. The pluck of his fingertips playing with a single lock of my hair made my eyelids heavy.

"Will you stay with me, in my bed tonight?" His deep voice sounded vulnerable with the ask. "I can't bear watching you walk out of my door again." His finger lifted my chin, his eyes swearing to mine. "I promise, Charlie."

I knew the promise. He wouldn't push me. It wasn't enough.

"I don't know if I make a good sleep companion." I cast my gaze over his shoulder, staring down something far away, long ago. "You may wake up with my hands choking your neck." My stare shot back to his. "And that's not a joke."

He let a pause ricochet between us. "Well then." His lips drew closer to mine. "I'll have to hold you so tight that you can't fight me."

CHAPTER TWENTY-TWO

CHARLIE

"I don't like it, y'all. This perverted fucker is smart."

I peeled an orange, always eating one to quell my fear.

Rob, Joaquin and I sat crammed next to each other in front of my laptop. Jeremy appeared on the screen. Our midweek morning meeting wasn't official until—wait, there it was—Jeremy clicked his damn pen.

Something had been agitating me for days. Like I was looking for something, fearing I held it in my hand the whole damn time. So, I started scoping for a new angle.

"Kierra's home with Malcom and the extra detail we sent over this week, right?" Jeremy asked, not expecting an answer. "Our bloody budget is blowing up over this now."

Jeremy could bitch about budgets till the cows came home. But it wasn't about money for him. I knew he worried about Kierra and the escalating tactics targeting her.

So did I.

We played it off around her. No reason for the girl to

suffer in constant fear. But when we found private moments like this? It made worry sweat from our pores.

"We've got nothing on the fake Instagram account." Jeremy rehashed what we already knew. "No prints on the car, the necklace, or the note. Even the window screen and sill came back clean."

"Fucker must be walking around with latex gloves in his pocket," I said before devouring my first bite.

"We know he worked on season one. We know he's on set now." Joaquin took the pragmatic approach. I liked him. His lithe body hid his best weapon. Like me and Rob, the man had multiple belts in martial arts. The fact that he had a cute Madrid accent was just a cherry on top. "I think he may be local. He knows the terrain well."

"Maybe," Rob said. "Tough to be sure. Hell, half the cast and crew live here six out of twelve months anyway. One thing is for certain. He knows his tech well."

I peeled another section away, watching the tiny white fibers release their hold. "I think it has something to do with Kierra's boyfriend too."

More of Jeremy's pen clicking. "How's that, Ravenel?"

"Kierra's boyfriend is of Pakistani descent. He's all over her Instagram. I checked. The day the necklace was left with handcuffs, Kierra had posted about her boyfriend. The day of the message to her account about the necklace, Kierra had posted about her boyfriend." I popped more fruit into my mouth, chewing and talking. "And guess what? The day season one wrapped. The day of the threatening note—"

"Kierra had posted about her boyfriend." Rob nodded. "Good catch, mi prima."

"You think it's about jealousy over a boyfriend?" Joaquin asked. Only his accent could make that ugly word sound tolerable.

"Or race?" Rob asked.

"I think I'm not going to assume a damn thing," I said. "We're just going to keep Kierra safe until he does what all men do eventually." A third section popped in my mouth. They waited me out until I said, "They all fuck up."

Joaquin started laughing. Jeremy's pen stopped clicking with his own amusement.

"That's just what you tell yourself about men, mi prima, so you'll be eligible to join a convent next year," Rob said.

Then we were all rolling.

"CAN I GET YOU ANYTHING, CHARLIE?" Lorenzo asked me later that day, walking toward Daniel's trailer with an espresso in his hand. "A café con leche? A foot rub?"

"Do your job Lorenzo and I'll do mine." I smiled at his reliably sweet-to-yucky comments, all while keeping my eyes on Kierra grabbing her lunch from the catering truck. Joaquin waited down at the truck too, getting his lunch while covertly shadowing her.

Over my left shoulder I heard Lorenzo's *tap-tap*, then *tap-tap*, on Daniel's trailer door. Daniel had been in there the entire hour I stood here outside Kierra's.

He bounded out a few seconds later, thanking Lorenzo for his daily caffeine delivery. Then he stepped to my eleven o'clock just a few feet away, dropping his backpack to the ground and sipping from the small paper cup.

"Ms. Ravenel." Daniel spoke in a public voice. "Joining us for skeet tomorrow?"

I glanced over at him.

It felt odd seeing him in character. Carric's look promised pain. He was not the romantic man I'd gone to bed with last Friday. The one whose embrace anchored me down into sleep with no nightmares. The one who rose before dawn for his workout, leaving me a cute "You slept like a beautiful angel, and I slept like a devil with a stiffy" note and a pot of hot coffee.

He'd been asking me to come back ever since, but I had to pace myself.

One night in his arms threatened to become a habit I couldn't afford.

But today, his question sounded harmless. Everyone knew he shot skeet with the cast and crew. I had heard the talk in the green room and knew the plans. Mason had been boasting about his new Browning shotgun, goading the guys on for some stiff wagers.

I stepped closer to him so as not to yell. "Sorry, Mr. Pierce. I have other plans." I was covering Kierra, the only one shooting tomorrow. Even my sense of duty didn't dampen the thrill of teasing him with rejection though.

Both his eyebrows ticked up at my smackdown. "I see." He leaned over, plucking his phone out of his pack's front pocket.

I checked back at catering. Kierra was walking back. Mason lurked by her side with Joaquin a few steps behind. As their steps drew near, I could overhear their conversation.

"Why are you so special to have your own meal prepared?" Mason was either teasing her or pissed.

"Because." With an overdramatic flip of her hair at the taunt, Kierra replied, "I have an allergy to shellfish. So, they make a special paella for me."

Their path took them right to where I stood. "Paella today?" I asked, trying to neutralize whatever was transpiring between the two.

Mason cut his eyes at me. A slow grin smeared across his face. "Smile more, Charlie. It makes me feel safe *and* happy."

"I'm not responsible for your emotions, Mason. Just responsible for everyone's safety."

Mason always did this, provoking everyone. The arrogance of his youth, beauty and fame gave him a long enough rope to get away with it. But I'd yank a damn knot in it if he tried that shit with me too often.

He squinted at my rebuke. I could smell it on him, knew exactly the kind of man he was. If misogyny had a brand rep, it would be Mason.

"Charlie, they have flan for dessert today too." Kierra knew it was my favorite. I wondered if she was also trying to smooth over my tension with Mason.

"I'll be sure to get my share," I said. "Thanks, chica."

Lorenzo knocked on Anders's trailer. Transpo carts for the long drive across the massive lot to the sound stage pulled up.

My phone vibrated in my back pocket. I pulled it out. Daniel's name appeared over a screen of texts.

If not skeet tomorrow how
about another tantric dinner
Saturday

BTW. Colleen cleared my
calendar for hiatus. I'm all yours

And she's tasked with finding our
island of 100 fucks. Don't worry.
We can trust her. I know for sure

I turned to him, not but fifteen feet away, his guilty grin burning a heavenly hole through me.

Another teasing Tantric dinner? My clit loved the idea. But my ego signed the papers now to have me committed.

I turned back, checking Kierra.

The carts had stopped. She sat propped up on hers, scarfing down paella with a fork from a cardboard food container. Same as Mason, who sat on his cart, joking with Lorenzo about something they "scored" last night. All waited on Anders.

Quick replies fired from my fingertips.

Is that what you've been up to for
the past hour?

Fantasizing about another Tantric
tease from me?

BTW. If you're a man capable of
100 fucks in 1 week, you're cast
on the wrong show

Nose down at his phone, slowly taking his seat on the cart, he grinned like he'd won the damn lottery at my replies. His fingertips fired up again.

Yes, thinking of you for the
past hour. You know how you
& your Tantric reading school me

Can you let a man at least try
for a dinner & 100 times? I'll
drop to my knees & beg for both

Finally, Anders burst out of his trailer. I replied:

It's a deal if I get to take a
picture of you kneeling
between my thighs

Daniel's grin was permanent, replying:

Please do

A smile held my face hostage while Anders walked over from his trailer to ride on the cart with Daniel.

"What's so damn funny, Char?" Anders paused, glancing left. I didn't answer. Daniel, with phone also in hand, had the same fuck-me smile.

A chuckle swayed through Anders's beard as he jumped on the cart beside him.

Rob texted me that evening.

I'll cover tomorrow

I replied with a simple:

Why?

Switch with me.
I need Monday off

That's BS fucker.

Anders wants you to shoot
tomorrow. I'll cover Kierra
Say yes, stubborn fucker

Kierra really didn't need me tomorrow. She'd be in the special effects chair for hours and then on the green screen stage. They were shooting fun solo scenes for her, magic and alchemy shots. It would be one of the few times, if I called with a change to our schedule, Kierra wouldn't mind.

Besides, I suffered Mason's big mouth too that week. I wanted in on the big scheme Anders had up his sleeve. I agreed, typing:

Copy

ANDERS COULDN'T WIPE the criminal smirk from his face, and I relished being his accomplice. When Daniel turned to see us strolling up to the shooting club pavilion, he tossed his head back, declaring, "I think we should lower the losing wager now."

Lance said, "I agree."

We walked out with our rifles to the first station. Lorenzo was taking practice shots on the field. Mason stood behind him, rubbing his rifle like it could fire more than his rounds. The two took their earmuffs off when they saw our approach.

"We got one more," Daniel said.

"You shoot?" Mason questioned me, spitting tobacco and condescension on the dirt beside my feet.

"A little." I twitched my nose. "Mind if I play?"

"Welcome." His tone did it like a fart in church.

We took our stand at station one.

"Ladies first." Mason's Texas drawl made it sound like the insult it truly was.

"Oh, make no mistake, Mason. I'm no lady. Just a bitch with a rifle." I stepped back. "You boys play first."

Lance started, followed by Lorenzo, then Daniel.

While Daniel fired his rounds, I admired his ass absorbing the recoil in his jeans.

Mmm and grabbing it between your legs the other night.

Stop it. Focus on the shot.

After Daniel, Mason stepped up to go next, but Anders aimed for maximum effect. He already told me he wanted Mason to shoot right before me.

"May I, mate?" Anders asked.

Mason retreated. Anders took his stance. He shot seven out of ten clays. Not bad, usually he did better.

Mason got seven too. He crowed, "Hell yeah" at matching Anders's score.

While he chest-pumped Lorenzo, seeking the praise he craved, I glanced at Daniel. He gave me a wink.

"All right, Char." Anders walked back even farther to enjoy the show. He positioned himself to my right, able to watch Mason's face.

Lorenzo stood on my left while Mason lurked beside him, his testosterone and cold-water cologne filling my nostrils. And Mason was eye-fucking me again.

I glanced at Daniel beside Anders and Lance. Daniel seethed back at Mason like a snot-blowing jealous bull, taking red aim for him. I walked forward and took position with the rifle in my grip.

Closing my eyes, the men ceased to exist.

Except him. Six years ago.

Firing two center mass through his chest. No! Focus.

One deep breath cleared my head.

A brown Kufi cap. One head shot.

Stop it! I squeezed my eyes harder. *Don't go there. Clear your fucking head! Now... and open your eyes.*

Exhale. Call. Mount. Move. Fire. Cycle. Move. Fire again. Cycle.

Both clays. No recoil.

Silence. I dismounted my rifle.

You fell. Blood in your mouth.

No! You're here. I shook my skull. *It's now. Not then. You're still fucking standing.*

One breath in. I gave another exhale. *Call again.* Two more clays. And again, and again, until I got all five pairs.

I turned back to the guys. To Mason's eyes blinking in shock at the clay dust in the air. To Lorenzo professing in a low voice, "I think I'm in love."

The rest of the guys gave me high-fives and, "Hell yeahs."

By the time we were done, and I scored the highest, we stood under the pavilion... and my right hand shook. My body still had the physical stamina for this, but my mind and memory were shot.

I said, "I gotta bow out," giving Anders a look he'd recognize. "I got calls home I have to make tonight."

I lied.

Anders nodded, just once; he understood. "Your chariot awaits."

Once we were in the car, he put on some Miles Davis jazz. I appreciated his gesture, letting me sit quietly, calming my breath and shaking hand.

"Thanks for coming out, Char. I'd pay five thousand euros to see that look of your arse-beating on Mason's face again." Anders stopped the car in front of my villa and patted my shoulder gently.

A text from Daniel chimed in my bag.

"You're welcome, you red-headed devil," I said. "Thanks for scheming with Rob to make it happen. I actually had fun with you guys."

I hopped down from his car before turning to grab my bag off the passenger floorboard.

"All of us guys, or just one *god* in particular?" Anders delivered a you're-busted smile. He said, "I've known you too long. Your secret's safe with me. And it's about fucking time."

That was true.

I felt myself fucking blush but wouldn't confirm it. "Night. Love you."

"Night, love you too." His laugh roared louder than the car engine as he drove off.

I checked the text once I got in the house. It was that sexy name again on my screen.

DANIEL
Save the euros you won today.
I can think of many tantric teases
to win mine back Saturday

CHAPTER TWENTY-THREE

CHARLIE

"You mix them together like this." Rob squirted a swirl of ketchup on top of a dollop of mayonnaise in a cardboard food tray, showing Kierra one of his concoctions. "And voila!" He dunked a French fry in the goop before shoving it in his mouth, making Kierra laugh, exclaiming, "Ewww!"

It was our Monday lunch. We waited by the catering truck for our burgers. I leaned against the metal humming hub of activity on set, watching up the path to Mason's trailer. And Daniel's. Both were no-shows for burgers today.

It scared me. How I actually missed Daniel.

His sister had surprised him, showing up Friday night for a visit, squashing our Tantric weekend plans.

Still, I made the most of my time off. A late Saturday morning flight had me meeting Juliette in Nice, France, where she was filming. We had a raucous night out with lots of drinks. But not enough alcohol in the world could get me to confess to my best friend about Daniel.

If I told Juliette about him, then it would be real.

And all I knew of life was that anything real got ruined.

"Charlie, your burger's ready, boo." Rob grabbed the food carton off the stainless steel countertop. He was playing with me today too.

Daniel's trailer door opened. Hand beside his ear, he talked on his phone. He had told me how he couldn't get a good signal in his trailer. His head hung guilty, down as he aimed between the trailers, his and Kierra's.

"Hang on a sec." I glanced at Rob. "I'll be right back."

Kierra would think I needed a bathroom break. Rob's look back knew otherwise—I was hunting intel.

A few steps up the path and I ducked behind the hair and makeup trailer. Working my way up the alley behind the wardrobe truck, I minded my steps this time over cords everywhere. The bustle of the studio. The carts putting up and down the path. The murmur of generators. It all masked my approach.

Daniel wasn't in the alley. The sound came from the tunnel between the two trailers, amplifying his side of the conversation as I neared.

I paused, hiding behind Kierra's trailer, close enough to smell him around the corner.

"I know, Mum." A low pitch of pain hummed in his voice. "I'm sorry." A long pause. A shuffle of his feet over the pavement. "You say it's not my fault but it'll always feel like it is though."

Fault? A fingernail scratched my heart, raising the hairs on my arms.

"No, I don't need to talk to her," he aid. "Sod all to say now. All this time."

Another long pause. My pulse tripled in such proximity. *Who is "her"?*

"Mum, I can't keep doing this. It's too much. It's too painful."

Doing what? Something too painful. Charlie Girl, this is a betrayal. Eavesdropping like this.

No matter my motives, this was not how to find out what Daniel hid. Not like this.

"We both need to let him go, Mum. Just bloody let him go." Sand scratched over pavement under his boot. "Mum. Mum... I'm sorry. I'm not cross with you, but I'm on set now and I can't get into this. I know how many years it's been. I know it's today. And it troubles me too. Every fucking day. But I don't want to talk about it. Not today. Not anymore."

An anniversary of something.

I marked dates too. I didn't need to look at a calendar. The cells in my body knew as light changed with seasons.

October twenty-eighth with long autumn shadows; the call from Pop, my dad's best friend, that my parents were dead.

February twenty-third with not enough daylight; Kai was killed.

The day before, February twenty-second and its eerie dusk; I was shot.

You never forget the day—and the two minutes measured within it—that change your life forever.

I stood there. Swimming in it. Vision blurred. Gaze to the ground.

A presence tingled beside my shoulder. "I gotta go, Mum." Daniel's voice hovered over me.

I jumped back. The look in his eyes—terrifying.

His nose was down, along with the phone descending from his ear. The question flowed like lava from his burning glare. "What are you doing, Charlie?"

I didn't recognize the man standing in front of me. My

pulse shot up more, thoughts darting as fast as my eyes, searching for a lie. "I was checking the window behind Kierra's trailer and I heard a voice. Yours..."

His nostrils flared. The rest of his face? Dead still. The air in his lungs heaved with breath. Like he was holding back something ruinous.

"...I didn't know what to do, Daniel. I'm sorry. I didn't mean to eavesdrop."

That's a lie.

My ass stood right here because I was snooping, tempted to violate his privacy, needing to absolve him of guilt. For what, I had to know. Because innocent, he wasn't.

His left cheek twitched. The entire mass of him towered over me. One raise of his fist and he could put an awful hurting on me. Not one I wouldn't fight. And not one I'd lose. I sifted through the heavy energy between us, not knowing which way this would go... and not backing down.

He took three pummeling furious breaths—I counted—before he spoke through his teeth.

"I thought I could trust you."

"I know."

Fuck, the only thing this man had done was lavish me with patience and care. That was my only evidence. So why the hell couldn't I shake it? He's done something. Bad.

Yeah, so have you. Wanna add hypocrite to the list of your sins too?

Honesty spoke. "I'm sorry, Daniel. I heard the pain in your voice, and it stopped my tracks. It broke my heart for you."

His exhale started at my mention of his pain, of my heart for him. His words followed. "It's my twin brother." The charge of the air around us moved from anger to anguish.

"Your twin brother? You've never mentioned him."

"I don't talk about him." Only his lips moved. "He died when we were ten. Pulmonary atresia. A heart defect. He got an infection from surgery, and it took him from me, from us."

The exhale that relieved my lungs next filled the space between us with compassion. Death. That was it. Something else pulling us together.

I said, "I could say, 'Sorry,' like what they say to me all the time... but that doesn't bring him back, does it?"

"No." The fact blinked his eyelids and dropped his chest. The burden, slouching his shoulders. "It doesn't bring him back. And it doesn't change that I was there, in hospital with my mum, when he died. I saw the whole thing."

His fingertips reached for mine, pulling me into his chest with a crushing hug. "At least I got to say, 'Goodbye,' to him. You never did with your parents."

The lump in my throat seared. I swallowed down pain for us both. "What's his name?" I asked the same question he had to honor my parents.

That's why he wasn't full of platitudes when I told him about their death. When death meets youth, it marks you unique. It's a special hell club with its own secret etiquette.

Tightening his grasp around me, he said, "Flynn Caspar Pierce." The cotton of his shirt dampened under my cheek. "He was so funny. So clever. But so weak. In and out of hospital his whole short life." His lips grazed through my hair. "When I told you the night we met that acting was the only thing that made me happy, Flynn is why. He's why I do this. Hiding in roles. Hiding from his ghost and trying to make up for all he never got to do. All at the same bloody time."

Wrapped in his arms, I risked the ask. "Who is the 'her' you mentioned?"

It took moments before he answered.

"My counselor. I saw her for a while, as a teen, but then I stopped. Much to my mum's concern."

The phone in my back pocket vibrated. Rob was looking for me.

Pulling back from his clutch, I met his gaze. "Can you come over tonight? I hate leaving you now, but we have no choice."

A tilting dive of Daniel's lips took mine—surprising me.

The risk we could get caught—completely disregarded by his mouth, grabbing for mine like his last breath of air would be found in my lungs. His fist wrapped tight around my ponytail, tongue snatching, grumbling desperate moans from his throat. His other palm clung around my tender throat. We were fucking losing it, losing our minds to each other, to our tragic and tempting bond. Daniel clutched me to the point of sweet pain, so hard my ribs seized, thighs blazed, and arms dangled helpless in his bind.

This force tumbled us together. The ice of my solitude. The jagged rock of his pain. It became a fucking avalanche melding our bodies, our past, our lives. It was more than the pummeling descent of our lust upon first recognition. It was a mass of suffering, sliding uncontrolled, burying us. Together.

Laughter hit the air. Kierra and Rob approached from the other side of the trailer, just feet away, upon us at any moment.

Daniel ripped away from me, both of us gasping, both of us drugged. With his nose to mine, he whispered, "Eight o'clock."

With a nod, I twisted from his grasp.

Shocked back—the next sight was my wrecking.

Lorenzo stood right there. Behind Mason's trailer. The look on his face told us...

He saw the whole thing.

CHAPTER TWENTY-FOUR

DANIEL

Say It - SG Lewis Remix by Flume

Her villa had a simple elegance to it. It was very Charlie: white walls, terra cotta floors, plants and Miró prints. Candles glowed everywhere. Her speakers poured out an ambient, sexy playlist. The stationary bike with a screen intrigued me from its spot in front of the sliding glass doors that led to a small courtyard.

I loved it here.

Taking another sip of wine, I doused my anger into only annoyance with her, for what she'd done that day. Not for one second did I believe she was checking Kierra's trailer. She spied on purpose.

It made me think of the adage, "There's no honour amongst thieves." Indeed. She hid to find out what I was hiding. With another big sip, I tried making it feel fair. With one glance over at her beauty, cooking dinner for me, it started to work.

"Now I know your secret." I leaned against the kitchen countertop.

She stirred grits. A food new to me but one I'd devour for her. "Which one?" she asked, grinning.

I caressed her ass, nodding toward the bike. "How you get a bum like that."

"Imagine your ass if you rode that thing for a couple of years." Her eyebrows edged up. "It would cut diamonds."

I gave hers a smack. "Challenge accepted."

"Ride it and see if you like it. Try to beat my rank, Pierce."

"I just might." I circled behind her, pressing into everything I craved. "There are other things of yours I'd rather ride first."

"Wait." She wiggled, pushing me off. "I hate my grits cold."

I chuckled, giving another playful swat to her bum before reclining back against the counter, patiently waiting for her to finish. I loved watching her "switchin' in the kitchen" as she called it. Another Charlie-ism saying for my list.

"You eat that with prawns?" I watched them sauté in the pan.

"With *shrimp*." Her tone corrected me. She ladled the creamy, buttery grits into wide blue bowls. It looked like polenta before she laid the shrimp on top. "Welcome to the Lowcountry, Daniel Pierce. Meet Shrimp 'n Grits."

"I do look forward to your low country, Charlie Ravenel."

I couldn't resist playing with her. Couldn't resist the promise of her and the joke. Any chance to fix the day, to make her smile. There it was. Sparkling back at me, fucking knocking me over.

All night, I joked and relished the new dish. The quaint table we sat at with dimly lit candles almost felt like a proper date in a cozy restaurant. That was a simple joy I had long since forsaken for fame, always having such romantic moments stolen by photos taken.

We polished off a bottle of Ygay. I rose to uncork another with no care for the hour, no concern for sleep. The elation of her company could buy me days without rest.

"We need to talk more about it." The pitch of her voice sang lower than normal. "About what happened today."

"I said it earlier." The cork easily gave way to my twisting force. "I'm not worried about Lorenzo. He won't risk running afoul of me."

I didn't want to sound arrogant, but this was how I used my power on set—to keep my secrets. After a quick side conversation with Lorenzo over espresso, a promise from me to put in a good word to the producers, the young man's mouth was sealed. His career depended on it.

"We can't make that mistake again," she said. "We can never get caught together. Not like that. Some of your trusted team knowing, or a couple of my best friends is one thing. Anyone else and we're fucked."

Another bad mood threatened, one that was all my fault.

I shouldn't have lost control like that, kissing her on set. The two of us at the gym with Rob was innocent. My lips taking hers in yet another breathtaking, passionate kiss? It was not. But I was overwhelmed with a feeling for her; so new, so powerful, I had to have her right then.

It left me mad again, mad at another one of my impulsive, horny cock ups.

"Are you still mad at me about today?" she asked. Fuck, and she could read it on me. "Mad at me for eavesdropping?"

"I'm trying not to be." I refilled her glass first. "I know we both have flaws and pain. So, I guess I'm glad you know now. Just don't ask me to talk about him."

"Why won't you talk about your brother?"

"The same reason you won't tell me more about the scar on your face."

"They're not the same thing."

I looked up, deflecting. "How so? Will you ever tell me, Charlie?"

She gazed down at her bowl. "I don't like talking about it."

"Well, that makes us uneven now. You spied on me to find out my pain. When is it your turn?" I challenged her back, feeling like a righteous hypocrite. I was.

Her eyes fired back at me. "Fine. Yes, I was spying. But when will you tell me your *whole* story, Daniel?"

Fuck. It was like she knew.

Right this ship now, Pierce, before you sink and lose her forever.

I softened my tone and heart toward her. "You said it the night we met. Let's not let it ruin this one. You were right. The truth hurts too fucking much. Let's just leave it in the past where it belongs."

Silence filled the air while I filled my glass next, anything to keep from looking her in the eye.

"Daniel..."

The twist of my wrist stopped my pour at her tone. I glanced up.

Charlie stood, awkward and halting. "I need to do something." She pointed to the ruby armless chair in her tiny living room. "Can you sit over there, please?"

"Charlie, please. Let's move past this. I'm not mad. I forgive you."

Please no more pain today.

It had hurt too much already. How she almost caught me. How I could have lost her. It gave me no choice, exposing one half of my damage, losing my twin. That part, that pain was true. But Flynn died January fifth, twenty-seven years ago. It was April. The other half of me? She could never know.

And the "her" Charlie asked me about? The counselor?

I never saw one.

If Charlie was ending us because she thought I was mad at her or because Lorenzo had caught us, it would destroy me.

Something foreboding filled the warm air while my steps trudged toward the chair, leaving the glasses behind on her breakfast bar, fearing I was about to take a seat in sure pain.

She closed the path between us, standing inches from my knees. I sat tense, gazing up at her beauty... ready for ruin.

CHARLIE

"DANIEL, I'm sorry I spied and exposed your scar today. You're right. It's only fair I do the same." I felt so connected to him. Through guilt. Through grief. And lust. My determined hands trembled, pinching the knot of my wrap sweater, releasing its bind over me, over my fear. "But I can't leave my pain in the past. I wear it on me."

I was tired of it. Tired of hiding. Tired of the ache. Tired of the fear.

If Daniel, or any man, wanted to know about my scars, it would be on my terms. Not by accident; not with pity.

Peeling my black sweater off, I dropped it to the floor, revealing more than my black lace bralette underneath. I stood vulnerable in his gaze. He sat before me in his soft T-shirt and cotton pants, but I couldn't read his hard eyes. They seemed overwhelmed, drinking me in. His lips parted. In horrified shock? Or to speak?

"Please don't say anything."

My shaking hands pulled the elastic band of my long silk skirt lower to where it hung below my hip bones. His eyes followed down my body, steaming tingles over my bare flesh.

I turned my back to him, draping my hair over my left shoulder and bowing my head.

Standing quiet and exposed before him, I let him read the story written down my body. I could feel his gaze caressing my skin, my wounds, my heart. Each breath I drew in the silence with him...

Terrifying. Awakening. Liberating.

"Charlie..." The velvet rope of his voice turned me back around, his eyes searching mine, his head shaking. "Listen to me. I don't deserve you. I'm too fucked up."

"Shhh." I lowered myself, straddling his lap, responding to his confession. "We both are."

I pulled my fingers through his hair, taking him with as deep of a kiss as he did to me that day. His tongue, his lips, the groan from his throat echoed mine, our mouths ripping our breath away.

He pulled back for air, "Charlie," sighing my name. His thumb grazed over my lace, under the swell of my breast. That tensed my nipples, dizzying my brain, my eyes following his touch. "God, how I want you," he sighed.

He wasn't wearing boxers. His thick erection was free and seeking me, annihilating my resolve and taunting me to try. I rolled my hips, hard and slow up his length.

"*Fuucckk*," he groaned tensing at my movement. "Please let me touch you."

I cupped his palms to my breasts, making us both moan. Grinding over him with no shame, I listened only to my body, not to my fear, not to any warning, craving only this exhilarating, terrifying ride. Closing my eyes, I focused on the pleasure. Back down and up his cock, I guided Daniel's fingers over my lace, to gently pinch, to pull me there, to a place I'd forgotten.

"Fuck, you're so beautiful." His words and touch started to make my body tremble, recognizing where we were going. "We can stop." But his hands didn't.

I opened my eyes. He was watching me... not my scars. "No."

"No to what?" He suspended his touch. He wasn't pushing me.

"No, I don't want to stop."

I hiked my skirt up high, pressing my pussy over the ridge of his hard cock with only his thin cotton pants and my panties between us.

"Oh, fuck yes," he growled while his hands locked over my hips. "It's your turn tonight." His grasp rolled me over him, hard, the pressure letting me hunt for my release. "Is this what you want, Charlie? Do you want to ride my hard cock 'til you come?"

My clit screamed at his naughty question and hard length, desperate for both.

"Yes," I said, my fingernails hanging on to him, on to the verge, afraid to fall for him. But I was. "Will you wait for me?"

DANIEL

"ALWAYS." Fuck, I didn't recognize the man in my skin, beholding her above me, crushing lethal blows to my ego regarding her body, her beauty.

She tugged at my shirt. I obeyed, pulling it over my head and throwing it on the floor before leaning back again.

"Damn, Daniel," she sighed, clutching my pecs. The greed in her starved hands drove me mad.

I spread my legs, making hers splay wider. Glazing my hands up her silky, naked thighs, I searched under her skirt and found she was wearing a thong, filling my hands with her firm bum, filling me with greed.

The snatch of my fingers opened her cheeks to me, to spread her open to feel more. That put her chin down, amping up her unrelenting friction across my cock.

"I want you," she sighed.

"I can tell." She was soaking through my pants to my cock, making me lose my mind, lose it all for her. "You're getting so fucking wet for me."

She hesitated. "Is it too much?"

"Never." I swore, looking down at her pussy hidden by soaked lace, gliding up and down over the cotton covering my swollen cock, then gazing back up at her, beguiled. "Give me more."

She started playing with her nipples in front of me. Fuck, a sudden urge owned my body. "Yes, like that. I want to watch you get off." I held it back, marveling at her erotic show for minutes until the breath in her ribs shallowed with lust. The way she pinched her nipples like I wanted to—with my fingers, with my mouth—I fought the hunger rising, wanting her, waiting for her.

But I couldn't, not for much longer. I pulled her hair back so I could watch her eyes. Begging. Insisting. "Come for me, Charlie."

The swirl of her hips rocked even faster over my cock. She sighed, "I love it when you say it like that," sinking her fingernails into my flesh, giving me sweet pain as she braced for it. "Do it again. Say my name and tell me to."

"Come on my cock, Charlie." I craved the words too because she was getting closer, a beautiful surrender taking her face, lips trembling, eyes heavy. Then she hesitated, slowing her ride. "Do you want to come?"

She was holding back, fighting it. Fear in her eyes. Lust in her quivering breath. "Yes," she confessed from her very edge.

For the first time, it wasn't about me. It was *for* her. Pleasure I could give her, could tell by her quaking thighs that she hadn't felt it in so long.

Not anymore. I'd take her with me, her hair tight in my grasp, my molars clenching, her eyes locked to mine. "Then come for me." My other hand guided her hip, hard, to ride me fast. "Let go and come so fucking hard and wet for me, Charlie." I thrust my hips hard into her saturated knickers, yanking her hair, yanking her hip in my hand.

Her thigh shook violently in my grasp. Throwing her head back, she cried out, "Oh God, Daniel. Yes!"

The explosion, it snapped right down, pouring a flood

from her, soaking my pants and drenching my cock. Her head fell forward, biting my shoulder, moaning with no control, body heaving with another wet wave over me.

Fuck me, I never made a woman come so wet before, her cum trickling down my thighs. It took me so damn hard. "Oh fuck, Charlie." The words growled loud up my throat, escaping along with the eruption of my own pleasure barreling through me, taking my sight, taking my mind. My grasp found her face buried in my shoulder, bringing her lips back to mine, sweet shudders racking our bodies and kiss until we found our breath.

She touched my face, "Thank you for waiting for me," still panting.

"You're worth it all." My eyes clung to the sight of her, in awe. "I can't believe you're with me." The beauty of her, spent and soaked for me, in my arms, she erased all my pain.

Then I remembered. Hers. How I could see it before my eyes. "Hang on to me," I said. She wrapped around me as I stood up, seeking the few steps toward her bedroom.

Laying her down, I rolled alongside her, resting on my elbow. I pulled back to study her in the lamp light, to see now. Her scars. My fingertips sought the circular one above her hip.

She revealed what my eyes now knew. "I was shot three times. My face is a bullet graze," she explained, letting tears roll down her cheeks, wetting her hair. "I got hit through my right deltoid and humerus." Her fingertips touched my hand lying on her hip. "And here, above my iliac crest through my external oblique. Names of bones and muscles I didn't know I had until bullets pierced them, changing everything."

She rolled onto her left side, exposing the exit wounds again. The one through her shoulder looked no bigger than a fifty pence coin. But the scar on her lower back was a jagged light pink, irregular concave circle the size of a large grape where the tissue was forever gone.

Her hand shook, reaching back, taking my fingertips and resting them on the scar below her waist. "If you want me, Daniel, then know all of me."

I traced over the scar, over the void.

Years of playing soldiers or heroes with guns, pretending to shoot and kill people, and get shot myself, it was all for money, for show. And yet, I'd never seen a real gunshot wound, certainly never touched one.

All I ever knew—bodies were controlled, used, forged into solid weapons of impervious strength. But now it confronted me. What bullets actually did to the fragile tissue of a human body. I bit my lip at the tragic reality, at the beauty of the body underneath my touch, a body I more than adored.

She turned back, facing me, holding my hand in hers. "February twenty-second is my anniversary. A Tuesday. I was fucking lucky that day. It's what I've told myself ever since. He got me where my Kevlar jacket and plates didn't protect me." Her hand shook in mine. "But I'm okay now."

No, she wasn't. Her words didn't match her eyes. It made so much sense now. Why she had pushed me away. Why she covered herself, struggling under my touch.

I triggered desire and trauma at the same time.

Now all the words from our first night broke me open. To be defined only by your body could be a painful, lonely place. Did I suffer too? Yes. She saw it in me.

But not like this. Not like what she'd been through.

Humility mauled me. "Charlie. When I say you're beautiful, please know, it's everything about you." I touched her cheek. "You're so much more than"—I paused, recalling her words that first night—"more than an object to me."

"I'm not a victim. I survived. And I don't want this to define me anymore. Sometimes, I *do* want to be an object." Her fingers lingered down my chest. "What did you say? A hundred times in a week? To be the object of your desire."

She had no idea.

I crawled on top of her. "Oh, you are, Charlotte Ravenel."

I cherished her terrain, pressing my lips to her shoulder scar, traveling down, touching them to the one above her hip. Then I focused my desire on her entire belly, to what skin my lips could thrill not hiding under black lace or silk. My adoration made her back arch, grasping for more of my kiss. The sweet aroma of our last orgasms filled my senses, pure lust making me crave more.

God, how I wanted to take all of her, every shred, every breath from her. Now and forever. And it would never be enough. Still, I had to try.

I had to have her—the right way.

Catching my breath, twisting back on my side, I said, "We leave Friday."

She exhaled a frustrated sigh, "I know," rolling to her side, teasing with her touch down my abs. "Let me get washed up before dessert." She started to get up.

"Can I join you?" I gave her my best shot, striking a pose with my shirt off, lowering the waist of my pants to expose my left hip bone.

She grinned by the foot of the bed before turning away. "You're such a gorgeous clit tease, Pierce."

"Revenge is sweet," I called out to her as she disappeared into the bathroom, closing the door behind her. "You will be mine. You can walk away now, Ravenel, but you will be!"

She showered and dressed before stepping back into the room. I lay there all the while, heart pounding, marveling at this new world with her.

"Hey beautiful," I said at the sight of her in the steamy doorway.

She stood before me. Wet hair falling free. My sweatpants hanging low on her hip bones. A cropped athletic tank showing off her strong body and scars.

"Hey, sexy." Her hand reached out for mine. I met her touch. "It's your turn."

You'll never let go of this hand, Pierce. Never.

CHAPTER TWENTY-FIVE

CHARLIE

I tapped Kierra's trailer door. "It's Charlie." Giving a few seconds before pulling it open.

"Good morning, love." Kierra's mom stood at the kitchenette. "Coffee?"

Anne and I were getting close too. We were all bound together, running this haunting gauntlet.

"Yes, please." I needed caffeine more than oxygen after last night.

I slept alone at my place, thankfully, because I woke up to my own cries. Nightmares that left me feeling raw, hands scratching over the rough fabric of my pants until I finally occupied them, sipping the steaming cup Anne offered and waiting for Kierra who still hid in the restroom.

The lull since the sick message a few weeks before found me waiting in that space between lightning and thunder.

It tried my patience.

Never before had I waited this long to catch someone.

The incidents and threats I intercepted on *Fated* protecting Juliette were rapid fire. I took down one after another.

Rob had wondered aloud yesterday if this stalker was finally bored, satisfied or moving on to someone else.

I didn't think so. I could sense it.

Kierra's stalker was preparing for something. The tension waiting for it was a perverse gas-lighting, knowing Kierra's world well, knowing just how to taunt her without getting caught.

His torment of Kierra tortured me too, wearing me down.

And when I became weak or triggered, the worst could happen.

That's what I feared when Jeremy called me for this job. If I had a PTSD flashback or hallucination, I'd be helpless, unable to protect Kierra.

That was my greatest fear.

All this strain while the entire production was stressed that week on an intense shooting schedule before everyone left on hiatus Friday. The principal cast had numerous scenes together. The one scheduled for today, Wednesday?

It haunted me.

I hated the day. My parents died on a Wednesday. Kai too. I always held my breath until the dawn of every Thursday.

Today they were shooting a difficult scene. An attempted rape of Kierra's character, Brigid, by a Roman soldier. Her brothers, Carric and Herne, catch the crime in the act. A fight between Carric and the soldier ends with Carric strangling him before he slits his throat, avenging his sister while Herne shields Brigid from the brutality.

"This is going to be a rough day," Anne said, taking her seat across from me at the banquette table. "I already spoke to Jennifer. She promises they'll get it done in as few shots as possible. And the counselor the studio hired should be here any minute."

Having counselors on set for such difficult scenes, particularly for youth, was protocol. The entire production did everything to minimize any trauma from the scene.

"I'm glad Jennifer's the one directing," I said. "And Thomas is a nice guy. He'll be sensitive to Kierra."

I met Thomas, the actor playing the soldier, yesterday. No creep vibe on him. He was a true professional.

"I just don't know how much more of this Kierra can take." Anne sighed. "I fear for her safety and her sanity."

That comment gut punched me, matching my fear. For Kierra. For myself. "I promise you, Ms. Williams. You have no idea how far I'll go to keep her safe."

Kierra stepped out of the restroom in her trailer, already in makeup and costume.

"Hey chica." I faked calm confidence.

"Howya." Kierra wore a weak smile, fear covering the rest of her angelic face.

"We have a few minutes," I said. "Wanna go for a walk?" Sitting and waiting only made it worse.

Kierra nodded.

We walked around basecamp, chatting about what I knew would cheer her—Harry Styles. I glanced over Kierra's shoulder. Lorenzo was walking across the lot to fetch her. Before he was close enough to hear, I reached for Kierra's hand, catching her attention too.

"You got this," I said. "You're a damn strong actor. Focus on your job." I peered into Kierra's eyes, steeling nerves. Whose nerves? Both. "Don't let him get in your head today. Okay?"

"Yep." Kierra raised her chin. "I got this."

It took a few hours. Shooting moved quickly through the struggle between Brigid and the soldier. Kierra and Thomas worked well together. It didn't seem to bother Kierra as much as I feared. The crew took a break for lunch and we came back for the last shots of the day, the scenes with Daniel and Mason who joined us.

They got through a wide shot of Carric and Herne entering the home, discovering Brigid fighting with the soldier. They set up and shot two more middle shots of their approach to Brigid with Carric pulling the soldier off her before Herne knelt to protect her.

But as we waited for the last setup, Kierra started fidgeting, thigh bouncing, eyes darting, getting anxious again. The counselor chatted with her by the edge of the stage building, returning to tell the director that Kierra was fine but ready for it to be over. Jennifer thanked her, assuring her that if the next shot went well, it would be the last.

The assistant director called, "Quiet on set."

I sighed, ready for this to be over. Standing behind Jennifer and the script supervisor, I watched Kierra but was drawn to the monitors.

The lens was going for a tight shot on Kierra's face, one where Brigid went from fighting and yelling, "No!" to her brothers rescuing her.

Jennifer called, "Action," immersing me in the pixelated struggle on the monitor, tasting the terror in Kierra's eyes.

The camera focuses wide on Brigid's face. Carric's hands appear, grabbing the soldier and throwing him off the girl. Herne comes into frame, kneeling down on one leg, touching Brigid's face, asking her if she is okay. Then both look to the distance, horrified, watching the fight unfold. Herne keeps one arm in front of Brigid, ready to protect her himself.

I watched the show.

My mind strobed. *Brown eyes.* My throat tightened. *Screams.* My ears started ringing. *Tears and pleas.* My heart raced for what was next...

"Cut!" Jennifer shouted.

My eyes stayed fixed on Kierra on the screen. Something was wrong. Then. I needed to protect her. Now. Kierra needed help. The counselor and her mom saw it too.

I snapped my gaze to the director, Jennifer, certain. "I need to help her. Did you get it?" Jennifer nodded yes, and I shadowed Kierra back to the green room.

Anne reached her hand out for Kierra as she approached the cast chairs. Kierra shook. I did too. Anne put her arm around Kierra. "All right, love. Well done. Let's go now."

Kierra, her mom and her counselor walked out of the stage building, back to basecamp. I followed behind them for the long walk we needed, taking deep breaths while my eyes swept the horizon, on guard.

They sat down on the sofa in Kierra's trailer. I took a seat at the banquette, clasping my hands together, hiding their tremors.

Anne eyed them. "Let's have some tea." She turned to put the kettle on, setting out some chamomile for us.

"Do you want to share anything?" the counselor gently asked Kierra.

"I just kept thinking about him. About the stalker." Tears fell over her lashes. "I was fine during the scenes with Thomas, the soldier. But this afternoon"—Kierra put her gaze to the ceiling—"with more men around me, all I could think about were those handcuffs, those nasty messages and those notes. That he took my knickers. I could imagine that's how he wants to hurt me. That's what it would feel like."

The girl's fear. The horrific vision she shared. It took all air from my lungs, burning my throat.

"It won't ever happen, Kierra." The promise bolted from my mouth. "He'll never lay a hand on you. I swear it."

Kierra wiped the tears from her cheeks. "I'm trying to be strong. To be a professional." Anne sniffed back her own tears over my shoulder. "But I just get so scared sometimes."

"It's okay to be scared." The counselor softly added, "It's okay to talk about it too."

"I get scared too, Kierra." I shared.

"You do?" Relief filled her face.

"Yes. I feel it every day. But I also try to feel joy." That was really my hope, a future I didn't know yet. "We can't let it ruin our lives."

"I'm proud of you, dear," Anne said, handing her daughter a cup of tea. "We'll get through this."

"You did a great job today." I piled on the love for the girl. "You looked strong on the monitor."

"Yeah?" Kierra asked. "I hope so. I love Brigid. She's so brave, and I want to do my best by her."

Feel that sick twist in your gut, Charlie Girl?

Kierra was brave. She had done a great job. Until that last scene.

Why?

There weren't "more men" around Kierra when she got triggered. The only three men nearest her on set? Thomas, who'd been there all day, and then Daniel and Mason.

I didn't know what to make of it. In that moment I was too flooded with my past, too busy trying to keep my head above the water for Kierra's sake.

"It was a long day," her mother said, offering me tea next.

"Thank you." I reached out to take it, glad to see my hand wasn't shaking anymore.

We chatted a bit more. When Kierra started talking about the plans she'd made with her boyfriend over hiatus, that was my signal. She'd be okay for now.

My phone vibrated. I checked it. It was Rob.

Sup fucker.
Gym today?

Yep

"All right." I stood up, smoothing my pants down. "You headed home now?" I had to be sure once more Kierra didn't need me. Joaquin would take over next and accompany them home.

"Yes, dear," Anne said. "We're fine now."

Kierra jumped up suddenly, lurching for me with a hug. "Thank you, Charlie." Her cheek nestled against mine.

I bit it back, all the tears in Kierra's tender embrace.

It was my job.

No, it isn't. I hugged her back. *It's my everything.* I would fucking end anyone who hurt my girl.

No matter the cost. No matter how. No matter who.

CHAPTER TWENTY-SIX

CHARLIE

I leaned against my trunk. "So, mi primo. I gotta tell you something and you can't freak out. Okay?"

I arrived at the gym ahead of Rob, but within seconds, his car had pulled up next to mine. While he grabbed his bag from his trunk... I had to tell him. Rob was one of my best friends. I trusted him with my life, with any secret.

And my emotions were stretched too thin to hide anything that afternoon.

"All right, mi prima." He glanced up, worry pinching his face. "Bring it."

"Daniel and I have been kinda dating."

I couldn't help it. I smiled.

"What?" He slammed his trunk closed, "Finally," and yanked me into a crushing squeeze. "I called this years ago. Remember? In Ibiza? I showed you his picture and you lost your horny mind." Confronting my eyes, his squinted. "And when we were at Anders's, you could smell the lust in the air between you two, you sly bitch. I want some mother-fuckin' details."

"There are no fucking details. Literally." I slung my bag over my shoulder as we headed toward the gym door. "We're going away on hiatus together, that's it."

"Uh-huh. You keep telling yourself that, boo."

Daniel stood inside, talking with Armand in the gym lobby and waiting for us.

"Please be chill," I said, "or I'll rip your nuts off. No one can know about us. We're just colleagues, friends working out."

"Oh baby girl, I got your back, always. But I'm gonna want some tea after you get back. Deal?"

He could tease but he'd never betray me. Rob knew why this was a big step for me.

Still, this would be fun... sharing a dirty secret with him.

"Deal," I said, opening the gym door.

When Daniel glanced up, greeting me with a heart-stopping smile, my stomach did a delicious butterfly flip.

Yum. Focus on him now.

Rob followed me, calling out, "Ten minutes at a fifteen incline at a six pace or higher." Starting our game as we disappeared into the locker rooms to change.

When I stepped out minutes later, meeting them in the hallway, Rob was shocked. "Damn, baby girl," he said. "Where you been hiding all that? You're looking ripped as hell."

My black and white graphic print sports bra and shiny black leggings didn't hide my scars. I was done with that.

"Feast your eyes," I said. Not to Rob. To Daniel.

Even though he hid his famous face under a red base-ball cap, I could see the knife and fork in his gaze.

We hit the treadmills hard, though we couldn't find any

side-by-side. From the far end of the gym in the cardio theater, I could see it was packed.

And I could see all the women. None of them approached Daniel. But all walked the runway across his line of sight.

Damn ladies, need a pole? Usually, I'd find it funny. Not today. Everything dug beneath my skin.

I tried getting into my music. Running an incline helped sweat dilute my anger. It drenched me by the time I finished. It did all three of us.

I called it next. "Forty punches in one minute on the bag. Three rounds." I needed to hit something. We all had gloves in our bags. Thankfully, the heavy bag swung unused. Shoving my left hand in the glove, I used my teeth to glove up my right.

The hard bag became someone's face I could rip off. Rob held the bag for me while Daniel did jumping jacks. My punches and jabs landed strong. But when I put my core into my swing—along with my rage—my hooks and uppercuts were brutal, knocking Rob back a step.

Something was looming inside me and I fought like hell to hold it back.

Rob, then Daniel took their turns. Next, Daniel called, "Thirty banded deadlifts."

I went first since the guys would add more plates to the bar. Watching my form in front of the mirror, anger fueled my exertions.

But after a few reps, I caught Daniel's eye in the reflection. He huffed behind me, doing high knees with Rob. A shit-eating grin owned his face, admiring my ass.

So now, nice and slow, I bent over for him, holding at the bottom, giving him a gander at my cleavage. Then I powered back up, giving my glutes an extra squeeze at the top, true to good form... and tease.

Daniel lost his rhythm, stopping to wipe his smiling face with a towel like he could wipe his dirty thoughts away too.

Rob stopped and started laughing. "You two need to get a fucking room. Literally."

I put the bar down, confessing to Daniel's reflection. "He knows."

Rob said, "Careful before this whole fucking gym knows."

Were we caught? Fucking each other with our eyes in front of at least forty other people and the ten fans who kept sharking by Daniel like he was fresh meat in the water... my fresh meat.

In the mirror, I clocked it.

Members were watching us, particularly two women whose eyes were blowtorches on us.

Nope. It'd only be a rumor. I wouldn't give them the satisfaction of catching me and Daniel with any PDA.

Just working out with my guys, bitches. One is my bestie and the other I'm gonna fuck till I can't walk, I joked to myself, keeping a friendly distance from Daniel.

I caught the eye of one of the women and smiled. *Fuck you.*

Rob did his reps while Daniel and I huffed out mountain climbers. Then Daniel did his deadlift reps with his navy gym shorts straining across his famous ass.

"Damn," I muttered, starting jumping jacks.

"Damn," Rob followed, declaring in a low voice. "Lucky bitch."

Daniel heard us and about lost it. Laughing and lifting weren't a good mix. Still, he refocused and finished.

We stood together, taking water and a quick towel while

Rob looked around, deciding what was next. He called, "Arnold presses. Thirty. Three sets."

Two benches sat open by the racks and mirrors. Mainly guys filled that side of the gym doing bench presses. Beside them, a group were going super heavy with clean and press reps, lifting a bar loaded with plates from the floor and pressing the weight up to above their heads.

I sensed it—all eyes scoping us as we crossed the gym.

Daniel didn't seem to notice. Or maybe he'd stopped caring long ago.

But I hated it—the sensation of being watched by all, hated by some. It was all too haunting, too familiar.

Like being a Marine in Afghanistan.

I did my reps with thirty pounds first, dropping down to twenty-fives to protect my shoulder. Daniel and Rob did fast feet for their plyo, looking like two linebackers behind me.

In the mirror, a few people behind us watched with menace in their stare. It was the same two women and one man whose look slithered up my spine. He gawked at Daniel with his creepy dark brown eyes.

Or was he leering at me?

Daniel followed next. I started fast feet with Rob.

The effort made my head fuzzy toward the end. I shook my skull to clear it away, my heart pounding against my lungs. Daniel racked his dumbbells back. Rob grabbed a pair for his reps. Daniel resumed the fast feet beside me. I blindly followed suit, keeping quick pace with him. Rob started his count.

Bang! Bang!

Heavy metal plates and a steel bar crashed to the floor. One of the meatheads had lost strength under the bar in his clean. He hadn't used collars, so the plates dropped from the bar like bombs.

The whole gym turned to look at him. The guy waved "sorry" to everyone.

"Charlie?" Daniel shouted from far away. "Are you okay?"

He couldn't reach me.

I was gone.

TEA RETCHED UP MY THROAT. I didn't taste it.

I only smelled fried bread and the dirt road beneath my boots with my hands wrapped around my rifle.

I didn't see Daniel kneeling beside me.

I saw a face.

Dark brown eyes aimed at me. I aimed mine back. Answering his smirk with my own.

Then a dark barrel of a gun rose, targeting me.

The percussion from the shot gave me permission to...

"Fire!" my dad yelled.

Shouldering my M-16, a sting whizzed across my cheek.

More shots. I found him in my sight. A shock hammered my shoulder. Another shock punched my torso. I aimed and fired. And fired again. And again. My bullets found their mark. Blood splattered as his head jerked back.

"Roberts!" Jax yelled at me.

My right leg crumpled. With a heavy thud, my body hit the road. I rolled onto my stomach. My right arm wouldn't move. I pushed with my left boot, grabbing ground with my left hand, scratching with my fingertips, crawling for cover, dragging the rifle strapped by my side. Dirt mixed with the blood seeping into my mouth. The smell of grease on the road filled my nostrils.

AK shots.

I looked over my left shoulder. Jax's ankle exploded. He fell on his side. Miller and Perez fired, trying to suppress the enemy. Jax was crawling for cover.

Something felt wet. I looked back down. Dark blood trailed behind me. With one final push with my boot, I found cover. More shots from Miller and Perez.

All was heavy. I laid my head down. Sand grated against my cheek. The shots stopped.

"Roberts!" Steph shouted my name, rolling me over. Steph's hands searched underneath my Kevlar helmet. Then under my vest. Then she pressed down on my waist.

"Hang on, Roberts." She pressed hard. It hurt.

"Roberts, look at me!" Steph's wet hand grabbed my chin. I smelled my blood on her hand.

My heavy lids fluttered open to Steph's ebony eyes. Sand gritted in my teeth along with the iron taste of my blood filling my mouth.

"They're coming." Steph pressed even harder. It hurt. "You're gonna be okay."

A heavy pull. Taking me. Under.

"They're coming, Charlie Girl." My dad's silhouette knelt over me. I wanted to hug him. "Everything will be all right."

But I let go.

And fell into the black.

CHAPTER TWENTY-SEVEN

DANIEL

"Charlie," smoothing her sweaty hair back, I knelt over her body collapsed on the floor.

She lurched up and started gagging. Quickly, I rolled her on her side, supporting her shoulder, letting her vomit without choking. A puddle formed under her lips. Still, she didn't wake.

"She's out," Rob said. "I've seen this before." He took command. "Let's get her out of here."

I acted fast, scooping her up. "Hospital?" I cradled her like a child in his arms. She was sweaty, cold and stained with vomit. I didn't care.

"No," Rob said. "The sounds and smells make it worse for her."

I carried her across the gym, to the front door. All eyes on us. Phones too.

"Get her to your car. We'll take her home," Rob said. "I'll get her bag." He darted toward the women's locker room.

I wanted to protect her, getting her away from prying eyes and loud noises. Armand ran to hold the door open while the words hissed from my mouth. "Some fuckers are filming us."

"I'll take care of it," Armand said. "Is she okay?"

"She had a sugar drop," I lied. "Keep them away from these doors, and don't let anyone take pictures of my car."

Simon glanced up through the windshield. He jumped right out and opened the back door.

"What happened," he asked. "Is she hurt?"

"Not physically. Wait for Rob and we'll take her home." The 4x4 was big enough for me to climb into the backseat, careful not to hit her head.

I sat down. "Charlie." Gently, I cradled her skull. "Charlie, babe. Open your eyes."

Her lids fell low, her cheeks were pale, her mouth hung open. Oh God, seeing her like this. She looked lifeless. Like my twin brother. An ominous fear rose in me. "Charlie, please wake up, babe. Please." I heard panic edging into my voice.

I was aware of Rob running out of the gym, of Simon closing the back door, of Rob jumping into the front passenger's seat. "I got all three of our bags. Fluids for her. And here." Rob handed me a damp towel.

Simon had the car moving by the time Rob closed his door.

I carefully cleaned Charlie's face with the cool towel. "You've seen her do this before?"

Rob answered, "Twice. The first time, during target practice in L.A. I took her to the hospital then and it made it worse. She hallucinated for hours that she was back at the hospital in Germany. The next time, we were working at the London studio and someone dropped a big light. She grabbed my arm. I barely got her into her friend Juliette's trailer. She crawled into her shower, threw up, and passed out there. Then she woke up, hallucinated a bit, but not as bad."

"She hallucinates?"

"Sometimes she talks to Jax. He was on patrol with her the day she got shot. She says other names from her platoon. Steph. Miller. She talks to her dad. She talks to Kai." Rob's eyes darted up to mine. He suddenly stopped. Like he'd said too much.

I looked down at Charlie in my arms. Her eyelashes started fluttering. "How can I help her?" I asked, smoothing the hair back from her face.

"If she starts talking to people who aren't there, stay calm. Ask her what's happening. Don't argue with her. Just tell her gently she's hallucinating. She told me to get her in the shower. The water brings her back." Rob wiped the sweat from his brow. "Last time she just laid there, talking to other people for a while. Juliette and I soothed her. Then she got quiet for a bit... and looked at us. And I could tell. She was back."

"She told me she had PTSD." Tracing over her dark eyebrow, I wanted to bring her back to me. "I had no clue it was this bad."

Rob assured, "I have it too. PTSD. In one year at the U.S. Embassy in Kabul, we got fired on over thirty-five times. I used to get fits of rage, of paranoia. Had a pretty toxic drinking habit trying to numb it. Time helped. And my support group. And when I partnered with Charlie, our workouts and talks helped too. That's how we got so close. She even started me on meditation. But still, it gets you, man. It's never completely over for us."

I glimpsed out of the window at my gate approaching.

When Rob had said, "Take her home," I immediately thought of mine. Maybe we should've gone to Charlie's villa. But it was too late.

Simon parked by the front door and rushed out, opening my car door and helping me step out with Charlie in my arms. Then he ran ahead, up the stairs to unlock the front door.

"Rob, please stay," I said.

"I'm never leaving her, don't worry." Rob leapt out with our bags and a sports drink.

"To the shower?" I carried her upstairs.

"Yep." He followed me through my bedroom and into the bathroom with its huge shower.

I walked right in with Charlie in my arms. "Would you get the water, Rob?"

He turned on both shower heads. It washed over us with a warm downpour.

Charlie stirred. Would she thrash? I didn't know and she was becoming slippery to hold. Carefully, I knelt on the shower floor with her.

She started mumbling.

Rob talked to her. "Charlie, mi prima. It's Rob." He gently touched her foot dangling over my knee. "I'm right here, boo."

She didn't respond.

I tried. "Charlie, wake up babe. It's Daniel. I've got you."

She moved to sit up in my arms. I set her down, kneeling behind her. She crawled up to her knees, facing the shower wall in front of her.

Rob studied her face and said, "She's hallucinating."

Charlie

"Charlie, what's happening?"

I heard the voice. It was familiar. Safe.

"Kai's dead." Tears streamed down my cheeks. "Kai's dead and it's my fault."

"Where are you, Charlie?"

"I'm in the hospital in Germany. With you, Jax." I sobbed. "It's my fault." I retched, hunched over on my hands and knees.

"You're gonna be okay, baby girl. You're hallucinating. Talk to me now."

"I shot him, Jax. I had to." I looked up into Jax's warm eyes from my wheelchair, pleading for him to understand, begging for his forgiveness. "I had to kill him, Jax. It was the only way."

I hated seeing Jax like this—lying in a hospital bed—a void under the blanket at the bottom of his left leg.

"I know. It'll be okay, Roberts." Jax reached out his hand for mine. It was sandpaper wrapping around my fingers. "I'm okay."

"I'm so sorry." Another sob. "It wasn't supposed to be you. It was supposed to be me." I retched.

"Don't be sorry, Roberts. You did the right thing. Damn, the whole platoon knew what was going on. It's not your fault." He squeezed my hand. "Hell, I wanted to do it too. But you're the best shot." He smiled at me, trying to joke, to cheer me up.

Jax was my Lowcountry brother. We were practically neighbors. Everyone in the platoon made fun of our accents, and we didn't give a shit. We talked fishing, making big plans for when we got back home on the Calibogue Sound. He told me all about Ara, his wife. How we'd get along like two peas in a pod. I told him about Kai, swearing I'd never get the two guys off my boat once we were back.

Jax patted my hand. "I'll be up and fishin' with y'all in no time. I promise ya. I got a long road ahead of me, but ain't nothing keepin' my ass down. We'll be home soon enough and on that boat. You just buy me a fifth of SoCo and we'll be even. Okay, Roberts?"

I shook my head "no" at his plans. "Jax, I'm not Charlotte Roberts anymore. Kai is dead. He's dead because of me." I retched again. "I'm Charlie Ravenel again."

Spasms twisted my stomach. Spit dripped from my mouth.

"Charlie Ravenel." Jax said my name. It wasn't his voice. "Charlie Ravenel, you're hallucinating," my dad said. "Let Jax go. You can talk with him later." It wasn't my dad either.

"Open your eyes, Charlotte." My mom stood right behind me.

"Charlie, wake up, boo." I heard it.

Now.

I found my fingers. They felt wet. Smooth tile was under them, my fingertips grazing over grout ridges.

"Charlie, sip this drink." A safe voice said beside me. "You need fluids. There's nothing left in you."

Something cool touched my face. My hand reached for it, finding a plastic bottle in my grasp.

"Take a small sip." A deep voice in an English accent. "Please take a sip, Charlie," it said.

Kneeling. Putting the bottle to my lips. Liquid poured across my tongue. Grape taste. Cool down my throat. Warm water blessed my head. Hard tile hurt my knees. Cedar and apple scents tickled up my nose. I smiled hearing a shuffle behind me.

My vision cleared and white marble appeared. A shower. I turned to the right. Rob sat there with a relieved smile on his face. I turned to my left, looking over my shoulder. Daniel knelt behind me, soaking wet in his gym clothes... looking like he'd seen a ghost.

"Oh, shit." I groaned, vomiting the grape right back up.

"Charlie, what do you need, babe?" Daniel held my wet ponytail back.

Taking deep, four-count breaths, I let the water pour over me, grounding myself into the white marble tile of the shower floor. "I'm okay, y'all."

Daniel let out a sigh of relief.

"Rob, what happened?" I asked.

"It was like last time. You're gonna feel like shit from the vomiting, so please drink up."

I sat down on the shower floor, leaning my head back against the cool tile wall, letting the water wash it all away. I was in Daniel's shower. I could smell his soap, the smell of his skin.

"Can I have a real shower now?" I could smell the vomit on me too.

"Yes, boo. I'll help you." Rob had done this before, stripped me down and helped me clean up.

Through pure exhaustion I grinned at him. "Thank you, fucker."

I looked over at Daniel, reaching out my hand for his. He smiled, taking it.

"Hey, Sex God." My voice sounded hoarse from retching. "You still have to wait a couple days to see all this sexy stuff." I barely gestured to my crotch. "Real sexy now, isn't it?" I laid my head back against the wall. "Though I think you've seen about all of me, haven't you?"

I had no energy, looked like shit and didn't give a fucking damn.

Daniel crawled over to me and wiped my face clean. Lifting my chin up, "You get more beautiful every day, Ravenel," he said before kissing the tip of my nose.

Rob cooed from the shower door. "Aww, you two are so cute."

"I'll be in the bedroom," Daniel said, although I could tell he didn't want to leave me. "I'll find you some clothes." He got up and stepped out of the shower. Grabbing a towel, handing two to Rob, he clutched his shoulder. "I'll take a quick rinse down the hall and be right back and leave them at the door."

After he left, Rob blurted, "Holy shit. I can't stand it. You are such a lucky bitch." Crawling into the shower, he started helping me take my sneakers off. The movement twisted my stomach.

"Hang on." I held it back, breathing a few minutes to get control. "Okay." Giving him the green light, Rob finished with my shoes, and slowly, I sat up.

"Help me." My arms were weak, lifting them above my head so he could pull my sports bra off.

I had to lie back down on the shower floor.

"And he really hasn't seen your booty yet?" Rob asked while he helped me shimmy out of my leggings next.

"Not yet." I was naked now.

"Damn baby girl, I'd be on that dick 24/7/365," he teased, handing me the bottle of soap I liked so much, looking for shampoo next.

I sat on the shower floor, lathering up in the suds while Rob washed my hair. Then he took the nozzle down to rinse it.

"Your man even has conditioner." He sniffed the bottle

before putting it in my hair. "You're gonna smell like him. Smell so good maybe I'd consider fucking you myself if I close my eyes."

He was on a roll, making himself laugh with this.

"Yeah, right. The next man fucking me is Daniel Pierce," I said, at first as a comeback to Rob's taunt, then happily realizing it was true. "And he's not my man."

"You didn't see how he worried about you." Rob laughed. "He *will* be your man once he taps that Dominican ass of yours. Mi prima, you're gonna have that man on his knees."

"I'd rather be on *my* knees." *Damn, is it Friday yet?*

Rob squeezed the water from my hair. "You and me both." He always did this, joking with me about sex to make me feel better.

"Me first, Vasquez."

"Well, you may need some pointers and coaching."

Now I laughed out loud. "I don't need instructions on how to suck cock, Vasquez. And ain't nobody got to cheer me on to fuck Daniel. It's been six years. Don't you worry. I'm not gonna get off that D for a week."

Rob turned the shower off. "Oh, you'll be getting off with him over and over again. The whole world does."

He leaned down, helping me stand up. My legs were still weak though some balance was returning.

But he was soaked. He sat me down on the shower bench and stripped down, taking a quick shower himself before handing me a towel, and wrapping another around his waist. Cracking the bathroom door open, he peeked at the floor and reached down, retrieving the two piles of clothes Daniel left for us.

"Look at this. He's so sweet on you, mi prima." He helped me out of the shower, offering one stack to me, taking the other for himself. We dressed while Rob started to muse. "Think of all the twisted-ass, hot, kinky shit the two of you can do to each other in one week. Talk about a Disney Park of sucks and fucks."

"Oh, I have."

"You better pack toys and have you two dirty outfits a day. Make the most of it. It's a minimum of three fucks a day." He was planning it all out. I was too. It made me happy through an otherwise miserable state.

He kept smiling, devising. "I hope you come back barely able to walk because he fucked the hell out of you." He pulled a sweatshirt on. "And you fuck that D raw. He needs to be lusciously hurting too."

"That's the plan."

I laughed, glancing down at the ensemble Daniel had plucked from his wardrobe. His sweatpants and shirt fit Rob of course, but his gym shorts hung off me like culottes. I pulled his huge T-shirt on, twisting the hem into a knot at my waist. Toothpaste was on his vanity. I used that to finger brush my teeth, rinsing my mouth until I only tasted mint. Then I combed my fingers through my wet hair while Rob gave his a quick shake.

He laughed, holding onto my waist, going for the door and joking aloud. "Well, look at us now. This makes two of us getting into Daniel Pierce's pants, bitch."

We pushed it open to find Daniel sitting right there, on his bed, waiting for us, his right eyebrow cocked up with an amused smile.

I jumped back. "How much of that did you hear?" By the pornified charm on his face, all of it.

"Not a word." He grinned, scooping me up. "Let me feed you both."

"Daniel Balthazar Pierce, quit fuckin' carrying me

everywhere." I kicked my feet for him to put me down. "I can walk, but I don't know if I can eat."

"Shut up, boo." Rob chuckled. "Let the man carry your weak ass and feed us both." He walked behind us out of the bedroom, his gravel voice rumbling low. "Daniel, you can carry me around anytime you want."

"You sure you've got this?" Daniel asked me at the top of the stairs.

"Yes." He had no idea.

He set me down, holding onto my hand instead.

CHAPTER TWENTY-EIGHT

CHARLIE

Under a blanket on the sofa, I curled up by the gas fire in the living room, watching Daniel across the open room in the kitchen washing dishes.

He had found some leftovers for Rob and Simon. I had nibbled bites of bread. My stomach finally stopped cramping, so I ate the leftover roasted potatoes Daniel warmed for me next.

Simon took Rob back to the gym for his car. Not before Rob gave me a big hug. "I love you so much, mi prima. Have a great time." Kissing my cheek, he had whispered in my ear, "And I want fuckin' details."

"I love you too, fucker. Beyond words," I said, safe in his embrace.

I thanked Simon too, apologizing for scaring the hell out of him.

"Please don't apologize, marm," he said, smiling at the

hug I gave him. "I've dealt with worse when Daniel and his mates get plastered."

"Oi!" Daniel had shouted in protest. "When's the last time I got plastered?"

Now we were alone and Daniel came over to sit with me on the sofa, gesturing to my empty plate. "What else can I get you?"

"I'm fine, thank you." I scooted over, making room for him. "I'm sorry for everything. To be so much trouble today."

I noticed it. How he didn't flinch. How he seemed to thrive caring for me. Still, would he want to risk repeats? Did he have second thoughts about our trip?

He curled up next to me, pulling some of the blanket over him too. "Don't worry. I'll be posting you a bill in the morning." Tilting his head, he played with my hair. "Excessive water use."

"I don't remember anything that happened between fast feet with you and waking up in your shower. If it scared the shit out of you. If you want to run away screaming, here's your chance."

"No matter how hard you try, you can't push me away, remember?" He twirled a lock of my hair around his finger. "But Charlie, can I ask you some questions?"

"Can you pour me a drink first, please?" I needed it for where this was going. "Something strong and neat."

"I'll make two." He patted my leg before getting up, heading toward the bar at the edge of the kitchen. "I have a bottle of Michter's 10 Year Elaine gave me for Christmas." He opened it, pouring us both two fingers worth.

He handed me a drink and sat back down. I turned sideways on the sofa, wedging my feet under his warm legs.

He smiled. "Do you need another blanket?"

"No, I like you keeping me warm." I raised my glass. "Ask me anything. It's okay. No more secrets."

He took a few moments, staring at the ceiling, before he asked, "Who is Kai?"

I took a sip, letting it coat my sore throat. "Can I start from the beginning? I think I'll answer your questions. If I don't, just ask."

I set the glass down on the coffee table.

With a deep inhale, I traveled back a lifetime in two seconds. "After my parents died, I wanted to run. Away from home. Away from college. I thought maybe I'd join the military. Do something else responsible with my life, to help and protect people, but still escape."

I held his hand over top of our blanket.

"So, I met with a Marine recruiter on campus and found out about the Platoon Leaders Course. Guess the tomboy in me loved the idea. It made me want to be an officer, so I had to stay in college."

I paused, remembering the grueling program, how I found it fun. "I guess I also wanted something to push me like my dad always did." Bittersweet memories of graduation, all the milestones my parents missed played like a stinging slideshow in my mind. "I think I also needed family, so the Corps became mine."

My free hand reached out for my glass.

"After Quantico, I was off to the Defense Language Institute for Pashto. That's where I heard about the Female Engagement Teams training at Camp Pendleton, and I volunteered. They needed interpreters, and I liked the idea of working with other women, trying to help them."

I explained to him how we were called "FETs." As female Marines, we were allowed into the mud huts and compounds in Afghanistan where the male soldiers weren't.

That's where the women and girls lived. FETs could go in and try to help with community building, medical treatment, or other things the women may need. We were also in a position to gather a lot of intel from them too.

Daniel smiled, squeezing my hand. "Sounds like you. Helping girls like Kierra."

I sucked my teeth with the next sip. "Yeah, but we were pretty fucking naive in some ways. The people of Afghanistan are used to having their country occupied by foreigners. We handed out dollars for everything. Some men allowed us in because they appreciated the help. Others did because we came with lots of handouts, and it was part of the game. In many ways we did important work, and in other ways, we got played."

I tossed back the last sip. "I think I'm gonna go through the whole bottle of this delicious potion you poured me tonight."

"I have a whole bottle and the whole night."

When he gave me a kiss, I wanted to stop my story right there. But he took my glass, and got up to pour us another.

He returned, holding the crystal tumbler out for me. "Here you are, Major Ravenel."

I cupped the glass, "No. Not a major. I made captain just before this," gesturing to my cheek.

He sat back down and reached under the blanket, rubbing my ankles and calves to warm them. Even by the fire, I was still cold and drained from the day.

My long sigh greeted the haunting part of my story, the one of my nightmares.

"I was on my second tour in Helmand when I befriended a girl. Well, she was actually a wife. A fourteen-year-old wife and mother named Paksima."

My pupils fixated on the flames in the fireplace. "And

Paksima's husband was an evil son-of-a-bitch. Farzad." I hated speaking that name.

"They had a little baby, Esin. She was a little over one by my guess." Tears started to fall down my cheeks remembering Paksima's laughing brown eyes and Esin's giggles when I'd play with Esin, and the little stuffed teddy bear the FETs gave the toddler. "They were both just little girls. One painfully young mother and her beautiful little daughter."

Daniel took his hand warming my feet to hold my empty hand again atop the blanket.

"I was in and out of that compound talking with Paksima and the other women for months." Tears pooled down into the corners of my mouth. "I noticed numerous times the bruises on Paksima. Her pain. Her fear. A couple of times she was lying down. She couldn't even stand up and I knew it—he was beating and raping her."

I set the glass down before wiping away the deluge down my face. "It happens everywhere. All over the world. But there. There's little you can do about it. It's part of the culture. Young brides. It made me sick."

"I can't imagine," he said. "My little sister, Tess. Being married off at fourteen. God, I couldn't stand it."

"I never got used to it. I don't think any of us did." I looked down at my hand in his. "The last time I was there, little Esin was sick. She had this wail. A high-pitched, vibrating screech of pain that made Paksima frantic. It made her grab my hand, pleading for us to help her baby. But Farzad wouldn't let us take her for medical care.

"Steph was on my team. She had medical training. She asked to examine her, but her father wouldn't allow it. The little baby girl just kept grabbing her privates, screaming until she lost her voice."

A sob escaped my throat. "We knew then exactly what was happening to them both."

Daniel reached for me, "Oh, God," pulling me to his shoulder. "I'm so sorry, Charlie. I'm so sorry." He kissed my hair.

I crunched my molars so hard, holding back a torrent of sobs. If I let them go, I'd never stop, and I had to finish. I couldn't be with him or anyone who didn't know my truth.

And if it drove him away, so be it.

Better to know now.

Pulling back from his embrace, I tipped my head back. "He knew we knew and he didn't know what we'd do. Not that we could do a damn thing. But maybe it'd mean no more handouts. No more cash for the bullshit intel he fed us."

My tears stopped as I turned to stare at the fire.

"He hated everything we stood for. I think what he hated most was that we were women. And then we were Marines. We were occupiers in his home and his homeland, and now we knew. He wouldn't have bribes or honor with us anymore."

My mind was thousands of miles and years away, but my head shook with the same sure resolve.

"And I knew he'd keep torturing and hurting those girls. He was never going to stop. So, there was only one thing I could do."

My eyes were transfixed, gunning for the flames in the fire.

"I knew if I could get him to shoot at me, I'd be justified in killing him."

CHAPTER TWENTY-NINE

DANIEL

Mallorca by RY X

My breath seized at her confession.

I sat silent, reeling and listening for more.

She said, "We were on patrol two days later. Me, Steph, Miller, Perez and Jax. We led the platoon through the Marjah bizarre. Jax was out in front. I was behind him. I knew we were close to the fried bread stand where Farzad and his brothers would often sit, smoking and drinking. I purposefully didn't wear my headscarf that day under my helmet. I figured if I tipped it down on my head, he'd see my blonde hair. He could target me. And I could target him."

She raised her chin up. "Steph, Miller and Perez stopped at the snack stand about thirty feet back from me and Jax. They always talked with that man. He had a pet monkey, and they thought it was funny. I stood out toward the road with Jax."

I stood right there with her, imagining it, my heart pounding while I focused on the scar across her cheek.

"I saw Paksima's husband, Farzad, sitting beside the stand," she said. "I looked him dead in the eyes. He stood up. I don't know how long we stood there, killing each other with our eyes."

She closed hers. "Then he smirked at me and I saw it—the pistol rising from his vest pocket. But I wasn't afraid. I just waited to hear the shot I needed to have permission to fire. And I did.

"I heard my dad's voice yell 'Fire!' I shouldered my rifle, felt something sting my cheek. I got him in my sights while I heard multiple shots. I felt the hit to my shoulder, another to my waist. I thought I fired back three times. The report said I fired five rounds total. Hitting him three times. Two center mass. One to the head. Like we're trained. The report said he had an Army issue M9. Stolen or bought. Lots of men carried pistols or AKs. They found five rounds left in his magazine. He shot three down my right, so luckily seven bullets missed me. Spray and pray."

That crude comment knocked me back.

I knew Charlie was an incredible shot, but to plan a killing and then carry out the plan? While getting shot herself?

This was a Charlie I hadn't imagined.

But it was a part of her. The scars down her body. What I saw of her today in the shower.

It forced me to confront a world, a brutality I lived sheltered from.

"Truth is"—she tilted her head to the side, twisting her mouth—"I don't know who planned it. Me or him? Maybe it was an ambush and he waited for us. We varied our times and routes, but not enough. And maybe the others could've made the shot too."

She paused, taking a long sip of rye, sucking it back through her teeth, before setting the glass down.

"Or maybe," she said, "I set it up. I gave him a chance to take the shot because I just needed justification to kill him... and I did."

I let go of her hand, pulling mine down my face. "Who knows about this, Charlie?"

"Not many. It's confidential in a mission report. I've read it. It says I took fire by a hostile threat with a suspected association with the Taliban. I fired back and killed him, taking three shots myself. Apparently, another man who had an AK was there with Farzad. He started firing at me next, but Jax protected me, suppressed his fire so he turned on Jax, hitting him twice at close range in the ankle."

Her gaze met mine and she shook her head like she was ashamed. "Jax lost his foot because of me. I don't know what I thought would happen. Maybe it was going to anyway, and something prepared me. Or maybe I planned it, and something protected me. I've searched my soul for years, and I don't know.

"But I remember my dad was there. Like his spirit guided me. I know he yelled 'fire' before that first bullet left his chamber, before it hit my cheek. I was ready for it." Her shoulders collapsed. "And I know, when you take someone else's life, you lose a piece of your own. No matter why."

She paused and searched my eyes with hers. "Do you hate me?"

"Hate you?" Like she needed absolution from me of all people.

"I don't know how to read the look on your face right now."

"I don't hate you. I'm just listening, taking it in." I reached out, touching her scar. The trail of a bullet across her cheek. If it had been two more millimeters to her left, I wouldn't be talking to her today.

"Charlie, people say 'I can't imagine,' when someone shares something horrible. But I can and"—I stopped, overwhelmed—"I have no words." I offered my embrace instead.

She laid her head on my chest and we sat silent for a few minutes. But still, I had a question, something I had to know.

I pulled back to question her. "Who is Kai?"

Sorrow creased her face. "Daniel, Kai was my husband. A Marine. He was killed in Sangin one day after I was shot."

Everything made sense. "And you think it was your fault he got killed."

"I did." She nodded. "I still do, I guess, on some subconscious level. My head knows we lost a lot in Sangin. But I'm afraid he was worried about me, distracted because he wanted to get back to me. I don't remember being at the FOB hospital. My next memory was the hospital in Germany and I kept asking for him. Finally the chaplain came in to tell me and I lost the next year of my life after the words fell out of his mouth."

My arms flinched to reach for her, then I paused, worried. "Can I hold you?"

"Why are you asking me that now?" She looked hurt. "Because of what I did? Or because I'm a widow?"

"No. That's why I want to hold you. I just remember how I felt when Flynn died. I didn't want anyone touching me."

She nuzzled into my chest, wrapping her arms around

my neck. "Well, I'm holding you and your pain now, all these years later."

That slammed my heart so hard, biting back tears and years of letting no one hold me, missing my brother, my young heart aching and lonely.

So, I held hers now. And let her hold me. So tight. Both disappearing in our thoughts. She, quiet with visiting her memories, while I wrestled the magnitude of what she'd done.

"You would've liked Kai," she said after a while, pecking my cheek. "He was a closeted introvert like you. Preferring books and family. And handsome like you."

"If he was married to you, he was a very special man." I imagined the man it would have taken to marry a much younger Charlie. Like a horse whisperer with a wild mustang. Very kind and calm, but in control.

"What was his last name?" I needed to put this last piece together.

"Roberts. Kai Roberts. I was Captain Charlotte Roberts. There was too much pain in that name for me. I had to go back to my maiden name."

I conjured the pain of losing the love of your life. With Charlie in my arms, it wasn't hard.

Anyone from the outside could reason that she didn't cause Kai's death. It wasn't her fault. But to hold such guilt was living hell.

I knew guilt all too well.

"So Kai is the only other man you told me about?" Humility flooded my heart for the memory of a real hero I'd never know.

"Yeah. He was my first... everything."

"Why do I get to be second, Charlie?" It had bothered me for weeks. In quieter moments when lust didn't dominate my thoughts, my conscience did, mocking my worth of her. "You deserve better than me. I haven't been the best man I should have. You called it the day we met and neither one of us were impressed with what you saw."

She sat up, challenging me with her eyebrow raised. "Daniel, do you think I'm a stupid person?"

"No." That made me laugh. "Quite the opposite."

"Well then. I'm smart enough to know we're both pretty fucking flawed. That's what I meant the day we met. And despite how you like carrying me around your house like I'm helpless, I can take care of my damn self. I know exactly what I deserve and why you're second."

"All right then. Why? Why me, Charlie?"

The gaze in her eyes aimed at me softened with her voice. "Because you laughed at my mouse voices."

That smallest moment crushed me, cracking me open. What I felt that night too? How that one instant had altered the orbit of my world, pulling me closer to her sun.

It ignited in me now. Drawing my mouth to hers, I lay us back on the sofa, cradling her face in my hands, finding my lips on hers, over and over.

I wouldn't insult her again. I knew my why. Why I wanted everything with her. Why she would be my last, my always, my body waking next to hers, urging to connect like my next breath. Then my heart, aching for hers, remembered. Today at the gym. Tonight by the fire. Everything she'd been through.

My kiss hovered over hers. "I don't want to rush you. We don't have to go on holiday."

The demand in her eyes, the heave of her chest under mine, the part of her lips all declared, "I know what I want, Daniel." Her hand reached down, grasping my hardening cock. "I want you."

"Oh, fuck." I groaned surprised, roused ready by her stroking grip. Her hand gripping my cock felt so good. Her kiss seemed so fearless. Like she was free now.

She opened her thighs. I climbed between them. She tugged at my shirt. I sat up on my knees, pulling it over my head. When I looked down, she was the most magnificent sight—lust swimming in her eyes, taking me in her tight grasp, stroking me over my pants.

Urgency took my lips to hers, then her neck. My finger-tips drew teasing circles around her hard nipples under her shirt before giving a gentle pinch like I'd been dying to do. The sinews on her neck tensed under my kiss in a craving wail for my touch.

The sound of her pleasure detonated through me. I craved it more than what my body demanded. I did it again. She writhed my name with a moan, her hand slipping under the waistband of my pants, the soft skin of her palm gliding over my bare ass before her fingers clinched my flesh with such need, her hips lifting, opening for me. A torrent of lust surged through every nerve in my body, knowing what could be next. One or two more hasty moves and we'd both have exactly what we ached for. Each other.

God how I wanted to bury my cock in her so deep, to see how wet I could get her, to feel her streams down my thighs. I bet she'd come so hard I'd have to fight to stay inside of her. Fuck, I needed her.

But not like this. Not tonight. I had to find control. I wanted more. All of her. Always.

Lifting myself off her in a daze, I huffed. "We have to stop. I want to wait too. Till our holiday."

She groaned with a loud sigh of frustration, "*Fuck-ingggg hellll.*" It was so cute.

With an amused whimper, she opened her eyes. "Okay,

dammit. We'll wait." Her palm kept caressing my ass cheek. "Just stay here for a minute so I can enjoy the sight." But her hips lifted in sneaky circles under me, trying to break my resolve.

"You've trained me well, Ravenel." I grinned with a slow thrust into her swirl. "I can do your tease all night now."

"Promises, promises."

"Seven nights to be exact."

"And days. Rob's got it all planned out."

I blushed at overhearing their conversation, leaning down for a kiss before I lay alongside her. "I seem to remember something about toys and naughty outfits too."

She shifted to her side, facing me, her cheeks still flushed from our near fuck. "Oh, is Daniel Pierce into naughty toys and outfits?"

"Naughty toys and outfits? With you? Fuck yes."

"You keep saying the word 'naughty' to me in that goddamn accent and you're getting more than you bargained for."

This was torture. "Oh, does Ms. Ravenel like being naughty?"

"Hell yes. After six years, naughty is just the appetizer for what I want with you." Her eyes danced with plans. "Any requests? I'm going shopping tomorrow."

"I wish I could go with you." I craved a day shopping with her. That wasn't possible. Simple public joys got ripped from my life long ago.

"Text me what you want, and I'll be your personal sex shopper, Mr. Pierce."

"With you, Ms. Ravenel, the list is long. And if you please, I'm in dire need of new swimming trunks too."

"Oh, that'll be fun."

"Whatever pleases you. Size large, but please with a drawstring or they won't stay up."

"I thought that's the plan."

A thought blitzed through my mind at the mention of "the plan." Twirling her hair, I tried to think of how to ask. "Um, in regard to provisions for this week of exquisite debauchery, what other items should this gentleman bring?"

It took a few seconds for her to catch on. When she finally did, she gave me a knowing grin.

"We're covered." Lifting her right arm, she brought my fingertips to feel the birth control implant under her bicep. "And I've been in a sexual convent for so long my hymen has grown back," she joked. "But you're the Sex God. I'm the one who should be asking you."

I breathed bittersweet relief she was covered. Touched actually, that she'd been alone all this time. And to be the second person for her? Lying next to her now, so honest and laughing at her abstinence with every noble reason why, I suffered that same bloody truth that I didn't deserve her.

"I've been monogamous for over two years and completely alone with my hand and thoughts of you since I've been here. And I get everything poked, prodded and tested every year."

She grew quiet at my answer. I worried. Would I have to tell her now? "Do you have any questions for me?"

"Yes." She twirled my hair. I held my breath. "Will you hold me so tight again tonight that I can't fight you?"

CHAPTER THIRTY

CHARLIE

A note was left folded on his pillow for me when I awoke alone the next morning.

My Captain Sex Goddess,
This truth doesn't hurt. That I am the luckiest man in the
world to spend a night holding you in my arms. You told me
the day we met that I've paid a price for this life. I have. And
I'm strong enough to pay it all over again if it finds me again
with you, watching you sleep by my side. My only regret? I
didn't get to see your smile this morning. Have one for me
please, Friday at 4.
D, 24/7/365
P.S. Elaine and Colleen are downstairs
P.S.S. Enjoy shopping for us

Wearing a smile along with his clothes from last night, I found Colleen and Elaine in the kitchen, having tea and going over his schedule. "Good morning," I said. Both looked up at me. "Sorry to interrupt."

"Good morning, Ms. Ravenel." Elaine's muted grin stamped her approval on my overnight stay as Daniel's guest. "It's no interruption." She reached for a cup and saucer. "Coffee?"

You'll need a gallon in your veins in a minute.

"Yes, please." I took a seat at the island. "And please, call me Charlie." I appreciated the gesture of professional respect, but that ship had clearly sailed. This was business and pleasure now.

Elaine asked, "Cream and sugar, Charlie?"

"Yes, please. Thank you."

"Charlie, you have such a lovely accent," Colleen said. "May I ask where you're from?"

"Yes ma'am. I'm from a very small island off the South Carolina coast. Daufuskie Island." I opened my phone on the counter and shared some photos with Colleen and Elaine.

"Looks like you have another destination to add to your retirement travel list," Elaine said to Colleen.

We had an easy chat getting to know each other. I asked for suggestions on which shops I should visit for Daniel's swim trunks. Elaine asked about my military service. It was easier now, telling them the official version of my tours and injuries.

"Charlie, I'm glad you brought that up, dear." Colleen paused, clearing her throat with a delicate cough. "Daniel's publicist called a couple hours ago. Daniel wanted to phone you himself but didn't want to wake you."

My grip on the coffee cup threatened to crack it in my bare hands.

Oh fuck, please don't say it.

But she did.

"A video of Daniel helping you yesterday leaked. His publicist has issued a statement—he was a Good Samaritan to an anonymous woman who had a medical event at a gym. But I'm afraid a few people are posting some unkind words and..." She stopped, unable to finish.

Distress was written all over Colleen's face.

She had clearly navigated Daniel's storms of press about the latest woman *on* his arm before, along with a few small scandals. Fucking ironic now it was a story about the woman passed out *in* his arms.

This one would be legend.

I measured out a long sigh, making sure to set my coffee cup down before I pulverized it. "Can I see, please?"

Colleen laid her tablet down in front of me. I caught both women exchanging a regretful head shake before I scrolled through the posts, videos of Daniel carrying me through the gym.

Oh shit, we're going viral.

Social media was blowing up with the epic spectacle of #danielpierce saving a woman draped helpless over his bulging biceps like a goddamn romance novel cover.

The comments and posts had rumors flying. The distress on Daniel's face was obvious, even under his baseball cap.

My face and scars were on full display. Internet trolls posted zoomed in shots of the scar on my cheek and the bullet wound through my shoulder. Some memes and hashtags were brutal: #gunshots, #bulletholes, #whoisshe, #savemedaniel, #danielpiercedme, and on and on.

Some were innocent "Daniel the hero" posts. I didn't care about the damsel in distress press. Even the asinine comments and hashtags didn't bother me. I was tough enough to take it.

But it shocked the psyche to see myself in Daniel's arms.

It's disturbing enough to see a video of your own limp unconscious body. It's even more haunting knowing where your mind was at the same time.

I hated it. I'd been so helpless, so exposed.

Elaine put her hand atop mine. "I'm so sorry."

Colleen chimed in with her expertise. "Trust me. It'll die down in a few days. Someone will have a baby or a break-up. These people have the attention span of a gnat."

"Is my name out?" Security was always my first thought.

Elaine patted my hand. "No. Your name isn't out. The gym owner saw to that. He deleted your name from the membership database. He's a good chap. He knew what to do."

"Just be careful today, love, when you're in the city center shopping," Colleen said. "You may be recognized."

I nodded, knowing how to make myself stand out like prey and how to camouflage for the hunt.

"Daniel asked that you please phone him this morning," Colleen said. "He's quite numb to this by now, but he sounded worried for you." Her request also rang with a warmth of approval.

I gave them both thankful hugs. They rang for Matt to give me a ride back to my car at the gym. While he did, I called Jeremy, reporting in.

I stuck to the truth. Sort of. How Rob, Daniel and I were working out. How I got triggered by a loud noise. How Rob and Daniel brought me home.

Jeremy said, "I'm glad they were there for you. You'll

take a couple of days, yeah? Let Rob and Joaquin handle things."

I wasn't his only employee with PTSD. Jeremy told me he respected that it came with qualifications for the job. He still had no idea how much of a demon it was for me. If he had known, he'd have seen it as I did. It was my greatest asset for the job and my greatest liability.

"I'm fine. I'll be on set within the hour."

"It's not a request, Ravenel. You *will* take these last two days off and let Rob and Joaquin cover things.

"Yes, boss."

His pen started clicking. "And don't be daft and think you'll sneak on set. I'll find out."

Fuck. It sucked having a smart-as-hell boss. "Fine. Can you just make sure the studio keeps my name out of the press? And I wanna know immediately if anyone starts digging."

It pissed me off to start monitoring my own digital footprint. I had none until now.

There was no social media in my maiden or married name. No news articles. Not even a mention of me from skeet competitions I won as a teen. They were too long ago. There were only military records, most you had to get permission for.

I never wanted to be found.

And for good reason.

For six years I hid under a different name, in the dark shadows of a stage building or on my remote island home. No one could find me. And I planned to return to that safety and anonymity.

Soon.

But now—even though my name change may still be camouflaged—my face had been revealed.

With one #danielpierce, my distinct scars were everywhere online. It was a nuclear bomb drop of my image for millions across the globe. And it was *millions* in the tally of shares, posts, retweets, and likes... and clicking up.

Two months in Daniel's world and I went from never showing my scars, to the entire online world making bullshit hashtags and comments about them.

"Copy. I'll keep you posted," Jeremy said, breaking my lightning speed mental rant. "Have a good break. That starts *today*. Where you going? On a proper holiday, I hope."

"Some place with a lot of blue water." That wasn't a lie.

Jeremy laughed. "Good for you. Have fun." We wrapped up our call as Matt pulled up to my car.

In the ten minutes it took me to drive back to my villa I debated—should I go to set or not? How pissed off would Jeremy be if I disobeyed him?

I was already taking the biggest risk tomorrow traveling with Daniel. If Jeremy found out, he'd be clicking his damn pen and reassigning me off Kierra's detail so damn fast my fucking head would spin.

With my phone cradled in my neck, I unlocked my front door, giving Daniel a quick call to leave him a voice-mail. It shocked me when he answered.

"Are you okay?" he asked quietly.

"Yeah, I'm fine. I thought you would be shooting," I replied softly, knowing if I spoke too loudly, anyone near him would recognize my voice on his phone.

"I'm on set, but you're more important." He paused. "I'm so sorry."

"I'm a grown ass woman, Pierce. I can take it. Let's just get the hell out of here for a while."

"We will. Far away. I promise."

"Moscow?"

His low rumbling laugh warmed me. "It's a surprise."

"Thank you for my note."

"Thank you for the company and whatever you buy us today, captain. Gotta go. Sorry." He hung up.

Fine. If I was banned from work today, I was going shopping, paparazzi be damned.

"No FUCKING way you're coming to work, boo," Rob said when I called him later.

During my shopping spree, I stopped to enjoy a café con leche and a couple rosquillas. I had called Kierra's mom to check in. Kierra was supposed to be on hold that day, at home and relaxing. When Anne told me that Kierra got called in for reshoots, I silently blew a gasket.

I protested Rob's dictate when I called him next. "Jeremy told me to take the day off, but he didn't know Kierra would be on set today. I need to be there for her."

"It's just a reshoot, mi prima. One scene," Rob said. "The script supervisor caught that Mason knelt on the wrong knee for the close-up shot. That's all Kierra has to reshoot today."

"Fine. Then I'm coming in."

"Joaquin and I are already here, outside her trailer. Her mom and counselor are here too. Relax bitch and have some fuckin' fun. And some fun fuckin'."

His jokes usually amused me. Not today.

My whole world started spinning off its axis.

First, my fucking face was viral. And now, I was being told I couldn't work.

"How much longer will she be there?" I asked.

"I think they're almost done. Maybe two p.m.," Rob answered.

Well then. Jeremy didn't say I couldn't meet Kierra at home. So, I did. I popped by for a goodbye hug before hiatus. It was another time my stubbornness paid off.

Because all hell broke loose.

I chatted with Kierra in her bedroom about our hiatus plans. When Kierra asked about mine, I only divulged I'd be sitting by a pool for a week. That was partially true.

"Kierra, have you checked your bag yet?" I noticed how Kierra just dropped it on her bed, zipped, and hadn't checked it like she should.

"Ah, yeah. Right." Kierra unzipped it. She started unpacking items, nonchalant at first, then frantically ripping them out. "Charlie, I put my hairbrush in my bag. I did what you said and remembered everything. But it's not in here."

Air pulled sharply into my lungs but I kept my face stoic. "Was your bag in your trailer all day?"

"No. I was too distracted having to reshoot that scene. I didn't realize it until we were leaving set, and I couldn't find it in my trailer. Joaquin finally found it in the makeup trailer. I'd left it there."

Probabilities fired through my logic. The number of people who belonged in the hair and makeup trailer was very small, the cast and just a few of the crew. Not that someone couldn't sneak in. Transpo unlocked the trailer every morning. Lorenzo was supposed to keep an eye on it. Still, the strongest probability? He belonged in there today, noticing Kierra had left her bag behind.

It was a dumbass move. It put him right next to Kierra. Like he couldn't resist her anymore, even if it was a risk.

"Is anything else missing?"

I stood beside her, watching Kierra remove the last items. Coconut lip balm. Peony flower hand lotion. A rainbow hair scrunchie. Nothing else was missing. All he took was her hairbrush. Kierra's trademark long, copper hair, that's what he craved.

The bag was empty now. Except for a bulge in the interior pocket, zipped shut.

Kierra turned to me with terror on her face. "I didn't put anything in there." She pointed to the pocket straining with something inside. "I can't do it, Charlie. You check it. Please."

I grabbed a pen from the nightstand, using it to pull the zipper open. If prints were left behind, I didn't want to disturb them.

Slowly, the pocket opened... and white cotton appeared.

Kierra gasped, fingers to her mouth. "My knickers."

I pulled them out with the pen. A folded note fell out along with them. I pushed open the crease of paper, enough to read the black ink, handwritten in odd block capital letters, like to disguise someone's natural penmanship.

I ENJOYED THESE IN MY GRASP.
WILL SEE THEM ON YOU. SOON.

The afternoon descended from there. Kierra sat on her bed, shaken to tears. Anne started throwing things in their luggage. Rob and Joaquin came over. The Madrid detectives too. I conferenced Jeremy in on speaker phone. All knew what to do. And I knew what we'd find.

Nothing.

After a couple of hours, everyone left. I stayed behind. Anne was in her bedroom stuck on a call with the airline trying to get their flight home to Galway moved earlier.

I found Kierra in her bathroom, sitting on the edge of the tub with a tear-stained face, trembling hands but fury in her eyes.

"I'm coming back, Charlie," Kierra said, shaking her head, refusing to surrender. "I'm going to fight like you do. He's not doing this to me."

I squatted down, taking both of Kierra's hands in mine. "Are you sure that's what you want to do?"

"Yes." Her lips quivered. "I can be afraid here, working and trying to be happy like you said. Or I can be afraid at home and miserable."

Pieces of my heart broke off. Kierra was right. Home safe, but miserable? Or working afraid and trying to be happy? I had lived both. The wisdom of this girl exceeded her years. But the risk to her was not one my soul could tolerate.

"Kierra, there's no shame if you choose your safety over anything else." I brushed back a wisp of her copper hair. "All that matters is for you to be safe."

"I won't be safe until he's caught."

"You're right. And I'll keep you safe until then. I'll catch him. But you don't have to do this. You don't have to prove a damn thing to anyone and suffer like this."

Kierra squeezed my hand holding hers. "I'd rather be afraid with you by my side than alone and terrified."

I clenched my jaw, tears welling up in my eyes. Again, the wisdom and resilience from this girl. All girls. It was far greater than the world gave them credit for. I listened to it, respected it.

"All right, then." I grinned, letting a tear slip down my cheek, not afraid to let Kierra see that a woman could have tears and strength at the same time. "Tell me what you want to do."

"I'm coming back after hiatus. I've worked too hard. I'm not letting some sick wanker ruin it."

Her stubbornness made my smile grow. Proud. "All right. I got your back. That sick wanker can do all his tricks, but he's not touching you. I promise. Over my dead body."

CHAPTER THIRTY-ONE

CHARLIE

S imon knocked on my door Friday, promptly at four p.m. There was no way Daniel could be spotted outside my villa now. Unease for the reason why threatened my excitement for this trip.

I opened the door and Simon insisted on taking my bags. Distracted with other concerns, I let him.

Kierra was safe in Galway. I had talked to her that morning before her flight. It seemed Kierra was more focused now on the excitement of seeing her boyfriend than what had happened the day before, her capricious teenage nature serving her well.

But now I faced risk.

If I thought Daniel and I had to be careful before, now we were at DEFCON 1. Okay, maybe only DEFCON 2, but my paranoia had its own scale. A sighting of Daniel Pierce traveling with the same woman with a scar on her face would throw a full gas tank on this bonfire.

Stepping out of my safe villa, a new sensation crawled over me.

I crossed over. Crossed into a world of lethal risk. Threats I couldn't rationalize; I could only feel the warning across every certain nerve in my being.

Rushing for safety, I opened the backdoor to the SUV myself.

"Hi beautiful." Daniel sat waiting for me inside, leaning toward me as soon as the door closed.

I smiled through his kiss. "Hi sexy." My relief to see him surprised me.

"When do I get to know?" I held his hand while Simon drove us through Madrid to the airport.

"When we get there, my lady," Daniel belted out in a Shakespearean actor's voice. "It's an adventure!"

I joked back. "More like, it's a testament to Colleen's meticulous planning."

He raised my hand, grazing his lips across my knuckles. "Indeed, between her skills and my money, prepare to be spoiled, Ms. Ravenel."

"I don't require money or spoiling, Mr. Daniel Pierce."

"I know," he said. "That's what makes it so fun doing this for you."

We pulled into a private airport. I pointed out the window to the luxury private jets. "Are we flying in one of those little things?"

He smiled with pride at his surprise. "For the first leg." Then he flinched. "Bloody, Charlie. I'm so sorry. Your parents. It didn't occur to me about you and flying."

A buzz of anxiety tingled my scalp. "That's not it. I'm not a happy passenger on anything. I get nervous. I like being in control."

"You? Wanting control? Imagine that." He kissed me with a deep tongue tease before Simon opened the door.

Once we stepped onboard, I had to admit... the plane's luxury was like a Xanax. Two rooms traveled down the middle of the plane, leather seating and decor in ivory and black in both. The forward room had an office while the back room was for sleeping with plush recliners. It was not the tin cans on wings or the loud, shuddering Ospreys I was used to.

We sat back in recliners opposite each other, drinks in hand, ready for take-off. Out of the airplane window, I watched Madrid beneath us disappear.

White panties. Knickers, as Kierra called them. Had he kept them in his pocket just waiting for his chance? No. If he was a cast member, he would've been in wardrobe. So, he had to have kept them in a bag, a backpack maybe. And a missing hairbrush. What was special about Kierra's copper hair? And zip tie handcuffs. Did he have a fetish for control? What was next? Kierra's tear-stained cheeks.

That sight was all I saw as the landscape below traveled from urban building tops to dotted rural green. The sensation of flight and the sure threat to Kierra raised my heart rate.

I closed my eyes.

Stop it. The girl is safe at home in Galway. No crew or cast members are there. I took another deep breath. *And you've waited so painfully long for this. Leave your fear behind and enjoy just one week.* Another deep breath. *It's just one week.*

We reached cruising altitude. I glanced away from the airplane window to find Daniel smiling at me. The look on his face suddenly put my clit in drive, all other thoughts gone. "What are you staring at?"

"Are you going to be in control this entire week, Charlie?"

I gestured to the plane around me. "Clearly not."

He unbuckled his seat belt, rising in front of me, his hard desire at my eye level. I peered up at him. "Would you like me to be in control this week, Daniel?"

Kneeling in front of me, he pulled my hips to the edge of the seat, tongue teasing me with penetrating kisses before he stopped to share. "I'm hoping we take turns at control for the win."

The grip of my fingers latched through his dark waves, yanking him back to my lips. The control I took over him made him moan. His hand grasped, yanking my seat belt free before pulling me off the chair. We knelt, unleashing our mouths and exploring hands all over each other.

He begged in my ear, "Please tell me our week has finally begun."

"Right here, on the plane? You want to start?"

Talk about flying the friendly skies.

He jumped to his feet, pulling the privacy slide between the two rooms closed. We sat in the back of the plane while the staff were up front with the pilots. He tapped the touchscreen, turning up the soft jazz lulling through the speakers.

The erection under his dark jeans knelt back down in front of me. He said, "We have two hours, and I won't even need one."

"Are you telling me where we're going?"

"No." He took my hands, cupping them over his massive, straining cock. "But I'll tell you where we're going in the next hour." His hands guided mine, stroking over his need. "We start now because I want you too fucking much."

My fingers outlined the contours of his erection, my

body wanting this but my heart not quite ready to jump. "How about a soft launch, Pierce?"

"What does that entail?"

"Only hands. No bare skin."

"You first, Ms. Ravenel."

His hands roamed over my braless breasts, over my silk black tank, teasing my nipples with the games his fingers could play. My neck curved open for his mouth, for his lips clinging down my skin while his touch painfully pleased me, circling, twisting and yes, gently pinching. Oh fuck, that gets me every time. With no more fear, a moan of surrender took my body. Sneaking up fast, desire reigned over me.

I pushed him off, provoking his wanton eyes. Unzipping my white jeans, I slid them down to my knees, spreading my legs open and revealing my white lace thong.

"Damn, babe." He sighed at the view.

Grabbing his right hand, I thrust it between my thighs, over my panties. His fingers pressed one skimpy layer of lace away from claiming me, my pussy already soaking it through. Shamelessly riding his hand, his palm was my saddle, and I was at full gallop.

"Fuck yes." He groaned at my impatient lust.

God, he felt so good. Whenever his hands were on me, his lips on mine, all else disappeared but his touch. Fear? Warning? That haunting instinct? I was free of it. He was my new drug. Making me start, quickening my nerves, a sweet flush igniting my clit. The firm heat of his hand caressed the entire journey between my thighs, the ridge of his middle finger rubbing against my exact tiny, divine spot.

He asked, "Do you like this, Charlie?" Pressing harder against my clit, his thick, strong finger was drawing me closer. "Do you like my hand making your pussy so wet?"

Fuck, his voice did it to me every time. "Yes, Daniel."

He rubbed even harder, rattling my clit while he growled, "Then show me how much you fucking like it." His command snatched me over the edge.

"Oh shit, Daniel." I grabbed his shoulders, my whole body shaking, drenching his hand and my jeans.

He rushed to unzip his with dripping fingers, revealing his cock towering under black boxer briefs.

"My turn." I tore his jeans down farther over his ass to his knees, teasing my fingers over him before gripping him firm with both hands.

"No, our turn." He surprised me, spanking his fingers against my clit, making me cry out. "Now and all week long, I'm going to enjoy making you come. Over and over."

I stroked his cock faster. He delivered another playful tap to my clit. Our racy competition went back and forth, over and over and making me bold. "Do you like my hands stroking your thick cock, Daniel?" With every spank he gave, my grip tightened its pump.

His breath grew shallow. "Yes, Charlie." His chest muscles tensed up. He peered down at my hands milking his cock over his thin briefs, his breath panting while he issued another tap to my clit, making me shudder again.

The erotic contest clenched my jaw. "Then show me how much you fucking like it, Daniel." One hand pumped his cock while my other playfully twisted his nipple under his T-shirt. He thrust into my hand, his breath dragging across his throat at my brute touch.

His middle finger rocked hard against my clit spanked tender while the rest of his hand seized what was within his grasp. "Come for me again," he said. "So fucking wet like you do." With his tease of my nipple I did, moaning his name, my thighs quaking, my lust flowing over his hand.

"Watch, Charlie." He shook, looking down at my hands fisting his cock, resting his forehead to mine. "I want you like this." Two more thrusts and he gasped, and gasped again while we watched him fill my hands with my creamy reward seeping through his boxers.

Lifting my chin up, he brought my lips up to his. "God, I needed that with you." He grinned through our kissing. "We're not even on the ground Sex Goddess, and you're already rocking my world."

My breath panted, recovering from my own orgasms. "We better not be flying to a roach motel in Russia."

He chuckled. "Far from it."

Our short flight connected to a long one from Istanbul to the Seychelles. Then with a quick, heads-down exit of the airport to a waiting car and we were here, on the flybridge of a yacht for the final leg of our journey.

Daniel wrapped his arms around me while the boat glided across the pristine water. I loved the raw beauty of my island home, but this place was that of luxury travel magazines, wishing you were here.

Our trip concierge, James, joined us, pointing to the island on the horizon. A white beach wrapped around it while a small mountain of outcrops covered in tropical greens crowned the top. The water around the island beamed electric turquoise. Four one-story, luxury villas were tucked into the landscape, steps from the water. The only thing nearby? Small uninhabited granite islands, perfect for snorkeling their shores.

I offered Daniel my lips. "Okay. You can spoil me now."

"Two kids on a no-name island." He invoked the day we met before cradling my face for a deep kiss, mic-dropping the romance.

We were greeted on the dock with towels scented with

Ylang Ylang, two flutes of champagne and skewers with slices of the best mango I ever tasted. The island staff introduced themselves, all a thirty-minute cart ride away from any request.

"The island is all yours. No other guests," James said.

My jaw hit the alabaster marble floor when I took in the view from the wall of windows in our villa's living room—a sweeping vista of a beach dappled with palms disappearing into a placid ocean of brilliant blues with small outcrops to the south.

"Consider us both spoiled." Daniel squeezed my hand. "Colleen outdid herself."

James said, "Two luxury bedrooms are on either side, a chef will deliver your meals, a private gym and a spa are just down the hall." He gave us the tour, showing us the touch screen where our next wish was one tap away.

Daniel asked for our luggage to be put in the bedroom with the infinity pool outside. I chimed in, "Can you put my bags in the other one, please?" Daniel's face crinkled with concern. "Can a gal not surprise a guy?" He smiled back, intrigued.

Colleen had requested the chef prepare brunch for our arrival. We were starving and thankful for her foresight. James poured us a second glass of champagne as the chef prepared eggs, fresh fruits, and grilled fish.

When we were finally alone, Daniel raised his glass. "Here's to an island to ourselves where we will apparently school the fish on the definition of wet."

I laughed at his recall for my lines. Lifting the flute to my lips, closing my eyes for a long sip, I drank in the bubbles and deep relaxation. It took me a few moments when I opened them to notice the white velvet box on the white linen tablecloth. It had appeared out of nowhere. My chin snapped up at the surprise.

Daniel stood up, taking my hand to join him. "Charlotte Sophia Ravenel, I wanted to give you something as beautiful and rare as you." Cracking the box open, he revealed four natural blue Akoya pearls on a thin pendant, hanging from a platinum chain.

Oh God, it's beautiful. Watch out, it's too much. Put it on.

He stepped behind me, brushing my hair over my shoulder, clasping it around with a kiss to my neck.

Blue pearls? A gift for island kids. His symbolic choice softened all my edges. And heart.

What was that beautiful feeling called again? I searched for a parachute not to fall in it. I couldn't find one.

"Daniel." I turned to him, all jokes abandoning me. "Thank you. For all of this." Touching the pearls at the hollow of my throat. "I've never been given jewelry before. I even picked out my own wedding ring because Kai was too unsure what to choose."

"I know I'm not the first at everything with you, but I'd like to try." He gifted me with kiss after kiss.

Yep, I was falling. "You sure know how to sweep a woman off her feet, Daniel Pierce. Are you trying to get lucky or something?"

His reply and kisses trailed down my neck. "Whatever *you* plan, Ms. Ravenel." They landed on the pearls over my skin.

"Can I make a joke about pearl necklaces now?" I opened more than my throat to him while his chuckle pressed against my flesh.

With a couple more sips of champagne, we wrapped up our brunch. He held my hand while we walked up the hibiscus lined path to our villa. Entering the door into the sprawling living area, he turned to me with an eager question on his handsome face. *What's next?*

"Give me just a minute." I disappeared into the other bedroom to search through my suitcase, returning with a black gift box tied with a matching ribbon. "Per your request, sir."

He took the box, pulling the ribbon. It tumbled to the floor. Opening the gift, it took him a second until he let out a happy laugh. "You are a sexy devil."

They were the swim trunks he'd requested, but probably not what he had imagined. I bought him three matching black, Aussie rower swim shorts with drawstrings. They'd leave nothing to the imagination, highlighting his every muscle and bulge.

He said, "You better have something equally revealing to make this fair."

"Meet me in the ocean in fifteen minutes." I disappeared again into the other bedroom, closing the door behind me.

CHAPTER THIRTY-TWO

DANIEL

A gentle breeze greeted my almost naked flesh as I crossed the pool deck, stepping down the grassy pathway to the beach. I tossed my sunglasses on the blanket and pillows left for us on the sugar sand. Ten steps into the breathless water and I dove in. Closing my eyes in a back float, every ounce of stress left my body.

This was heaven. Not because of the paradise surrounding me.

Because of her.

Never had a woman seeped relaxation into my pores like this, all sensation returning to me.

Yes, I had forgotten who I was, selling pieces of myself off along the way, moving through life a smiling, numb shell. And yes, I had to be numb given what I did. The guilt would break me if I let it all in. But not with her. Charlie redeemed me. Every part of me was awake with her.

Where was she?

I stood up in the navel deep, tepid water. "Bloody hell,

there is a God," I murmured at the sight walking across the pool deck. It swelled my cock.

I had hints of Charlie already, using my imagination for the rest. This was the real thing. A tiny, white crochet bikini hugged her tan skin, revealing more toned muscles and curving, feminine temptations than it covered.

Throwing her sunglasses on the blanket, she kicked off her shoes. Water lapped her thighs as she waded in with a grin before diving under, emerging just within my reach.

With a hook of my arm around her waist, I drew her near, gazing down and admiring hundreds of string holes in her bikini. "That's a fair bargain." My hard appreciation of her suit was obvious.

"You look fuckable to the millionth degree in those rowers, Daniel Pierce." She clasped her arms around my neck, wrapping her legs around my waist.

My hands caressed her bum while I licked the salt water down her throat, over the necklace. "Right here in the water?" I suggested between kisses to her cleavage.

She dropped her arms, falling back to float with her legs tightly ensnared around me. "I thought you were gonna try to beat me at the whole Tantric thing."

I worshipped the sight. Blue water reflecting in her eyes, blonde hair fanning around her, strong abs and legs engaged, squeezing me in her grip. To have her like this would be divine, but I played along. Hands up in surrender, I let go of her ass. "You're on, Ravenel."

With a playful laugh, she relinquished her hold and stood up. "Let's go check that out." She pointed to the outcrop down the beach.

We swam over and explored the boulders ascending above my head. They extended from the shoreline into the water. It was a great spot to snorkel, hinting to the magic of this place all around.

"Let's take the boat out snorkeling tomorrow," I said.

"Sounds fun. We don't have clear water like this at home." She swam up to the beach to explore the shallow part of the outcrop.

I swam around the other side, charmed by the school of fish that neared, then darted away. My stare above the liquid line let me watch her bending down, examining shells in the sand. I considered her scars. With hardly a stitch of clothing on her backside, her hair falling down her front with her back to me in the bright light of day, I couldn't avoid them.

It strangled me again. What she had said about her real story. *Spray and pray.* A crude but accurate description of what an untrained shooter did to their target. One I witnessed now. The spray pattern that pierced down her right side.

Her story had obsessed my mind over the past couple days, shocking me at first, taking a while to process her sacrifice—willing to die to protect two girls. Did she plan it or was it an ambush? Maybe both. Either way, a smile sparked deep across my being, watching her, more than lust pulling me to her.

You know what it's called, Pierce. Now go show her.

Sneaking up from behind, I wrapped my arms around her. "Let's save that for tomorrow."

It startled a laugh from her, dropping the shells from her hand. "What are we doing?"

"It's a hard launch now."

CHARLIE

OH, hell yes. Your willpower is all game and gone.

He led me to the outdoor shower on the side of the villa. With a turn of the knob, warm rain from the nozzle fell over us. Dappled sunlight heated us through the canopy of palms above.

My hands wandered down his glistening chest and abs, treasuring the dusting of dark chest hair over his pecs that mapped down his eight-pack abs in a seductive trail, leading to my reward.

With a whisper in my ear, pinching the end of both strings to my bikini top, he asked, "Is this what you want, Charlie?"

I jumped this time, completely free and falling into the yearning. "Yes."

With his pull, the strands tied around my neck and back snapped free. A sigh escaped his lips to the flop of my top to the floor.

His gaze and hands took forever across my exposed, tingling flesh. Tracing over every inch of me, his worshipping eyes, words, and hands made me shake.

It almost overwhelmed me. How lonely I had been. How much I needed someone's touch. How much I wanted him, so bad. God, how he could make me come just like this.

A brush of his hand glided down my midriff, stopping at the string holding my bottoms. He pulled one to tension, asking, "Do you want this?"

It wasn't an answer. It was a demand across my entire being. "Yes."

He held my gaze, pulling the string. Cool air rushed the spot between my hip bone and where I ached for him. The back of his fingers skated over my bare flesh, tickling the strength from my knees. He reached for the other side, urging in my ear, holding high the tip of the last string with his fingertips. "Tell me what you want, Charlie."

"Unwrap me, Daniel."

We watched his fingertips coax the last string until it unleashed its hold on my bottoms. They fell to the shower floor.

"Yes." The word hissed faintly from his lips at his first glimpse. "So fucking beautiful."

Watching him drink me in with his eyes, an intoxicating mix of shyness and desire washed over me. So exposed. So aroused. "Is this, okay?" I mimicked him, pulling at the drawstring of his bathing suit.

"No." He gently grabbed my hand, his other turning the shower off. "Ladies first."

"Don't you dare treat me like a lady."

"All right then, Sex Goddess." Keeping hold of my hand, he took two white plush towels at the shower exit and led the way. "Come with me."

Oh, I'll be coming with him. Many times.

He approached the four-person, chaise lounge bathed in noon sunlight. Lowering all backs flat, creating a large, white canvas platform before casting a towel across our impromptu bed, he dropped the other to the ground.

"Lie down, Charlie."

Greed for this found me crawling across the plush cushions, turning over and spreading my thighs open for him.

He asked, "Do you remember what you made me promise on our first date?" I paused to recall. Once he gripped his cock under his bathing suit in front of me, I remembered.

Sliding my hands down my belly, "Yes, I do"—I stopped before the spectacle he craved—"but we do it together."

He returned my smile, eyes on mine, pulling the string loose on his shorts. In one slow tug down, his wet suit hugged his muscular thighs. He stared at me, appreciating my reaction.

Because oh hell, did I have one. An impulse to touch myself with a sigh at the sight of his hefty cock eager for me. Good God, he looked more exquisite than his fans guessed, and my imagination had allowed. My fingers slid slick over where he focused on me with ravenous, aqua eyes.

"Do you like watching me touch myself, Daniel?"

He stroked off, watching my glazed fingers dip inside. "Yes, Charlie."

"Have you been thinking about me like this?"

"Every night. And morning." His fist pumped fast. "Just like this."

"Show me what happens to you when you think about fucking me."

No shyness found inside, I only had pure lust for the sight before me. His lips parted, his cock swelling even more, captivated by my solo pleasure for lush moments. Then he stopped.

"Not yet. You've waited six years." He stripped off his suit before climbing over me. "I told you what I'm going to do to you all week to make up for it." His body braced above mine like the steam off hot, wet pavement. The weight of him. The beauty of him. Everything in me opened to him. "I want to spoil you."

"How?" The hard heat of him held inches away. Away from the part of me that hurt with desperate need.

Kissing me before he answered, lips pressing to my ear, he asked, "Can I taste you, Charlie?"

Leave it to Daniel Pierce to turn sexual consent into a hot game, one I'd let him win. Weaving my fingers into his sopping hair, I pushed his mouth down. Losing all to him as he kissed, licked, nibbled, and teased his way below.

Grabbing the other towel, making a pillow for his knees, with a tug, he pulled my hips across the cushions so he could relish it all.

Wandering his fingertips, he explored every inch of my flesh but the one crying for his touch, making me writhe with urgent ache.

"What do you want, Charlie?" His question beckoned me up on my elbows to the sultry scene before me. "I want to hear you say it."

Oh God, Daniel Pierce is kneeling between your legs, his bowed lips hovering over your pussy. No more waiting.

I spread my thighs wider for his kiss. "Put your mouth where it belongs, Daniel."

He did. With a warm wide lick up, a gentle puff of cool air, a soft suck, and then a playful, hard spank of my clit—he shocked ecstasy right through me, making me cry out. Shocking any of my hesitation away. Over and over, he indulged me with generous spasms while I kept moaning for more.

His eyes met mine, his smile emerged, his mouth glistening with my lust. "I'm going to do this to your beautiful pussy all week." He plunged two fingers into my soaked walls, returning to his onslaught with a circling tongue over my clit.

A moan from my depths escaped to feel his touch inside me. "God Daniel, you're making me come." To feel him, any part of him, inside of my starved body took me to the edge, rolling my hips over his mouth, my eyes closing heavy with desire.

He stopped and demanded, "No. Watch me. Watch me eat your pussy, Charlie. Watch how I make you come."

I did. It was a beautiful, wanton sight. When his black waves returned between my thighs, his tongue flicking with zeal across my clit, a tremor quaked my legs. He responded, thrusting two fingers harder, faster. Forcing my eyes open through gasping pants, I struggled to keep still under his hungry mouth and hard touch. The strength of his other hand pressed down on my mound, securing his control of me. Then his beautiful eyes locked on mine with relish in them, lavishing me like this, like he was starving for me. His command over my pleasure and body freed the apex spasm.

"Daniel, God!" It burst. Pouring from me. Making him moan at the taste of my little ocean. I fell back, gripping his silky, wet waves between my legs. Convulsing under his unrelenting purring tongue and pounding touch, he consumed me through one licking wave after another, moaning into my pussy every time I flowed over his mouth.

Where the fuck are you? How long can he do this? Don't care. Just let him.

His touch became my only world, my only sensation. His thick fingers, his soft tongue, his sucking lips, his hard chin, my God, he wouldn't stop. No time existed while he tapped my well so long, so many times, so fucking deep with need until I whimpered with happy, grateful tears, confessing I was spent.

He stopped and found his way back to my mouth. "See how good you taste, Charlie?" His kiss shared my intimate flavor until I caught my breath.

I glazed my fingertips across his shining lips. "It's your turn now." His hard dick urged, dripping against my thigh.

"Not yet. I'm taking my time with you." Such devilish delight, such heavenly awe was in his eyes. "I've never made a woman come like you do. Fuck, it turns me on to drink you, to feel you dripping across my flesh. To know that I can please you like that, you're my new obsession."

"Well, you can obsess all week, Mr. Pierce."

"Oh, I will." His ardent kiss disclosed the depth of his words. Then he slowly got up and I watched him walk nude across the pool deck into the living room, aiming for the bar inside the sliding glass doors.

God damn. He is a fucking Greek God—no, a Sex God—with that flexing ass, cut body, incredible cock and generous mouth.

I stretched out in the sun. Warm air and sunlight blanketed my naked body. Pure satisfaction greeted the tide Daniel had created between my legs, a lush lagoon I'd swim in all week.

Careful, Charlie Girl, that man is waking more than your body.

CHAPTER THIRTY-THREE

DANIEL

Never did I want to erase the tingling taste of her from my mouth, but we deserved to raise a glass. With two full in my hand, I offered her one along with a kiss before reclining next to her inviting nudity.

A surprised "yum" fell from her lips at first sip. "I didn't take a sophisticated Englishman for a Cuba Libre fan," she said. "You're drinking like the masses."

"I'm not as stodgy as you think. Feeling quite liberated with you, actually. Have you noticed my penchant for flip-flops now?"

"Yep. Next thing you know, I'll have you holding a red plastic cup in your hand at the Freeport Marina." She laughed at the apparently ridiculous premise of me on her side of the Atlantic.

"How close is your home to Williamstown, North Carolina?" I asked.

"Williamstown? I've never heard of it. Why?"

"There's a movie studio there with water tanks."

"Oh, you mean Wilmington, North Carolina. Depending upon traffic and ferries, it's about a seven-hour drive." Her gaze dropped. "Why?" She swirled her drink; fear flexing in her voice. "Are you shooting something there?"

"Probably," I said. "I think the studio is still negotiating. Meanwhile Elaine is researching a rental for me." I paused, noting how the pleasant air suddenly shifted to eerie around us. "Seven hours? Why don't you work closer to home? At that studio or all the shows filming in the States?"

"Jeremy bugs the shit out of me with offers. Georgia mostly. But I won't work any detail close to home. Too many damn guns."

Something dark traveled in her eyes. "Charlie, what did I say to upset you? Is it the guns?"

"Maybe." She paused, looking away at the water. "I just got this sudden sick feeling. Like I'm losing control over everything." She glanced back at me. "Have you ever noticed the moon in the day sky?"

An odd question. "Yes, I suppose I have."

"I notice it. All the time. It haunts me. Like it's threatening something." Her ribs heaved with a loud breath. "Like it's warning me to keep my two worlds—my home and my work—far apart."

"So, I'm work to you? Shooting a film near your home? And that's haunting for you?"

That stung. I wanted to be her home. Not her work.

She didn't mean to hurt me. I knew now what she'd lost. Why she was afraid. Why she could only give me this week. I hoped to change her mind by the end of it. It left me honored and heartbroken at the same time.

Nothing but hurt creased around her eyes too. "Daniel, you know you're more than that to me."

"Do I? All I've ever known is people using me, Charlie. For profit or pleasure. What are we?"

It angered me. Why did I need for it be different with her?

"Please don't do this," she said. "I'm here risking my job to be with you. I'm here after six years of being alone, and now I'm sharing myself with you. The second person for me. Doesn't that say enough?"

Stop it now, Pierce. Don't push her away with your desperation.

I smiled, surrendering though my heart ached. "Yes, it does."

"Besides, by my measure of distance, Wilmington *is* close, like home." It was like she'd realized the wound she'd made, grazing her fingertips over the exact spot on my chest that hurt, assuring me. "It's close enough for you to come have a beer at the marina with me."

A glimmer of hope. "Only if they serve Guinness in red plastic cups."

That made her laugh. And me. It was all I wanted, her joy, for however long I could have it.

She threw the rest of her drink back before asking, "What's the project?"

"It's about a Navy SEAL team with a sleeper agent."

"Let me guess." She flipped over to her stomach, propping up on her elbows. "You're the sleeper agent."

"Contractually I can't reveal any secrets, Ms. Ravenel."

I skimmed my hand over the rise of her bum. Bloody hell, how her flesh rose to attention under my touch. Wild thoughts entered my mind.

"Mr. Pierce, I'm the trained professional. I know how to

get the intel I want." She rolled back over, descending her hands down her nude body, stopping between her thighs. "Tell me I'm wrong."

"Oh, you being wrong is so fucking right." I leaned over, kissing her while my hand met hers between her legs.

Snatch! She grabbed my wrist. Twisting under my touch, leaping on top of me and pinning both down by my side.

Damn, she moved fast and strong. And fucking hell, it turned me on. A lot.

Her lips played paths down my body, my cock getting so hard awaiting her descent. The fragrance of her desire mixing with vanilla from her strands marked my memory. Damp ribbons of her hair mopped down between my legs, her restraint of my wrists magnifying my lust.

Watching me starve for this, she finally arrived. My eyes beheld her tongue. When it flicked the sensitive underside of my tip, a groan threw my head back. Another wet flick. Oh God, and another.

Then the pleasure ceased. I looked at her.

She was grinning up at me. "Tell me I'm wrong."

"You look far more hard-core than I ever imagined with my hard cock in front of your glossy lips, Ms. Ravenel." She teased with a lingering lick up my length, still pinning my wrists down. "Is this a torture tactic they teach you in the Marines?"

Her grin, shameless as she circled her tongue over my crown before she replied, "There would be world peace if they did."

Ironic, because I'd wage a war for her mouth right now.

"Tell me I'm wrong, Daniel," she demanded again before brushing her lips against my begging tip.

Was it possible to moan in lust and laugh at the same time? I did. "Fuck's sakes. Yes, Charlie, I'm the guilty one."

"I knew it." She pounced off me in another darting move, laughing with her dive into the pool.

The saucy little minx, I loved every minute of the hunt. I jumped up after her, diving in, breaking the surface and grabbing her, squeezing a laugh from her ribs.

With a slippery turn in my grasp, she asked, "Do I need to feed you lunch?"

"Lunch is the last thing that needs to be eaten right now." I pressed heavy against her belly with exactly what was on the menu.

She agreed, taking my hand, picking up our towels, and leading me from the pool into our bedroom. We walked across the marble floor to a sitting area where a massive teakwood, full length mirror stood, propped against the wall.

Realizing her plan, I released a conquered moan.

She folded and dropped the towel on the floor, making a pillow for her knees between the mirror and me.

"Charlie." I gazed down at her. "I'm not going to last like this."

"I'll make it last so you can enjoy it, Daniel, because I don't usually kneel to men." She peered up at me without a touch. "Breathe."

I closed my eyes, inhaling deep breaths for control. But with the first touch of her tight grip and wet mouth around my cock, lust and urge surged right back. I watched our reflection like porn, her long blonde wet waves and that fantastic bum kneeling before me. Then I looked down to the most orgasmic vision—her, fingering herself while sucking me off. The sight dominated me, whipping a loud moan of my coming release.

She abruptly stopped, pulling away her touch. "Breathe."

I struggled but found a way back. She did this to me so many times I lost count, the tension, my orgasm climbing higher each time, restraint quaking my thighs.

Then she issued the same command I gave her. "Watch me suck your cock, Daniel."

Hell yes, I watched, willing myself to remember it forever. By the quickening rhythm of her hand, she was getting as close as I'd been for the past eternity. Then her throat suddenly took all she could of me in one merciless plunge. A cry escaped my lips at the swift sensation. The vibration of her moans thrumming over my cock made me insane as she took me again and again.

I had to hear it. "Are you getting off sucking my cock, Charlie?"

Her onslaught continued, almost taking me, then she stopped, her lips dripping. "Yes, I will. Now tell me what *you* want, Daniel."

Almost broken with desire, I could barely speak. "I want us together, Charlie." In every way.

She put my hands to her hair, letting me control her. Fuck yes, with a primal groan, I clamped her mouth down on me. Moans came from her full throat, ravaging me with shameless glucking sucks of my cock.

I shook in awe, shuddering through every tissue in my body. I gazed down at her, at that delicious look in her captivating eyes. At how she was getting off on my pleasure like I did for hers. At how even on her knees, she ruled me.

"Make us come, Charlie," I pleaded. A deep groan thundered from her throat, mouth quivering over my cock while she shook, raining her orgasm over her hand.

It ended me too.

"Fuck, Charlie! God!" I struggled to stay on my feet, losing strength in my legs, stars filling my vision, heaving rush after rush into her mouth. I staggered back but her latch held tight, swallowing everything from me—my breath and mind gone.

I gasped, "I need to lie down," smiling at my weakness, pulling us down to the rug underneath. I took her in my arms and she held me, soothing her hand up and down my back while my heart raced against her cheek.

"Are you okay?" She softly asked, sounding worried.

Was I okay? No. I was falling apart. Bit by bit. Into her.

I lifted her lips to mine, savoring my taste in her mouth before I confessed, "I'm blissfully destroyed by you, Charlie Ravenel."

Her fingertip tickled down my nose. "Will you let me save you now? With food this time?"

She was so bloody cute. I rolled onto my back. "Yes, please."

"Let me get it." She stood up. "Meet me on those big sofas out on the veranda."

I crawled up to stand on weak legs, noting the cute way she almost sighed the word "veranda" with her accent. Plucking the towel from the floor, I wrapped it around my waist. Dazed for focus, I found the spot she'd suggested and the plush sofa sank underneath my weight.

The moment closed my eyes, relishing magnificent gratification. Everything about her. With her. Worth the wait. Worth my life.

CHAPTER THIRTY-FOUR

CHARLIE

Sliding my black silk slip on, I found the kitchen. Our chef left lunch prepared. I carried the tray out to where Daniel waited. He started to stand as I approached. "Let me help," he said.

"Hush your fuss." I set the tray down on the ottoman. "I got this."

He plopped back down. "I'm starting a list on my phone of your Charlie-isms."

"Charlie-isms?" I nestled down onto the sofa beside him with my plate.

"Your cheeky little phrases like, 'hush your fuss.'" He grabbed his plate. "Or 'switchin' in the kitchen' or 'faster than a hot knife through butter.'"

"Damn, you sure do have a good memory for lines."

"Come on then," he taunted, loading up his fork with a bite of fish steamed in banana leaves. "Give us another."

After a generous mouthful of fish with mango salsa delighting my tastebuds, I said, "Well, my dad would say I was so mule-headed I could start an argument in an empty house."

Daniel howled back. "*That* is the dog's bollocks."

Our banter volleyed while we savored the meal. Once full, he rested against the arm of the sofa while I reclined opposite him, propped up on throw pillows.

"So, did you plan that? The mirror?" A satisfied grin took his face. "I think I'm still regaining the strength in my legs."

"I noted it during our tour this morning. A Marine adapts, remember?" My legs coiled around his. "What about you and those erotic little clit spanks that drive me wild?"

He told me how he'd been a good student, reading up on Tantric sex, getting informed and randy daily. "If school had been this much fun, I'd have a bloody PhD by now."

The mention of sex and school made me curious. "Tell me about your first, first whatever, but tell me about her."

I had strong guesses about a teenage Daniel. After the pictures I saw of his debut modeling campaign when he was barely eighteen, I could imagine his love escapades.

Daniel already knew about Kai. That was all to know about my sexual past. He, on the other hand, was a book series. *Daniel: The Early Years* interested me. I didn't care to read *Daniel: Last Year*.

"Ah, that's a corker," he said. "The first and last time I got my heart broken." The look squinting in his eyes blew in a sudden dark storm. "Gemma Evans."

"What did she look like?"

I had a hunch. The photos of him with women HGR had compiled in his profile were catalogued in my mind. Knowing exes was protocol. They're often the source of threats. And for him, the bevy of exes over the past twenty years warned me of a pattern. Staged photos at premieres. Shots snapped in a restaurant. Holding hands on the streets of London or rushing through an airport.

Daniel had an M.O. He wasn't private with his dates. It was like he wanted to be seen with them.

But I didn't see anything from the past couple of years, which puzzled me.

He did have a type for a while though—young, and seemingly jejune.

"Gemma Evans was a tall, beautiful copper haired ginger who gutted me." His smile was bitter. "We started dating when I turned sixteen. She was a year older and had me absolutely gobsmacked. I lost my virginity to her at her family's Christmas party. We hid in her bedroom for the whole five minutes it took. After that, I followed her like a rutting bull, trying for every chance at sex or whatever."

He raised his glass to me. "She gave me my first blow job."

I smiled; confident I set the bar highest now.

His mouth twisted, saying, "I fell so blind in love. I believed we'd be together forever. I spent all the money I'd saved on a ring for her. We made a promise to get engaged as soon as I turned eighteen. But later that summer, I went on holiday with my family to visit my Gran in York, and she went on with my best mate, Harry."

I winced, knowing pain from teen years could hurt like hell, even years later.

He shook his head. "What gutted me was I was such a fool, wasn't I? Gemma was cruel. When I came home, I had no idea. I would ring her up, and she wouldn't phone back. I would ring Harry up; he'd do the same. Finally, I saw them and our mates outside the superstore. She barely spoke to me. Harry acted all dodgy. Like he wanted to tell me.

Everyone did. But Gemma told them not to. She wanted me to look like a nob in front them. She was a nutter that way."

His fist mindlessly punched one of the throw pillows under his hand. "She tortured me for weeks. Finally, my sister Tess told me she saw them at the park. How Gemma was all over Harry. Tess wanted a major punch-up with Gemma but I told her no. I didn't want to give Gemma the satisfaction of knowing she'd hurt me so much."

He stopped punching and stared at something distant over my shoulder. "I don't know what gutted me more. Losing my girlfriend. Losing my best friend. Or being made a fool. She was the first person I let hug me after Flynn died." Pain poured down his face. "I felt so bloody betrayed. Furious actually."

His last sip poured over his strained lips before he said, "I went from hurt to hate pretty quick. She tried many times to give me a bell as soon as"—he gestured to the opulence around us—"all this began. Once I started modeling and getting attention, she wanted to get back together."

"Did you?"

"No," he said. "But I wish I had so I could hurt her back like she hurt me. Again, and again."

A wicked energy lashed from his last words. He was quiet for a moment before it left his face. "A thousand years ago," he said, his eyebrow raised over a resigned smile, staring back at me now.

"That was the only time you got your heart broken?"

How many broken hearts had he left in his wake? Maybe indirect revenge? Fast calculations of all the pain he must have caused if that was true.

That was it. Whatever Daniel hid, it was about another woman. But how bad could it be? All I knew from him was the most alluring cocktail of care, sexy and strong.

"That's hard to believe," I said. "What have you been doing these past twenty years then?"

"I told you, I haven't been an angel." His eyes followed the back of his fingertips brushing up my shin. "I never gave my heart away again."

Up, his gaze met mine. Like that wasn't true. Like something had changed for him. Like past wrongs sought right in my eyes.

"Want me to find Gemma and kick her ass for you?" I crawled across the sofa to straddle him.

He kissed me, trapping me on top of him, his lips skating over mine, saying, "The only thing I want now is you, Charlie Ravenel." The intensity of his grip and next kiss seared.

I returned his passion with mine before coming up for air from his grasp, urging, "Take a shower with me."

He took the tray back to the kitchen while I wandered into his bathroom. With a twist of the shower knob, steam soon filled the air. I gathered toiletries. The hosts had left shampoo and conditioner on the vanity.

Remembering the aroma I adored, his soap, I spotted his cognac leather dopp kit on the countertop. It was worn with years of travel, like a keepsake, bulging awkward with all he must lumber from home to set, to location and back.

My fingertips pinched the aged bronze zipper. The sound of the rain shower falling to marble tile and the slow tug of a zipper filled the air.

"What are you doing?"

I jumped, glancing up to see him in the reflection. "Looking for your soap."

With fast steps toward me, he said, "I'll get it." The weight of his palm landed on my hand, halting me from opening his bag, lips distracting my efforts, tickling through my strands. "Can I wash your hair?"

"Yes."

"I'm right behind you." He swatted my ass, directing me toward the shower. I heard the quick rip of his bag's zipper open, then the fast rip back to close it.

When he met me in the shower, his grip held a black bottle.

CHAPTER THIRTY-FIVE

DANIEL

Beneath Your Beautiful by Labrinth

Shampoo bubbled through her long tresses. I was enthralled by the intimate ritual, relieved she didn't open my bag, that she didn't find what I hid inside.

She'd know upon sight of it. Would know my sin. And this would all end.

I wouldn't allow it. Not when I stood this close to having her.

The shower sprayer in my grasp washed my worry and the suds away before I followed with conditioner. It made her hair fall into a sheet of gold down her back. Fuck me, she was so beautiful.

A racy thought stirred within. I curled my hand around, cupping her breast, teasing her nipple while pressing the nozzle between her legs, taking her neck with my lips. She moaned back against me while all three sensations seized her body. My thumb flipped the dial, the head pulsing now.

She groaned, her knees buckling. I held her so tight in this pleasure she couldn't escape it, whispering in her ear, "Please tell me you brought some toys for this trip."

She squirmed, turning around in my wet grasp. "Pace yourself, Sex God." Stroking my firm cock, she said, "All I want is you right now."

I dropped the nozzle, "Charlie," and cupped her face. "You have to tell me exactly what that means and what you want because I don't know where this is going, and I won't push you."

I could play games with her, be teased and tortured for days upon end, but I wanted her given fully to me, never taken. Not her.

She reached her lips for mine. "I'm ready, Daniel."

I met her kiss. "Are you sure?"

"Yes. Now."

"Here in the shower?" My palm traveled between her thighs.

She stopped its descent. "Not here." Turning the water off, she reached for our towels and handed me one. I dried my hair, following her into the bedroom, expecting her to stop but she kept walking, through the open sliding glass doors, outside.

"Are we going to fuck all over this house?"

She cooed over her shoulder, "We're going to fuck all over this island."

Following her nude ass swaying to the veranda in the late afternoon glow, she aimed toward our favorite sofa. I ducked inside the living room doors, pouring us a sip of Brugal rum. I knew she liked her Tito's, must have sipped it for years alone. But rum would be for us now. Together, and always.

I handed her a glass before crawling into the double-deep sofa beside her. We took sips then with a deep kiss, our tongues shared the sweet flavor. While we finished our drinks and kisses, I saw the change in her eyes.

She was doing it again. Wavering. Afraid.

"Are you sure about this?" I played with a wet lock of her hair. "After six years and everything. Just tell me and we can stop anytime."

She took my glass along with hers, setting them on the ottoman before turning to straddle me. "I want to try with you, Daniel." Cradling my jaw in her hands, her gaze assured me. "*This* is how much you mean to me."

Gesturing for me to move away from the back of the sofa, she wrapped her legs around me. As she sat on my lap, I crossed my legs underneath her, sliding my hands up her back.

What she already meant to me, I pressed my forehead to hers, diving into her marine eyes. Nuzzling my nose against hers, it was sprinkled with freckles that disarmed me. I gazed at pink lips that had ripped me open the night we met. My thumb gently traced the scar that humbled my colossal ego. This truth redefined me the moment she dawned in my world.

This was the only place for me. With her.

Lacing my hands through her hair, I had to hear it, I had to be sure. "What do you want?"

"This." She put me where she opened for me. "You." She held me and my eyes there... for as long as she wanted. The sensitive tip of my cock felt how wet, how ready she was, but she didn't move for minutes except for kissing me with those transcendent lips. The pressure, throbbing and barely inside of her, matching breath for breath—it captivated me and welled tears behind her lashes.

I cradled her cheek. "Are you okay?"

"I forgot how beautiful this feels."

Forgot? I never felt this power before.

"I'm not moving without you, Charlie." Every part of me ached. "For as long as you want."

Suddenly she descended, "Now, Daniel," taking every inch of me.

"Oh, God," I groaned in shock. Her sex and thighs clamped tight around me. I could barely move and didn't want to. She started a deep grind over me, shuddering, gasping, surprising me. This wasn't Tantric.

I pulled back and saw it in her eyes. Yes, she was going fast, with no control. With me buried deep inside her, I braced myself. This was for her, she had waited dearly for it and I found my will to hold on.

Wrapping my lips around her nipple, I sucked, taking her to the edge. The sound of her gasps and clasp through my hair held me there. I made her cry out with tremors. I pulled off, latching on to the other, doing the same with an intensity that made her growl so low, so enticing.

She arched her back, contracting every strong muscle around me. I had to see this, pulling my lips away, clutching her shaking waist, watching her beauty, watching her tense up to unleash. But she was holding back, quivering afraid until I gave her the words she craved. "Come on. All over my cock and so fucking wet and tight. Come for me, Charlie."

It was so strong. Quaking her lips, shaking her body, eyes crying as her pleasure poured down my shaft, drenching my thighs. With a tight flex and wild moan, she did it again, freeing another wave across my lap.

I forced myself to anchor to my edge, her full walls constricting around me, over and over. She wouldn't stop. Never had a fuck wet me like this before. It frenzied my mind. "God, Charlie," I cried out, holding back with all I had.

The crush of her legs unwrapped around me. She insisted, "More, Daniel." I held onto her, rising to my knees and lying her down under me. Holding back, I relished the sight, how her pussy still pulsed, dripping ready for me. She writhed, begging, "Please. Now."

Yanking her hips underneath me, she moaned at my control. Finding that spot again, right at her opening, I teased us both with halting movements, for minutes, the full tip of my cock driving her into crazy thrashes.

"Daniel, *please*." Her fingernails scratched my ass. That ignited my hips, plunging into her, unrelenting. Fuck, I wasn't going to last. I waited too long, wanting her too much. And she felt too fucking good, so slick and tight and swelling for me.

Sweat glossed our bodies. Spreading her legs wider with my knees, I hammered her clit with my thrusts, relishing the sweet smacking sound of lust between us. The power of it making her rise, widen and latch onto me.

"Yes. Fuck me harder, Daniel."

Oh God, that sound. My name, aching through her honey voice, giving that perfect command, I found an even greater force, rewarding us both.

The soft, warm skin of her perfect body melding into my curve wasn't letting go. Never had a touch pulled me in like this, so pure, and taking me... to more than fucking her. I was disappearing. My flesh, my heart, hers.

"Charlie, please." I held there, overwhelmed by it all. Grasping, tugging her hair to turn her face toward mine, to witness this. Her lips parted at my possession; her gorgeous eyes locked to mine.

I never wanted to leave this moment, taking her with

one hard pound after another. It owned us, her eyes urgent with it, me begging her, "Come *with* me."

That did it. Her neck arched. Growling my name, she bucked under me with clenching spasms, drenching me again. She took me, my free hand stilling her hip while every part of me groaned deep into her, the sight filling me, of her taking everything from me. Everything. Everything. "God, Charlie, I..." A gasp with another pulse choked me, stopping me from confessing more. Because it was so much more.

All her waiting. All my wanting. I stayed inside of her, kissing her lips through gasps. With a gaze down, I found tears falling down her sweet face, making her eyes burn bright blue.

"Charlie?" It crushed me. "Babe, are you okay?"

Wrapping around me, "Daniel," was all she said, nodding "yes," pulling me down to hold her. I rolled us on our sides, embracing her tighter.

Her shoulders shook with quiet sobs, tears that wouldn't stop, wetting my chest, dousing my heart.

Every breath for every future moment, I held in my arms then. It was her. I wouldn't breathe without her by my side, in my embrace, in my life. Always. And it was the same for her. I knew it. How she let me hold her. All she had; all she'd lost. I'd spend the rest of my life to be worth her.

"Shhhh, it's okay, babe. I got you. It's okay," I said through her soft cries. Over and over. Holding it all for her, as strong as I could be, I cradled her in my arms, staying inside of her until my soft exit. Still, I never let her go.

CHAPTER THIRTY-SIX

CHARLIE

My mom shouted in my ears, "¡Abre los ojos Charlotte!"

I did. My eyes flew open.

Lying perfectly still, I searched around. Dawn appeared over a tranquil ocean through glass doors. White sheets lay under my hands. A weight trapped my body. A tender soreness ached between my thighs. Breath warmed my shoulder. I lifted up, turning my head. His arm and leg were draped over me.

I remembered.

Daniel.

He slept peacefully behind me. Heavy eyebrows and thick lashes serene with slumber. Bowed lips beckoning me to kiss them but I couldn't bring myself to wake him. We were both tired from our travels—and I recalled with a satis-fied smile—all we shared the day before.

Sliding out from under him, I pulled the covers back over his naked body, admiring the sight. Bare feet silently crossing the floor, I closed the bedroom door behind me with a gentle click. Taking in the magnificent view, my heart was still racing from my nightmare.

I wandered into the other bathroom, my body craving a shower after last night. The memory tickled my belly. My first time with Daniel on the veranda. A naked dinner in the same spot. Laughing through stories in the glow of twinkling deck lights. Skinny dipping in the pool. Teasing each other, playing games that turned into lust. Disappearing into our bedroom for another union on our bed.

That time, so sensuously slow, bodies wrapping into a dozen positions, the sex so indulgent it tranquilized me into a content sleep.

Until my nightmare.

Hot water pelted me. I closed my eyes and had to do this, conjuring the dream that woke me.

My nightmares used to give me a flu for the day. Aches. Fever. Pain. All in my soul. Now they were my first cup of coffee in the morning—a bitter, daily ritual.

I had dreamt of Kai. Of our first camping trip at the Grand Canyon.

How he set our backpacks on a picnic table before we started our descent down the switchback trail. We had packed our own gear. Thankfully, he knew to check mine before we started. I protested. He replied, chuckling, "Lighten your burden, angel, or you won't make it." He made me laugh while we repacked it, relieving the weight. I adored his umber eyes, rich with love, always watching out for me.

Then something shifted, splintering from that moment to the next. His laughter morphed. Umber eyes turned raven—black with malice through the sight of my rifle.

Farzad's arm was rising; a pistol was in his hand, aimed at me.

In my dream, time had stopped in the space between a heartbeat. The mesh of my eyelashes closed, opening again through a slow blink... looking past Farzad's barrel... behind him for the first time.

Jansher, his brother, stood behind him. His hands lifting an AK tucked under his vest.

"Open your eyes, Charlotte!" My mom had commanded, and the memory returned.

I slammed my hand against the shower wall.

It was Jansher.

Jansher had tried to kill me too. He was the one who shot Jax. Jansher was Farzad's older brother, living in the same compound with his own wife and their two sons.

It was Jansher we had suspected was moving weapons. He was the one we tried getting more intel on, knowing he had ties to the Taliban. But his wife kept her distance from the FETs. She'd talk just long enough, taking what bounty we brought, then she'd disappear, keeping her boys with her. Steph and I once peeked into their sleeping quarters, surprised at the amount of technology Jansher hid. But we couldn't engage him, only report back what we had observed.

I washed my hair, processing it.

I had to tell Jax the next time we went fishing when I was home. He wasn't allowed in the compound like I was. He didn't know their faces as well as I did. And that day happened like a lightning strike. A sudden flash and then Jansher disappeared between the stands, down the street in Marjah.

It felt surreal. To live in that world, consumed with my work with the FETs, on my daily patrols... then waking up in Germany. Never to return. It seemed like one of my bad dreams if my memory and body didn't testify to the truth.

A truth I thought about daily—the two girls, Paksima and her daughter, Esin.

Paksima would be married to Jansher now. It haunted me with worry he'd be no different than his evil younger brother. But instinct told me, *No. He's different in many ways. More powerful. More calculating.* He'd have no time for girls. Instead, he'd focus his hatred on his real enemy, the occupiers, and all we stood for.

I tried toweling off the water and the memory.

Water droplets wiped off my skin. Still, it clung to me, seeping into my bones ever since that day, mocking me... *that war isn't over.*

That's enough! I dropped my towel. *Let it go. For once, just fucking let it go and let yourself be happy for a few days. Then you can go back. Back to your lonely hell.*

With a deep breath, I forced myself into the present moment.

And it was a splendid one.

My sobs last night with Daniel, liberating me from a crushing ache of solitude. The delicious sensation I squeezed now tight between my thighs, my need so satisfied. I smiled, looking out of the window.

Six more days of pleasure.

I clasped the necklace back on, touching the four pearls. Island kids. Something about it made my soul soar.

Sliding my slip back on, I padded barefoot down the hallway to the kitchen. We left our phones charging on the counter, promising each other we'd rarely check them.

It'd been a day. Time to check.

I tapped the screen. Jeremy had called. Twice yesterday. Shit. That wasn't good.

I had to prepare for this call.

Because now?

I was in up to my neck in guilt and would have to lie. With zero tolerance for dishonesty, I was about to suffer the bitter sting of hypocrisy—standing on an island in the Seychelles, spending a week fucking the hell out of the one man I wasn't supposed to.

At almost thirty-three, my head knew better. But my lonely heart and body rebelled.

I wasn't flippant about my job, took it too seriously to be honest. If I got taken off *The Druid* it'd be my biggest regret, of not protecting Kierra until I caught her stalker.

And I was so close. Proximity to the threat festered in my bones, both forces growing equally strong for me. Kierra and protection. Daniel and pleasure.

If I ever had to choose? No question what I'd do.

It was almost ten o'clock here. Six o'clock in London. Jeremy would be awake. Three seconds in and he picked up the call.

"Ravenel, how's the holiday?"

"Fucking gorgeous. I'm staring at an infinity pool calling my name."

"Sorry to keep ringing you up in paradise, wherever that may be, but you insisted."

"All right." I braced myself. "Lemme have it."

"The studio has been getting a lot of calls about *the woman* and *the incident* at the gym."

My eyes rolled at the word "incident." But Jeremy didn't know better.

He continued. "Seems the press got word from witnesses at the gym that you were there *with* Daniel Pierce that day. So, they started calling members of the crew, asking about a woman who works on the show with..." He paused, reluctant to say it.

"Scars." I helped him.

Jeremy knew what had happened to me in Afghanistan. I included a brief narrative of it in my personnel record, having to explain my scars and service. The official events surrounding the shooting of Captain Charlotte Roberts and Corporal Neil Jackson had cleared investigation, so I shared what was official—the undamning version of it.

"Yes, scars," he said. "Someone on the crew pointed the press our way. Told them you work cast security. So, now they're asking us if you'll do an interview about being rescued by Daniel Pierce. And about your scars." His words paused, frustrated, the incessant clicking of his pen filling my ears. "It's sick how they use people and their pain for a story and a few quid.

"But there were a couple of unusual calls that got our attention." His tone changed. My interest piqued. "Blocked VPNs from Russia, asking for your name. Asking if you're American. If you're former military. Odd actually. Not like most press outlets to use blocked numbers, but not unheard of, especially for rag reporters. They can be pretty bloody hard."

My records were under lock with HGR. They'd never violate my privacy. And on *The Druid* set? Only Rob, Joaquin, Anders, Kierra, and Daniel knew about my military background. And only Rob and Daniel knew about my other name, my married one.

But some news outlets had been caught hacking in the past. And I didn't put it past some assholes to try again.

"You know, Ravenel," Jeremy said, "you might want to avoid working out with Pierce. Paparazzi and fans hunt him like bloodhounds. If you're friends with him, out in public, they will be all over you too."

It pissed me off, considering what Jeremy warned... and the implications.

Just friends with Daniel? My boss had no clue.

But he was dead on about the paparazzi and fans. No fucking way I'd do an interview, but a statement might shut this shit down.

"All right. Thanks for the heads up. Let me think about what to do." Blue water sparkled in front of me, redirecting my thoughts. "If that's all boss, I'm diving in now."

"That's all. Have a good week. Chat with you Monday." He ended the call.

I put down my phone, instinct crawling up my neck with questions.

Who outed me as cast security? Who cared if I was former American military? The only connection I made to Russia? Not rag reporters. Afghanistan—a country the Russians had occupied for over a decade.

What the hell did that have to do with me being sighted with Daniel Pierce? And his A-list celebrity life? It was worlds, years, and cultures away from Afghanistan.

Now? All I was sure of?

My boss may not suspect me with Daniel, not with my nun-like past. But the paparazzi and his fans? They might. The staff on the island? They all had signed NDAs. My closest friends and his team? We could trust them.

But I'd tell Daniel to switch us to separate flights home. We couldn't travel publicly. I could never risk being sighted with him again.

Or my doomed fate would be sealed.

At least we were hiding here for the week, secluded from it all. At least they didn't have my name yet. Colleen had predicted the story would die down. I sure fucking hoped so.

Until then, I'd enjoy this little time.

The fancy espresso machine on the counter beckoned me to concoct café con leche. It wouldn't be the same as in Madrid, but I loved trying. Steaming the milk in the small metal pitcher was fun. The hissing and frothing sounds delighted me. But when I tried twisting the cup filter full of ground espresso into the machine, it didn't want to go in.

"Need some help?"

I jumped. Fuck, the man and his baritone voice entered a room like the best surprise party.

Glancing over my shoulder, *holy shit*, he hit me with another jolt.

Daniel's nude body roamed toward me. A black tendril fell over his face still soft with sleep, but the rest of him was tensed with hard desire. Brushing hair off my shoulder, he kissed the thin chain of our necklace. "I was hoping to wake up to your smile this morning." He pressed into me with his hefty hopes. "And my new, wet addiction under me."

How this man quenched my draught. After six years alone in a barren dessert, a dearth of sex or another's touch, all I had now was thirst. For him. Like an oasis. One drop across my tongue and I dove in. His touch, releasing my wet tears and desire. I earned this. Needed it. To be doused with pleasure.

My breath changed with his touch. "I wanted to serve you in bed," I said.

The dip of his hand plunged between my thighs. "Bend over and I'll drink you right here, if you please."

And he did. The espresso machine? Not the only thing dripping.

CHAPTER THIRTY-SEVEN

DANIEL

"The dream makes sense to me," she said, peeling the layers off a croissant, eating one at a time.

We sat on our favorite outdoor sofa enjoying the breakfast tray from the chef. I devoured almost the entire quiche while she told me about her dream—a memory recalled—and her call with Jeremy.

"Dreaming about Kai after last night with you makes sense." She stopped, her eyes flicking up at me suddenly.

"Charlie, your memories and marriage to Kai don't bother me." I rubbed her foot lying beside me. "Please don't fear sharing them."

"I feel like an asshole admitting it to you, but I think of Kai every day. Something will remind me. But I've never had a man in my life who had to deal with the memory of my first husband." She grimaced. "Dead husband."

"I don't mind you talking about him. I like it, actually. It's a way to honour him. Honour you both." I nodded toward her phone on the ottoman. "Do you have any pictures? If it doesn't upset you, I'd love to meet him, so to speak." I traced the high arch of her foot. "We have something very special in common."

"I only keep three in here." She picked up her phone and scrolled a bit. "This is the day we met. We were on the recruitment tour at Quantico. He kept smiling at me during the info sessions and asked me to dinner that night, so I guess it was our first date."

She handed me her phone.

Shock tensed my cheeks up at the image. "Wow, look at you two."

They were a vision of young love.

Charlie looked almost the same, except for smile wrinkles now. With Kai's arm wrapped over her shoulder, they appeared innocent of sex and war. Not anymore. I was thankful for it.

But something was different. I could see what she meant about her life before the scar on her cheek. How people had a hard time getting past her pretty face to take her seriously.

Now her scar forced respect. And her eyes have changed. Strength supplanted innocence, making her stunning now.

The image of Kai surprised me. I had imagined a muscular white, blond guy. Wrong.

Kai had long, straight black hair casually parted down the middle. High cheekbones under thick eyebrows and happy brown eyes. A thin regal nose. White teeth and full lips. He wasn't light and he wasn't dark. He wore a black shirt with a necklace of turquoise and silver.

The picture of Kai punched my heart, first with jealousy, then with grief. This beautiful man was gone from this world. I asked, "What kind of name is 'Kai'?"

"In Navajo, 'Kai' means 'willow tree.' His father was, is, Navajo, and his mom is white." She paused. "I never know what tense to talk about him in."

She reached over, swiping to the next picture.

Their wedding photo. They looked serene, holding hands. Charlie wore a white sundress with turquoise jewelry and a belt. Kai wore black pants, a long sleeve white button up shirt, his military-buzzed head wrapped in a traditional Navajo scarf. Standing under a grove of trees, both were barefoot in the grass.

"We got married in New Mexico," she said. "It was too painful getting married at my home since my parents had died, so his family took me in. I still talk to his parents sometimes. But it's hard. It only makes them sad. I know they'd be happy for me. But still, we don't talk as much as we used to."

She swiped to the last picture. "This is the hardest one for me. The last one we took so I made myself keep it. It was at Camp Leatherneck, six weeks before he was killed."

I glanced up and caught the grief in her eyes before looking back down to study the picture.

They were dressed in their cammies, standing in front of a beige trailer. A tight bun strained Charlie's hair and face back. They smiled, but I noticed... they weren't holding hands.

"Do you miss him?"

"That's hard to answer." Her gaze turned to the ocean. "Miss makes it sound sad, and I don't feel that anymore. Guilt, yes. For surviving when he didn't. But sad? Not anymore. My mom used to say, 'Remember the roses and not the thorns in life.'" A softness relaxed her face. "And I do. I have a lot of happy memories with him. He was a loving man. Quiet, but funny. Strong, but gentle. And he had a ridiculous obsession with Reese's Peanut Butter Cups." She smiled at that memory.

"I'm thankful for my time with him, but it feels like a lifetime ago. And it's hard to admit, but we grew apart in our last couple of years." She looked at me, gently shaking her head. "War does that to you. It puts a distance between you and everyone you love. And it's hard getting back to where you were before, if ever. And we both changed so much. Not that I didn't love him anymore. I just didn't know him. Hell, I didn't know myself anymore."

She sat quiet for a bit while I rubbed her foot. Then she said, "But he'd get a big kick out of me here with you though."

"Would he?" I liked the idea of Kai's blessing.

"Oh yeah, y'all would get on like a house on fire once he trusted you weren't a celebrity asshole." She slid a slice of mango over her lips. "You both have me and my mouth in common." Throwing her chin up dripping with mango juice, she laughed. "Whoops, I meant my *smart-ass* mouth, but you can take that pun literally too."

"Celebrity asshole, huh?" I chuckled at her naughty pun but wondered. "Like what you thought of me the night we met?"

"I didn't think you were an asshole when we met. I thought you were coming on to me. And now you know why it scared me. And I'm sorry, because I was the asshole, pushing you away."

I'd forever be thankful for that night. For the push and pull between us. How she was raw with pain, and I was numb to it. How sitting with her now, together, I never felt so alive.

She continued. "I'll confess. I did think you looked a hundred percent fuckable, but I've worked with lots of pretty men. And I know looks don't mean a goddamn thing. In fact, it can make someone pretty on the outside very ugly on the inside if they're arrogant. Then only a fool would suffer them."

"Oh, that's spoken from experience. There's a story there. Let's hear it."

"It's nothing. Just assholes not knowing how to take rejection. And one time, one guy wasn't so easy to reject."

"In a bad way?" It bothered me; the thought of a man making advances at Charlie on set tightened my grip over her foot. "Who?"

"No, not in a bad way. Sweet. Tempting for a hot second. But then absofuckinglutely not." She shook her head, resisting our conversation. "Shit, I shouldn't have said anything."

"Oh, come on. You can't say that and then not tell me."

"All right, fine, but this door swings both ways. If I ever ask about your past, you have to tell me."

"I'll tell you whatever you want to know."

"Lucky for you, Daniel Pierce, I don't wanna know. I have my flaws and jealousy and insecurity aren't on the list. I got my own damn past haunting me. I refuse to take on someone else's."

"Well, my offer still stands."

I took a sip of coffee, relieved to avoid her interrogation of my sexual past. She wouldn't like my answers, would see through my omissions, would walk away and never look back if she knew all my truth.

The threat of her leaving me was far more powerful

than my guilt. All I wanted was her. Even if it took silence and secrets to have her.

But I couldn't resist knowing this. "My question still stands. Who actually tempted Charlie Ravenel before she succumbed to my charms?"

Her eyebrows shot one inch up her forehead. "Oh, is that what you did? Charm me, Daniel?" She did that thing again, tonguing her back teeth. Made me fucking wild. "What if it's the other way around? What if I planned this all along? What if I charmed *you*?"

"Either way suits me fine. Charm me all week. I'm not complaining." I grinned, rubbing her sole, getting turned on by her stubborn banter. "And you still haven't answered my question."

"Okay, fine." She rolled her eyes. "When I worked on *Fated,* one of the actors crushed on me and asked me out for coffee. I actually considered it for a day. But then, I had to turn him down. For lots of reasons. He acted mature about it, but it was obvious for the rest of the season he had a thing for me. Finally though, he moved on, started dating someone else and it was fine. And now we're just good friends."

Some poor actor on set, smitten with Charlie? It was easy to imagine. She didn't blend into the landscape on any crew or location, catching any man's eye. She'd certainly caught mine. And more.

The question crawled out of my mouth. "Do I know him?"

"Yeah, you've worked with him."

"I did? Who?"

It was that boiling feeling again, same one I had for Rob. And I knew him? Someone who tempted Charlie before me? What the fuck? Why did it make me so raging jealous all of a sudden?

She said, "You seem far more interested in my past than I am in yours."

"Perhaps, but you have an unfair advantage. My past has been quite public."

"Indeed, it has." Smacking her lips, she cocked her head. "And yet, I'm sure there's much more to know about you than is orchestrated for the public eye."

"Indeed, there is. Like this week with you."

The ball of her foot squeezed pliable in my hand, her verbal resistance making me hard. "You still haven't answered my question. Why won't you tell me?" A wicked combination swirled through me—lust and jealousy.

"Because you worked with him. And Rob already made you jealous." Her marine eyes aimed right at me. "And I told you, I don't do jealous. It's a fucking ugly emotion. And I can see it in your eyes and hard cock right now."

I let go of her foot. "Yes, I'm jealous. To be honest, it's a new emotion for me," I confessed, tickling my finger up the sole of her little foot.

She yanked it back in an impulsive giggle. Fuck, turning me on more "Can I tickle it out of you?"

"No, dammit. Tickle me and I'll knee your balls up to your throat." She pushed her foot back into my hand, smiling. "But keep massaging me and muzzle that male ego, and I'll tell you."

I obliged, kneading my thumb into her arch. Dark jealousy went up in smoke at her laughter and promise to tell.

"Alistair Campbell," she said.

That name threw my head back in a huge laugh. Indeed, I knew Alistair well. We did the second *Zeus* movie together. Alistair had played Apollo.

"Well done, Ravenel." Yes, I was insecure and amused by the intel. "Very charming and fuckable indeed. Why didn't you?"

If I were into men, I'd be allured by Alistair. His blond waves, bedroom blue eyes over full lips always licked with sheen, shredded body and devilish smile made a lot of people weak in the knees.

"Why?" She chuckled, her eyes growing wide. "A thousand reasons why. Too young and naive, being one. I like my men grown. And I wasn't ready to be with anyone for all the reasons you know." She stopped, stoic and looked at me, not laughing anymore. "And getting caught fucking with the cast is a career killer for someone in my position."

I sighed at her truth. "It'll be okay. Only our trusted people know we're here together."

"Jeremy, my boss, says everyone is asking about me. There're even masked calls from Russia. It's too fucking weird. I was nowhere online, and now I'm everywhere, passed out in your hashtag Daniel Pierce arms." Her hands carved through her hair, pulling with tension, holding it back from her face. "I'm debating about releasing a statement. Give them what they want to make it stop. But I don't know. My instincts are all off when the fucking spotlight is on *me*."

"Probably not a good idea." I massaged the tips of her toes. "That gives it another news cycle. Let it die down. Somebody will get married or die, and we'll be long forgotten."

"I hope you're right. I just have a bad feeling this is gonna get way out of hand."

I had to tell her. Because it just may.

"Charlie, I need to tell you something. It's not a big deal but since we're on the subject." So much dread was in her eyes. "Lorenzo approached me our last day on set before hiatus. He wanted money to keep our secret."

"What? That little fucker. Acting all innocent. I knew we couldn't trust him."

"Trust isn't the currency on any set. So, I gave him what is. A hundred thousand euros and he signed an NDA. In my trailer. That day. It's done."

"A hundred thousand euros? Daniel, that's a lot of money to pay a blackmailing son-of-a-bitch."

I laughed. "No. It's not. Not in this industry. Millions are exchanged for secrets. You know that. And I would pay any amount to protect you. It doesn't matter if I get caught with you. I can do what I want. But I didn't want anyone hurting you."

She tilted her head with a soft smile, like she wanted to leap across the sofa to thank me, but concern strained her brow. "Still. What's to keep Lorenzo from telling a loud-mouthed asshole like Mason our secret? Hell, he probably did five minutes after he caught us."

"I was in Mason's shoes years ago. Trust me. One, he knows better than to fuck with me. And two, he's interested in fucking around with young women, not us."

"I hope you're right."

I sat up, putting our tray on the ottoman. "I know I'm right." Climbing over for a kiss, I laid her back on the sofa. "And your first impression of me was right. I am very fuck-able." I took her lips and then my favorite spots on her neck, stopping to kiss the pearls resting on her throat.

She squirmed under me. "Someone is feeling pretty full of himself this morning."

"I'm feeling something full, that's for sure." I started taking my towel off, my hard cock craving her.

She snapped her forearm to my throat. "Look here, Sex God. Someone also said something about snorkeling today."

The pressure against my jugular hurt, but the sight of her below me kept taunting. The pain she gave? So intoxicating when she mixed it with pleasure, saying, "Let's go show some fish just how fuckable you are, Daniel Pierce."

CHAPTER THIRTY-EIGHT

DANIEL

Talking Body - Gryffin Remix by Tove Lo

We met the water sports manager at the dock. He greeted us with welcome smiles, offering lifejackets to find the right fit. Then he presented the key to the boat to me.

I laughed, pointing to Charlie. "No, mate. She's the captain. Literally."

"Oh, right! Yes, sir." The manager apologized, handing the key to Charlie. He showed her around the helm, pointing out a good spot to drop anchor, referring to the laminated chart they kept onboard. After a quick check of the radio, he sent us off.

She stood at the wheel, backing out to clear the dock. I watched her fingers caress the throttle like they do my cock.

"Oh, I feel like I'm on the line at Daytona. Ready, Pierce?"

"Hit it!"

I kicked back in the front seat with my neoprene booted feet propped up on the dash. She looked out over the bow and grinned. I saw them too, small waves begging to be jumped.

For a woman who didn't like flying, she was fearless on the water. We spent a half hour zig-zagging across the low rolling swells before she slowed to approach a small granite island. After killing the engine, she started lowering the anchor.

"How often does that happen to you?" I asked. "That thing with the manager and the key? When someone assumes the man is in charge?"

In between enjoying Charlie deftly commanding the vessel across the water and looking bloody fit in her black and white bikini doing it, the question struck me.

She crawled out onto the deck bench over the stern to put on her fins and mask. "All the time." Dipping her hand in, she tested the water. "The first time Rob and I arrive anywhere; they usually think it. They sure as hell thought it many times in the Marines." She spit into her mask before rubbing it around the glass. "And all while growing up. Being blonde doesn't help either. I want a dollar for every fucking dumb blonde joke I've sneered through."

She slid the strap of her fin over the back of her bootie, adjusting it for her small foot. I crawled over to sit beside her, starting my ritual, prepping to dive in.

It made me a bit cross at the world, realizing I was guilty of doing it too. But she seemed to be enjoying her thoughts actually.

"What's so funny?" I asked.

"It's not so much wanting to be the boss." She threw her sunglasses onto the upholstered bench behind us. "And I don't give a shit about folks who call me a bitch when I'm in charge. They're right. Cross me, and I'll show you a bitch. But I don't need to be in charge all the time. I just insist on respect. I might know a fucking thing or a hundred."

With a snap, her other fin was on. "But the joke's on them in the end." She pulled the mask and snorkel on, letting them rest high on her forehead. "The dumber they think I am, the harder they fucking fall." Laughing, she slid her mask down and splashed back into the dazzling blue water.

I caught up with her, pointing toward the hard coral before reaching for her hand. We were like kids playing in tide pools, watching schools of yellow and blue fusilier fish and the clown fish shyly poking out from the coral. Stunning black, white, and yellow butterfly fish swam by. When she pointed to the white-tip reef shark swimming about six meters over my shoulder, I jumped with a startled yell into my snorkel, which had her laughing through hers.

We worked our way back around the small outcrop, exploring other spots for over an hour, until we emerged, taking off our masks.

"Whoops!" she exclaimed.

The sight of the boat floating out into the bay greeted us. The anchor didn't hold, and the boat drifted far from our drop point.

I appreciated the spectacle of her goof with a delighted smile.

Laughing at herself, she rolled over in a back float crying out in her heaviest Southern accent, "Save me, Daniel! Save me!"

"It's going to cost you, Ravenel." I grinned, throwing her my mask and snorkel, taking off toward the boat in a fast freestyle. I knew my way around boats too, not as well as Charlie, but I enjoyed having something over her now.

She was still laughing when I pulled up alongside her, killing the engine. And while tossing our gear in before she climbed up the ladder. Squeezing the water out of her hair, she chuckled, asking with a guilty smile, "Got any dumb blonde jokes for this one?"

I held the wheel while she rose up on her toes to kiss me. Slapping her wet ass before giving it a firm grab, I asked, "Do you want a buck or a quid?

CHARLIE

I LOVED the hunger a day on the water gives. It's always deep and pure. We were rewarded for our snorkeling, and two more hours spent boating and splashing around, with a late afternoon picnic lunch. The chef left coconut curry rice with shrimp and scallops for us in a basket on the beach blanket, steps from the small waves lapping the shore.

For dessert, Daniel ordered more rum and cokes while the chef also left us a treat of coconut ice cream in a special frozen container. It was only partially melted by the time we opened it, and absolute heaven.

Sitting cross legged next to him, licking my spoon, the sunlight dancing in sparkles across the water mesmerized me. His sigh broke my stare, making me glance over my shoulder.

Daniel was reclining back on the pillows, one hand behind his head, the other cradling his drink. Hair dripping with salt water and sex, his body was a muscular adult amusement park ride with those tight black rowers outlining his generous package.

Good God, if the world could see this picture. They'd go ape-shit, orgasmic over it. Talk about breaking the internet.

I dipped my spoon into the creamy dessert with a playful thought. "I like this ice cream." I turned to kneel over him. "But I'd really love to eat it like this." It dripped off my spoon onto his belly button.

The cold drops made his abs flinch, but his grin proved he loved it. "Are you hungry for a real dessert now?"

I answered by standing up and stripping off my bikini, watching him get hard at my show. "I'm fucking starving," I said with a greedy grin, dropping to my knees and lapping up the ice cream on his belly while pulling his wet rowers down.

With a glance up, I moaned as he was full in my mouth. The grip of his fist held my hair back so he could witness how much. I darted my tongue across his most sensitive spot, making him twist, confessing, "God, I love watching you."

"Do you now?"

"I'd beg for a photo if I could."

I smiled, glazing kisses over his fat tip before asking, "You wanna start a spank bank with me, Daniel?"

"I don't ever want to forget this week." He nodded toward the beach bag on the blanket. "My phone is in there."

The thought of him filming me flushed my body with next-level desire. And I deserved this ride. "Okay. Video. No faces or names."

He sighed, throwing his head back. "How did I get so fucking lucky with you?" Reaching for the bag, he turned back to me with his phone in hand and desire lathered over his face.

You've never done this before. Yep, and you don't need anyone's damn permission to try.

"You're the director." I rose up on my knees. "Tell me what you want."

He aimed his phone at me. "Make this your erotic debut."

"Before you press a damn thing on that phone, you better promise me this is secure."

"I'm schooled every year on how to protect my devices and leave no footprints. This is for us only. Just like this week." His eyes swore to mine. "I won't ever hurt you, Charlie. I promise."

A choice faced me, racing my pulse but wanting to trust him.

Another thing I hadn't done before, not since Kai—trust a man. But it was too powerful, this pull to Daniel. It made me lose my grip, letting go of the fear that kept me safe for so long.

For the first time, ever, I chose lust over alarm, indicating everything below my chin. "Below here is your X-rated frame."

He turned his phone horizontal to record it all, pressing the screen with a *ping*.

The lens started at my hand plunging between my legs. Teasing my sex, my fingers spread it open for his view, my middle finger toying my clit.

"Fuck me, Charlie." It groaned deep from his throat. His focus on me and this risk, it ignited my pleasure. Slowly, he panned up my belly, to my other fingertips gently tugging my nipple, stopping at the blue pearls dangling from my throat.

All I focused on? His hard-on flexing for me. "Tell me what you're thinking about," he said.

I divulged what I had imagined, touching myself and thinking of him. How I even did it years ago to one of his pictures. His breath panted shallow at my salacious recall, panning left to capture his other hand, jerking off at the audio of my confessions, then panning back to me.

The sight of his fist pumping his cock was hot, but I warned him. "No, sir. That's for me."

He stopped. "Then give me your best, bad performance." Pinching the screen, he zoomed out. "Are you being naughty with me filming you...?" His voice stammered not to say my name.

My lips sighed at the truth and his accent, "Yes," fingers plunging inside. I was so fucking wet and grazing over my clit, my eyes staring at his beauty.

"Does it get you off knowing I'm going to spank to this, to the sight of you, every day, moaning your name while I come?"

"Yes." I was going to break my fucking wrist to the tenor of his beguiling voice and his mighty cock waiting on me.

"Do you like me watching you finger yourself, Charlie?" There it was again. His voice taunting me. "Are you going to come for me right now?"

I threw my head back, jerking my hand, "Fuck yes," giving him and the camera the dripping, quivering act they lusted for.

Admiring curses murmured over his lips, turning into sighs of praise as he shot the spectacle of me crawling on top to ride him next with the blue water and horizon behind me.

Taking him between my legs, barely letting him inside, gripping his length firm, I swirled over his tip.

The veins in his neck groaned, his aqua eyes urging me. "Please..." he said, struggling again not to utter my name.

My sudden descent made him cry out. Unleashing lurid rolls, hard grinds and snapping hips, I fucked him and played with my tits in a raunchy display for him and I relished the sight.

How he watched, filming it, looking shattered below me. How his eyes were out of control with lust. How his strong body writhed helpless beneath me. How his lips parted with gasps and moans. His wide cock circling inside me; he was under my control.

"Do you like watching me?" I danced on my edge.

"Fuck yes," he growled.

"What will you do? Watching us fuck?"

With no shame, no fear in his eyes, he said, "I'll moan your fucking name and come so hard for you."

It rocketed up in me. "Watch us close up..." I almost said Daniel.

His hand shook, holding his phone closer to where our bodies joined. Rising on shaking thighs, letting him flop heavy out of me, I cried out, the camera forever archiving my lust for him, showering over his glazed cock beneath me.

"Fuck, please, Ch..." He held it up with his free hand, begging to be back inside of me.

I slid back down with shudders of frenzied desire. The tease done, I started seeking what I lost for six years. Like I could ever get it back but tried so hard with tight pistons over his length. The whole world disappeared except for him inside me, because only him now, because with him I wouldn't stop. I couldn't stop. Bracing my hands against his steel stomach, I moaned his name, watching his aqua stare while I rode him hard, greedy for each crashing wave after another over me, each streaming down between our thighs.

He dropped his phone. Holding onto my hips through his curses and strained moans until he finally seized them, trapping me on top. His chin threw back, opening his sinewed throat to me in a sudden thrash that arched his back, his lips loudly straining out my name. His entire body went still, except for his groans and pulsing against my walls.

I laid down on his pounding chest. He wrapped his arms around me, asking through clinging breath, "Charlie, how am I going to say goodbye to you after this week? I don't know how to let you go."

Sudden terror seized my heart. With his question. With his need.

What did I fear more? The risk of getting caught with him or the threat of falling for the one man I shouldn't? Knowing I'd lose more than my career to him. To be with Daniel Pierce? It would risk my life too. It would mean no more hiding, no more safety.

My haunt and his celebrity would hunt us for years.

It's why I forced myself to promise only this week. For both of us. Until now.

I rose up to find my breath and answer.

He gazed so vulnerably, so fucking beautiful up at me. My long pause seemed to scare him. He filled the silence.

"I know I just broke the unspoken rule between us, but I can't help it. Tell me, Charlie." There was no performance in him, only his raw truth screaming desperately from his gorgeous eyes. "If you're leaving me, tell me now. I've already lost people I love. I can't take much more."

The truth thundered through me. Everything my head told me. Gone. Everything that warned me. Disappeared. All that breathed in me now, in my heart, in my body, was him.

"We don't have to say, 'Goodbye,' Daniel. And we won't make any promises for forever either. Let's just be careful and live in between."

His hulking chest exhaled in relief at my answer. But even after the words fell from my lips, with his lavishing mine in overwhelming kisses and his massive arms wrapped around me, a torrent of panic rushed through me, my instinct whispering...

He will be your end.

CHAPTER THIRTY-NINE

CHARLIE

A grasp shook my shoulder. "Charlie." It yanked me out of the darkness. "Charlie, wake up, babe. You're having a bad dream."

My eyes opened with a heart pounding gasp, sight blurred, burning with hot tears. Was I awake or still in the nightmare?

"Charlie?" I twisted over suddenly. A silhouette loomed over me. Like the haunt I just left in my dream. Like the terror that promised to arrive.

No. It's here.

"Shit, Daniel." I let out a frightened sigh, trying to catch my breath. "God, I just had the worst dream."

I collapsed back, shaking my head "no" to free my mind of the vision. It reeled, remembering it again, making my chest rise and fall in terror.

"Come here," he said, opening his arms to me. "I can only imagine the nightmares you must have."

I rolled over to find my favorite spot now, resting my

cheek between his shoulder and chest. Breathing with him, I slowly calmed.

"Do you want to talk about it? Was it Afghanistan?"

"No." I soothed myself, running my hand across the thin blanket of his chest hair. "No. It was weird. Different." I closed my eyes, trying to recall...

Where was I?

"It was the same feeling from the day I got shot," I said. "But I wasn't there. I was somewhere with lots of blinding, white light."

"Did you see anyone?" He rubbed my back. "Hear anything?"

"No sound. Just my breath. My heartbeat in my ears. But you were with me. Holding my hand. And then you let go of it and"—I paused, the strangulation in my throat, the race in my heart again—"and I was falling. That falling feeling you get in dreams."

Tears slid down my cheek onto his chest.

Don't tell him the rest. He'll think you're a lunatic.

No blame if he did. I feared I was.

"Aww, babe." He lifted my chin up to look at him. "It was just a bad dream. You're processing a lot after all this time. We're sharing a lot of new things this week." He smeared my tears away with his thumb. "Let's dry your eyes and just go back to cuddles and holding hands. Nothing else."

A half smile cocked his lips at his sweet joke. God, his beauty when he did that, only wanting to make me smile too.

It worked.

"You're funny," I replied softly, kissing his chest and lying back in my spot. "Do you ever have nightmares? About your brother?"

His muscles tensed under me at that question. "Yes. I do," he said. "It's always at hospital, of him in the bed. It terrified me seeing him go like that. It wasn't expected. It was sudden." He squeezed me even harder. "Sometimes it's not him though. But I'm still standing by a hospital bed. Devastated. Losing someone I love."

I tightened my grip on him. "Why don't you talk about Flynn more?"

"I've spoken more about him to you in a couple of months than I have to anyone in decades."

Going from silence to sharing? I understood. It was the most terrifying leap of trust.

Nestled in his embrace with his arms tightened around me, I tried to shake the foreboding fear my nightmare roused. I couldn't. Because it was more than a nightmare. Or a memory.

It was my instinct again, rising like the day moon, hunting the world. Coming for me.

I lay there, accepting my truth.

If the end is coming for you, these moments with him are your consolation prize. Cherish them. They won't last. Nothing ever does.

We didn't go back to sleep. We just lay there in the silence and comfort of the other. Finally I arose, kissing his chest and asking, "Are you ready for an early breakfast and a lot of *hand-holding* today?"

It made me chuckle at the ridiculous thought. Abstaining from anything sexual with him? No. I'd share it all. His chest shook beneath me, laughing at the absurdity too.

SHIT. Later that day I checked my phone. I missed three texts from Juliette over the past two days while it was turned off.

One text, a quick request to chat. The second, a "Where the bloody hell are you?" The third, a panicked warning that a call to the police was next.

"I gotta call Juliette," I told Daniel while plopping down on a barstool at the kitchen island, going for a face chat so Juliette wouldn't think I'd been kidnapped.

I'd been an asshole friend not telling her about him yet. And Juliette stayed offline, hadn't seen the viral gym picture. Because if she had, she'd be blowing up my phone with more than texts.

Daniel nodded. He was busy, fussing with a shrimp curry for our lunch, trying to master our chef's cooking lesson from the night before.

Besides, he knew Juliette. They did a film together years before. I watched it last month, curious to see if my best friend had any chemistry with him. Juliette and Daniel never hooked up off-screen, I knew. But their on-screen chemistry gushed.

Juliette starred as a quirky teenager living in her diary fantasies of a hot boy at school, all while ignoring the best guy friend who adored her. Daniel had played the fantasy boy, of course. I also found press photos of the two of them at various events in London over the years, chatting, smiling friendly with champagne flutes in their hands.

Honestly, I feared what my best friend would think.

Yes, Juliette had been telling me to give up my lonely, safe world for at least a date. What would Juliette say when she found out I slammed down the damn gas pedal—racing from her suggested coffee with a nice, local guy to a week of erotic sex with one of the most famous men in the world?

"Your randy cunt made you lose your fucking mind." I could hear her now.

I tapped Juliette's cute face on my phone, launching the call.

"Bloody hell, there you are." Juliette appeared on the screen with panic etched across her brow melting into a smile of relief. "Dodgy bitch, you scared me!"

"I know. I'm sorry. I'm fine, chica." I leaned on the countertop with my phone aimed at my guilty face and the sparkling pool behind me. "I just now checked my phone."

"I don't know where you are and that's not the deal between us. Girl code, my love."

We always told each other where we were going if it was out of the norm.

"My bad. Is everything okay? You said it's important."

Juliette explained how she had her schedule now for the mini-series, *Dark Shores*. She'd be filming at the studios near London from November until next spring.

"It's a great role and important story," Juliette said. "But it's going to be pretty raw for me. I wanted to see if you could be with me. If you're not on *The Druid* next season."

My eyes darted up at Daniel, checking his wide tapered back poised in front of the cooktop. By the angle of his neck, he was listening to our every word.

Quick calculations shot through my mind.

I replied, "You know I want to be there for you." Torn in two, I wanted to protect my best friend, but I had to stay on *The Druid* to protect Kierra from her stalker. The fucker was sly. If it meant staying on through season three to protect Kierra, I would.

But it wasn't like me to abandon someone. I had two now—a girl and woman—who needed my protection.

"I'll do what I can," I said. "I'll ask Jeremy and see if we can figure out a time frame. I'll try to make it work."

"Oh, sweetie, please don't stress it. We'll get it sorted, and I love you no matter what..."

Right as that last word left Juliette's mouth, a loud *clang* and curse stormed the background.

"Fuck!" Daniel exclaimed, dropping the hot pot lid for the rice on the floor. He grabbed it without a mitt.

"Who's that?" Juliette shot right up on her sofa. "I just heard a man."

I glanced up over my phone at him... and smiled.

"Oh! My! God!" Juliette's voice rose three octaves. "Charlie! Who is it?"

I beckoned him over with a side nod. Daniel shook his burning hand, grinning in agreement.

I smiled back at Juliette on the screen, not needing to say much. A live video would say it all.

Hold on to your knickers, Juliette.

"He whisked me away to the Seychelles." I held my phone farther away for a wide shot. Daniel came in for a kiss, blocking the camera first with his black waves and naked, shredded torso. Then... he turned, facing the screen in a dramatic reveal.

It shocked a scream from Juliette.

We laughed, kissing again while Juliette hit her sofa with her fists, repeating, "Bloody hell!" over and over. Her head started shaking no, furrowing her brow. "Oh my God, you two!"

I watched it all cross my best friend's face, a hundred correct assumptions in seconds, then a sudden flash of warning in Juliette's eyes. Why?

"I'm taking good care of her, Jules, I promise," Daniel

said before pressing his lips to my hair still drying from our morning swim.

"Too bloody right, you'll take care of my girl, Daniel Pierce." Juliette cocked her head, warning with serious eyes contradicted by her famous, full-lipped smile. "How are you two avoiding the paps and people snapping pics?"

I explained how we had the island to ourselves. All three of us knew the game and how to hide.

"Try not to come back with any scratches or love bites on you, Daniel," Juliette said. "Makeup wouldn't appreciate that."

"Only in the places he loves, and they never see," I quipped, peering up at him and his guilty grin. It was already true.

"Oh, you two! Go have a blinding fuck. And call me soon, hun. Love you. Cheers." Juliette hung up.

We dutifully followed her instructions right there on the kitchen island.

LATER, our depleted bodies rested after an afternoon kayak race, lying on the beach blanket underneath the shade of the palms rustling above. He wrapped his arm over me, lacing his fingers with mine.

I closed my eyes, wanting to relax into his warmth, wanting to surrender to the tranquility. But the look on Juliette's face—delight and fear—it wouldn't let me.

I knew exactly what Juliette was thinking, cheering me on for one howling orgasm after another and worried I'd pay a painful price for each one.

What did my best friend know that I didn't?

Once his body lay heavy with slumber, I slipped out

from under its weight. My steps headed back for the kitchen and my phone.

Juliette answered the video call with wine in hand. "You should be fucking right now and not phoning me."

"Please tell me," I said. "Tell me what you know but don't want to."

Juliette sighed, setting her glass down on her coffee table. "Are you happy, sweetie?"

"For now, very. But I need to know, Jules. I saw it on your face."

"Charlie, I just want you to be happy. Not hurt. Not anymore." She shook her fingers through her tawny tresses. "And it's rubbish, really. Just beastly gossip and that's all it is."

"Then please tell me what you know." I kept glancing up to the windows in case Daniel appeared, looking for me.

"What I know is that Daniel has been nothing but the warmest gent since I met him ages ago. He met my brother when we were filming, always asks after him years later."

That sounded like the Daniel I knew. Juliette's brother had Downs Syndrome. With what I knew about Flynn now, Daniel's twin, it touched me that he always asked after him.

"Still," I said, "there's a 'but' in your voice a thousand miles wide."

"*But* I've heard things over the years. It's been a while now, but how he can be on set. With other women. The young ones."

"How young?"

"Not *that* young. Not illegal. Just, you know, with all the hot, lady-candy on set. How he would go after all of it. And get it."

I felt sick. Suddenly so fucking sick. Juliette must have seen it wince my face.

"Charlie, listen to me. It's rumours. That's sod all. You heard the ones about me. That Seamus and I were fucking. Never. That I'm secretly a lesbian. Nope, I'm bi and proud. Or the one that had me in a threesome with our Alistair. I fucking wish. They're all just rumours. Not true."

"Have you ever seen anything, Jules?"

"What I have seen is Daniel is one of the nicest blokes I know. Yes, he dates around. Yes, he fucked around with women on set. You can't be that fucking gorgeous and not. But no one I trust has ever said a bad thing about him."

"I don't know how to do this." Tears sprang up over my lashes. "I don't know how to date or just be with someone casually. Not after everything. I thought I could spend just one week with him. But I can't. I'm falling for him. But all I know is married or alone. And I can't be either with him."

"Oh, love." Juliette started crying too. "That's what you saw on my face. I'm not worried about Daniel hurting you. I'm worried about you hurting yourself. I thought we talked about small steps. Of just getting you in a bikini. I didn't know you were ready to jump naked out of a plane and land on Daniel Pierce's gorgeous, famous, hard cock."

That made me laugh through tears at my friend's wisdom. "Well," I said, wiping them away with relief, "it is a beautiful cock to land on. It almost makes waiting six years worth it."

"I bet. Just be careful. Not with him. With you. With your heart." She picked up her glass, adding before she took a sip, "I can tell you this. I've known that man for many years. I never saw the look in his eyes with some random date that he had for you on a bloody video chat. He's gobsmacked, so you two just need to go slow. That's all."

I glanced back up. Speak of the beautiful devil. He was walking up from the beach, flopping his tendril back and looking for me. "You have no idea how slow I've been going since I met him."

"Well, you two could be smashing together. Just don't get caught with him. You'll get sacked." She shook her head, not joking. "And if you debut as his girlfriend to the world, forget it. Game over. You won't recognize your life anymore."

That was it. What I really feared. Ex-girlfriends or fucking around on set? I didn't really care about.

It was losing my life to the limelight of Daniel Pierce's.

DANIEL

I FELT LIKE A KID AGAIN. A happy one.

Trailing Charlie. Teasing her with kisses and pinches on the bum, we explored every beach and trail on the island. With our neoprene booties on, nothing was off limits. She had me crawling over rocks, finding small pools of urchins. I had her marveling at the flowers while we hiked up the large granite outcrop that rose like a four-story tower at the center of the island.

We stood astonished once we reached the summit cleared for guests to enjoy, nothing but neon aqua speckled with cerulean all around. I offered her our water bottle first while I closed my eyes at the gentle breeze rewarding our climb.

"Take a picture with me," I said, holding my camera up with my arm around her, kissing her with blue heaven behind us.

After I snapped several pics, she said, "Those can never go on your Instagram." Pulling back from my lips, her face grew serious. "I don't want to deal with what your fifty-two million fans think about us together."

I turned and kissed her again, lowering my phone. "You're too special to me, Charlie. For the first time in my life, I don't want us public. I want to protect this. What we have together. I don't want to share you, or us, with anyone." A lock of her hair fell over her face. I tucked it behind her ear. "I wish we could just stay here."

I put my phone down on the boulder before swimming my fingertips down the sweaty small of her back. I couldn't get enough of her today. She seemed the same. Once in bed early that morning. Another time in the pool after a late breakfast. And again, right here, with her legs wrapped around me.

This ended tomorrow, and we didn't want to let go.

We cooled off with a naked swim in the pool at our villa before enjoying a late lunch on our favorite sofa in the shade.

She rested on my chest; her eyelids heavy with exhaustion.

My fingertips played with her damp strands, lulling her to sleep while I stared at the beach and ocean beyond.

Time was slipping behind the horizon.

I only had a few hours left with her, fleeting moments with the certainty of her body beside mine. A night without her filled me with dread. I didn't want to ever wake up without her in my arms, or just a few steps away, with the promise of her smile.

All this time, my life had been a toxic void of meaning. No purpose. No direction. Just me stumbling from one ego boost and massive paycheck to another. All that praise and pounds, and nothing had filled me.

Until her.

Her body relaxed next to mine. Her palm rested on my chest, her other hand tucked underneath her, touching my side. Her tan leg draped over mine. I gazed down at her cheek. It rested in the valley carved between my shoulder and pec. Her eyelashes fluttered underneath serene eyebrows while her soft breaths moved across my heart.

I wanted to wake her, for her to know. To promise words I said before but only now felt the meaning of. I grieved because I couldn't. We had time together, but not a life.

Her words said otherwise, but I saw the truth in flashes she tried to hide.

We had joined again and again this week, connecting every part of us, erasing every boundary separating us. I knew she felt it too, from the moment we met to every first we shared. Her lips would never confess it, but her body did, her stunning smile or crying eyes did.

Still, too much lived between us, layer upon layer of rules, secrets, memories, pain, and fear. I could change for her, and it wouldn't be enough. I would only find myself with nothing left but my love for her... and her fear of loving me back.

Saline trickled over my lips as I held her tight. I knew... and didn't care.

You will make this happen one day, Pierce. No matter what.

I was hers.

And she would be mine.

CHAPTER FORTY

CHARLIE

Holding a razor to his throat, I slowly dragged it down over the thick stubble.

"I'm trusting you so much right now," Daniel said.

"I really don't want to do this. You look so damn hot in this almost beard."

Nine days' worth of whiskers on his face from hiatus was turning into a sexy new look for him. One I loved the tickle of between my thighs.

"It's got to come off today, babe. I'm on set in two hours and I'd rather you do it than hair and make-up." He snuck a shaving cream kiss to my lips. "And lucky for me, I shoot nothing shirtless this week or I will be raising eyebrows to the delicious scratches you put down my back."

"Yeah, sorry about that. But you begged me to do it."

We did get carried away our last time on the island—a

hard and hot fuck on the bathroom counter before the staff came to pick up our bags for the trip back home.

"I love it when you do it," he said. "You just have to keep it to my arse though." The look in his eyes tempted me to meet his request now. "And we still have more toys and outfits to enjoy. We never did get to play with them all."

My grinning lips covered in foam asked, "Are you complaining?"

"Not at all. I wanted you naked and on my hard cock all week. We can add more accessories to our sex this week." He pecked my cheek, leaving a dollop of shaving cream behind. "And the next." Another white slathered kiss to my other cheek. "And the next." And on my nose. My smiling face was covered now.

A sudden *ring* hit the air. I recognized its unique tone.

Kierra.

"I gotta get that." I pushed him back, jumping off the bathroom counter and dashing toward my phone on the nightstand.

It was early Monday morning. Four a.m. First day back from hiatus and Kierra's call time was in two hours. Other than Daniel's shaving cream on my face, I stood ready for work.

"Hey chica," I answered the distinct tone.

"Charlie, it's Anne."

My stomach dropped for the fact Kierra's mom was calling on Kierra's phone *and* the immediate tone of "oh shit" in her voice.

"We got a package," Anne continued. "The guard at the gate dropped it off. It was delivered while we were away, addressed to Kierra, but I knew to open it. Her blue scarf that was stolen and some pictures were inside."

"Pictures of what?" I whispered, heading down Daniel's hallway into his guest bedroom so as not to be overheard.

"They're pictures of Kierra. Here at the house. Taken from outside of her bedroom window."

"Call the detectives now. I'm on my way."

I raced back into Daniel's bedroom, wiping the foam off my face, smearing the residue off on my tactical pants. I didn't give a shit. I had to get to Kierra. Grabbing my bag off Daniel's desk, I raised my hand goodbye to him standing naked, surprised by my whirlwind departure.

The stalker took the photos two weeks ago. I examined them closely as they sat on the kitchen table at Kierra's house before the detectives took them away as evidence. I remembered the exact day they were taken. Brigid, Kierra's character, had had a ritual scene that day. Her hair was intricately braided. Kierra wore it home still adorned, loving the look and taking selfies for her boyfriend.

The time was late dusk—dark enough to see inside but not prompting Kierra to close her blinds yet. The pictures didn't catch anything compromising. That didn't matter.

He lurked. Outside her home. Watching her.

I checked the postmark. He mailed it from here in Madrid on the same morning they shot the assault scene of Kierra's character.

The pictures were taken the evening before because I remembered that too. It found me alone in bed, full of dread for Kierra and that coming scene, plunging me into an onslaught of screaming nightmares.

No note accompanied the package. The timing said it all—the day of the assault scene. The violent message was clear.

The detectives collected the scarf as evidence too. Secretly, I hoped for disgusting physical evidence from the stalker, semen found soaked into the fibers of the blue cloth. Maybe we'd finally have a DNA sample. But still—nothing to match it with. No samples were found on the panties left before hiatus. The box was taken in as evidence too.

Yet again, I already feared it, making me sick... there would be no trace of him.

The detectives found the main power line to the security system of Kierra's house cut. Like he knew about security and cameras such that none captured his presence. No one had any idea how he got into the supposedly secure community.

Though fear and frustration screamed through my nerves, I kept my face stoic, wrapping up the report given to the detectives then calling Jeremy, Rob, and Joaquin with the update.

Anne and I waited for Kierra to come downstairs. Kierra knew about the package. We had told her as soon as I arrived. Kierra had said nothing, just resumed brushing her teeth, gaze frozen to the mirror.

Her lack of response disturbed me. Kierra was too young to be numb to this. Too innocent to be used to this. Too much at risk not to register the danger.

When Kierra appeared in the kitchen just after the detectives left, her face matched the emotionless one I held on mine.

"I'm ready," Kierra said.

"I don't want you going to set today," her mom replied.

"Mam, we talked about this. I'm not giving in. No matter what." Kierra tightened the scrunchie holding her hair back in a ponytail. "It's like what Charlie said to me the other week. 'Always fight back. Never give in.'"

I cringed.

Yes, I said that to Kierra while I taught her tricks. How

to snap free from zip ties. How to punch a dick or a throat. I tried to embolden the girl, to take her from scared to angry. Because angry kept you safe and alive.

But I didn't mean for my lessons and fighting words to be used in defiance of Kierra's mom.

Anne pursed her lips, looking at me, not angry, just auditing the situation. "Charlie, what do you advise now?"

"It's up to you and Kierra. Nothing will happen to her when I'm here. And we'll have extra detail on the house now, even when she's not here. Twenty-four hours a day."

"See, Mam. It's fine. If Charlie and the team are here, we're fine." Kierra yanked the zipper on her floral bag closed.

I clocked it. Kierra's hand shook. Fear *did* find her.

"Kierra," I said. "No one can be more stubborn than me. I get it. But you can be stubborn *and* scared. And leave anytime you want."

It twisted Kierra's angelic face. She was fighting back tears. "No. I won't leave." The shake of her head grew passionate, enraged. "I won't give in to him."

I didn't know if I was staring down a willful teenager or a strong, young woman. I reached my arms around Kierra, hugging both. "Okay then. Let's go to work."

The girl in my arms filled me with tragic pride and regret. Hating that Kierra had been robbed of the innocence of safety. Certain though—with Kierra's beauty and fame— it was better this way. She may spend her whole life with someone targeting her.

I lived that reality too.

CHAPTER FORTY-ONE

CHARLIE

Sunday found me at Anders's estate. After a long week on set, with Kierra resolved not to let the threats get to her, or to at least *act* like they didn't, I tried to finally relax too.

And these were my closest friends and colleagues. We had shared so much and now we shared my secret—the one about me and Daniel. It felt safe, good to have my friends' support and smiles. But that's as far as this secret could ever go.

"I wanna know how many times." A coy grin lay on Rob's face along with his body on the lounger next to me. "By my count it should be at least twenty-one, but by the way you're walking like you rode a stallion across Europe, I'm guessing it's more like forty."

The hot spring day had me reclining beside him and Maja, watching the kids splash in the pool, trying not to blush at the questions about my holiday with Daniel.

But they started an X-rated Spanish Inquisition that had us all amused.

Maja raised her curious eyebrow. "I want to know if he really *is* a sex god."

Daniel stood in the pool, throwing Erikson up in the air to his squeals of delight.

Rob said, "I wanna know how many times he made you yell 'God!'"

I adored Daniel from behind my sunglasses, swearing, "You two are so fucking bad."

Rob wouldn't relent. "No, bitch, the only 'fucking bad' around here is all the kinky ass shit you two did, and that you will now divulge to us. You promised me tea and fuckin' details, remember?"

"Are those scratches I see across his back?" Maja asked with a tone about to laugh.

"Sure are," Rob confirmed. "They match the fading hickies on the inside of Charlie's thighs."

That made me laugh, quickly crossing my bare legs, making Daniel smile as he glanced across the pool to where the three of us sat. He threw Erikson to Joaquin and swam to the edge near our chairs.

Jumping out of the pool like a wet lynx, he asked, "Should my ears be burning?"

Rob lowered his sunglasses. "Daniel, I hope it's only your ears burning and not your crotch after all that hot fuckin' you and Charlie did on hiatus."

Daniel shook his head with a guilty laugh, giving Rob a wink at his wisdom.

Then he sprang in surprise, grabbing me up and throwing me over his shoulder, his wet hands giving my ass a smack that shocked a squeal of delight from my lips.

"Come on Sex Goddess," he said, "let's put these flames out," plunging us into the pool.

Later, Rob and I taught Erikson how to dive into the deep end. I treaded water, spotting Erikson while Rob coached him from the edge. Peeking back over my shoulder, I took in the adorable scene.

Joaquin sat with Daniel on a pair of loungers. Little Linnea sat on Daniel's chest, delighting in their new game. She would put her pudgy palm over Daniel's mouth and he would blow raspberries back, tickling her hand with the funny noise, making her chortle a deep belly laugh that made the men laugh just as hard.

Maja and Anders lay back on their loungers by the patio doors, clearly enjoying the sight of their children and friends, and the break they got from being human jungle gyms on a daily basis.

After a while, Linnea lay down to rest on Daniel's chest, sucking her index finger. He cradled her head there, talking to Joaquin about Real Madrid football.

I watched Maja get up, walk over to Daniel, noting her daughter's light drool over his chest.

You drool over his pecs too, Charlie Girl.

Maja said, "I think Zeus has charmed another one of my children. Do you want me to take her?"

His massive palm touched the downy brown curls on her head. "Aww, this is the bee's knees. I'm fine."

Maja shrugged, handing him a baby blanket. He covered Linnea up just before Anders took the chance, scooping Maja up and leaping them into the pool.

I asked Joaquin to take my spot as a diving coach. Jumping out of the water, I dried off, walking over to Daniel.

"Looks like I've been replaced," I said, plopping down

beside him, thinking he looked transcendently sexy, bare chested in the sun with a little girl asleep in his arms.

"Can you blame a bloke?" He grinned, holding the toddler tight, but stretching his face toward mine, seeking a kiss.

I leaned in, letting him take one from my lips. And another. And then another kiss so craving from his mouth it stammered my breath.

Anders laughed from the shallow end. "Hey you two, keep that up, and you're going to have one of your own."

I met Daniel's gaze. It captured me, the yearning in his eyes. It was warming... and terrifying. Then he turned, asking Maja, "Should we put her to bed for you?"

"That would be nice," Maja said with Anders still wrapped around her.

Anders added, "Take care of that little human bumble bee too, so I can take my wife up to our bed." Maja swatted in pretend protest at his suggestion.

"It's your house, mate. Feel free," Daniel said. "It looks like the guys have the bumble boy covered."

All this... while I sat frozen, hearing their banter from a million miles away. Fear sharked in circles of dark water around me, swirling terror through my soul, the current, pulling in the wrong direction, away from my safe shore.

Daniel's hand patted my knee, pulling me back. "Want to help me?" He stood up with Linnea asleep in his arms.

"Sure." A smile failed me.

I followed Daniel up the stairs, cradling a child in his arms this time. Though we climbed the curving steps, I kept falling into depths of fear.

Daniel and a baby. And the certain wish in his eyes aimed right at me, telling me it's what he wanted.

Why does something so beautiful feel so terrifying?

Why? Because you don't trust a future with anyone. Because everything you ever cherished got taken... and buried.

He helped me peel Linnea's bathing suit off, throwing her wet swim diaper in the bin while I dried her. Linnea protested with a whimper, not wanting to wake. I calmed us both with a soft, "Shhhhh," stroking the back of my fingertips over her curls. Daniel handed me a fresh diaper and a pair of cow print pajamas from the dresser.

Feel this is heaven, Charlie Girl? Bliss. Feel your heart pounding? Panic.

I dressed Linnea while Daniel turned on the night light and turned off the lamp. The warmth of his body stood beside me while I kept soothing Linnea until she fell back to sleep.

Daniel turned, putting his hand to my scarred cheek, whispering, "I'd like to do this the right way this time." Drawing his lips closer. "Ms. Ravenel, may I please kiss you?" He waited inches from my answer, melting my fear away.

"Yes, Mr. Pierce. You may."

God, everything's so right about him. It must be wrong.

He kissed me softly first, then with a growing passion. Linnea stirred and I grinned, lifting my lips from his.

"This is how it happens, Pierce," I said with a warning nod over to the baby girl in the crib. Pulling him out of the nursery, I quietly closed the door behind us.

Daniel's next kiss took me so fast, pushing me gently against the wall, urging hard against my body and reaching for my heart, for my future. Stopping for breath, his eyes fixed hard on mine while his rich voice proposed, "I know what happens next, Charlie."

The first time he tried kissing me, a few feet away from

where we stood, the same terror hit me. And he saw it. The fear I couldn't hide.

"Don't worry," he said. "We're protected." His lips skated up my neck before whispering in my ear, "But I sure do crave breaking down your defenses. You can't fight me. Remember?"

I TRIED. That night. Lying on his bed. Not to fight it.

He stood at the edge, pulling me to him, resting my feet against his shoulders, hugging the backs of my thighs close to his chest. Our sighs matched his wet dive into me, grinding slow circles into my depths.

It threw my head back at the most tender spot he discovered inside. Using the strength of my hamstrings, I lifted myself up higher on him for more, the intensity taking us. He kept gasping at the new descending angle while I moved in a coaxing spiral, enveloping all of him.

"Oh God, Charlie." It was in his voice. In his aqua eyes. In his panting at the sensitivity of his cock, buried and swirling against my swollen walls. In how he leaned over me while I braced my strong legs back against him. In how he couldn't be any deeper inside of me as I rose up to him, again and again, securing our pleasure.

The way he gazed down at me; he wasn't fighting it. The way he shuddered, speechless with breaths of primal satisfaction climaxing inside me, it was like he was letting go of something, never wanting to reclaim it again.

I wanted to join him there.

In the soaking pleasure, I did. In the sweet surrender, I couldn't.

CHAPTER FORTY-TWO

CHARLIE

My eyes slid open before dawn. His warmth wrapped around me, so close his chest hairs tickled my back. I lay in the darkness, caressing his hand. He slept peacefully while I cried at the whirlpool of thoughts that had shaken me awake.

You fucked up. Big time.

You saw his eyes when he held Linnea, peering into yours, speaking a thousand hopes and dreams.

You hear it almost tumble from his mouth every time he lies spent inside you.

You sobbed, vulnerable in his arms, letting him in the first time. So many times.

And now the only moments you're free from fear is when his body is connected to yours.

You're not in control. You've fallen.

This wasn't only attraction, or a week of desire fulfilled or something in between. This was so much more.

You must decide. Decide before the decision is made for you.

I could be a fool.

Forgetting every warning I sensed for our future, I could settle into this present peace. Enjoy the laughter at our play every day and the pleasure that consumed us every night. I could rest in his arms, talking with him about everything and nothing. Letting him sweep me off my feet, adoring me until my last breath.

No matter how soon that may be.

And so, my life would intertwine with his. So much so that mine would disappear.

Daniel Pierce's world owned anyone in it. From the homes he bought his family. To the cherished team he employed. To the frenzied pace of his celebrity life that possessed millions of people's hearts and the press to hunt him.

A life with him would force me to forsake everything— my privacy, my home, my career... my safety.

I hid so that no one could pursue me. No one could ever find me.

How long could *we* hide? While we were colleagues, yes. But after that? If I took Daniel's public hand, standing beside him in the spotlight, it was like Juliette said, I wouldn't recognize my world anymore.

I'd lose my life to live in his.

Or... I could be smart.

Leave and never look back. Save myself from annihilation like before, crawling back through the pain, time and again to find myself. Back to who I was without anyone. I loved that woman. I didn't define myself by anyone else. I never could. I could walk my beach every morning, alone, safe, and never get hurt again.

You were naive to think you could control this. No one can. You will have to be together forever, or you will have to leave him behind.

Biting my bottom lip, I tried replacing tears with blood, one pain for another, knowing...

I couldn't live in either world.

He stirred behind me. His arm lifted off me, turning over. The glow of his phone lit up the room as he checked the time. Slowly he got up, tucking the covers back over me. Through half-closed eyes, I watched his silhouette move through the darkness into the closet.

My tears fell for him now.

I couldn't change my past, and he wouldn't change his future.

He jotted a note for me on the desk in his room while I watched. Watched how he was both powerful and tender. Which seduced me more? How he cared for my wounds and worshipped my strength? Or how he shared his own with me too?

Peering down at me in the darkness, he set the note on the nightstand. Bending over for a kiss, I feared he'd find my cheeks wet. His lips grazed my hair instead.

He walked out, gently closing the door behind him and quiet sobs racked me. Burying my face in his pillow, I inhaled his smell.

How did you let it get this far? So far, that either way, you're going to hurt him. You're going to rip the last beautiful part of him away. His heart.

Every fiber in me wanted to protect him from every punch of pain. Even the one I was destined to deliver. And every thought in my head promised...

If you sacrifice yourself for him, you'll be the one hurt. You're a conflicted, fucked-up, selfish mess, Charlie Girl.

With one certain truth.

I'd take a bullet for any girl or woman, but I wouldn't give my life away for the love of a man.

You were always meant to be alone.

The sound of his car's tires crunched out of the pebbled drive. I made the bed before grabbing my jeans, panties, and tank top from the floor. In his bathroom, I got dressed. He'd left his T-shirt and sweatpant shorts folded for me on the bench by the shower, the ones from the day I collapsed. He insisted I keep them. I stuffed them in my duffel before cramming my toiletry bag in on top and zipping it closed.

Before I left, I picked up the note he'd written.

Over and over again, Charlie. I won't fight it.
I'm yours. 24/7/365
D

Carefully, I folded it and slid it into my back pocket... and left.

DANIEL

I LOOKED for Charlie on set, but she didn't come. Kierra was shooting in a different stage building. No doubt that's where Charlie was and belonged. It was okay. I'd see her at home. We all wrapped around six.

Simon drove while I occupied myself gazing at the photos I'd taken of Charlie on holiday, then going through other ones I'd taken recently, deleting the ones I didn't want to archive.

My front door swung open to a dark house. I called out

for her. Silence. I walked into the kitchen, flipping the lights on, then checking the garage. No white Tic Tac car. Plucking my phone from my back pocket, I texted her.

I'm home babe
Where are you

I waited for her reply, taking dinner out of the fridge, heating some up for her too. Maybe she was delayed with Rob or running an errand. Her chime rang through the air, lifting my spirits until I read the sting of her reply.

I'm home. Need to do
laundry and get sleep

I tried shaking off my disappointment and ate dinner alone, watching episodes of an architecture show until my eyes grew heavy. I smiled, walking past our bed. Charlie made it every day, something I hadn't done since I'd left home. Part of her military training, she joked. I tried forcing myself into a good mood, until the shower bathed me in eerie emptiness.

Her clothes were gone. The top of the bathroom vanity was clear of her things.

My phone sat on the nightstand, tempting me to text her, or call her. Is something wrong? But I didn't want to be that kind of man again. I respected her boundaries. She had stayed over every night since we came home from holiday.

This was only one night without her.

I crawled in bed alone, hugging the pillow. The aroma of her perfume on the white cotton pillowcase calmed me to sleep.

The next day I didn't see her either. No texts or calls. I

shot with Anders and the horses all day. The banter between Anders and Lance was a mild distraction from her void until I arrived again to an empty home.

For months I lived here by myself and I was fine. Now? Only a couple of days without her—everything felt wrong. I had to know.

Charlie, where are you?

Are you okay?

Are we okay?

I wandered into the kitchen out of habit, finding no appetite. Snatching my keys from the countertop, I jumped in the Volvo on a mission.

When I got to her house, her car wasn't parked outside. Lights were on inside her villa, but she had them on timers for safety. She'd told me I should do the same.

I watched for movement in her front window.

Nothing.

Fuck this. I whipped the wheel around in a quick turn, gunning for Rob's place. Or maybe she was with Maja. But why hadn't she texted back by now?

Fear consumed me. I yanked the wheel over to the curb. Texting her:

Let me know you're okay.

I'm about to knock on every door

until I find you

I tried controlling my breath. Like she'd taught me. That thought of her, that memory, it caught in my throat and clenched my jaw.

The phone lit up in my hand.

I'm okay. At Rob's.

A stuttered sigh dissolved my fear, only to be replaced with a sick disquiet. I tried admonishing it away.

Calm down, Pierce. Don't be a nutter. You'll frighten her away, if you haven't already.

Can I cook for you tomorrow?
You pick the song

I drove back home.

Swallowing down mindless bites of dinner, I waited, hoping two fingers of rye and a book would distract me. The glass emptied over my lips, but I didn't read a single page. I poured another and sat back down, staring at the empty courtyard where we had danced. The drink finished in three gulps. And then another. And another.

Closing my eyes, I was desperate for her reply or to pass out drunk. Anything to stop this bloody feeling, the one of being abandoned. Like I felt when my twin died. I could never bear it. It brought out the worst in me.

Finally, the typewriter sound. I checked my phone.

Yes

A wave of relief exhaled from my heavy lungs. She'd be back tomorrow.

I stumbled going upstairs, stumbled into the shower, my skin buzzing with memories of our week. The urge in my body and the ache in my heart for her overwhelmed me.

Her absence was painful. Stroking my cock and thinking of her, like she stood here with me, a storm of desire and loneliness raged within.

My voice reverberated in the tile surround. "Please, Charlie."

CHAPTER FORTY-THREE

CHARLIE

How To Let You Go by Benson Taylor

I sat in my car, parked at the curb a block away from his estate, already a half hour late for the dinner he was cooking for me.

Was I breaking up with him or going home to him?

You can't do this, Charlie Girl.

Fuck you, it hurts either way.

I had tried two days without him. Staying focused on Kierra during the day, doing TikTok dances with her, keeping Kierra smiling and distracted. Then I rode my bike for two hours after work before occupying myself chatting with Juliette. Still, thoughts of him drifted through my mind.

I missed him.

That numb daze that kept me safe from emotions for so many years. I tried conjuring it back, turning it on like a light switch. No power.

Face it. This is gonna hurt like hell.

The night before when I saw his texts, frantic for me, I had choked back tears. And guilt. I had a plan. Hurting him like this wasn't it.

I heard his car creep up to my house. Mine was parked around the block so he wouldn't know I was home. I had watched him from the darkness of the window of my guest room, anguish twisting his beautiful face before he spun around, searching for me.

I searched too. For my truth.

What do you want?

Not the bright lights, the burning sun of his celebrity life. Not the dark, lonely moon of my haunted world either.

You want him, not his life.

You want to be safe, but not alone.

And I knew this...

He was hiding something. I sensed it the minute I laid eyes on him. Why wouldn't he just tell me? That hurt. How I had told him everything, all my pain and loss. I let him in, trusting him. So, why wouldn't he trust me too with his darkest secret?

Maybe he needs a chance. You got another one. Give him one too.

Maybe if I gave him time to tell me, or a reason to, he finally would. Circumstance had forced me to reveal my story. Somehow, I trusted, the same would happen for him.

With a "yes" to his dinner invitation, I decided to trust the one thing that had betrayed me so much—fate.

When my car pulled into his garage, his dark silhouette filled the open doorframe. My heart leapt, then tightened. We greeted each other with desperate lips that turned into him shuddering inside me with my legs wrapped around him on his bed. He cried out for me with more than pleasure, demanding I leave marks again on his backside. I clung to him with a drenching, aching ferocity. I couldn't fill the emptiness without him now.

He held me tight afterward. We lay in silence. I dove into my private fears, sensing he swam in his until he broke the spell.

"Can I spoil you with dinner now?"

"Yes," I murmured, trying to shake our tenuous mood with a kiss.

I sat at the kitchen island, watching him make Gazpacho. He refused my offer to help but filled me in on his travel plans.

"I'm off to London Friday for a preview show for Logan MacGregor," he said, slicing some rosemary bread to accompany our meal. "He's after me all the time now for events. Ever since *The Druid* started, he says he's been inspired. A proud Scot and all."

Daniel had been the fashion designer's menswear brand ambassador and model for years. I'd seen the numerous photoshoots and articles of Daniel in Logan's threads. The co-branding of fashion with film was gold for both men.

But this trip was news to me. "Aren't you shooting through Saturday?"

"Colleen sorted it with production. She'll travel with me Friday morning. We'll be back Saturday evening. I don't want to miss you or Erikson's birthday party Sunday. I sent Elaine out today for a present from us."

He walked around the island with bowls in hand, setting one down for me, then him. I sat silently. Not sure what to say with all the plans he made. We needed to slow down. We needed to be careful.

"I wish you'd go with me to Logan's party." He lifted my

chin up for a kiss. "I'd be so proud to walk a carpet with you."

His lips met mine while a shock of fear shot across my mind at his wish.

Everything about walking a red carpet with Daniel under the deluge of white light terrified me.

I tried covering, politely pulling away from our kiss and going for my first slurp from the spoon before declaring, "I'm sure our bosses would not be happy with the shitshow that would cause. We always have to be careful, Daniel. Everywhere we go. No one can know about us."

Lorraine had hired Jeremy, who'd hired me to protect Kierra. Walking a red carpet with Daniel Pierce, Kierra's co-star, was not in the cards.

And even if we weren't colleagues forbidden to date, Daniel's celebrity world would be hell, my hell—the biggest and maybe the last mistake of my life.

My eyes fell on the stack of folders on Daniel's counter-top, searching for something to change the subject. Something to shift this painful mood between us.

"Are those the design folders you mentioned?" I nodded toward the glossy booklets marked with sticky tabs in a pile on his kitchen island. We had lengthy talks on vacation about the renovations of our respective homes—mine on Daufuskie, his in Cornwall. We shared thrill and frustration with the process.

"Colleen told me she can't get you to make up your mind," I said. "Might be kind of nice to let her wrap this up for you. One final project completed before she retires."

Daniel's gaze considered the pile of architectural draw-ings on vellum paper, booklets, and folders he had procrasti-nated over for a year.

"Huh, I never thought of it that way," he said. "She was

with me when I bought the estate to renovate, and she's been on my case every day since to finish it. And that's why. One last thing for me before she retires." He delivered a soft peck to my cheek. "How'd you get so beautiful and smart?"

"It's called fucking common sense, beautiful man." I grinned, hovering my hand over the folders. "Speak now or forever hold your peace. You said on vacation you wanted my help with this, and I'm a hurricane. Once I'm on my path, watch out."

"A force of nature, indeed, Hurricane Charlie." He smiled at my hand suspended over his house plans. "Be my guest. I'd love to have my life completely wrecked by you."

He got up, pouring us another drink. I started asking him questions about what design style he liked, what he wanted to feel in a space.

"Aren't you just going to pick something out and say 'here'?" He walked back, glasses in hand, standing beside me with a grin. "Just help me pick between dark blue and even darker blue."

"No way, Pierce." I stood up too, taking our bowls to the sink. "If you want my touch in your home, you're going to have to work for it."

I came back to stand beside him. Opening all the folders and booklets to review, I asked about the light in the house. The water on the horizon. The landscape around the home. I filtered through all his choices until it lay before us.

He wrapped his arms around me while we regarded the palette of lush blues, dark teals, rich blacks with muted brass, velvets mixed with light, botanical textures, all surrounded by pure, warm white.

"I think you missed your calling, Ravenel." He admired our work, squeezing me tighter. "Thank you. Really. That's a huge weight off my shoulders, and Colleen will be thrilled to finally finish this." His lips aimed for my neck, asking, "When do I get to see your home and all your hard work?"

Daniel in your family home? On your island?

I closed my eyes at the thought... and saw the moon in the day sky.

Never.

His nose nuzzled my hair, not witnessing the dread in my eyes. "I don't think you'd enjoy slumming it in my neck of the woods, Daniel."

Turning me around, he kissed down to my collarbone, opening my robe with one flick of his hand, unwrapping his next as easily. "You're so wrong." Dropping to his knees, he swore, "I'll prove how much I love getting dirty with you."

He buried his mouth between my thighs. It was too strong, the desire his curling tongue and practiced fingers could conjure in me. Gaze locked on each other's, I held him there as tight as he devoured me. He undid me every time, ripping my fear away in a loud gush, letting me forget tomorrow for just one more night.

DANIEL

I DIDN'T GO to the gym the next morning, needing the time by her side instead. We lay awake, hearing Colleen come in downstairs, happy to know what she'd find waiting for her on the breakfast bar.

Charlie lingered on my chest while I rubbed lightly up and down her arm. I traced the exit wound on the back of her shoulder. "Does this ever give you trouble?"

"It can." Her fingers drifted over my pecs. "Reaching up

for things over my head can be difficult. But down, kayaking and paddling, that's easy. At home, I go out on the water every day the weather allows. I look out my bedroom window, and if there are no white caps, it's a day on the water for me."

I admired the distinct curve of her strong deltoid, remembering how we raced each other in kayaks on our holiday. I had power in my strokes, but she was light and fast.

"Is that where you're going after we wrap?" I asked. "Back home?"

We had a month and half left shooting. Production was scheduled to wrap just before Comic-Con in late July. The cast and executive producers would all go to the convention in San Diego, do the press circuit there, then disperse until the following February when pre-production for *The Druid* season three would resume in Spain.

I tried imagining my life after July. I couldn't. Not without her.

"Yeah. I go back to Daufuskie. I may be with Juliette in London this fall. I don't know what's after that."

Her words were neutral. Her voice was neutral. I waited for her to say something else, to offer hope for what could be next between us. Telling myself there was still time to work the future out with her.

Trailing my fingers over the hourglass of her waist, I memorized her contours. She did the same, tickling her fingertips down my trail, down my abs, down to what we both wanted.

I pulled her on top of me. To remember. How her nipples woke to my touch, to my sucking mouth. How her pussy glazed my cock, gliding up and down. How her beautiful eyes almost closed when she moaned with me, ready to come. How her lips trembled, crying out my name while her lust rained over me.

I let her take me. Every time. If only I could keep her, always.

We were due on set, so we showered together. We shared the bathroom mirror while I brushed my teeth, and she brushed her hair.

"Late dinner tonight?" I tried to sound relaxed, to sound confident in her answer. I wasn't.

She looked back at my reflection in the mirror, and I felt my heart as naked as my body. I froze and saw it in her eyes. The way she blinked and paused.

She faked a smile for me. "It's a crazy couple of days. Let's do dinner when you get back from London."

The weight on my chest lightened when she promised hope. I turned toward her, standing beside me at the vanity. "It's a date." I pressed my minty lips to hers.

"You're going to be so late, Pierce." She gave me a swat on my bare ass. "And so am I."

I wouldn't press her for more. I didn't want to scare her away. Dressing in boxer briefs, jeans and a navy knit shirt, I confirmed, "All right, babe. See you in a few days, yes?"

Walking toward the door, I looked back one more time. She sat, perched on the edge of the tub, lacing up her boots. She replied, "Yeah," without glancing up at me.

My bag landed with a thud in the waiting car. I caught the look of surprise from Simon at my tardiness. But guilt about that didn't burden me.

All I could feel was a surge of hope. And fear.

Charlie was pulling away from me, slowing us down. Why?

My heart had hope. I was doing everything to keep her. Sharing everything with her.

Except that one thing. Your secret. Your guilt.

I feared I wore it like my own gashing scar across my heart.

Maybe that's what happened. She could see it. She saw everything else about me. Did she know my crime too?

But how could she? She never opened my leather wash bag. As soon as we returned from holiday, I hid the damning evidence in an old pair of boots in my closet.

Maybe she had already snooped? Maybe she did find it? Maybe she already knew and maybe, with no words spoken about it, she already forgave me. Forgave me for my compulsions. For my shame.

Either way, it didn't matter.

I'd drown before letting her go.

CHAPTER FORTY-FOUR

CHARLIE

A Tibetan chime filled the air. I stretched, waking my muscles and mind. Staring at the ceiling, I planned my day—meditation, a bike class, a trip to the bakery for some rosquillas for Erikson's party tomorrow.

I smiled. And Daniel would be back today.

His flight from London had him home around five.

I know we left things precariously, even with plans for dinner. My inhale thinned at the powerful question between us. I promised myself I'd confront it tonight.

It's time for a long talk and the truth.

I reached for my phone and saw three texts from Juliette. One from Maja. One from Rob. All to call them. ASAP.

"What the fuck?" My back shocked straight up, throwing my feet to the floor. Hands trembling over the screen, I called Juliette back while my toes automatically aimed toward the kitchen.

Please God, please God, let everyone be okay. Please not another person ripped from your world.

Juliette answered quickly. "Charlie!"

"What's wrong?"

"He was drunk, Charlie. I was there, and I mean he was plastered."

"Who?" A fast second. "Daniel?"

"Yes, Daniel. At Logan's preview party. I—"

"Is he okay?" God, was he hurt? Or worse?

"He's fine. Should be fine. Just check your laptop, hun. Just search it, please. You'll see."

I opened my laptop on the counter. Putting my phone on speaker, I set it down. Hands shaking, afraid to type, afraid to know; my fingertips struck the keys anyway. "Daniel Pierce Logan Preview Party London." With one tap of the cursor, I clicked "Images."

A gasp dropped my heart. It shattered against the shock. "Jules,"—I could barely breathe, hot tears forming over my lashes—"who is she?"

Who was the sexy, tall, auburn-haired woman on his arm? On his lips last night?

Juliette said, "I asked around. Her name is 'Kathy Fields.' She's the account director for Logan's brand. She works for the same P.R. firm that reps Daniel. Someone said she and Daniel have been together for two years now."

A tsunami of pain washed away my voice.

"Charlie? Love, are you okay? That fucking, lying twat. Did he not tell you about her? About his girlfriend?"

"I never asked," was my stunned reply.

"I don't know what to make of it. I saw them on the carpet ahead of me. Then when I went into the hall, she was whispering in his ear and he was shaking his head. I couldn't tell if they were in love or in a row over something.

I watched him leave later with another woman, older, with her arm on his elbow. He was stumbling blotto, eyes bleeding red. I texted you several times but—"

"I went to bed early." I'd taken an evening walk to clear my head. After a shower, I silenced my phone and went to bed, excited to see Daniel the next day. Today.

"Oh, sweetie. I'm so sorry. I wish I could be there with you. I'd jump on the next flight if I could, but I'm fucking stuck shooting here in Nice for the next five days."

"I'll live. Thanks for telling me." I wiped the wet pain off my face. Time to rebuild all my walls. Time to rearrange my life yet again after devastation. "I need to think, Jules. Can I call you later?"

"Yes, of course. Call me whenever. I love you."

"Love you too. Bye."

At least my world was certain now. I knew what I wanted.

Throwing on shorts and a sports bra, yanking on my socks, and running shoes, tears fell as I flew out the door.

I wanted to be alone. Again. Always.

DANIEL

I PARKED my bike by Anders's garage Sunday afternoon, my head pounding along with my heart. I pulled off my helmet and looked around. Her car was parked on the circular drive.

Talk to her, Pierce. Fucking fix this.

I already tried calling and texting her a manic number of times the day before. I woke up, hungover in my London townhouse. After I got my head out of the toilet that morning, I saw the text from Colleen.

Ring me first thing

A text from Kathy glowed underneath.

You owe me the truth

I had struggled getting my memory to catch up to my phone. Bits of Friday night clicked through my mind like screenshots of a drunken car crash.

Click. I arrived in London. Colleen went to a late lunch with a friend. I went to Logan's house for pre-show drinks. Way too many drinks.

Click. The state I was in when I got to Logan's. In two days, I had only two texts from Charlie. Their tone left me panicked, broken.

Click. A bottle of Bombo 40, my favorite rum from Cornwall was on Logan's bar cart. Pouring into a crystal tumbler, I didn't stop until I felt better.

Click. Until I felt nothing. Remembered naught.

Oh fuck. You cocked up. Majorly.

I had phoned Colleen.

She answered quickly. "You need to check your media and talk with Scott."

I'd heard this refrain from her before. We both thought I was past behaving like this. A morning call to Scott, my publicist, usually only meant one thing, and it wasn't good.

"You may need to make a few calls today." She didn't need to say to whom. I knew.

I checked my tablet while she spoke, opening the pictures Scott had emailed me overnight.

"Bloody hell." I swiped through photo after obnoxious photo of me sloshed over Kathy. Kissing her like cameras didn't exist. Grabbing her bum with a drunken smirk. Eyes bloodshot. Hair disheveled. The whole world had the proof and I recalled none of it.

I cringed. Colleen didn't like having to get involved in my messy, personal affairs. Literally.

"Thank you, Colleen." She had gotten me home safely, had saved me many times. But no one could save me from myself. "I'll make the calls."

I had phoned Kathy for a call long overdue, confessing it all.

Yes, I didn't care for her the way she deserved. Yes, work had mattered more to me. And yes, I'd only phone her when I felt lonely or horny. I tried with her at Christmas. Tried having a proper dinner date and later that night fucking my way back to feeling something for her. I couldn't.

She had told me she hoped we just needed time apart. Even though we hadn't spoken in months when I stepped out of the car for Logan's party, she could tell I was plastered but seemed happy to see her. So, she kissed me. She thought we were back together. When we got inside, she tried to hold me, telling me how she missed me.

"But you kept slurring, 'We're over, Kathy,' and pushing me away." She cried in a strained voice to my ear. "You played games with me, Daniel, embarrassing me in front of everyone."

"I know, Kat. I'm sorry."

"There's another woman, isn't there?" Her tone had changed to cold calculation. "It's that woman who was passed out in your arms, isn't it? You are *not* a Good Samaritan, Daniel Pierce. Far from it. You're in love with her."

I had confessed everything to Kathy... but this. I couldn't tell her about me and Charlie. No one could know about us. If there was even an *us* left.

I had said, "I don't know what anything is anymore, Kat."

That wasn't a lie.

When I got back to Madrid yesterday afternoon, I told Simon to take me straight to Charlie's villa. I rang her bell, knocked on her door. She was home. Her car was there. Keeping my back turned from the street, I quietly begged her to answer, only hearing in reply people passing by on the walkway. I couldn't be spotted at her villa. I left, head hanging low, masking my face smeared with shame.

All the cast and crew were invited to Erikson's birthday pool party. I hoped to talk to her here, to explain everything.

I pulled Erikson's present out of the bag on my bike. A stuffed *T-Rex*. Music beckoned me around the back to the pool. There were lots of people. Working my way through the crowd, I forced a smile, suffering through the small talk.

Mason grabbed my arm. He stood with Lorenzo, both with beers in hand. "Damn, Pierce. You reached a new level of famous this weekend. You were tore up, dude, and all over that hot ass ginger."

Drunken nights were Mason's M.O. I hated being reduced to his level.

Lorenzo raised his eyebrow, smirking. "Too bad the secret about *that* woman is out."

I wanted to punch the smug grins off their faces. But I had to suffer it. I did this all to myself.

I glanced over Mason's shoulder. Rob, Joaquin, Anders, and Maja stared dead at me. They knew.

Stepping to cross the pool deck toward them, I had to

make this right. The ripple effects of hurting Charlie would hurt our friends too.

"Zeus!" Erikson came running out of the house, directly at me.

I had to stop to avoid mowing the little boy down. I knelt, glad to see someone who seemed happy to see me.

Erickson asked, "Did you bring me a present?"

"What's this?" I held out the box with its dinosaur wrapping paper. "It's from me and Auntie Char. Happy Birthday, buddy." I used my American accent, wrapping my arm around Erikson's little, boney back in a hug.

"What is it?"

"You have to wait to blow out the candles first." I set it on the gift table behind me.

"Will you swim with me again?"

"I didn't bring a suit, little man. I'm sorry. Next time, okay?" I lowered my voice to almost a whisper. "Where's Auntie Char?"

"She's getting my rings from the garage so we can swim for them." His tiny chin lifted to Zeus with pride. "I can dive in now."

"Can you? Well done! I'm proud of you." I tousled the boy's hair. "I'll go help her find them."

CHARLIE

I BENT over the bin in the garage, digging through the pile of pool toys.

"Charlie."

The sudden resonance of his voice made me jump. I spun around.

"Fuck, Daniel!" The brute sight of him punched my heart. "You scared the shit out of me." But I refused to flinch at its pain.

"Charlie, we need to talk."

"There's nothing to say." I bore into his aqua eyes, ignoring his beautiful face. "I saw all I needed to. No words needed."

He stepped closer. "Charlie, I didn't fuck her. She's my ex-girlfriend and *she* kissed me."

Hate seethed calmly over my teeth. "Daniel, I have flaws but dumbass ain't one. There were multiple pictures, multiple kisses, not just one. But it was the ass grab that sealed your fate." I sneered. "And keep your voice down. I don't want anyone to ever know that I gave you a chance in hell, that I ever even knew you."

"Charlie, please. I got plastered at Logan's house. Then Kathy was waiting at the party. She was right there when I stepped out of the car. She took my hand and kissed me first. I sorta remember that part, but I was pissed, so fucking drunk. She kissed me again and I guess... I guess I just went with it. It was familiar to me. She was familiar to me."

That plunged a knife in my heart, but I didn't intend on shedding another tear over this man. "Well, I'm fucking happy for you two to be reunited now."

I had Erikson's dive rings in my hands. I moved to push past him, to go back outside.

"Charlie, we're not reunited. We're done. She isn't the one I want." But he stood in my way, his empty palms opened to me, pleading. "She said she missed me, and the only person I missed was you. Over these past few days. This past week, Charlie. You've been pulling away from me."

I wouldn't hear his explanation through the angry tears

bleeding from my eyes. I couldn't stop them.

"Charlie, please." Another halting step toward me. "Kathy was a bad habit because I didn't want to be alone. But I haven't spoken to her since Christmas. Since I've been here shooting and met you." His arm rose, his hand reaching, his gait closing the distance. "I'm so sorry. You know what you mean to me. You're the one I want. You know that."

I slammed the heel of my palm into the damp heat of his chest, wanting to fucking claw it open, making it bleed like my heart suffered now.

"No, Daniel." I glared up through my eyebrows, clenching my teeth. "What I *know* is I don't need you to take care of me. I don't need you to fucking carry me. And I don't need you to save me."

I resented the pain washing over me. It hurt worse than bullets piercing me.

Desperation ricocheted across his eyes. I didn't care. I aimed and fired.

"I don't need you, Daniel. I don't need a father. I don't need a hero. I don't need anyone." Escape battled my feet back while rage launched from my mouth. "And I don't need"—my fist grabbed a familiar pain, my aching, lonely chest, my heart bruised and suffering again—"to be hurt like this ever again. All I did was trust you, and all you did was rip me apart."

I knew how to survive this pain. It hurt so bad... but it wouldn't kill me.

Tears poured a numb calm. Cold down my face. Ice over my heart. Through every sure muscle, frosting down my being. "I'm dead to you, Daniel."

I brushed by him.

And didn't look back.

CHAPTER FORTY-FIVE

CHARLIE

Fallen by Harry Styles

A double knock hit my hotel door. I checked the peephole before letting him in.

"Sup, fucker." Rob added a hulking hug to his greeting. I needed it. This afternoon was a shitshow. Even more of a shitshow than this past awful month.

I squeezed him back. "Sup, fucker."

"Joaquin's at her door." Rob updated me on who was guarding Kierra.

I pointed to the open laptop on the table by the window in my hotel room. "And Jeremy's on with us."

Three videos taken of Kierra on set had leaked online early that morning, and "going viral" was an understatement.

Photos and videos from set were strictly forbidden and almost everyone obeyed. Whoever shot these had to have been devious about it. Drawing closer. Closer than my nerves tolerated.

One video creeped three long minutes, zoomed in on Kierra's lips while she sat, unaware, on her transpo cart, relishing flan. Her eyes, happy, off in a daydream. Her lips savoring bites. Her tongue licking the creamy dessert off a spoon.

The other was shot with the afternoon sun behind her, light shining through the loose white linen tunic her character wore. Kierra stood talking to someone while the camera captured her silhouette from the side.

The video started at her feet. Slowly, it panned, crawling up her wispy legs. Fondling over the curve of her bottom. Up her belly. Trespassing to her breasts. Groping their pert curve for two minutes. Then stealing back down, following the copper waves down her back. Almost four minutes total it spent ravaging Kierra's image.

The last was Kierra laughing. The camera zoomed in on her smile, then it zoomed out, capturing a woman laughing with her. A woman with a pink scar across her right cheek. It lurked there. For three minutes. While Kierra and I shared a moment, and the camera stole it from us.

"They're scrubbed." Jeremy updated us. "They dropped this morning, 3:04 a.m., Central Europe time."

"No footprint," Rob said with a groan of frustration.

I studied the videos, watched them several times while my guts twisted.

These felt different. Different from the photos taken outside of Kierra's house. These were meant to torment Kierra, yes. But these videos seemed more depraved, the lewd lens groping, begging for an intimacy he couldn't have.

I put earbuds in. Listening carefully. He had edited the

audio. All three videos were silent, except for his huffing breath. Except for the last one with me and Kierra. In the last five seconds of the clip, I heard it in his electronically altered voice. "Soon."

The promise in his wicked word dropped heat through my muscles, poising me ready to strike at his imposed timing.

Production was almost finished this season and these videos were a demented guarantee. And posting them on a fake account—@thedruid.brigid.is.mine—it was a perverted Ode to Kierra. Some of the comments under the fake profile were vile. Mostly men it seemed making perverted statements, using graphic descriptions, and shameless sex emojis about Kierra's body.

Not caring she was only sixteen.

Relishing it actually.

Posting them online not only violated Kierra, it violated the security of the entire show. By that afternoon, the account was shut down. But it was too late. Reposts spread like wildfire.

The studio got calls. All wanted a comment from Kierra and others about how someone leaked creepy videos online from the supposedly secure set of *The Druid*.

"They were shot last Wednesday," I confirmed to Rob and Jeremy. "I recognize some of the day players in the background, and catering makes flan on Wednesdays."

None of us liked the timing of their drop.

At the studio in Madrid, we had more control, more safety. Or so it seemed. Now the production was shooting locations on the Mediterranean island of Menorca for nine more days. Security presented even more of a challenge.

The studio had put the cast up here, all in the same

luxury oceanside Aparthotel. Joaquin had suggested it to production given its remote location and gated parking lot. With the ocean front on one side and the enclosed parking, it was easier to secure. So, the cast and crew rented the entire building. HGR put us on detail here too, requiring all hotel staff to sign NDAs protecting everyone's privacy and security.

I had to admit the property was beautiful—on the oceanfront with a huge infinity pool surrounded by white canopy covered loungers. I promised Kierra we'd lie out tomorrow since we had night shoots the rest of the time here. With these videos leaked, I wasn't leaving her side.

"I'll go talk with her and her mom," I said. We all knew I was the only one who could comfort Kierra right now. "And Rob and I are on transpo and location tonight."

"I want the principal cast in the same van with you both," Jeremy said, banging out an email to the producer coordinating transpo. "It's safer and cheaper. Who's shooting this week?"

"All four," Rob said, giving me a look. "Kierra, Daniel, Mason and Anders."

Fuck this. Rob seconded with a knowing glance.

Menorca was a magical location for the exterior scenes of the last two episodes being shot now. Unadulterated beaches on a rugged coast. The greens. The terrain. It was perfect for the sacrificial storyline.

But it meant no full basecamp at this location. It was too expensive and a logistical nightmare. So, the production rented half a dozen camper vans and pop-up tents for all. Transpo had to take the principal cast from the hotel to the location and back again.

With another incident and cost always a factor, the cast

would be corralled together in one spot on location, and in one transpo van for the rest of the time here.

There's no avoiding him now.

DANIEL

THE NIGHT BEFORE, empty glasses had littered the table in front of me. I'd ordered Cuba Libres, two at a time with double shots. Usually, I avoided bars while filming, but it was my third night straight at a sleek roof-top bar and pool in Menorca, a gaggle of fawning Spanish groupies and European tourists surrounding me.

I'd watched through heavy eyes, vision blurred.

Mason up on some smoking hot brunette.

Lorenzo chatting up some bird at the bar.

I sat alone, dripping with fuck-off vibes. Crowds had danced around me. Women swarmed. Chatting. Giggling. Taking selfies and videos with me in the background. A few dared to approach. I swatted them away with a slurred, "No, gracias."

I was a dick to everyone and didn't care.

Closing my eyes to another familiar sip, I saw Charlie the moment they shut.

Her blue eyes with blue water behind her. Her small hand, held in mine in bed. Her smile covered in my shaving cream. Her face during our hypnotic first time together, after our rum kisses. Her tears, threatening mine.

Every night I tortured myself with the video we made. Swimming in a wicked mix of desire and pain, stroking my cock off, revering our touch, hearing our sex, it ended me in a pathetic lonely release.

Work was cruel. I craved seeing her on set. But when I did, a hell of hurt ravaged me.

She wouldn't even look at me, didn't laugh like she used to, not even with Kierra. She kept her hat low over her eyes, standing stoic in the shadows of the stages behind our cast chairs—close enough to do her job but away from my gaze.

When she relented, stepping into my view, I saw the pain I caused on her face. It was killing me.

"I'll never hurt you." I promised her on the beach that day.

I lied.

A drunken tear slid down my ruddy cheek at my broken word and heart.

"Dance with me."

A voice had commanded me in English with a Spanish accent. My eyelids, weighing a ton, cracked open to a blurry silhouette, to a blonde in a black bikini. Blue lights from the pool sparkled behind her. A touch to my hand. Something powerful moved me to stand, to follow her across the pool deck.

To dance with her. Her fingertips pressed to your back. Yours traveling down to the small of hers. Swaying with her in your courtyard. Her long hair grazing your cheek. The warmth of her face nearing yours.

Opening my eyes.

It's not Charlie.

"No." I had stumbled back from strange lips, tripping over a chair behind me and crashing back into the pool. The water smacked me with the hurt I tried to numb, blue light and misery surrounding me with a muffled commotion above.

You could drown and end all your pain.

Instinct won. I broke the surface, gasping for air. A sob

had escaped with my coughs, tears and pool water dripping down my face.

Simon stood at the edge of the pool. "You all right, mate?"

I had pleaded with a tongue thick with rum, "Get me out of here."

CHAPTER FORTY-SIX

CHARLIE

"Kierra, I think it's time you give your Instagram posts a break," I told her, flanking her right, with Rob on Kierra's left, her mom and Anders in back. We rode down on the elevator, on our way out of the hotel to the transpo van.

Kierra had posted again that day, hours after the videos dropped. It was her boyfriend's birthday.

I had checked. Most comments were birthday and heart emojis. A few read nasty. Jealous. Perverted. Kierra's boyfriend posts triggered the stalker. Every time.

And I had had enough. Of everything.

"For how long?" Kierra asked. Not petulant. Like it was sinking in with her too.

"Until I get my hands around his neck," I said.

In my periphery, Rob grinned.

Production rented a black Mercedes luxury van. It waited outside of the hotel's double glass doors that evening. Daniel and Mason idled in the lobby, noses down to their phones. I walked past them, whistling at them like dogs to follow, not giving a shit for their ego or status.

I put Kierra in an aisle seat up front. Rob sat beside the driver while I sat beside Kierra, blocking the window. Anders was across the aisle, next to Kierra's mom. Daniel and Mason entered, sitting behind us.

Both were hungover. It took five minutes into our drive before they snored all the way to the location, filling the small van with their booze breath.

Anders got up and lowered the windows over both for fresh air.

In the month since I ended it with Daniel, I noticed the change. How he hung out with Mason and Lorenzo on set, making plans to go out to clubs or parties. How he showed up to set late, hungover and sullen to everyone around him.

He had tried one time to talk to me. Two weeks before, he approached me in the parking lot at the studio. "Please just talk to me, Charlie," he said, hiding his pained eyes under the brim of his red baseball hat.

That hat. The one he wore when he carried me out of the gym, holding me and my pain that night. It brought it all back. "Please just leave me alone, Daniel."

I could barely utter the words before escaping into my car. And then the tears flowed. He stood for a minute, watching me while I cried, while I stared out of the front windshield. Eventually, because he couldn't make a scene... he walked away.

Kierra took her phone out in the van and started scrolling. She paused on cute posts of puppies and showed them to me. I smiled, watching her search on the screen. Scrolling was fine. Posting wasn't.

Then Kierra stopped on an image in her feed that shocked us both. It was Daniel with his navy shirt and jeans soaking wet, staggering through a hotel lobby with Simon beside him. He was clearly drunk with bloodshot eyes and a slack-jawed face.

Kierra swiped to the next picture.

Daniel stood fully clothed in a pool with Simon perched by the edge. She scrolled down through the comments in Spanish that she couldn't read without translation. I could. It brought bile up my throat.

When Kierra touched the #danielpierce, hundreds of photos populated her screen. Posts and reposts of Daniel, Mason and Lorenzo getting smashed at some rooftop bar here on the island.

I noticed at first, in most of them, Daniel sat alone at a table.

But Kierra scrolled down.

A video reel played of Daniel dancing intimately with a blonde in a bikini, leaning down to kiss her, then stumbling back drunk into the pool.

It punished me all over again. The heart punch of pictures of him with Kathy a month ago, and now this back-handed slap across my face.

Who is this man?

Not the Daniel who gave me rare blue pearls and an ocean of lush memories. Not the Daniel who shared his pain and my secrets. Not the man who swept me off my feet, promising he'd never let me go, that he'd never hurt me.

Yeah, well suck it up. You always sensed this about him. You were just so lonely, horny and hellbent, you chose to ignore it.

I bit my lip, hard, to keep tears from rolling down my face. Kierra didn't notice. She kept scrolling through her phone at the hundred damning images.

I glanced at Anders.

He sucked his teeth with a knowing shake of his head. He saw the posts too and looked pissed off. Once the van pulled past the roadblock to the location, Anders stood and gave both Daniel and Mason a shove to the head. "Wake up you bloody cock-ups."

When they wrapped shooting at two a.m., I sensed Anders was calmer. He had taken his anger out on Daniel and Mason in the scenes; it played well for the camera. We all moved quietly, loading back into the van, taking our same seats.

But Mason still seethed at Anders's wrath. I overheard Mason protest to Daniel on set, bitching how they'd done nothing wrong. They went out for drinks and ass. What was everyone so pissed off about?

Nice, Daniel Pierce. Apparently, you're no different than Mason Hunt. Peas in a drunken, arrogant, asshole pod.

"Shit," Rob said.

His curse shook me from my sickened thoughts. I focused out the front window of the van and saw it too.

A small crowd of people had amassed outside the gate of our hotel. The hotel security guard tried pushing them back, but he couldn't control them. Once the crowd spotted the van on the horizon, driving toward them, they started screaming.

I stood up and walked toward the driver, peering over Rob's shoulder to get a good look. Counting heads. Scanning them.

Eight young Spanish women yelling for Daniel. Two Spanish teen girls screeching for Mason. Five young men shouting for "The Druid." Two older guys bellowing for "Carric" and "Brigid." They sounded Irish.

"This is a clusterfuck." I fumed as the crowd

surrounded our van trapped outside of the gate. "Llama a la policía," I instructed the van driver.

Blam, blam, blam! Two guys smacked the van's door window, making Kierra jump with a scream.

Anders got up, taking my empty seat beside her. "It's all right," he said, patting her hand like a dad would for his little girl. Her mom looked over, nervous.

Kierra's fear set me off. I exploded in rage. "You wanna fuckin' tell me how the hell they knew we were stayin' here and comin' back tonight?"

My eyes shot daggers at Mason and Daniel.

Mason looked like a deer in headlights. Daniel cringed, closing his eyes, shaking his head in shame.

"Hey, you little fuckboys." I aimed my fury at them. "You chasing tail to fuck all over this island just fucked us all now."

Rob looked up at me, surprised. It wasn't like me to be unprofessional and curse in front of Kierra, but I was right. They'd done this.

Mason hissed. "Chill out, Charlie. We can do whatever the fuck we want." He threw his arm over the seat in front of him to stand, to challenge me. "Who the hell do you think you are?"

But I blitzed to his chair faster than he could blink. "Sit your fucking ass down, Mason." I glowered over him. "I'm the bitch in charge of keeping everyone safe. Fuck with me and my job, and I'll rip your goddamn pretty face off with my teeth."

Mason's stance wavered with venom.

I mocked him with a raised eyebrow and a calm, cold snarl from my depths, my truth dead aimed at him. "Come on, Mason. Try me. All I need is a reason."

Mason retreated, falling back into his seat.

Then I turned my neck, focusing a hard glare on Daniel who sat, face in shock.

Get a good look, Pierce.

This is the Charlie who planned it. This is the Charlie gleeful to take any pain to protect her girl. This is the Charlie you don't fuck with.

Blam! "Carric!" *Blam, blam!* "Brigid!"

The guys smacked the glass over and over. I looked back over my shoulder at Rob staring back at me from the passenger seat. We gave each other a nod. Rob jumped out first, slamming the door behind him.

I turned to Anders. "Keep them in here. No matter what."

Rob pushed the guys back from the side door. I cracked it open once it was clear, sliding out and slamming it back. The driver quickly locked it behind me.

Hotel security struggled to corral the crowd away to clear the gate.

The two drunks who were banging on the door window took offense at Rob's gestures to move them back. One guy shoved Rob, then took a swing. But Rob caught his wrist mid-air, twisting it, forcing the man to flip around, his arm trapped against his lower back. Rob kicked him in the back of his knees, taking him to the ground.

The guy's friend lunged to take on Rob, but I covered him. I stepped in front of the guy, putting my palm up.

"Stop, sir," I calmly said.

He shoved my shoulder with his left hand. "Fuck you, bitch."

He's a Southpaw. I grinned, palm still up. "Step back, sir."

His left hook slowly sailed through the air. I saw it coming, didn't even duck as it landed across my face.

I wanted it.

"Charlie!" Daniel called out from the open van window.

I raised my fists, positioning my feet in fighting stance. Laughing.

The guy in front of me stood, eyes wide that I didn't fall at his punch.

His left shoulder twitched back to throw another hook.

As predictable as the sunrise.

I ducked now and wove left. Charging back up, I punched a knife strike across the front side of his throat with a fierce right.

He dropped cold.

From the open van windows, I could hear it.

Anders started laughing.

Mason wondered aloud, "What was that?"

Anders answered, roaring, "A woman you don't fuck with."

Daniel's voice answered Mason, "A brachial stun. Show her some bloody respect or you're next."

Police cars had arrived. Two officers helped push the crowd away, clearing the van's path through the gate. Another officer cuffed the guy Rob had on the ground. Another helped me, kneeling over my victim while I gave him not-so-gentle slaps to the face to wake him back up.

The van pulled through the gate. It closed securely behind them. Rob stayed with the officers to give statements but I told the officers, "Un momento, por favor." I had to get back to Kierra.

Before I passed through the security gate door, I turned toward the small crowd. "¡Basta! ¡Váyanse!" I shouted, pointing them away to disperse, giving them a look to fear.

Then.

It was here.

Firing me out of this crisis.

Into my own.

I peered through the thinning crowd, into the darkness behind them, an eerie shiver dripping down my neck, recognition rising across my flesh. The certainty chewed the space behind my eyes, flaring my nostrils at the proximity.

Someone lurked in the shadows. Staring at me.

Instinct told me. *He found you.*

My eyes disagreed, seeing nothing.

The present moment commanding—*protect the girl.*

I turned away.

The van driver kept everyone on board until I arrived. I slid the door open, motioning for Kierra and her mom to come with me, moving them quickly toward the hotel doors.

All while I could hear Anders's voice booming, schooling Daniel and Mason. "You fucking tossers. This shit ends now. You're risking yourselves and the fucking show." A pause. "You know the right thing to do."

He must have said that to Daniel.

CHAPTER FORTY-SEVEN

CHARLIE

A low glass wall stood between me and the waves crashing against the rocks below. I picked a lounger for me and Kierra. One that gave me visibility to the ocean on one side and the hotel pool on the other.

I pulled half of the canopy back so I could get some rays while Kierra sat on the shaded side. Kierra couldn't let herself burn. The alabaster look for her character had to stay consistent. Still, we could enjoy the soothing sound of the ocean and a girls' afternoon together.

Setting my pool bag and towel down, I took my linen cover-up off and tossed it on the table beside the lounger. The same black and white bikini from my vacation with Daniel barely covered me. It was the only quasi professional suit I had here.

"Charlie?" Kierra's voice sighed soft with shock.

I looked over my shoulder. Kierra stared in distress at

my scars. I turned to sit down beside her, reaching for her ivory hand. "I'm okay, chica."

Kierra was accustomed to the scar on my face. She'd told me many times she thought it looked "deadly"—ironic Irish slang for fantastic. Kierra didn't know any better at the time. But now she saw my other scars and tears welled up in her eyes.

"I got them six years ago," I told her. "They hurt like hell to recover from, but it was worth it."

I held Kierra's hand, sharing the official story. About the FETs and our work. About a strong girl I knew named Paksima that reminded me of Kierra. But I stopped there. Kierra was maturing but deserved to keep any innocence she may have left.

My story prompted Kierra to ask, "Did you always want to do this? To protect girls?"

"I guess so. One day in high school on the school bus, I stood up to some guys picking on a pretty girl." I lowered my voice. "I punched one of them in the dick."

That made Kierra smile.

"I've been kickin' ass ever since." Deploying my rebellious grin, I said, "That's why you're safe with me. Me, crazy Rob and sweet Joaquin."

That made Kierra chuckle. "Rob can be a bit of a nutter trying to make me laugh."

I rested on my stomach, wanting to dive in the pool, but unwilling to leave Kierra's side. Instead, we waited quietly in the sun for our lunch order of virgin piña coladas and ceviche to arrive.

The bruise throbbing on my right cheek made me wince, so I turned to rest on my left, closing my eyes for a few deep breaths, trying to relax.

My mind had other plans.

What was that last night? When I sensed someone stalking me? A premonition or a promise fulfilled? Was it finally here? Did it find me following the #danielpierce viral photo? The pulse in the bruise on my cheek troubled me otherwise.

Maybe it's something else, Charlie Girl. You have another scar. The one on your mind. It confuses threat, time, and place. Careful what you trust as real.

My next exhale conjured Daniel. Finding memories of moments we shared. The mouse voices. Our first kiss. The way when he held me; I knew he didn't want to let go. Neither did I.

A painful surge fluttered an off-rhythm beat in my heart. With it my mom's voice whispered in my ear, "Abre los ojos, Charlotte."

I opened them, glancing up at the hotel behind me. At the corner suites with luxury, ocean-view, glass balconies rising two stories above us.

Daniel stood right there, watching me.

I didn't look away from his stare. The sun bathed my body, but it was his gaze that warmed me with a storm of feelings.

As someone trained to observe, to understand the all too predictable behaviors of the human animal, I was no fool. Just blinded by pain. For a while.

I had seen on the video how he pulled away from the strange woman's kiss, falling back into the pool. I had studied the pictures of him and Kathy until they became neutral, until I could see that his explanations were possibly true.

Yes, he fucked up, and he was flawed. Was that what he

was hiding? That when he got drunk, he got out of control, that he couldn't trust himself or his memory?

Or was it something else?

My mother's wisdom and warning echoed through my mind.

Open your eyes, Charlie Girl, and see the truth.

DANIEL

STANDING ON MY BALCONY, I peered down through the pain between us. I'd been admiring her. Every svelte muscle. Every nimble move. Every tender smile shared.

I was aching to go to her then, and every day of the seven more we shot in Menorca. But I never did. It would only bring us pain.

After leaving set each day, I locked myself in my hotel suite. No more drinking. No more hurting myself or the ones I cared for.

My time was occupied reviewing the script for the Navy SEALs film this autumn. It was confirmed we'd shoot at the studio in Wilmington, North Carolina. Being so close to Charlie's home would be too hard on me. I asked the producers for a schedule to shoot me out quickly so I could leave by mid-November.

I wanted to go home to my family in Cornwall after I was done. To enjoy the result of my home renovations. A thought that reminded me all over again of Charlie, making me suffer.

Fuck, I can't escape her.

From excruciating hours on set, silent beside her, to

painful lonely ones in my hotel room without her, the Mediterranean island was paradise for most. Hell for me.

On the flight leaving Menorca, I forced myself to leave all hope behind too. I lost Charlie. I had to find a way to live numb again.

Back in Madrid for our final nine days of filming at the studio, the only comfort I found was that Anders had warmed to me again.

Mason still acted like a petulant arse though. His hatred for Charlie was palpable on set. It made me glad this was Mason's last season on the show.

We were days into shooting through the pages. Through the last script of the last episode of the season—the dramatic conclusion where Mason's character, Herne, volunteers to be sacrificed to appease the gods.

Herne, the youngest son, is desperate to quell the wrath of the gods raining down upon his Morrigan family and the wrath of the Romans advancing across their lands. Arzur, the father, weeps, agreeing, seeing no other way to save the family from near destruction. If he offered one son to the gods, surely they would bless the other, Carric, his eldest son as the next Arch Druid.

All three men are blind to the truth. The anger of the gods comes from the men's denial to see that Brigid, the girl, is the chosen one to save them.

The dramatic final scene concludes with Arzur blessing Brigid and Carric with sacred mistletoe, cutting their right hands with his ritual knife of iron and wood. Their blood blesses the rope for their brother's neck. Arzur weeps, tightening it around his younger son's throat. The rope forces blood to constrict in his neck. Tears fall down Carric's scarred warrior face, grieving for his little brother. Brigid rises, stepping back in dismay, certain this is wrong, but helpless to stop it.

With one final cry to the gods, Arzur slices Herne's throat. It erupts in a hallowed fountain of blood across the altar. Racked by sorrow, but sure in their faith all will be blessed now, Carric and Arzur turn at the sound of Brigid's steps. Her leather-sandaled feet are sliding away from the cursed pool of her brother's blood flowing toward her.

The final shot falls upon Brigid.

Her eyes pierce the camera lens with an omniscient glare of defiance. She feels it. She's finally been granted a power greater than any man's. The camera dramatically pulls back to a wide shot of Brigid standing proud as her first woman's blood dawns on the front of her white priestess tunic.

Fade out.

We had rehearsals today with stunts, props and special effects, practicing with the prop knives and rope for the final sacrificial scene.

Tomorrow, we'd film the scenes with the mistletoe blessing, the cutting of Brigid and Carric's hands, and the blessing of the rope. It required multiple set ups and shots with special effects.

Securing the top-secret script into my backpack, I reluctantly found myself walking with Mason as we left the set, headed toward the car park at the edge of basecamp.

We turned our heads to peals of laughter.

Kierra and Charlie stood beside Lorenzo, amused by something he showed them on his phone.

It burned right through me. How Lorenzo was a good-looking bloke, cunning in how he enjoyed the women Mason's fame lured over. I saw it myself when I went out with them. Lorenzo was more than handsome. He acted harmless but was calculated in his pursuit.

And now Lorenzo's eyes lit up. I seethed, knowing why.

Lorenzo wanted to fuck Charlie, who returned his smile. And Kierra? Her giggle was nervous, revealing she was clearly besotted by Lorenzo's charms as well.

And the fucker had been trying to blackmail me even more to keep my secret. And I'd been paying out.

"Sucks, doesn't it? Wanting something you can't have," Mason affirmed, standing beside me, taking in the same spectacle. "Makes it even better when you finally get it."

I turned away in resolve.

CHARLIE

MY PERIPHERAL VISION clocked Mason and Daniel heading toward the parking lot.

I wanted to talk to him, but Lorenzo and his puppy videos distracted us.

Kierra had been stopping to talk to Lorenzo a lot lately. It made me smile, seeing her happy. It was harmless flirting. Lorenzo was too old, too much of a player for Kierra. Flirting was all this would ever be with me around.

Besides, when Lorenzo's gaze turned toward me, I caught the invitation in his bedroom eyes. I smiled back. I had to stroke his ego to protect the secret Lorenzo knew about me and Daniel. Though we were over, I couldn't afford for that to get out.

I wasn't getting reassigned. I wasn't leaving Kierra.

Turning away from Lorenzo, I looked back at Mason and Daniel walking away.

Tension rippled across his back muscles. His pace, hunting slow and deliberate. His fists were shoved in his jean pockets. His head was down and growling low.

Fuck, he's jealous.

I didn't trust jealousy.

It was deadly.

CHAPTER FORTY-EIGHT

CHARLIE

The set was crowded. I didn't like it. It made my job harder. And it seemed everyone, from every department, was here today.

I shadowed Kierra as tightly as possible.

They completed the mistletoe scene before the lunch break. I didn't eat. I stayed stationed outside of Kierra's trailer. That meant I stood beside Daniel's too, steeling myself against the constant hurt of seeing him.

When the door to his trailer swung open and he stepped out, it forced my sudden inhale. He looked right at me, face muscles tensed, mirroring mine. There were no words, only torment between us. Only did I exhale after he turned his back and walked away.

I escorted Kierra back to the stage building for the series of shots with the hand cut. Jennifer Adams, the director, gave directions to the cast while hair and makeup finished their last looks and special effects glued prosthetic skins over Kierra and Daniel's palms, hiding blood squibs underneath.

An unease slid up my neck. Tension arced across my shoulders. Heat fired across my nerves.

I scanned the stage and set—dozens of crew members were prepping for the scene. Taking them all in, I trusted my instinct to find where I needed to aim.

I noted Kierra's mom in her usual chair in the corner of the green room. She gave me a nod. Her readiness to have this done and take her daughter home strained her face.

"Action!" The first shot was called.

Carric and Brigid kneel side by side. Both bow their heads, offering their hands up to their father while Herne stands peacefully in front of the altar.

Arzur picks up the sacred knife from the altar, turning toward his daughter.

Anders took Kierra's right hand into his left. He poised the knife to follow the hidden slit already cut into the prosthetic across her palm, focusing as they did in rehearsals, making sure only to pierce the squib. The hidden blood pack would slowly emit a dramatic trickle of blood down Kierra's hand.

The knife in his hand!

I ran toward Kierra, just as Anders applied enough pressure and—

Kierra flinched, yanking her hand back with a yelp of pain.

Anders stopped and stared at the knife, balancing its weight in his palm before he dropped it on the floor while Kierra held her right hand against her chest.

I reached her, putting both arms around the girl, protecting her. The blood running down Kierra's bare wrist was all too real.

Jennifer yelled, "Cut," and the entire set erupted in chaos.

"Are you okay?" Anders asked. He extended a hand, but I shook my head, warning him off.

Daniel and Mason stood back. Anne reached us and I moved aside, helping Kierra stand and go to her mother. Then I squatted down, studying the knife Anders had dropped.

"What the hell, Charlie?" Anders said. "It's not... it's not—"

"Someone switched the prop knife out," I said. "Don't touch it."

The assistant director called for the medic and studio security. The props master rushed over and looked at the knife on the ground, then back at the props cart in utter dismay. The special effects artist peeled off the prosthetic skin so the medic could examine Kierra's hand.

The cut bled heavily, but the medic said, "It's not deep. Won't need stitches. I just need to dress it."

"Do it here," I said. "She's not leaving my sight."

The medic took a few steps away with Kierra and started dressing her cut. Anne stood by her daughter's side, and I stayed by my mark, scanning back across the crowd assembled. Hoping to catch the look of satisfaction across the fucker's face. And making sure no one touched that knife.

Finally, Rob and Joaquin came running into the stage building with a team of studio security.

"I called the detectives and police," Rob said. "They're on the way."

"Joaquin, take her back to her trailer." I wanted Kierra out of here and in a secured space. The detectives could take her statement there.

Kierra looked back once, not crying, and gave me a look of pure anger. Not at me. I was glad to see it in the girl's eyes. *Yes, Kierra, fuck him,* I thought it too. Then I turned back to the work at hand.

The whole scene changed into an investigation as to how this real knife found its way on set.

I felt relieved for both Kierra and Anders that the cut wasn't deep. Anders would never hurt the girl on purpose and no doubt would blame himself for not figuring out faster that the knife was wrong. But the cut on Kierra's hand wasn't the real wound.

Fucking asshole. He knew the wound wouldn't be serious. He got his rocks off on hurting Kierra just enough *and* with what he knew would happen next.

It stopped the entire production.

This was more than a threat toward one person. This was a calculated cut to end it all.

"I'm going to kill the fucker who did this," Rob said.

"No," I said. "That's my job."

And you will. You will fuck him up one side and down the other for hurting your girl.

The studio shut down for two days while security combed every stage, props and more. The police took the knife into evidence. They'd test for fingerprints, DNA, and to determine its possible origin. They requested Anders accompany them to the station to provide a sample of his fingerprints, and I knew, ask some pointed questions.

I had a good enough look at it to know the knife matched the prop in appearance. The wooden handles seemed the same, but the fiberboard blade of the real prop would have made that knife heavier.

The knife Anders dropped sounded lighter, like plastic.

My eyes told me it looked thinner; razor-sharp too. How did it get on set?

Lorraine Morris, the showrunner and executive producer, flew in that night to meet with Kierra, her mother and our HGR team at Kierra's home. Anne wanted shooting cancelled, but Kierra grew bold.

"Mam, he's not going to win," Kierra said. "Charlie, tell her."

"Kierra, you need to listen to your instinct and your mom," I said. "Sometimes you fight, and sometimes you take cover. You live to fight another day."

Tears streamed down Kierra's face. The girl could take no more. Her bravery melted into anguish. It made my eyes burn, holding back my own.

"If I give up and give in to him now," Kierra said to her mom, "I won't ever want to fight again."

"All right, love." Kierra's mom squeezed her uninjured hand. "We won't stop. We'll fight back."

That was where Kierra got it from, I saw it true. Kierra's fighting spirit came from her mom.

I swallowed hard. My dad gave me skills, but I got my fight from my mom. My heart ached. I missed her so much in that moment.

Local police, studio security and our HGR team stood on high alert when production resumed. Everyone on set acted unnerved. It made Kierra angrier that she was made to seem like a victim instead of a survivor. When she heard that production was thinking of cancelling their wrap party, she spoke up.

"Everyone has worked so hard this season. And we're not giving up now. If you want to support me, then we're going out with a bang of a party," Kierra announced on set to a round of applause.

The energy the last two days heightened, raising everyone's work up a notch. I stayed on the hunt through it all, scoping the eyes of everyone around Kierra.

Finally, in the last shot of the final scene, I saw the look wax and wane across his face.

I grinned. *I see you motherfucker.* I'd suspected him.

All along.

My trigger finger tensed ready but held smart enough to wait. Wait for the evidence that was coming. Wait because a powerful man like him didn't go down without dead certain proof.

And when you have it—take the shot. No matter how it hurts you too. Fucking end him.

CHAPTER FORTY-NINE

DANIEL

Thumping music greeted me before the elevator doors even opened. Lance and I stepped out into the summer evening, finding ourselves on a rooftop terrace bar overlooking Madrid. Bass beats pumped, vibrating the glass railing walls around the perimeter. By the noise level, the entire cast and crew were here at the wrap party.

It all felt bittersweet.

I sipped a beer, made the rounds, giving hugs and well wishes to everyone. Glancing over people's shoulders, searching the crowd for her, I didn't see her, but I noted extra security posted around. Swigging another beer, I swore this was the last one.

No public spectacle tonight.

Lorraine found me in the crowd, giving me a warm hug. We chatted about my film this autumn until I fell silent at the song drop.

"Bailando" played. The crew erupted, cheering to the

same tune from our dance party on set months back. I peeked over Lorraine's shoulder.

Found her.

Kierra was pulling Manuel to the dance floor. Beside them, Rob raced Charlie there too.

Her outfit mocked me. The red skirt from our first date. From the night I first held her, never wanting to let go. The thin black wrap sweater from our first kiss. And from the night she shared her scars. From the night I touched them and found my home. God, it hurt so bad.

Lorraine reacted to my distracted stare, turning around to see the dancing. "Oh, let's go!" She grabbed my hand, leading me to the edge of the dance floor. "Shall we?"

I couldn't turn her down. I'd give my best performance. If Charlie could do it, so could I.

Lifting Lorraine's hand, we did a decent job improvising through the pop Flamenco beat. Everyone clapped us along. While I danced with Lorraine, I stole glances of Charlie and Rob firing up the performance once again.

I grieved... she wasn't dancing for me anymore.

Another potent Latin beat took over. Lorraine gave me a hug saying, "You make a lady look good, Daniel. So much so that I need water and to catch my breath." She signaled to Jennifer and the two women started up their own conversation.

I turned back. Now was my chance. I had to talk to her.

I spotted Kierra dancing with Rob. The crowd moved. My stare shifted next to them.

No.

Charlie was dancing with Lorenzo. With his hand caressing her back. With his eyes sparkling with expectation. Her long hair swayed with him to the beat while her small hands held on to his tan arms. The worst part? I didn't need to see her face to know—she was smiling.

I staggered back to the bar in defeat.

Recognition raised the raven-haired bartender's eager eyes. She licked her lips to serve me. "¿Sí, señor?"

"Brugal, neat. Double." While I waited for my shot of rum, I looked over my shoulder at the dance floor.

Charlie's fingertips rested on Lorenzo's shoulders now. His ambitious hands traveled down, down to grasp her rolling hips.

My jaw clenched, ready to break the moment and their bind with my bite.

"¿Señor?" The bartender broke my focus.

"Gracias," I murmured. The douse of rum down my throat—mere mist over my fury. I ordered another before looking back again, watching my world leave me behind.

Remembering her smile and cherished mouse voices. Remembering her pain and our angry parting words. Charlie swore she was dead to me. But I was the one who wanted no life without her.

The sweet *thud* of a full shot glass hit the wooden bar. I turned, reaching for my new liquid home just as a heavy hand gently landed on my shoulder.

"Hey mate," Anders said, standing behind me. "Let me join you. I'll stick to Irish swill though."

I exhaled with sudden relief. Anders pushed the shot aside, ordering Guinness for us. Then he mapped my beaten glare to the dance floor while we waited for our beers.

"Ah, I see." Anders nodded at Charlie dancing with Lorenzo. Our bottles clunked down on the bar. He handed one to me. "You know, mate, you should talk to her."

"That's not going to work this time." I looked back again

to the sound of the song change. Charlie was laughing, hugging Kierra and talking with her mum.

"Maybe not," Anders said. "I know how fucking stubborn she can be."

That got my attention.

Anders took a long swig before adding, "But I also know this—Erikson wouldn't be here if I let one big row stand between me and Maja. I was an idiot arse our first couple years and I had to fight like hell to keep her."

Anders lifted his chin. I followed his gesture. Maja stood talking intently with Charlie now.

"We both know she's worth fighting for," Anders said. "And you know, mate. They give up a lot to be with us. To be in our lives. Almost everything."

He took another long swig, letting the wisdom sink into my thick skull.

"Question is"—Anders raised his eyebrow, challenging me—"what are you willing to give up to be in hers?"

"Everything," I replied without thinking.

Anders's big red beard and heart smiled at the obvious. "Don't you think she should know that?"

I sipped my beer. Fucking hell, I finally understood. It wasn't just my massive fuck-up making Charlie push me away again.

It was my career, my bleeding celebrity life she was afraid of. Every time I had mentioned my future, my fans, my next film—she had winced with fear in her eyes. Charlie worked on the darkest side of my world and wanted none of its blinding, paparazzi light, certainly not after all she'd survived.

If you want Charlie in your life, Pierce, you're going to have to change. All of it.

CHAPTER FIFTY

CHARLIE

I rolled my eyes at all the people sleeping peacefully around me. That included Kierra, in the aisle across from me.

Settle the fuck down. Close your eyes and sleep, or there will be hell to pay tomorrow.

We flew on the red-eye from New York to San Diego. Everyone else from the show had arrived at Comic-Con the day before, with Joaquin running advance security. Kierra was delayed because her father and brother joined the trip for a family vacation to the zoo afterward.

Rob and I traveled with them. We'd land, go straight to the hotel to refresh, then on to interviews there and *The Druid* panel in the big hall that night.

It would be a long day for us all, and I twitched, alone and alert in the maddening, humming silence of the plane.

On my other side, Rob slumbered like a big angel. I looked past his bulk, out the airplane window.

The full moon was my only company. It spoke to me from the blackness outside.

It spoke to me of home.

I closed my eyes, trying to imagine that moon over my island. Often, I'd walk out to the beach at night and stare at its spotlight across the water. At the rise and fall of the dark rolling waves pulling at both me and the tide.

I tried breathing in that movement now. Like I always did in meditation.

A wave in.

A wave out.

A wave in.

It didn't work.

The waves rose and with them, my sense of the storm brewing beyond the horizon.

Our plane flew straight into it.

CHAPTER FIFTY-ONE

CHARLIE

Army of Me by Bjork

My eyeballs hurt I was so tired. But I breath drew across a razor's edge, the pain of it keeping me wide awake.

Something felt off.

I stood outside the door to one of the hotel's numerous event rooms waiting for Kierra, Daniel, Anders, and Mason to finish their first interview. Lorraine, *The Druid's* showrunner had joined the interview too. I let her in over an hour ago.

What the fuck was taking so long?

Press walked by with credentials hanging from their necks. Clusters of cast members and their staff from other productions wandered past. Rob and Joaquin had walked down the long corridor to map the path to the next inter-view room. Joaquin would stay there and secure it while Rob would double back.

This half of the third floor had event spaces turned into interview rooms. The other half of the floor featured hotel suites currently being used as holding rooms for the various cast members to refresh, eat, and head off to another round of the same questions.

When Colleen emerged, I asked about the delay.

"They decided to shoot more interviews in here," Colleen said. "They're having sound issues with the crowd in the ballroom down the hall. So, while we wait for this crew to pack up and the other to start, I'm off to fetch Daniel some lunch."

"Okay. Thank you."

I tried not taking my displeasure with the situation out on Colleen. Grace, Kierra's assistant, was supposed to tell me if anything changed with the schedule.

We faced a lot of risky transitions through uncontrolled spaces at this venue. I had mapped most of them in advance early that morning. I had to know whenever something changed to protect Kierra.

Pushing the door to the room open, I saw Lorraine standing there, smiling, talking on her phone. The crew from one entertainment program were packing up their gear. Another crew waited their turn, their sound tech yucking it up with Anders about the Tour de France.

How did all these people get in the room?

"Where's Kierra?" I demanded.

"She went to freshen up and get her phone," Anders said.

"How?" I'd been by the door the whole time. "Where?"

Grace looked up from her tablet, grinning, not understanding the urgency in my voice. She pointed to the pipe and drape curtains on the opposite side of the room. "She just went back to the holding room to fetch her phone while we wait between interviews."

At first I didn't understand, but then a camerawoman pulled a panel of curtain back to leave, opening a concealed door. I didn't see that other door when I escorted Kierra into the room earlier.

Fuck my exhaustion. I missed it. Crossing the room, I pushed it open. It led to another hallway connecting the rooms and suites.

I turned around, trying not to rouse the notice of the press in the room, calmly asking Anders, "Where's everyone else?"

"Daniel went down the hall and Mason's getting lunch. They'll be back in a bit," Anders said. "Kierra should be right back too."

Fuck! No!

Aiming out of the hidden door, harnessing surging fear, I entered the hallway, letting the door slam behind me. The back hall was stifling, crowded with various crew and cast milling about. I walked, quickly pushing through, my pulse confirming...

It's happening. Now.

Go! Go! Go!

I cleared the crowd, darting right, down another hall, spotting a sound tech entering another room. I needed to run, but it would draw too much attention.

Kierra assumed she was safe from her stalker in these back halls and holding rooms.

She wasn't.

I knew who it was, suspected him at first and was dead certain now. This whole damn season—I waited for him to slip up—but not like this. Not when I wasn't around.

This was his chance. He'd take it... and take Kierra.

I broke left. A new hallway, finally leaving the crowds behind, my heart and elbows were pumping, sprinting now.

Mind flashing back. Paksima's tears. Esin's screams. I sacrificed it all for those girls. And I'd do it again for Kierra. Time was my only opponent. I just had to get to her. I could win this fight. I could take him. Yes, he had the size.

But I had the rage.

One more right turn. Down the hall. The suite door. Flicking my card in front of the sensor, it beeped. I slammed the door open and heard Kierra's screams. Running through the living room of the suite, I targeted the scene, one of the adjacent bedrooms.

They were on the floor.

He knelt over Kierra, his tapered back muscles straining under his navy shirt. Yanking down at the waistband of her white pants with one hand. A fist full of her copper curls in his other. The words growled up from his throat, "You're mine now."

Kierra was on her stomach. Digging her black sandals into the carpet. Crying, "No! No!" Trying to escape into the bathroom in front of them.

Bolting toward him, I leapt on his back, hooking my left arm around his throat and twisting to flip him off Kierra. The force crashed our bodies back together against the wall. I landed, trapped under his back but had him trapped in a rear naked choke.

He knifed his elbow into my ribs but I locked position under him, wrapping my legs around him, hooking them over the top of his thighs. Every muscle in my body contracted around him. My left bicep squeezed over his throat while my right hand pulled against my left wrist, securing its choking grasp.

Then I felt it—his back muscles tensing over my chest.

Shit, hang on.

He lifted up. I latched on to him. He jerked right, slamming my head into the door jamb of the bathroom. Pain blazed my skull. "Fuck you," I snarled because I wouldn't let go.

He did it again, pounding me hard into the wooden door casing.

It only pissed me off more.

"Charlie!" Kierra cried.

I glanced over from under him. Kierra was crawling like a frightened crab away from our fight.

Constricting my biceps even harder, I didn't need size. I had aim. My arm strangled across the artery in his throat, choking him in the exact vice of my tight grip.

"I can do this all day, motherfucker," I whispered in his ear, tasting his sweat, "but you can't."

He strained now, falling back on top of me, fingers scratching at my forearm, his muscles contracting. He mounted up again before brutally crashing my face against the doorframe once more.

"Do it harder," I dared him.

Heaving, he started coiling up for another strike. Just what I wanted. I snap-turned underneath him. The twisting momentum blocked the last flow of blood to his brain.

He fell limp in my grasp. I released his neck. His body lay slumped and heavy over mine. Pushing him off me, I kicked my legs free and crawled across the floor to Kierra leaning against the wall.

"It's okay." I knelt in front of her, soothing Kierra's tear-stained cheeks with my palms. "It's okay. It's over now."

Kierra sobbed in shock while I hugged her, keeping watch over his body sprawled across the carpet. I didn't have long before he'd wake back up.

The suite door slammed open with a furor. Anders ran into the room. "Charlie, what's going on?"

He stopped... and stared.

CHAPTER FIFTY-TWO

CHARLIE

Daniel rushed in after Anders with Grace and Lorraine behind him.

Mason lay lifeless on the floor.

"We're okay." I saw them take it all in. "Lorraine, call the police. Grace, get Rob and Joaquin in here." Grace stood frozen in place but my, "Now," made her move back from the doorway to find them.

They couldn't be far behind me. Once Rob found us missing from the first interview room when he returned, he'd call Joaquin and they'd head this way.

I had shared my certainty with Rob and Joaquin after the knife incident. We'd met in the security trailer, packing it up to wrap the season, prepping to cover Kierra's travel here.

"We need Mason's fucking prints on something," I had said.

"Not one physical piece of evidence connects him yet," Rob had replied.

Joaquin threw our files in a box. "Not even the scarf or panties had DNA. Just silicone lubricant on it."

"That sick fuck jerks off with latex on his cock and hands." I had crammed my laptop in my backpack, my mind focusing on his last chance. "He's running out of time and opportunity. He's going to make a move at Comic-Con. I know it."

We had Kierra covered from the moment we landed in San Diego. I was her protection through the interviews. Rob and Joaquin ran advance. Joaquin secured the next space. Rob would circle back to shadow Mason the minute we moved from one space to another.

But Kierra wasn't supposed to leave any room without me, not without her protection.

"He's waking up." Anders stood over Mason now like he wanted to kick the shit out of him. "What do I do?"

"Nothing. You have to stay out of this, Anders. I've got him." I still knelt in front of Kierra. Taking her elbows, I gently helped her stand. "Kierra, go with Anders." I passed her off to his waiting arms, making sure Kierra was secure in the adjacent room.

Mason stirred. "Stay down asshole or I'll fucking end you," I said, standing over him, but away from his grasp.

Mason coughed, rubbing his throat, rolling back and forth on the carpet.

Daniel stayed in the room. Concern wrenched over his face. "You're bleeding, Charlie." He reached out for me.

I turned away from his touch but could feel it. The pain in my cheekbone. Blood dripping down my cheek. The burning ache between us. "I'm fine."

Mason coughed through laughter at Daniel's observation. His voice hoarse but clear. "How do you like my bloody kiss on your face, bitch?"

Daniel pounced. I stopped him, slamming my palms against his concrete chest, the touch of him hammering my heart, but I wouldn't take my eyes off Mason.

"Go in the other room, Mr. Pierce. You can't get involved."

The last thing anyone needed was for one of the cast to assault another, regardless of the circumstances. I wouldn't put it past a fucker like Mason to press bogus charges, dragging us all through some serious mud.

Daniel stepped back but didn't leave. "You're fucking over, Mason." He sneered at Mason propped up on his elbow, struggling to sit up.

"Fuck you." Mason laughed even more. "She came on to *me*."

"Is that your story now, Mason?" I knew what he was doing. If he could say Kierra consented, even initiated their contact, Mason could maybe plea this down to a lesser charge. "You've got a mountain of evidence against you that burns your ass otherwise."

Mason rolled to his hands and knees. "I don't know what you're talking about."

"You know damn well what I'm talking about. And stay down," I warned him. "You make one dumbass move and the next ass beating will be worse."

I wanted to kick his ass over and over again, but I couldn't use excessive force. I had waited too long to build a clean case against him, no matter what shit he tried to pull now.

The suite door slammed open again. Rob and Joaquin ran in. I didn't offer any explanations. They didn't ask. There'd be time for that later.

"Joaquin," I said, "secure everyone else in the other room."

Joaquin nodded, gently pulling at Daniel's arm. Daniel looked back, one last time at Mason, and then at me before he retreated.

"Sup fucker." Rob noted my bleeding face. "That's gonna be pretty in the morning."

I nodded to Mason glaring up at me. "So is his neck."

"The police are coming up," Rob said.

Mason raised his palms in mock surrender. He sat with his back to the wall, rubbing his throat, but aiming his sadistic eyes up at me.

The hatred he fired at me only triggered my wrath. I wouldn't back down from his stare. "That was your best performance yet, Mason. And now the show's really over for you."

Mason's grin was wicked, dripping with perversity. "I'm not done yet."

"You're the one on the floor after my ass-kicking. You're looking pretty damn done from up here."

Mason's words weren't an imperative. "Fuck you," he hissed. They sounded like a promise.

I squatted down to his eye level, kissing his evil with my confidence.

"You'll be standing in a long line if you want to fuck with me, Mason."

Daniel

I couldn't calm my pulse. My chest pounded with rage at what Mason did to Kierra. And Charlie. I stood with Anders, protective over Kierra sitting on the sofa with Grace and Lorraine, respecting Joaquin's directive to stand down, but fucking hell, I wanted to rip Mason apart.

A knock tapped the door. Joaquin checked the peephole before opening it. Two police officers entered. Charlie appeared in the doorway between the bedroom and living room suite at the sound of their entry.

"We need rape detectives up here," Charlie said to the officers. "I've got an attempted rape of a juvenile, the scene and the suspect behind me."

One of the officers followed Charlie's gesture, pointing into the bedroom where she and Rob had Mason secure. The other officer stayed in the living room, making the call. Then she took a seat in the chair beside Kierra, asking if she needed medical attention. Kierra refused it. Her hands shook, clothes appeared torn, but she said she was fine.

"I'll see y'all soon," Mason said when he appeared in the room, hands cuffed behind his back, the officer guiding his shoulder toward the door with Rob joining him.

"Kierra darlin'," Mason cooed. "Tell 'em the truth. We're not a secret anymore. Tell them how we've been fuckin' all along."

Kierra jolted up. "That's a lie!"

"Shut the fuck up," Rob said, pushing Mason's other shoulder through the doorway.

The sound of Mason's evil, departing laughter polluted the hallway as the hotel door slammed behind them.

"That's not true!" Kierra still stood, looking at the officer now. "I've never done anything with him. Never. I came in here to get my phone before our next interview, and he came in seconds behind me. He said he was going to miss me. That I was beautiful, and he loved watching me. That I should be with him, and we would be the next *it* couple. And then he went on about how it wasn't fair he's off the show and I'm a lucky bitch to still be on it. That it's his show, he made it, and my character is a bullshit, dumb girl."

"It's okay," the officer said, trying to calm Kierra down. "The detective will take your statement in private as soon as they get here."

Tears fell down Kierra's angry face. She wiped them away like they annoyed her and kept going. "No. I want everyone to know."

Kierra looked at me and Anders. "I tried getting away from him," she said. "I ran into the bedroom, so I could lock myself in. So I could call Charlie." A sob left Kierra's throat. "I shouldn't have left without her." She looked over at Charlie standing in the bedroom door. "I'm sorry."

"It's okay, chica," Charlie assured her, walking over to hold Kierra's shaking hand. "We all know the truth. We know he's lying."

"Kierra, we'll defend you," Lorraine added, sitting on the sofa, looking up to Kierra and Charlie. "He's not getting away with what he did all season."

"What?" I asked. "He's been doing *what* all season?"

I knew Charlie was here to protect Kierra and for cast security. But I had no idea it was to protect her against Mason… all this time.

"It was more than the knife," Kierra said. "Someone's been leaving me notes. Taking my stuff. Stalking me all season. But Charlie's been protecting me. Coaching me. 'Always fight back. No matter what,' she told me. So, I did."

Kierra's face turned from mine down to the officer's. "It was Mason this whole time. And Charlie kept me safe. She told me she'd catch who was doing it. That he'd go to jail, and I would be safe. She said since I'm a minor, the crime would be kept from the press."

Kierra asked the officer, "Is that true? That no one will ever know what Mason did to me?"

"Probably, yes," the officer said.

"Kierra, you can keep it secret," Charlie said. "Maybe get Mason to sign an NDA. No one in here will betray you."

Charlie's chin went up. I recognized the look on her face. It was the same one when she told me about the girls in Afghanistan. The ones she took bullets for.

"Or," Charlie encouraged, "you can tell your story one day. If you're ever ready. Maybe it will help other girls."

Another knock at the door startled us. Joaquin checked and opened it to two plain clothes detectives who presented their badges. Kierra's mother rushed in behind them, her face distraught.

She pulled Kierra in for a hug. Kierra returned it but it didn't stop her. She stood by her mum and turned to all us adults holding sway over her world and future.

"Mason's not hurting me or any girl ever again," Kierra said. "We're doing the Comic-Con panel tonight. And once we're finished here, I will issue a public statement. It's my story. I'll tell it my way."

I followed Kierra's glance to Charlie. Tears fell down her blood-stained cheek. Kierra latched around her neck in a sudden hug next.

"I'm so proud of you," Charlie cried in her embrace.

A lump choked my throat at the powerful sight and story I knew.

On paper, guarding Kierra was Charlie's job.

But all I wanted to do then was take Charlie in my arms, wrap her in a blanket of esteem, knowing for her... it was much more.

It was her mandate. And her sacrifice. She'd take down anyone to protect her girls.

"Gentlemen, we need to ask you to please clear the scene." One of the detectives addressed me and Anders. "We'll take your statements outside."

I turned, following his motion toward the door but I looked back one last time. The other detective started taking pictures of Charlie's face.

And Charlie looked away.

Away from me.

CHAPTER FIFTY-THREE

CHARLIE

Better by SYML

The ride fifteen stories up in the elevator gave me enough time to breathe in my resolve.

We finished with the detectives. Joaquin had escorted Kierra and her mom back to her room where her dad waited with her brother. Rob was running advance on the panel tonight. I was going back to my hotel room to clean my face, change and rest up for the big event.

Silence filled the space around me. I tried inhaling its calm.

Kierra was safe. I was alone.

Only one of those facts filled me with peace.

The elevator dinged. I stepped into the hallway, turned the corner toward my room and gasped at the sight.

"What are you doing, Daniel?"

He sat right there, twenty feet away on the floor, waiting outside my hotel door.

My pulse sprinted away seeing him, but my feet stood firm.

"I want to talk with you." His hefty arms rested on his knees. "And I'm not leaving until we do."

An assault of emotions constricted my neck, but I pushed through. "I don't know what to say."

"Well, I have something to say." His large frame stood, and approached me, sucking the air from my lungs. "Charlie, I miss you so much. Every part of me hurts. I've been a fucking wreck without you."

"You made your choices, Daniel." I stepped toward him, angry now. "You're a grown-ass man. No one poured rum down your throat. No one made you and Logan get trashed. Or you and that sick fuck Mason whore it up all over Menorca."

He stepped toward me, just within my grasp. "That's not fair. I didn't know about Mason's shit. And I wasn't whoring it up. I haven't been with anyone. I haven't kissed anyone. Not since that bloody red carpet nightmare with Kathy." The veins on his neck raised with his voice. "I don't want anyone but you, Charlie."

His eyes burned bright with pain, searching mine for a reply.

I refused, clamping my jaw tight. It wasn't enough.

"Is that it?" Desperation threatened his eyes. "You're just going to walk away from us? I know I hurt you, and I'm so bloody sorry for it. But I was hurting myself, Charlie. You hurt me too. You fucking played head games with me. And then one vulnerable moment for me, one of my weaknesses, and you said you were dead to me. Like we both haven't buried enough people in our lives."

Every emotion stormed through me, but I controlled my face. No expression or words escaped.

"Goddamnit, Charlie. You're the best thing to happen to me. Ever. And you just fucking walked out!" His fist punched the air. "It was easy when we had the best week of our lives. The fucking pleasure is the easy part. But the minute you felt pain, you ran. You didn't even give me a chance. Give us a chance."

He stepped even closer; his massive body surged taut but I wasn't giving in. My stubborn silence made his nostrils flare.

"Did that week mean nothing to you?" he asked. "Did you fucking use me to get what you want? To have your fun? As long as you could control it. Part of your one-week plan, right? You got to fuck *Daniel Pierce* and leave me bloody gutted."

He mocked his own name, staring me down with eyes trying to hold mine captive.

My words escaped. "I didn't use you, Daniel. You knew the deal, one week, and then we both wanted more. But you couldn't go two more weeks before you left *me* gutted."

How dare he?

"You went back to your bullshit, A-list life where people use each other, get used and move on," I said. "That's not me, and you know it. Fucking far from it. My body bears witness to the kind of woman I am." I dared. "Can I say the same for you?"

My question hit him right back to the fated one that drew us together the night we met.

His shoulders thundered up at my strike. "I'm fucking human too, Charlie. You get to have your ghosts. Why can't I have my demons? Your pain is thousands of miles and years away. But mine is now. And nothing could ever compare to yours. Nothing. But you know that I can never escape mine either. It's every day. Living my bloody life in a goddamn prison of a fishbowl for all to take everything from me, laughing at my mistakes and pain."

He clenched his jaw, stepping to where I could hear his breath, smell his soap, skyrocketing my pulse.

"And I've done nothing but be there for you," he said. "Nothing but care for you. That's the kind of man I am, and you know it. You fucking know it! I waited for you. I was so honoured to. And we shared so much. And I never abandoned you. I'm right here fighting for you. So why the hell can't you do that for me too?"

Silence dominated me while agony threatened to drip over his lashes, his eyes searching mine for an answer that wouldn't come.

"Why are you running from me, Charlie? From us? Are you that afraid? Afraid for us to be together?"

Afraid?

He had no idea.

Once, when I was a teenager, when my parents and I moved back to Daufuskie, the local kids rejected me. Bullied me. My dad found me, lonely and stubborn with no friends. "I don't care," I told him. My dad put his arm around me. "Choosing lonely is easy. Braving love is hard, Charlie Girl," he said. "That's why your mom and I raise you strong. So that you're not afraid to love."

No, don't. Too late.

The memory. The truth. They forced tears down my mute cheeks.

Daniel's voice softened. "Charlie, I know you've been hurt. So much. You saved those girls. So when will you save yourself and live again? Are you going to push away everything in your life now if it hurts?" His hand reached to hold me but halted mid-air, empty. "You would rather be alone forever? Doesn't being lonely hurt too?"

That fact strangled me. Everything in my life. Yes, it was ripped away. My parents. Kai. Peace. Safety. Which was worse? Loss or lonely? Both stole the air for my voice away.

I couldn't answer him. I just stood still, terrified... because he was right.

His eyes kept searching mine, staring back at him. His fists raised in the air along with his voice again, pleading, "Please, Charlie. We have something so beautiful together. The most beautiful thing I've ever known." His deep voice boomed louder, echoing down the corridor while his fists tightened. "And I know you feel it too. From the moment we met. It's worth fighting for, but I can't promise you that it won't hurt sometimes."

A *ding*. A clatter of voices stumbling out of the elevator around the corner sounded over my shoulder. *Clicks* of doors opening in the hallway behind Daniel followed next. His baritone shouts and celebrity face would have the entire hotel floor witnessing our fight.

He yelled, "Please God, say something!"

"Daniel." I lowered my tone. "We need to go inside. They're watching us."

I didn't need to check to know eyes stared at us, sensing their halted breath and probably phones rising to record this viral, celebrity spectacle.

He looked up and over my shoulder, then back over his, seeing what I could sense. The small group peering nervously down the corridor and the guests sneaking a look out of their room.

"Fuck them." He turned back toward me. "I can't

escape them. This is my fucking life, and they ruin every-thing. But I won't let them ruin us."

His face bloomed red, filling his lungs to yell, "I love you, Charlie Ravenel, and I don't fucking care who knows!"

My dad. *Braving love is hard, Charlie Girl.*

My mom. *Open your eyes, Charlotte. See the truth.*

Kai. *Lighten your burden, angel. Or you won't make it.*

Crawl back to your truth. Time to live again.

It fell from my trembling lips. "I love you too, Daniel."

He bolted toward me, cupping my unbruised cheek in his shaking hand, lowering his lips to mine, tears salting our urgent kiss. Oh God, I had missed him. When his tongue found mine, it lifted a moan from his throat, the sound of his desire surging down my body.

The little group gathered in the hall clapped. Doors shut back, closed.

Pressing my hot cheeks to his, I insisted, "We need to go inside." He paused and made a bending motion. "Do not pick me up." I laughed, wiping my tear-stained face. He grinned back, holding his hand out for mine instead.

After my hotel door closed securely behind us, he scooped me up anyway. I didn't care. I only wanted him—what he was doing now. Carrying me to the bed. Laying me down.

He climbed on top of me, braced on one hand, staring down at me.

"I mean it, Charlie. I love you. I'm so fucking in love with you, Charlotte Sophia Ravenel." His fingers brushed across my cheek. "I wanted to tell you on holiday, but I was afraid I'd scare you away."

The sight of him above me, "I'm so fucking in love with you too, Daniel Balthazar Pierce," I never wanted him to leave. "I'm sorry I got scared, that I pushed you away. I shouldn't have hurt you like that. I didn't mean to play games; I just didn't know what to do." I reached up for his stubbled cheek. "Deep down, I knew you were the one. That you had me at the mouse voices."

My confession made his chest fall. He kissed my lips, blazing impatient for our reunion. "Fuck, I love you so much," he whispered down my neck.

I tugged at his damp shirt. "I need to shower," he said, rising to kneel over me. He peeled off the leather jacket he'd worn for interviews that day, lifting the T-shirt underneath over his head before tossing both to the floor. Damn, he was beautiful. His chest hair curled over sculpted pecs, drenched from his stifling clothes and our heated words in the hallway. "And we need to clean your cheek."

"No. I want you now, Daniel." I yanked off my shirt and bra. "And I love you all sweaty."

Then I remembered—my boots. Gently, I pushed him back so I could sit up to whip open their strangling laces.

He stood up at the foot of the bed, watching me. The seconds it took, making him laugh. "I do love waiting on you too, Charlie."

I chuckled, kicking them off then my socks before flopping back on the bed to strip off my pants. "Enjoying my show too?" I slid my white lace thong down next.

"I always do," he said, kicking off his shoes, watching me lie naked now on the edge of the bed. "God, look at you." He stopped, his eyes locked on mine. Then he shook his head. "Fuck, I missed you."

He did that gesture that coaxes me every time—licking his bottom lip before biting it. Staring at me, he said, "Spread open for me, Charlie, and show me what I love so much."

It thrilled me, opening my thighs even more for him.

The trust. The vulnerability. The lust. Only he could do this to me, with me. I wouldn't fight it anymore, lying there, for his ardent stare, for his breath lifting his ribs, for his cock straining under his jeans.

The stillness my body took for his adoration didn't match the craze of my desire, my desperate need for him tingling my exposed flesh. But we both indulged, slowing this down for just a moment so I could feel his gaze loving me.

He sighed," You're so beautiful. I can't get enough of you," with his hands going for his belt.

"No. I want to." I sat up, unhooking his belt, unbuttoning his jeans, then unzipping them. Fuck, tearing away these little barriers between us only turned me on more.

I dragged down the elastic band of his boxer briefs, desperate for what I craved underneath. Oh God, the sight of him again, his love, his body—all massive for me.

My fists took him first, releasing his moan. I gazed up at him, kneading his hard cock before my mouth plunged down on him, as far down as I could go and holding at where his mass hit my throat.

"Fuck, Charlie." He gasped. "I missed you."

I pulled my dripping lips off. "You missed this?" Plunging down again before dragging my tongue back up his shaft, licking the most sensitive seam on his tip.

"Fuck yes." He laced his hands through my hair. "Is it getting you wet? Sucking my cock again, Charlie?"

Grazing my lips over his fat tip, I answered, "I'm going to make us both drip, Daniel." My fist and mouth took him, tight and hungry, wanting his taste so much, indulging him, making us both moan. Giving him the show we desired, I sat on the edge of the bed, fingering myself while I sucked his sweet cock.

I knew his body, his breath. "Yes, Charlie." It was making him crazed, my mouth, my fingers, quaking his thighs while he murmured, "I can hear your wet pussy wanting me." I could taste how he ached for it too.

"Not like this, babe." But he stopped me. "Lie back. I'll show you how I missed you."

Pulling my lips off his cock, I ached for that too. "I never stopped thinking about you. About this, about how you fuck me." I laid back, wanting him now... and always.

"I do more than fuck you, Charlie." He knelt by the edge of the bed. "I make love to you every lewd way we want."

Throwing my legs over his shoulders, his fingers spread me open for his mouth diving between my lips, making me suddenly cry out, "Yes," my back arching tight at his ravenous tongue fucking me.

"Did you miss this?" he asked next before sucking my clit, hard, forcing me to cry out again, unable to control my hips writhing over his face.

I huffed, "God yes, Daniel," while he blew cool air over my clit before his warm flicking tongue frenzied my nerves.

But his grip over my thighs was too strong, holding me there. "Give me what I'm thirsty for."

His command made me open my eyes and watch my body fulfill his wish. It was easy, the touch of him again, that voice, that tongue, those eyes. He ripped my first orgasm from my core, all over his moaning mouth.

"Fuck, Daniel. Please." I shook, pulling at his waves, pulling him up to me.

"No. You have more." God, the sight of him. "And I'm going to drink it all." His lips and chin glistening from my desire went back for more.

I surrendered to him, to it all. Letting him roll his

tongue over my clit again. Letting him curl his long, thick unrelenting fingers inside of me. I let him lavish me, beckoning me into more twisting screams until my pleasure dripped from his chin and fingers.

How could I ever live without this? Without him?

It made me desperate to the point of pain. "Now, Daniel." I needed him. So much. "Fuck me now."

"I told you... I'm going to give you much more than *now* with me, Charlie," he said, crawling over top of me while I crawled back on the bed. "I'm going to give you everything."

DANIEL

RESPONDING to the urgency in her beg and body with her flavor in my mouth, she was driving me wild.

"Taste what we have together." I offered my slick fingers to her lips. She sucked them with no shame, only moans while she stared back at me. "This is why we belong together." I gave her my mouth next, sharing the taste of her pleasure swirling over our tongues.

Her fist seized my cock. Her ambitious touch lifted my kiss from hers, watching her eyes while she held me there, teasing my tip around her warm, dripping entrance.

"What do you want, Daniel?"

Oh God, how she turned the tables on me, on my life. Our power play was my favorite sport. She was more than my equal. She was my salvation.

"I want you to know that I'm going to fuck you until my final day, Charlie." I urged into her, the only place for me. "You'll be the last one I taste." Her welcome wrapped so tight around me. "The last one I touch." All the way in, where I belonged. "The last one I'll love."

She grabbed my ass, lifting her hips, promising me, "You'll be my home," rising to meet me, coaxing me even deeper.

"God Charlie, you feel so good." I reached for her other hand, holding it over her head, lacing my fingers in hers, descending into her. She was soaking for me, her fingernails, digging into the flesh of my cheeks, driving me harder.

Groaning at the stinging delight of her pain, fuck, I loved it, loved her, everything she made me feel—my life's addiction.

She writhed under me. "I want all of you, Daniel." Her gaze taking me too. "All or nothing."

"You have me." I delivered it with force, all she was scratching for. "Like this." My knees spread her thighs farther apart. "All of me."

I took both her hands, holding them over her head in my grasp, arching her back, tensing her breasts up to me, nipples grazing against my chest. The hotel bed slammed into the wall, matching the rhythm of my fierce strokes, of our loud aching grunts for each other. Filling the room. Filling the luscious time here.

I wanted all of her too. Staring into her eyes. Fucking her so hard I would forever lose my mind and heart to her.

"Is this what you want, Charlie? Like this?" I hammered my passion against her clit, as hard, as deep inside her as I could, knowing what we needed to hear, knowing that look in her eyes. "Say it."

"Yes, Daniel." Her head gently thrashed, body straining to twist more, but I pinned her down too strong. "I want you to fuck me." She spread her thighs wider, hanging in the air like she was to her edge. "And I want you to love me. So fucking hard."

"I will." Pounding her, I gave her more than naughty words. "I'm going to love you every day." More than the sex we craved. "I'm going to kiss your sweet pussy every day." More than the need we felt. "I'm going to fuck you every day." It was my desperate truth, my entire life for her. "I'm going to make you come every day." Not just now. "Do it, Charlie." I wanted forever with her. "Come for me." As hard as I could with savage force.

"Daniel!" She cried out, surging in a spasm so strong, fighting my control. But I was too strong, holding her down while it racked across her body under mine, rolling her eyes and drenching my cock with my favorite reward.

She always ended me. I groaned, erupting inside of her, quaking with release, taking my breath and pain away. All I could think. Speak. Feel. "I love you."

"I love you too." She pushed against my restraint. I let go of her hands. They wrapped around me. "So much, Daniel." Pulling me near.

Burying my face in her hair, catching my breath, the torment of our time apart released its strangle over my heart. I whispered in her ear, "You're the only one, Charlie. I promise. You brought me back to life. No one else."

She cradled my head there. "I promise I'll stay and try. I won't abandon you, no matter how scared I get."

"I want to figure out a way." I rolled us on our side, so I could swear it to her eyes. "I want to be with you. I know you hate my life, how it can be." Brushing her hair back from her bloody cheek, I anchored my gaze to hers. "But nothing means more to me than you. I'll give up whatever it takes."

"I don't want you to give up everything for me. You've

worked too hard. It makes you happy and it honors your brother. I'd never ask that. And I can't give up everything either. I fought too hard rebuilding my life, too many times. I won't lose it now for any man."

Her lips kissed mine before she explained, "I love you, Daniel, but yes, parts of your life terrify me."

"I know. They scare me too sometimes. You were right. The first day we met. I was numb to it. All it takes from me. And it took my soul along the way. Until I met you. Until you saw my pain and asked me how it felt."

I cherished the contours of her face. "I'll change what I can, Charlie. But I can't control everything." My fingertips trailed under the bloody cut on her cheekbone. God, she was incredible. "Just promise to fight for us. Fight for our love like you do for everyone else."

She reached out, twirling my sweaty hair around her finger. "I promise."

"It'll be easier now. People can know about us."

A cute grin slid across her face.

My lips curled up, knowing that look on her face. "What?"

"I think we just fucked so loud and long the whole hotel knows about us now."

"Well then." I mounted back on top of her. "Let's give them an encore."

"Oh God, you're sweaty." She smeared her hands down my back.

I wrapped her in my arms, rubbing my drenched naked body against hers, laughing. "I thought you loved my sweaty body."

She giggled under my wrestle. "I do, but it needs a fucking shower."

I relented and got up. "Come next door to my room and take one with me."

"Your room is next to mine?"

"Yep."

"Did you plan it that way?"

"Yep." I reached my hand out for her. Always. "I wasn't leaving San Diego without you."

CHAPTER FIFTY-FOUR

DANIEL

"**I** need to eat something. My stomach is squirrely," Charlie said, rubbing body wash over her belly. "And I have a headache the size of Texas."

Relief washed over me. Elation too. I had Charlie's luggage in my room. Her gorgeous body standing in front of me in the shower.

And her love.

"My badass Sex Goddess, look at me." I lifted her chin, checking her pupils. They seemed okay. Maybe not. "Do you think you're concussed?"

Earlier, I saw her blood smeared on that bathroom door. And the dent in the wall above Mason's body. Pride and concern for her filled me.

"I'll be fine. I just need a nap." She grinned and turned around, handing me the bottle of shampoo. "We've got three hours before the panel, and I'd like to sleep through two of them."

I looked down, smiling at the two dimples above her strong ass, one dimple right under the bullet scar on her hip. Fuck's sakes, she took my breath away.

"Did you always know it was Mason?" I asked, lathering the long rope of her wet hair until suds formed.

"At one point, I thought it was you."

"You did?" The assumption of guilt didn't bother me. I was guilty. Never of hurting Kierra or any girl. But guilt was my constant companion. "What proved my innocence?"

"My instinct." She leaned back into me, turning her lips toward mine for a gentle kiss before she said, "And when you laughed at my mouse voices."

I massaged her strands as she turned back. "When did you know it was Mason?" I asked.

"I had my suspicions all along." She reached for her face cleanser. "The minute I saw the picture of his note to Kierra, I knew she was at risk. I didn't want another job when Jeremy called. I was safe at home. And it was the anniversary of the day I was shot, like it was an omen."

She started cleaning the cut on her cheek. "But I had to protect her. When I got to Madrid, in my interviews with the producers, I asked about the week before y'all wrapped season one. The week Kierra's things went missing and notes were left in her trailer. Do you remember it?"

"A little, yes."

"Well, Lorraine told me how they told you, Kierra and Mason their plan to kill off Mason's character this season. Lorraine thought it was screenwriting gold. But when I asked about Mason's response—"

"He didn't say anything." I suddenly recalled that same meeting. "He just sat there."

"That's what Lorraine said. It sounded like a bizarre

response to me from a young man who traffics in drama daily."

She turned back around, wrapping her arms around my waist, tipping her head back to let me rinse the shampoo out. "It gave Mason a motive. He was jealous of Kierra's boyfriend and her lead role. Like he wanted to hurt Kierra and hurt the show. Two things he couldn't have.

"And then when I interviewed Mason," she said. "He felt all kinds of wrong to me. I saw his vellum paper and 3D printer. That's how he made the notes and the knife."

I squeezed a dollop of conditioner into my palm, feeling another guilt. This was a serious conversation, and I cared for Kierra like a little sister. And I respected the hell of out Charlie's job. But with her naked body pressing against mine, I wrestled with my focus.

She continued, "Mason had motive, means and access. I clocked a hidden camera in his living room. That fucker filmed everything. Even Kierra on set. He had enough money to bribe his way into Kierra's gated community. He had the time and access to sneak around, stealing stuff, leaving things behind. Lorenzo had to have seen him going into Kierra's trailer but probably thought Mason was just joking around with her. I don't think he had any idea what Mason was really up to."

I combed the creme down through her tresses with my fingers. "Did you?" Loving this part of our ritual. How it turned her hair into silk.

"I started adding it up. But Mason is as smart as he is evil. He knows how to manipulate technology, knows how not to leave evidence."

"Sounds like that twisted, psycho character he played in that sick film he did two years ago," I said. "Maybe that's where he learned the skills."

She shot her eyes up at me, worried. "Mason Hunt isn't done, Daniel. He's going to out us. He will tell everyone we were together when we weren't supposed to be. I know Lorenzo told him about us. I got him to admit it to me while we danced at the wrap party."

I confessed, "That dick, Lorenzo, has been blackmailing me more to protect our secret. I know the NDA works in court, but I didn't want to risk the immediate threat, the one to your job, so I paid him another one hundred thousand to shut him up for good."

"When was this?"

"While we were broken up."

"You did that for me? Even though you thought we were over?"

"I might fuck up sometimes, Charlie, but I'll always love and protect you."

"That makes two of us." She lifted her lips up. I gladly answered with mine in a deep kiss, ready for another round in the shower with her but she pulled away to say, "I have an idea. A way we can work this out and maybe not get completely fucked sideways by Mason's big mouth."

"Does this jolly idea involve me and you? Together now?" That was all I cared about. Lorenzo and Mason could go to bloody hell and back. I just wanted Charlie... with me and happy.

"Yes," she said, smiling at my lips nearing hers again.

"Then I'm in."

WE CURLED up on the bed, talking about what was next. It wasn't long before Charlie's eyes grew heavy. She stopped mid-sentence, exhaustion finally defeating her. I gave her a kiss and pulled the covers over her.

I couldn't sleep. I had to get dressed. Colleen would be here any minute for an emergency meeting.

I met with her in the other room of my suite, working to change my schedule. "I'm taking Charlie as my plus one to my film premiere next week."

Colleen smiled but shook her head, disagreeing. "Daniel, you know I'm relieved she's back in your life. But you must appreciate the repercussions if you walk a red carpet with her on your arm. Millions of your fans will love her. But thousands will vilify her and come after her. That sweet woman will be praised and persecuted the minute you go public, and it will never be the same for her again."

"We just talked about it," I said. "Now that she caught Mason, her work on *The Druid* is done. But with Mason and his vindictive mouth, we can't hide anymore. At least this way, it gives me a chance to make up for what I did."

She paused, considering my point.

I continued, "And let's shorten my press junket to New York only." I knew my contract. I had a minimum requirement and I'd meet it, nothing more. "When I introduce Charlie to the world, it will be even more press for my film. Either way, opening weekend box office numbers are not my concern anymore."

"Oh?" Her voice traveled up two octaves in delight. "Caring more for Charlie than your career? My, my, my, the times and my boy, they are a changin'."

"Yes, they are. I love her, and I'm going to be with her. I don't care what I have to change. The rest of the world can go fuck themselves."

I grinned now, remembering all the years my sister,

mum or Colleen told me I behaved too selfishly to find love. I had. But people don't change until they feel a love that inspires them to.

I stood up and walked to the bedroom door, peering in. Her body laid so serene. Sudden fear coursed through me. "Should we ring down to the concierge for a doctor? I keep worrying she's concussed. She doesn't usually sleep so still like this."

"Wake her in an hour, dear." Colleen wore an amused grin, clearly approving of me doting over Charlie. "If she's not well, she'll speak up, I'm sure."

"All right then," I said. "After the press and premiere, Charlie and I will disappear. We are off the grid until I report to the Wilmington studio in October."

Noting the time on my watch, we had one hour and I'd wake her. If she felt okay, we needed to get ready for tonight. If not, I'd skip the panel and get her to a doctor.

"Oh and"—I looked up at Colleen—"she is 'Charlotte Roberts' on any lists or in statements next week. We need to release that name before Mason starts talking."

It was part of our plan. No, Charlie's plan, but I went along with it, impressed with her strategy and pre-emptive strike. The world, and indeed Mason, wouldn't know what hit them.

"I'll sort it all, Daniel," Colleen said as I sat back down across from her, noting the view of the massive blue sky and San Diego Bay behind her.

"I can see how much you love her," she said. Her concerned tone and fading smile caught my glance. "And I want this for you. I want you two together. But you can't have love built on a lie. You must tell her. She deserves to know what happened."

Colleen was there ten years ago. She knew my guilt, my crime.

"I know. I will." I dropped my gaze down to the dark gray carpet.

But not yet, Pierce. You finally found the love of your life. Don't lose her.

CHAPTER FIFTY-FIVE

CHARLIE

Death of Me by PVRIS

My eyelids cracked open from a fatigue I'd never known. I didn't mind. I woke up to joy. To his warm body wrapped safely over mine, pressing so close his chest hairs tickled my back again. The hum of his soft snore soothed peacefully behind me.

My phone lay within easy reach on the nightstand. I checked it—8:08 a.m. Saturday, July 20—glowed back.

Daniel stirred at my movement, lifting his arm off me.

We had three hours before Colleen would knock. Before there would be no turning back. I'd call my boss and Daniel's to confess how I broke the rules.

And fell in love.

It made me smile, remembering my job and last night. How Kierra had taken the Comic-Con stage with confidence. I was so proud of her. Kierra seemed emboldened now, almost fearless having faced down the threat of Mason. And now, she was free of it.

It was a new beginning for us all.

My smile dropped for what would begin for me though.

Members of the press or a fan, probably both, would match my distinct face on the stage last night working security for *The Druid,* to the videos leaked on set with Kierra, to the woman passed out in #danielpierce's arms months before. And any day now... Mason would confirm it, exposing my relationship with Daniel.

And the hunt would begin.

I really would be a target.

Of the press. Of his fans. Of something else I knew was coming for me.

That's why I had a plan. If I could stay five steps ahead of any threat, we might make it. And like hell if I wouldn't die trying.

A sudden urge took me to have the one thing I wanted. The one thing that made me feel safe.

Him.

I rolled over. Daniel slept naked on his back. One bulging bicep resting above his head. His other resting heavy under my shoulder. Protecting me.

Charlie Girl, his beauty is much more than his appearance. It's in how he loves you.

Tickling my fingertip down his Greek god nose. Traveling it next across the hill, valley and hill of his cleft, prickly chin. It was endearing. How he shaved in the morning and had a full shadow by the next. And sexy as hell.

His thick lashes blinked.

I climbed on top of him. "Good morning, sexy."

His deep voice awoke. "Good morning, beautiful." His

morning cock was already granite under me. His hands knew exactly where to find my hips in his grasp.

I paused, adoring him. His love was worth it. No matter how the thought of his life terrified me. How what was next would send anyone running away with fatal fear. Not me. Not this time.

He opened his eyes and read my face. "Babe, what's wrong? You look scared."

I gazed down at his caring eyes. "I think I might always live scared. But I don't want to do it alone anymore. I want to live it with you."

He grinned, gliding his hands up my waist. "In one week, we are, Charlie. We're living together on your island."

He had acted so surprised, so happy yesterday when I suggested that after his film premiere and junket in New York, we spend the next two months on Daufuskie.

His fingertips traveled up to tease my nipples, making me ache for him. I asked, "Are you ready to get dirty and wet down in my Lowcountry, Pierce?"

"In so many ways." He nudged into my slick slit, seeking more. "You owe me a rematch in a kayak race, Ravenel."

I beat him on our Seychelles vacation and would gladly do it again. On my water, the Calibogue Sound, no man could beat me.

"You want to have your ass handed to you in another race, Pierce?"

His side grin and thrust taunted me. "I'll take your hands on my arse anytime." He sat up, tongue taunting my nipple, crossing his legs in front of him.

Yes, the urge hit me too. I moved to wrap my legs around his waist—

"Oh shit." I darted off him instead. Stomach lurching, I

bolted toward the bathroom. Crashing to my knees on the tile, I lost last night's dinner in the toilet.

"Babe, are you okay?" He rushed in behind me, reaching to hold my hair back.

"Yeah," I said, flushing it all down.

"I'm worried you're concussed." He wet a washcloth for my face. "You should see the bruise on your face this morning. There are nasty ones on your ribs too. You took some hard hits yesterday and now it's showing."

I sat back on my knees, grateful for the cool washcloth and his care. "I'm fine. I've been holding that back all week. Hell, for months. All my fear and worry for Kierra. The stress of it. I just needed to get it out."

I did feel better. More than better.

I felt loved. Again. Finally.

Slowly rising, I stood up in front of the sink, saw what he meant by the bruises and didn't care. He leaned in the doorway while I started brushing my teeth. I watched him in the mirror. The smile on his face wouldn't stop.

"I know what you're thinking," I said through minty suds in my mouth.

"I'm not thinking anything."

"Your lips can lie like a rug, but your pretty face can't."

He tossed his head back, laughing. "Another Charlie-ism." His amused gaze fell back to mine in the reflection. "Come on then. Read me like you always do. What am I thinking?"

"You hope you got me pregnant." I smiled before spitting out the rest of the toothpaste, rinsing my mouth and wiping it clean while I watched him. "I'm dropping all my defenses to you, Pierce, except that one. I'm protected, on birth control, remember?"

He came up behind me, turning me around. "*I'm*

thinking I'm loving every minute of tearing down your defenses." Lifting me up by my hips, he plopped me on top of the vanity. His smile and lips lingered inches from mine. "Do you feel better now?"

"With you"—I reached down, waking up his cock again —"I feel perfect." Stroking his heft, I said, "Come on then. Give it a go, Pierce. Try tearing them down more."

He yanked me to the edge of the vanity. "Spread your legs again because you know how I'll tear them down." His lips neared mine, saying, "All over us and the wet tile."

And he did. While he was inside every part of me, wetting my world alive. While his lips pressed to my ear. While he swore, "I love you so much, Charlie." My defenses fell to him, to the floor.

I wrapped what was left of me around him. My body. My heart. My love. My life. Looking over his shoulder, out of the window in his luxury hotel bathroom, vowing, "I love you too, Daniel," I stared right at it.

The future. The threat.

The moon warning in the day sky.

ALSO BY KELLY FINLEY

Come for Me Trilogy

Protect Her, Prequel Novelette

Pierce Her, Book One

Hunt Her, Book Two

Chase Her, Book Three

All for You Duet

After Him, Book One

With Him, Book Two

And more coming very soon...

Get more from Kelly Finley on Amazon

Anonymous

It's her.

Out of the corner of my eye, she always had my attention. How that woman's shoulders stood strong while she laughed with the girl, protecting her.

And that damn face of hers. The smile, disarming. The strands of golden hair, alluring. Those speckles across her nose with her pink lips sounding with rolling laughs, inviting. My gaze trailed down the vein in her neck, tempting me.

But it's her marine eyes. How they aim for you. How they pierce right through, claiming their target.

Defiance trails the air around her. Even her chin resists my rule. Either it's up, challenging me, or it's down, calculating her next move against me.

The urge. To follow her. To take her. To end her. It never really took me. Too many other things attracted my attention before.

But now with this viral spectacle, with the video and photos connecting her beguiling image to that global celebrity?

The glorious revenge would horrify millions.

The cost? The sacrifice to pursue her? Worth every risk.

A scent drops, the first spot on a trail, twisting my soul with a hunger driving me to have her.

The hunt has begun.

CHARLIE

"Are you ready for this, Charlie?"

Ready for what, I wondered. The hard cock urging between my cheeks, or the bundle of lit dynamite I was about to throw on my life?

Fuck it.

I'd do both.

His baritone British accent pressed into me, not asking about the meeting—the one in an hour that would have the world aiming for me. Adding one more maddening predator, the press, hunting to claim my sanity. And my life.

No, he was asking for more of me. His brute body steamed against my back under the rain from the shower above, hands caressing my wet cheeks, spreading them, gliding his eager, hard lust between them.

"Daniel Pierce, I don't know how you're ready again," I said.

We'd just fucked two hours before.

No, that round on the bathroom vanity was making love, bringing tears to my eyes at his gasps of love for me.

Because as of this morning... we were finally free.

Free to be together. Free to tell the world. Free to love.

And our ecstasy lasted only that blissful, orgasmic moment before it was shot away by the text *ping* that beckoned me to check my phone charging on the hotel nightstand. While Daniel started our shower, my index finger touched the screen.

And summoned hell.

Now, I was thankful he couldn't see my face. Lust and fear were smeared across it. A guise I wore daily since I'm with him, loving him.

His fingers descended between my thighs, expertly strumming me closer. To pleasure. To the edge. To him.

"I'm ready for you and our life together, Charlie Ravenel." The words hummed from his lips across my shoulder. Standing behind me, his truth was tempting. "It's all I want. You. Us. Our love," he said. "And no more hiding."

I was never supposed to do this. Months before. When I was hired to protect Kierra Williams—a sixteen-year-old actor someone was stalking on the set of the smash show *The Druid*. My mission was to keep the girl safe and to find out who was leaving notes, tormenting Kierra with haunting tactics.

But I fucked up. And fucked the one man I shouldn't.

Daniel Pierce.

The lead actor on the show. The A-list celebrity with almost sixty million followers. The one with a panty-melting face. The one with a profile of masculine perfection only a bit more recognizable than his I-don't-care-if-my-dad-catches-me-fucking-him perfectly sculpted muscular frame. And don't get anyone started on his amazing ass.

Our first fuck was an atom bomb of love dropped on my lonely life.

And now his hands wrapped around me, coaxing me, reminding every cell in my body that this is where I belong, even if it meant giving up everything to be with him. Not that I was the kind of woman who gave up a damn thing for a man. Fuck that. Never.

I had no choice. Not after the last forty-eight hours.

I told myself: *Nope, that's bullshit. This whole gorgeous, hot mess started months back.*

True. Daniel and I were a secret until that famous shot connected the two of us.

That shot? That video?

It was the one when me, Daniel, and Rob, my best friend and colleague, were at a gym in Madrid, Spain.

To the public eye, we were just friends. Friends who shared workouts and our work on *The Druid*, filmed at the massive studio nearby. Daniel was the famous face with constant cameras on him. Rob and I were his colleagues, cast security for the show.

All would have been peachy until a loud noise cracked

the air like gunshots across the gym. Some guy had dropped his heavy bar, but the sudden sound had dropped me to my knees in a PTSD blackout, shooting my mind back six years to when I was a Marine.

And shot three times.

Witnesses in the gym had recorded the spectacle with their phones—#danielpierce rescuing a woman passed out in his arms.

So yeah, that video? It struck fucking media gold.

Because I was no average damsel in distress.

Posts of the video went viral, revealing my distinct scars. The bullet graze across my right cheek. The shot through my right shoulder. Hashtags, rumors, and comments started. Millions of them. And fans and press have been hunting for the blonde draped over Daniel Pierce's biceps ever since.

And now this.

A stand-off.

A lethal chess game with the sadistic stalker I caught trying to rape Kierra Williams. The stalker was none other than Kierra and Daniel's co-star.

The beautiful. The famous. The evil. Mason Hunt.

"You can't fight me, Charlie." Daniel's digits focused me on this indulgence. One I needed like fire needs oxygen. The only thing that grounded me—that kept me sane—was his love.

His lips nuzzled down my neck, knowing my "hell yes" spot, the heat of his wet body, every part of it firm, and one even harder for me, wanting in. A whisper steamed over my ear, "I can't get enough of us," while thick fingers plunged into my thirst, the others teasing my tingling nipples.

Frisking hands apprehended my desire and heart with another beckon from his lips, "you're so fucking beautiful," in that velvet, bass voice. It could sell sand in a desert. A gentle kiss landed on my cheek. "God, I love you, babe. Come on. One more time to celebrate. We're finally free."

No, we weren't.

I read the text minutes before joining him in the shower. It slung me right back into a prison cell of fear. Crashing me back into the concrete wall of reality.

Unknown
I'm standing in line. Thinking
about fucking with you.
Today & always

It was a fatal secret I'd surely keep from Daniel to protect him. He never knew about such threats. I'd already been shot by such a man and prevailed. Never would I let harm come to Daniel, the rare gem of love I found again.

The last words I had said to the stalker? To Mason Hunt while he licked his evil "fuck you" lips and words up to me, promising he wasn't done? Tormenting. Stalking. Raping.

I had stood over Mason, after I kicked his ass, before the detectives came to whisk him away in cuffs. Squatting down, confronting his eyes and threat, I said, "You'll be standing in a long line if you want to fuck with me."

Now Mason's white-pretty-boy-celebrity-rich-ass made bail, paid a sycophant member of his posse to buy a bag full of burner phones so he could let me know... he was standing in line, waiting...

To more than fuck with me.

Warm water rained over me. Resting back against Daniel's cement chest, my tormented mind took this spot as a buzz of Xanax to my anxiety. If only for a short life. Or a night. Or a moment. Daniel was my harbor in a hurricane, and my squalling storm... all at the same time.

He stood behind me with more than desire. It was love. Love wrapping around me, asking to lavish me. And I wanted this. Needed it. Given how long I pushed love away. Feared it for six years. Until Daniel.

Could I really do it? Drop all my defenses given how many were gunning for me now?

Resistance twisted my shoulders. Fear deployed through my nerves.

"How do you reckon we're free now?" I asked him. "I'm about to lose my job by stepping out into white lights on a red carpet with you for the entire world to see and fuck my life sideways."

"Charlie." His shocked voice and gentle hands turned me around. Hurt by my comment burned in his aqua eyes. "You don't have to go to the premiere with me. I would never make you do a bloody thing."

Shit, I didn't mean to fire at him like that. My damn mouth needed a silencer sometimes. The fucking text from Mason had sentenced me to a vengeful mood.

Daniel wouldn't let go. "What's going on with you?" Confusion dripped from his face. "We talked about this yesterday. How we're doing this together. Are you having second thoughts?"

His hulking shoulders rose under his steel jaw, veins and sinews down his neck tensing in her sight. He said, "If we do this, there's no going back. Our lives. Our careers. Nothing will be the same." A small measure of his power squeezed my bicep. "I love you and I won't have you hating me, resenting me for it. What do you want, babe?"

"Daniel." My hand scratched over his sexy stubble. "I *want* to go to the premiere with you. I love you, and I *want* you to fuck me *and* my life sideways."

No smile back. He didn't buy it.

"I'm serious, Charlie. Don't muck about." Little droplets were clinging to his dark chest hair, while drip by drip, falling from his coal-colored waves. Even angry. Or hurt. He was the sexiest man to millions and the most beautiful love I'd known. "We don't have to go public."

"We already *are* public, Daniel. Your obsessed fans are connecting the dots as we speak. My scarred face and body passed out in your arms in a Madrid gym months ago. It's all over social media. And last night? The same scar across my cheek, on the Comic-Con stage walking behind you and Kierra, clearly security for the cast of *your* show. The connection is made." Certainty washed down my face, staring back up at his. "Tick fucking tock."

Was it his fault?

No. We both had a legacy of guilt.

He was an A-list celebrity at the pinnacle of his career whose feet couldn't hit public pavement without notice. Without risk.

I loved him. But hated his life.

I was an addict for protecting others, mainly girls and women. Years ago in the military and now as my job. My instinct kept us safe but always told me—*hide. Never seek the spotlight unless you're saving someone.* Only then, like before, would I stand in the fire.

He loved me but had no idea what we faced.

In four days.

I would take a swan dive into his celebrity life.

Exposure to the level of fatal, I feared.

His hand cupped my cheek. Goddamnit, that always disarmed me, and he knew it. "I know we're running out of time, babe," he said. "It's why we agreed to do it this way. On our terms. Out our relationship before the press or Mason can."

"I know." I held his hand caressing my face. "We're in this together. I promise."

God, how I wanted to tell him more. We had more to worry about from Mason than him leaking to the press that Daniel Pierce was dating, fucking, whatever, a member of cast security for his show.

That was salacious gossip. Nothing to fear.

The text this morning? To hell it was **Unknown**.

My instinct read it and stared down the next week, months, hell maybe the rest of my life. Knowing...

Mason Hunt was sinking his sadistic teeth into me now. Vicious because I busted him stalking Kierra. Obsessed with revenge for the ass-beating I gave him when I stopped him trying to rape her. Fixated upon a new target for his demented psyche—the woman who ruined his career.

I knew the minute I set my sights on Mason Hunt five months before that he was a predator.

And now... *I* was his prey.

But if I told Daniel, we'd both be robbed of peace. And I meant it. I loved him. Because, dear God, the man dropped to his knees and loved me so much in return.

Yes, on paper, I was the hero, the one who sacrificed. The one who gave her service and almost her life to help others. And I would till my dying day.

But what the world didn't know about Daniel Pierce was that behind his facade of hero, celebrity, and beauty, you would find a man capable of a love so great it tore down my every defense.

He could fuck me. Fuck my private life. Fuck my safe solitude all up.

It fired my DNA up—*protect him, always.*

From the terrifying truth. From my haunting, lingering instinct. It was always right. Warning me...

Mason Hunt isn't the only one gunning for you now.

The Come for Me series by KELLY FINLEY
KELLY FINLEY
PIERCE HER
KELLY FINLEY
HUNT HER
KELLY FINLEY
CHASE HER

A NOTE FROM KELLY

This book was inspired by real love, tragic events and incredible people. There's even more thrilling, hot fiction baked in too.

I share stories, interviews and more on my website at kellyfinley.com.

Here I will share—I had to have a Charlie in my life. Teaching about actual badass women for over twenty years, I never met many in fiction. Not women characters with big hearts, smart minds and mouths, with bodies that will proudly fuck someone up *and* shamelessly fuck in the same story.

My friends complained about the same thing. So, here she is.

I love these characters. They smear my dreams into a waking reality at 4 a.m. They talk to me when I'm trying to watch something. And they really demand my attention when I'm driving with my playlist on (shhh, don't tell anyone).

So, y'all got to know... there's more coming. Stay on this

thrilling, sexy ride with me. Your reads, reviews and messages fire up my pages. Thank you!

Before you go... please consider leaving me a review.

ACKNOWLEDGMENTS

For the man who brings me coffee, drinks, dinner, laughs, and lots of love. Kevin, thanks for putting up with me, my closed office door, and my slight obsessions. I'll go ahead and apologize now for only more of the same.

For my Amaru who ate French fries with me as I told you about a story in my head and heart. Thanks for telling me to put that shit on paper. You're my best creation and critic.

For my family who is so damn tired of listening to the same songs, but so thankful for all our trips to the island. Thanks for keeping me grounded and stomping my ego when needed. And thanks for skipping the steamy pages (wink, wink).

Mad love to my alpha readers: Sarah and Melissa. Thanks for the patience, texts, notes, phone chats, and drinks shared. To my beta readers, Angela, Ashley, Michelle, Bianca, and Victoria—y'all helped me shape this book from a hot mess into a hot story.

To all my friends and family who indulged my research and interviews. I'm honored to know people who served, people on set, and people who kick ass for a living.

Serious thanks to my editors, Judy Roth and Nora Esthimer, for the tough love and warm encouragement... and for your patience.

Big hugs to Deborah Richmond who proofs my goofs. As always, special thanks to Kat Wyeth on the other side of my world for your proofreading patience and magic. Such gratitude for Caroline Johnson who designs my sexy covers.

My humble gratitude goes to the women who have or do serve. This beloved character is informed and inspired by you. While brave women make up less than twenty percent of the military services in the USA and smaller numbers globally, they make it to even fewer romance pages celebrating them. Not anymore.

Above all, humble thanks to my readers. If this book made you smile once, swoon a couple of times, and shout, "Hell yes!" then I'm fulfilled. *Thank you.*

ABOUT THE AUTHOR

Kelly Finley hates writing bios but appreciates that you made it this far. So here you go...

She lives in the Carolinas with her sexy husband and cherished family. A rebel with many causes, she fancies black leather, dirty jokes, big hearts, and smart mouths.

Thrilled by a flipped gender script and ticked off by women portrayed as weak, she noticed how many badass, sexy heroines were missing, particularly from romance pages.

Her friends shared the same frustration and told her to practice what she has taught for over twenty years—women who kick ass.

Dedicated to writing books featuring heroines we champion and love—ones with shameless heat, brave hearts, and whip-smart minds—she's most likely at her keyboard putting the next one on the page for you.

amazon.com/author/kellyfinley

patreon.com/kellyfinleyauthor

goodreads.com/goodreads_kelly_finley

bookbub.com/authors/kelly-finley

instagram.com/kellyfinleyauthor

tiktok.com/@kellyfinleybooks

facebook.com/KellyFinleyBooks